DEVIL'S HOPE

S.J. Winter

Winter Publishing

I dedicate this book to all those who wander but are not lost.

Whose pasts are messy, but they keep on keeping on anyway.

Also, to all those I haven't thanked, but who have given me so much support in all of my writing endeavors!

CONTENTS

Author's Note

Dear Reader,

Before you embark on this journey into the world of "Devil's Hope," I wanted to share a bit about the inspiration and intention behind this story.

As a person who is not of Hispanic or African descent, I recognize the importance of cultural representation and the responsibility that comes with telling stories rooted in cultures other than my own. My fascination with religions and spiritual practices began with a vivid dream involving Voodoo, which led me on a path of extensive research and discovery. I had the privilege of knowing someone who was close to the religion who generously shared his knowledge and insights with me until his unfortunate passing. His guidance helped shape the authenticity and depth of the cultural aspects within this novel.

Voodoo, like many other religions, has often been misunderstood and misrepresented, particularly by the Christian church. My hope in writing this story is to present Voodoo and its practitioners with the respect and nuance they deserve, highlighting the beauty and diversity of their beliefs and practices. Through the characters and their experiences, I aim to celebrate the common threads of humanity that connect us all, despite our diverse backgrounds.

It is not my intention to speak over voices from the communities represented in this book but to offer a respectful and heartfelt portrayal that contributes to a broader understanding and appreciation of these rich cultural traditions. I believe that storytelling is a powerful tool for bridging gaps and fostering empathy, and I hope that "Devil's Hope" can play a small part in that endeavor.

Thank you for reading, and I welcome your thoughts and feedback as we navigate this story together.

Warm regards,

S.J. Winter

CHAPTER ONE

The light from the screen illuminated her features with the headline: "New Orleans Gripped by Terror: String of Strangulation Leaves City on Edge." Her brown eyes studied each word as she scrolled through the article, her brows furrowed with focus on each passing line. The armrest creaked as Cassielle's grip on them grew firmer as she leaned back. She shouldn't have been focused on something that was not on her to-do list for the day. She was accustomed to the sterile glow of her computer screen, the distant detachment of solving crimes. Nick used to joke how she must have ice water in her veins. Little did he know, she was good at faking her detachment.

Reflexively, she turned her phone over and glanced at the screen. An action fueled by a flicker of hope, only to find the screen empty of any new messages. None from Nick. He must have moved on by now. His life was probably entwined with a new investigative partner, possibly a new girlfriend, and a new path. One that didn't include her. Cassielle, on the other hand, had made the conscious decision to leave the world of murder investigations for the mundane task of finding lost pets, cheating spouses, business espionage, and other likewise inane jobs.

It provided her with a necessary change, a shield from the chaos of her former career. Despite its monotony, it offered a semblance of normalcy and a means to carve out her own space in the city. The promised increase in pay was compelling and essential for living independently.

Seven murders, each one a thread woven into the

tapestry of fear blanketing the city. It was all anyone could talk about.

Cassielle welcomed her detachment from the cases, grateful once again for not being entangled in the grim task of solving the murders plaguing the city. The escalating press coverage only added to her relief; the spotlight was never her ally. She preferred the quiet diligence of her work, leaving the media frenzy and public scrutiny to Detective Nicholas Rush's eager embrace.

As Cassielle's mind wrestled with her distracted thoughts, a sudden wave of memories crashed against the shores of her consciousness. She closed her eyes, allowing herself to be swept away by the tide of recollection.

In the dimly lit room filled with the scent of incense, Cassielle hesitated at the threshold, observing her mother's every move. Her mother, with her long, flowing hair and piercing eyes, exuded an aura of mystique. Her colorful garments swayed with her graceful motions as she commanded the space around her effortlessly. Her slender fingers danced through the air, tracing intricate patterns with a practiced ease. Despite the softness of her features, there was a quiet strength in her presence, a sense of authority that spoke volumes about her knowledge and experience in the mystical arts.

The room pulsed with energy, alive with the ancient rhythms of Voodoo magic. Cassielle felt a stirring in her chest, a mixture of awe and apprehension as she gazed upon her mother's ritual. She longed to understand, to be a part of something so powerful and mysterious.

But as her mother turned to her, her eyes alight with intensity, Cassielle felt a surge of fear grip at her heart. She knew she could never meet her mother's expectations. They were a burden too heavy to bear.

Her mother's sharp and commanding voice cut through the silence. "You have a gift, Cassielle," she said, her words both a blessing and a curse. "You must learn to harness it, to embrace the magic that flows through your veins. If you ask, Papa Legba will help guide you in whatever course Bondye would like you to follow."

But Cassielle could only nod, her throat tight with uncertainty. She felt her mother's gaze on her, a silent reminder of the path before her.

As the memories faded, Cassielle found herself back in her office, the echoes of her past still lingering in the air. She felt a pang of regret, a longing for a connection lost to time. But she knew she could never go back, the choices she had made had set her on a different path.

With a heavy heart, she turned back to her work. This business, her refuge from the storm raging within her, was her second chance. A chance to channel her skills into something constructive, something that didn't feed the addiction gnawing at her insides. Leaving the force had been the right choice, she told herself, the only choice. Now, if only she could believe it as vehemently as she had told herself.

Cassielle pushed aside the troubling thoughts swirling in her mind and minimized the news article on her laptop screen. With a few swift clicks, she pulled up the latest surveillance images she had captured earlier that morning. Each photo was a snapshot of a clandestine rendezvous unfolding in the park, the people within clearly illuminated by the morning sun.

As she meticulously edited the images, making them more apparent, her trained eye discerned every detail with precision. The couple in question appeared relaxed, their laughter evident through the still frames as they shared a croissant, oblivious to the lens trained on them.

Her client's concerns weighed heavily on Cassielle's mind as she worked. The woman had confided her suspicions of her husband's infidelity, citing his frequent travels and recent trips to New Orleans as cause for suspicion. Desperate for answers, she had enlisted Cassielle's expertise to uncover the truth.

Cassielle drafted a detailed email report recounting everything she had observed over the past three days. She attached the surveillance photos as evidence, each image a damning testament to the husband's indiscretions.

It wasn't Cassielle's place to pass judgment or offer reassurance. She just presented the facts as she uncovered them and let her client draw their conclusions. With a final click of the mouse, she sent the email into the digital ether, knowing whatever happened next was not her responsibility. All she had to do now was look for another job.

Cassielle's heart skipped a beat as she lifted her gaze from her email browser on her laptop screen. Her eyes widened at the sight of a looming figure before her. She felt a momentary sense of disorientation, and her mind raced to comprehend the intrusion. He stood before her like a phantom materializing out of thin air, his black robes swirling around him with an eerie grace. The antiquated garb clashed with the contemporary aesthetics of her workspace, casting a foreboding silhouette that seemed to ripple across the pristine surfaces.

His presence defied reason, yet there was something captivating about him that sparked a flame inside of her. Her initial shock ebbed away, replaced by a torrent of questions flooding her mind. Had she overlooked locking the door? It remained firmly shut, defying any explanation for his sudden appearance. How had he made it in? The feeble light struggling to penetrate the room wavered in his presence as if recoiling from the darkness cloaking him like a second skin.

With a furrowed brow, she shot a wary glance at the stranger before her, her eyes narrowing as they settled on the incongruous top hat perched atop his head.

"Nice hat," she remarked, her voice tinged with a hint of suspicion and disbelief. "Do you always get dressed up to break in?" She wouldn't let on how he had startled her, but her tone betrayed the turmoil beneath the surface. It's always best not to show fear in dangerous situations. Her hand slowly moved to her hip.

"Thank you," he said, his low, melodic hum reverberating with a seductive allure. "I find it adds a certain flair to my attire. I apologize if I startled you. I was hoping to speak with you."

Cassielle's hand subtly brushed against her gun holster at her hip as she feigned disinterest, her curiosity simmering beneath a facade of composure. With her fingers lightly tracing the grip of her gun, she replied, "Flair, huh?" Her words dripped with sarcasm. "Well, you certainly know how to make an entrance. Next time, maybe consider knocking. A locked door usually indicates the business is closed."

"Of course," he said, moving across the floor to take the seat across from her. " I will remember that for the next time I pay you a visit."

The stranger's look made her uncomfortable. "Ms. Cassielle," he began, his voice taking on a more serious note. "I was hoping to chat with the great-great-great granddaughter of the Voodoo Queen Marie Laveau."

Cassielle couldn't shake her distrust of him. He triggered something in her she didn't recognize or understand, and she both liked and disliked it. She felt the hairs on her neck prickle, a primal instinct warning her of hidden dangers lurking beneath his charming facade.

As the stranger's gaze wandered around her office, the room screamed Cassielle's profession and dedication. A cluttered bulletin board adorned one wall, its surface a patchwork of newspaper clippings, photographs, and notes, each item a tantalizing clue waiting to be deciphered. Opposite, a sleek, modern style grandfather clock stood sentinel, its steady tick-tock filling the silence with a sense of urgency, a reminder of time's relentless passage and mysteries.

Cassielle's breath caught at his words, a surge of anxiety washing over her like a crashing wave. Her stomach clenched in a familiar pang of loss. She had spent years running from her heritage, burying the memories of her mother's legacy deep within her soul. The last thing she wanted was to be dragged back into the Voodoo world, especially not by some enigmatic stranger.

"If you seek Voodoo assistance, you've come to the wrong place. I'm not a practitioner," she said, her voice steely and her resolve betraying the turmoil swirling within her. "I do private investigations. If you have a lost pet, loved one, or something someone stole, I can help. Otherwise, you've come to the wrong place."

Her chair groaned against the floor as she pushed back, the sound a familiar protest against the weight of her decision. Glancing at the clock mounted on the wall, its hands inching closer to the end of the workday, Cassielle knew it was time to call it quits. Dinner time. Or drink time? Liquid dinner for tonight, she decided, the weight of the day pressing heavily upon her shoulders. She just needed to get rid of this guy first.

The stranger observed her with a bemused smile. Cassielle casually shrugged and continued. "There's a Mambo down the street you could see... or if you're interested in something darker, a little further down, there's a Bokor who runs a small tea shop," she suggested.

"No, no, I'm not seeking Voodoo assistance, though that may come in handy," He flashed her a brilliant smile. Cassielle was instantly annoyed by how his smile made her stomach flip. She couldn't help but admire his profile. Even though he dressed in very old-fashioned robes, she could tell he was tall, lean, and had sharp, angular features.

"If you hadn't broken into my place of business, I would be more interested in talking to you. However, I'll let you leave in one piece if you leave now." With purposeful steps, she circled her desk, her fingers trailing along the familiar textures of the wood as if seeking solace in its solidity, her other hand still on her gun beneath the flap of her suit jacket. She approached her coat rack in the corner, a silent guardian watching over her domain, and reached for her rucksack with her free hand. The bag's worn straps were a comforting weight against her shoulder. She kept her eyes on him.

"Sorry, I was merely hoping to acquire your assistance," he responded, his smile radiant and his eyes holding her gaze in a hypnotic trance. "I wouldn't have come to you if you weren't who you are and descended from whom you are descended from."

He moved to follow her, yielding to her silent dismissal. Cassielle wasted no time opening the door, which was unlocked after all. Odd. He went out the opened door to the sidewalk out front. Cassielle followed and quickly pivoted to lock the door behind her. Once she heard the familiar click, she turned to face him again, a mask of determination firmly in place.

Passing him, Cassielle's movements became clipped, her pace quickening as if propelled by an invisible force. She glanced to the ground for a moment, avoiding meeting his gaze before looking back up at him, her jaw set in a tight line. "Well, as I said before, my office is closed. Good luck finding the help you're looking for."

Stepping out onto the sidewalk, she immersed herself in the bustling after-work foot traffic, the warmth of the setting sun a welcome embrace against her light brown skin.

"So, you're not into Voodoo?" His voice drifted from her left. He seemed to be following her like a bad penny.

Cassielle halted, turning to face him, her eyes narrowing in a silent challenge. "You don't take 'no' for an answer, do you?"

"Not really, no," he admitted with a charming grin, his words carrying an undeniable weight of truth.

"Well, that's a shame for you. You're in for a great deal of disappointment," she retorted. Her gaze drifted to the restaurant across the street, and the promise of a quiet drink called to her like a siren's song.

"I am rarely disappointed, Dawlin'," he murmured, his voice husky with a velvety undertone, a subtle invitation lingering between them like a whispered promise. She

7

mentally shook off the impure thoughts settling in. Something about him made her consider doing things she wouldn't normally consider regarding a stranger. She pulled herself together with a deep breath.

"Well, good for you then. Congrats." She put her thoughts to trying to seem as indifferent as she could. She lifted her chin and continued along her way. She wouldn't let him know how his presence affected her, and she had no intention of entertaining any further conversation.

But the stranger, unfazed by her lack of interest, persisted, his voice cutting through the air like a blade forged in the fires of determination. "Wait," his voice pierced the city's din, commanding attention with a quiet authority which bothered her despite her best efforts to ignore him. "There's something you need to know."

She stopped in her tracks, her muscles tensing with irritation and reluctant curiosity. Casselle didn't turn back, her gaze fixed firmly on the path ahead, yet she couldn't deny the pull of the stranger's words.

Undeterred by her silence, the stranger continued, his words measured and deliberate. "These murders, they're not ordinary. They're ritualistic, meticulously executed by different hands, yet all following the same sinister pattern."

Despite her efforts to ignore him, a flicker of curiosity ignited within Cassielle at the mention of the unusual killings. She hesitated, her back still turned to him. "And what does that have to do with me?" she finally relented, her voice betraying a hint of intrigue.

Seizing her momentary interest, he pressed on, his words weaving a tapestry of intrigue and danger. "You possess a unique understanding of this city's mysteries. Your lineage and connections render you more qualified than anyone to untangle this web of wickedness. Your mother trained you for a reason."

She gritted her teeth, resisting the urge to respond. She didn't want to be entangled in another murder case, particularly one shrouded in such ominous circumstances. Yet, beneath her resolve, a nagging sense of responsibility tugged at her. It was like a silent reminder of her past duty towards her city and its inhabitants.

With a heavy sigh, she quickened her pace as she sought to put distance between herself and the stranger. "What do you know of my mother or any training she may or may not have given me? My detective skills came from the academy. Not my mother. I'm not interested," she muttered, her voice firm and unwavering. "Curiosity killed the cat." Why couldn't this guy take a hint?

The stranger's words followed her like a persistent stalker, haunting her every step. As she stepped off the curb onto the street, the stranger's voice whispered behind her, a mere breath in the city's din.

"I wasn't referencing your investigative skills, though those are strong, too. I was talking about your magical abilities."

Her footsteps halted. Turning to face him incredulously, she opened her mouth to speak, but changed her mind, taking a moment to recollect her thoughts. She shook her head and waved him off. "I'm not interested in whatever you want."

He paused and a flicker of a reaction crossed his face. "Perhaps we will talk another time, then." His words, carrying a weight of inevitability, left Cassielle with a sinking feeling in the pit of her stomach. As she turned to continue across the street, she couldn't shake the feeling his intense gaze gave her. The confusing desire and fear.

She paused at the other side, her senses prickling with a sudden feeling of absence, like when someone leaves the room and you're suddenly alone. Yet she wasn't alone. She was on the street. There were other people around. When she turned to look, he was nowhere to be found, as if he had melted into the shadows of the evening, leaving behind nothing but unanswered questions.

CHAPTER TWO

The stranger's presence haunted her, leaving an unsettling and edgy feeling in the air. With a dismissive shrug, Cassielle shook her head to banish any lingering doubts from her mind. She had other matters to address, more concrete puzzles to solve than the mysterious stranger who had appeared in her life now.

It was unsettling when he brought up her mother. Still, anyone with basic computer skills could quickly discover her mother's identity and profession. Her mother would have given her some form of education in it. Many families deeply rooted in religion pass on their beliefs and knowledge to their children. He didn't know her mother. He was a wannabe master of deception.

Reflecting on the unusual sequence of events, she carefully considered her choices. A drink to forget the oddities of the day, or maybe she should consider reducing her intake. Alcohol had provided her a great deal of escape from her thoughts and emotions, but perhaps she needed to find a new coping mechanism. She felt the warm evening air wrap around her, creating a cozy embrace as she navigated the lively streets. Passersby hurried past her, their faces a blur of apathy as she made her way through the bustling sidewalk. She experienced a feeling of disconnection, as if she were navigating through a strange place. She was all too familiar with this feeling. Her heart was filled with aching at the thought. Loneliness seemed to transcend mere words.

As she rounded a bend, she found herself outside Lafitte's Blacksmith Shop Bar, with its cozy lights pouring onto the pavement, beckoning her to come inside. She opened the door and entered, greeted by the familiar aromas and the humid atmosphere.

The hanging lanterns emitted a soft, flickering glow, evoking the feel of the gas-lit streets of New Orleans. The interior exuded a warm and inviting ambiance, with just a few customers sparsely spread across the room. The atmosphere was saturated with the comforting scent of simmering spices and the subtle aroma of freshly brewed coffee. Soft jazz music filled the air. This place was a mix of comfort and unease. It was filled with a tangle of positive and negative memories. It was ingrained in her, whether she wanted it or not. The decor had a rustic charm, featuring exposed brick walls decorated with vintage posters and framed photographs of iconic New Orleans landmarks. Clusters of weathered wooden tables and chairs were arranged, each illuminated by the gentle flicker of candlelight.

Upon closer inspection, one could discern the faint etchings of names and dates on the wooden chairs and tables. Alba supported the act of vandalism. She desired to create a sense of everlasting connection for all individuals to LaFitte's history. The walls of LaFitte's were adorned with memories-some good, some bad-which seemed to take on a life of their own. She wondered if her own vandalism was still there. A carving: C & N, along with the date, 2/14/08—their first official date. She hadn't looked at it in a while. The carving was likely a permanent detail on the table where she and her friends used to sit. This wasn't surprising; Nick wasn't the type to erase such sentimental marks. He'd once said to her, "Our scars are what make us who we are."

Alba stood behind the bar, engaged in conversation with a man sporting long dark dreadlocks neatly tied back. Their voices disappeared in the cacophony of chatter. Cassielle approached them, feeling a surge of unease as she braced herself to reveal the details of her recent experience.

"Hey, child!" Alba's melodic Barbadian accent rang out,

her face instantly brightening with a smile as she spotted Cassielle. "What brings ya here so early?" She casually shifted away from the man she had been conversing with at the bar. Cassielle followed and sat down across from her, her mind still spinning from the unexpected encounter. She paused briefly, uncertain of how to approach the subject.

"I... I had an unusual experience at work today," she finally confessed, her voice soft and uncertain.

Alba arched an eyebrow, her face reflecting a sense of intrigue. "What happened?"

Cassielle shared the details of her encounter with the stranger as well as the disquiet which followed the encounter. Alba listened attentively, her expression a blend of worry and fascination.

"That sounds troubling," Alba commented, her brow furrowing in concern. "Ya alright, dear?"

Cassielle shrugged, feeling a lingering wariness deep within her. "I'm fine," she replied, her voice lacking confidence. She paused. "He brought up my mother and Voodoo. He mentioned how the murders seemed to be linked and carried out in a ritualistic manner." She took a moment to gather her ideas. "He's probably just another person with an interest in true crime who finds these gruesome murders intriguing."

Alba nodded, serving Cassielle a glass of unsweetened iced tea and sliding it over to her. "Ya would know more 'bout that than most. People are always fascinated with the dark side of life. Plenty of people got wrong ideas 'bout Voodoo, thinking it's a wicked and evil religion. But when they really look into it and understand it better, they see that those ideas ain't true and lose interest. Maybe he thinks some evil sorcerer behind it?"

Cassielle savored the taste of the tea as it danced across her palate. She hadn't come here for tea, but Alba usually knew better. It was flawless. "Well, you may have a point. He was even dressed up as if he were Baron Samedi."

Alba chuckled, "Looks like he's real late for Mardi Gras."

Cassielle laughed and took another sip of her tea, allowing the conversation to switch to other, more lighthearted subjects. Yet, Cassielle couldn't shake the nerves in the depths of her stomach.

As always, Alba seemed to know what she was thinking. "It's normal for ya to feel uneasy when someone talk 'bout your mother and Voodoo. Ya lost your mother when ya was young, and that hurt never fully heals." She raised her hand, halting Cassielle, who was about to argue she was perfectly fine. "It don't heal," she repeated, "It might hurt less over time, but the pain is always there. It's like a crack in a saucer that get fixed. Even though it fixed, ya still see the crack.

"'Bout him talking 'bout Voodoo, it's up to you if ya want to go back to practicing it. Ya mother was sad when you left. She didn't say much, and I didn't ask, and I ain't expecting ya to give me no details either. Believing in a religion is something personal." She smiled, "Bondye gave us free will. We can hold on to or let go of our beliefs. It ain't something we gotta carry forever. Voodoo's like a breeze in the wind. Always there, waiting for us to listen. If ya regret leaving, maybe part of ya want to find the comfort and wisdom of Voodoo."

Cassielle could feel tears welling up behind her eyelids. She would not cry. Taking a deep steadying breath, she composed herself. Somehow, Alba always had a way of sending her teetering on the edge of tears.

"Embrace the journey, dear," Alba smiled softly, "It's never too late to learn and grow from the past. We come to the truth in our own time."

Their conversation smoothly shifted. As she finished her drink and said goodbye, she felt as if a heavy burden had been lifted from her shoulders. She stepped out onto the sidewalk in front of Lafitte's and looked around as if emerging from a haunting reverie. There was a fire the stranger had ignited within her; one she wasn't sure she could put out. The city appeared to throb with vitality, its streets teeming with the liveliness of its residents. She strolled, lost in contemplation, her mind consumed by the meeting and the flood of memories it had awakened within her.

Cassielle's eyes moved upwards as she turned onto her street. She paused to admire the vast expanse of star-covered sky above. The stars twinkled and cast a gentle light, bathing the city beneath. She could feel her muscles relax as she breathed in the sweet summer smells and gazed longingly at the shimmering stars above. There was so much more out there than she could ever understand. She was just a speck in the universe.

She remembered sitting with her mother on their porch in the Bayou, gazing up at the celestial tapestry interwoven with the branches of the Cypress Trees and the swaying Spanish Moss. Her mother had always mentioned how the stars served as a reminder we are never truly alone. The presence of a higher power is always by our side.

Cassielle glanced up at the full moon, its silver light spilling across the landscape. Her mother always said the full moon was a time to let go of what no longer served you. Cassielle shook her head, slipping her hands into her pockets. Her mother had plenty of advice, but it didn't make it true. Cassielle would do what she knew best: keep to herself, do her job, and protect her loved ones from the darkness she was sure lurked inside her.

Cassielle resumed walking home, her mind wandering. She would not dwell on the mystery man despite the persistent yearning within her. She wanted to hear his voice, to find him, and to speak with him. Maybe she was losing her mind. She hurried down the street, eager to reach the calm refuge of her apartment, a stone's throw away from the majestic St. Louis Cathedral. However, the insistent pull of curiosity called out to her like a tune stuck in her head.

CHAPTER THREE

The sun filtered in through the blinds, creating a simple pattern of light and shadows across Cassielle's desk. Notes were piled in a cluttered heap around her workspace, and she sat hunched over her laptop, intent on going through emails and figuring out her schedule for the day. Her morning coffee sat forgotten just to the left of her. Despite her efforts to focus, thoughts of the stranger from the day before lingered at the edges of her mind like an unwelcome guest.

Cassielle typed on her keyboard, and the chime of an incoming message grabbed her attention. She paused, her fingers hovering above the keys, as she noticed the email notification at the bottom of her screen. She sighed and clicked the Outlook icon.

She saw a new case inquiry with the subject line "Desperate Plea for Help." The writer was a former client. Some may have been curious from the title, but Cassielle had seen so many 'desperate pleas' it failed to inspire her. However, she still clicked on the email and began to read.

It was from a woman named Adrianna, who explained how her daughter, Sarah, had gone missing when she did not come home after a late-night shift at a diner. Adrianna had filed a missing person report with the police but was worried, especially with the news full of reports on the recent string of random murders.

As she read through Adrianna's email, empathy rolled over her. Her thoughts unwillingly turned to her memories of her mother's unsolved murder. Uncertainty gnawed at her heart, a vicious reminder of the endless waiting and questions that would likely never resolve. Perhaps she could help alleviate a fraction of Adrianna's pain by finding some answers for her. Or even better, finding her daughter. Cassielle wasted no time in writing a response. She outlined her willingness to assist her as well as the cost of her fees and her availability to meet and discuss the case further should Adrianna choose to enlist her help.

Once the email was sent, Cassielle turned her focus to a different puzzle. A wealthy businessman had written to her a while ago with the delicate task of uncovering corporate espionage within his company. She found this case to be a challenge requiring her to pay close attention to detail and analyze the information she obtained.

She pulled up the surveillance footage his security department had sent her earlier. She hit play and leaned forward, her eyes glued to the screen, searching for any clues about the identity of the culprit. She spotted a man coming out of the businessman's office. She'd been watching their security footage for some time now and had been trying to note patterns between the comings and goings of employees. This footage showed the same man she had followed the other day to a strange rendezvous. She paused the video and looked to her right to find her notebook. Her fingers lingered on her notebook as movement outside her window drew her attention. Her gaze lifted, and through the glass, she caught a glimpse of a distinct silhouette-a top hat and long coat passing by. She shifted in her chair as a jolt of uneasy recognition coursed through her. She inhaled sharply, uncertainty flickering in her eyes as she watched the figure disappear.

She must have imagined it. Yet, the feeling he was the man from the day before lingered. She couldn't shake her thoughts about him; they even followed her into her dreams, dreams that left her aching for more.

He was either insane or really did know something about the murders. But this thought was ridiculous. The papers reported suspects were arrested in every case. But then there was his mention of her mother, which was equally ridiculous. He could have done a Google search for that information. She needed to stop thinking about him.

Cassielle redirected her attention to her office surroundings. The layout and decor held her like a familiar embrace, grounding her in a sense of belonging. This room felt more like home to her than her own apartment; after all, she spent more time here than anywhere else. She shook her head and pushed aside her lingering edginess about the stranger. She refocused on her desk, burying herself in her work.

As she settled back into the rhythm of her tasks, Cassielle's mind shifted gears. Yet, even amidst the familiarity of her workspace, a worry lingered at the edges of her consciousness. Financial concerns crept in, casting a dark pall over her thoughts. Good paying business had been sluggish of late, and the rent deadline loomed on the horizon.

Cassielle crossed one leg over the other, her foot tapping anxiously against the floor. Anxiety settled in her stomach, drawing her attention to the morning paper resting on her desk. Alba had handed it to her earlier, a gesture like a subtle nudge back toward her old life as a homicide detective. But perhaps Alba simply recognized her fascination with the recent murders, knowing her interest in true crime.

The murders weren't her concern. She forced herself to go back to her work, focusing on the surveillance footage. She studied each frame, her eye discerning every detail. Gradually, patterns began to emerge, and she felt a glimmer of hope she might be able to solve this case quicker than anticipated.

As hours passed, she engrossed herself in her work, her brow furrowing with concentration. Eventually, her progress seemed to stall, and she pushed away from her desk, running her hands through her hair. She couldn't figure it out. The answers were buried beneath layers of data and surveillance footage. Time blurred, the outside world fading into insignificance as she poured over documents and surveillance footage with laser-like focus.

A low rumble of thunder reverberated through the air, startling Cassielle from her intense focus. She pushed back from her desk, muscles protesting from hours of immobility. Glancing up, she noticed the ominous clouds gathering outside her window, with the first droplets of rain splattering against the glass. It was then Cassielle realized she had lost track of time. Checking the clock, she was shocked to see it was well into the afternoon, her neglected stomach growling in protest.

As Cassielle finished up her work and prepared to leave for the day, her eyes were drawn to the familiar folder on her computer labeled 'Case File - S. Madison.' It was a ritual she couldn't seem to shake, a quiet reminder of the unresolved mystery that tugged at her thoughts. With a sigh, she clicked open the folder, skimming through the documents and police reports detailing her mother's death years ago. Each page stirred a mix of emotions within her-a blend of grief, frustration, and an unyielding desire for closure.

Cassielle closed the folder and shut down her laptop. Dwelling on the past wouldn't solve anything. If she hadn't been able to solve it over the last 10 years, it was unlikely she would solve it today. Still, the specter of her mother's unsolved murder lingered like an unwelcome guest, a constant reminder of the case she couldn't solve. She was haunted by the image of the bullet piercing her mother's stomach and her doubling over, face twisted in pain and confusion. She rubbed her eyes, her fingers pressing hard against her eyelids as if trying to scrub away the visual etched into her mind.

With a resigned sigh, Cassielle began to stretch, each movement a desperate attempt to ease the tension in her limbs. Her gaze drifted to her phone, lying innocently beside her, its screen lighting up with a new message. Alba's name flashed across the display, a beacon of comforting familiarity. Cassielle typed in her passcode, and the message popped up on her screen.

"Hey, trouble. Didn't see ya for lunch today. Wanna come by for dinner?"

A grin tugged at the corners of her lips as she read the message, a surge of affection flooding her chest at the thought of seeing Alba. As she reached for her phone to confirm she would come to Lafitte's, she noticed another notification-a missed message from Brittany. Her heart skipped a beat as she read the simple yet loaded question: "Drinks tonight?"

Instantly, a pang of guilt pricked at Cassielle's conscience, accompanied by a wave of discomfort. She had been dodging Brittany's calls and texts more often lately, mainly since their conversations inevitably circled back to Nick. Cassielle couldn't bring herself to relive the messy situation, so she opted to avoid Brittany altogether, busying herself with work or finding other excuses to sidestep their usual meetups. Yet, even as Cassielle hesitated, a part of her longed for the familiar bond they once shared, the easy camaraderie that defined their friendship.

Cassielle let out a heavy sigh as she typed, "Not tonight. Busy with work. Tomorrow?" She closed the message and opened the one from Alba. She typed out a response, her thumbs dancing across the screen with practiced ease. "Be there in 10." She slipped her phone in her pocket, the weight of the decision bearing down on her. The invitation hung in the air, a silent reminder of the web of emotions she had yet to untangle. Despite her reluctance, she knew sooner or later, she would have to face the music. Tomorrow would have to be the day if Brittany agreed to it.

Cassielle gathered her belongings, her movements quickening with each passing moment. The prospect of catching up with Alba over a hearty meal at LaFitte's offered her some respite from her guilt. Maybe the fastest way to her heart was through her stomach.

As Cassielle moved to step out of her office and into the muggy streets of New Orleans, she pulled the hood of her jacket up over her head, preparing for the walk in the storm.

"Thank God for jackets with silk lined hoods," she thought. The air crackled with anticipation, heavy with the promise of rain. Thunder rumbled in the distance, a warning of the tempest to come, while flashes of lightning illuminated the darkening sky. The fat raindrops had started while she was inside now intensified into a relentless downpour, each droplet growing larger and heavier as they cascaded from the darkened sky.

Despite the ominous weather, Cassielle pushed her thoughts aside and forced herself to conjure optimistic thoughts. "Thoughts become a reality," her counselor's words echoed in her mind. Today was shaping up to be a good day, she told herself, though the storm clouds mirrored her inner uncertainty.

Cassielle hurried out into the rain, navigating the relatively quiet sidewalks of the French Quarter. As she sped up, she couldn't shake the sensation of being watched. With each step, the fine hairs on the back of her neck rose, her sense of foreboding tightening around her. She glanced over her shoulder, half-expecting to find the man lurking in the shadows, but she was met with only the deserted city streets. The only sounds were the distant rumble of thunder, the relentless drumming of raindrops against the pavement, and the pounding of her heartbeat in her ears.

At the street corner, she paused, savoring the shift from the warm, humid air to the cool, saturated atmosphere of the storm. She relished the change before a voice sliced through her peace.

"Stay out of it," the voice commanded, cutting through her thoughts like a sharp blade.

She turned quickly to find the source of the voice. She spotted a man slumped against the nearby building. His clothing was torn, and he sat on a broken cardboard box. A sign leaning near him stated, "Need food, please help." His gaze was averted as if addressing an invisible friend. Cassielle's brow furrowed. Had he been talking to her, or was he rambling to himself?

"He's no good, that Baron," the man repeated, his words carried an eerie foreboding. Who was Baron, and why did the homeless man seem so convinced of his malevolence? He couldn't be talking to her.

Attempting to shake off the encounter, Cassielle turned away, but the man's voice came again, pulling at her like an invisible thread. "Are you listening to me, Cassielle?"

CHAPTER FOUR

Startled, she spun around to face him. His previously averted gaze locked onto hers with an uncomfortable intensity. In the dim light, they appeared as black as the stranger's hat.

"Don't listen to him. Stay out of it," the man warned, his voice carrying a weight of ominous finality.

Cassielle's mind raced with conflicting thoughts as she grappled with the unsettling encounter. Should she confront the man and demand an explanation for his cryptic warning? Or should she dismiss his words as the ramblings of someone lost in the throes of drug-induced delirium?

She weighed her options, her gaze flickering back to the homeless man slouched against the building. His form seemed to blur in her peripheral vision, his words echoing in her mind like a haunting refrain. Was it worth engaging with someone who appeared so disconnected from reality?

With a resigned sigh, Cassielle rationalized the man must be in the grip of some drug-induced episode, his words a nonsensical manifestation of his altered state. Perhaps he hadn't even said her name-it had simply sounded like it amidst the cacophony of the cars and rain on the street.

Determined to put distance between herself and the unsettling encounter, Cassielle turned and started to walk away so quickly she nearly collided with a man in a hoodie. "Sorry," she murmured, her steps quickening as she hurried past him and across the street. The sound of her own heartbeat thrummed in her ears, drowning out the distant rumble of thunder. She needed to put this bizarre encounter behind her and focus on her rendezvous with Alba at Lafitte's.

As Cassielle glanced back at the corner, her gaze locked onto a figure who caught her attention. Tall and lean, draped in flowing black coat that seemed to dance in the wind, the man exuded an aura of mystique and intrigue. He sported the same top hat of the figure from the day before. His features, obscured partially by the shadows, appeared sharp and angular, giving him an almost ethereal presence in the dimming light. Was he following her now?

The clouds had darkened the street enough for the streetlights to come on, casting an eerie glow over the scene.

"This is like some bad horror film," Cassielle thought to herself as she decided and ran through the rain after the figure, the thunder adding a dramatic soundtrack to her chase. Each flicker of lightning outlined the figure, briefly illuminating his silhouette against the backdrop of the stormy sky. If he was following her, she was going to make him stop.

Despite the downpour intensifying around her, Cassielle felt a surge of determination coursing through her veins. With each step, the distance between them closed, the sound of her footsteps drowned out by the rhythmic pattern of raindrops.

As she drew closer, the man turned, his gaze meeting hers briefly before he disappeared around a corner, leaving Cassielle to navigate the slick pavement alone. Undeterred, she quickened her pace. She had to catch him, had to unravel the enigma entwining them both in its profound embrace. As Cassielle pursued the figure through the rain-soaked streets, her mind buzzed with questions, each step fueling her determination to uncover the truth. The man's connection to the recent murders gnawed at her thoughts like a persistent itch, urging her to delve deeper into the mystery. Yet, amidst the chaos of the storm and the urgency of her pursuit, she couldn't fathom why he had singled her out. What stake did he have in her involvement? In addition to that, why did she care? Why couldn't she let this go?

As Cassielle rounded the corner in pursuit of the mysterious figure, her heart pounding with anticipation, she found herself standing in a narrow, dead-end alley. The hooded man was nowhere to be seen, as if he had vanished into thin air, leaving Cassielle alone in the desolate space. Rain continued to pour down, drenching her to the bone and adding to her frustration and bewilderment. If he was so determined to talk to her and get her help, why was he running from her?

Something about the stranger was extremely off, and it made her stomach clench uncomfortably. Not for the first time in her adult life, she felt a deep longing for the feeling of safety and home. That feeling had been shattered fifteen years ago. She had gone back to the bodega more times than she could count until, finally, it went out of business, and she could no longer legally go inside. However, that hadn't stopped her from illegally entering. All so she could see and feel her mother's presence again, even if it was also the place where her mother was taken away from her. A futile attempt to feel safe.

Feeling defeated and disoriented, Cassielle retraced her steps, her soaked clothes clinging uncomfortably to her skin. With each splash of her footsteps against the wet pavement, she hurried back the way she had come, the distant glow of Lafitte's guiding her through the dimly lit streets. She had lost the mysterious stranger. There were still answers to be found, and she was determined to uncover them, even if it meant braving the storm inside of herself once more.

Arriving at LaFitte's, Cassielle pushed open the door to the cozy bar, greeted by the familiar sights and sounds of the bustling establishment. The aroma of sizzling food filled the air, and the low murmur of conversation blended with the soft melody playing in the background, broken up by the occasional boom of thunder.

Alba spotted Cassielle immediately and waved her over to a corner booth where she was already seated, a warm smile lighting up her face. However, as Cassielle approached, Alba's smile turned into a look of concern.

"Oh Larde! You're soaked!" Alba exclaimed, noticing the water dripping from Cassielle's clothes. "What happened?"

"I figured today was just perfect for a rain-soaked run," Cassielle said with a shrug. "Nothing like a free shower to brighten my day!"

"We'll get ya upstairs," Alba suggested. "I'll get ya some dry clothes, and we can dry ya hair properly."

Cassielle hesitated, but Alba insisted, leading her towards the stairs at the back of the bar.

"I'll be right back," Alba assured the bartender, who nodded in understanding.

As Cassielle followed Alba up the stairs to her apartment, a wave of nostalgia washed over her. This place held countless memories, some of which she'd rather forget. It was here she had lived during her rebellious teenage years, sneaking out to explore the abandoned buildings of New Orleans in pursuit of something darker than mere adventure.

The thought of those nights unsettled her. She pushed the memories aside, focusing on the present as Alba led her into the small upstairs apartment. Once there, she gratefully accepted dry clothes and a towel, feeling the warmth of Alba's hospitality envelop her like a comforting embrace. The harbor that had sheltered her during turbulent times of her youth was a refuge she found herself returning to even now. More often than she'd like to admit.

"Thanks," Cassielle said sincerely, touched by her kindness.

"Anytime, dearheart," Alba replied with a smile. "Now, we're gonna get ya dried off before ya catch a cold."

Not too long after, they sat at a corner table of the bar. They were both sipping on steaming cups of au lait coffee, the rich aroma of coffee and chicory mingling with the tantalizing scent of cooking food.

"So, what's been keeping ya so busy today?" Alba asked, her eyes twinkling with curiosity. "Anymore 'bout that stranger from yesterday?"

Cassielle sank into the plush cushion, her thoughts swirling with uncertainty. She toyed with the idea of confiding in Alba, her gaze drifting to the flickering candle on the table. How much should she reveal? Her trust in Alba ran deep, yet the intricacies of certain cases demanded discretion. And there was the matter of the puzzling stranger. She hesitated, her lips pursing as she weighed her options. Some truths were best left unspoken, especially when they danced on the edges of doubt. After all, could she truly trust her own senses, or were they merely leading her down a path of uncertainty? It wasn't the first time she'd experienced such ambiguity, her mind plagued by shadows of the past lingering like nocturnal specters.

"Just the usual," Cassielle replied with a casual shrug, deciding to keep her response vague for now. "A mix of surveillance work, background checks, and following up on leads." She paused. "There have been some other weird things…"

Alba raised an eyebrow, waiting.

"Some strange man on the street said something to me about not listening to someone named Baron and telling me or him to stay out of it… I'm not sure if he was even talking to me. And I saw the stranger again, but he took off running." She took a sip of her drink before continuing. "I chased after him because I'm starting to feel like he's stalking me…"

"Mussie…" Alba tapped her fingers against her mug. Cassielle waited. Alba only said the Bajan mussie instead of maybe or perhaps when she was thinking about something she wasn't eager to share.

"What are you thinking?" Cassielle watched Alba as she lifted her coffee to her lips.

"Could Baron be Baron Samedi?"

Cassielle coughed, choking on her coffee. "Baron Samedi? The Loa?"

"Well, the man ya described sounded like Baron Samedi and the other stranger said not to listen to Baron…"

"Alba," Cassielle took a breath. How could she say what she wanted to say without offending Alba and her religion?

"I know ya don't believe, but with all the strange murders, and the man turnin' up at your office?"

"When I was on the force all sorts of people would come out of the woodwork when newsworthy events happened... it doesn't mean anything." Even as she said it, she was squashing the little voice inside of her who agreed with Alba. How could one not think this was the case when they spent so much time practicing Voodoo?

Alba sighed. She clearly sensed she wouldn't get through to Cassielle, so she changed the subject, regaling her with stories from the bar and the colorful characters who frequented it.

As they chatted and laughed, Cassielle felt the weight of the day's investigations begin to lift from her shoulders. There was something about being in Alba's company always put her at ease, allowing her to forget the troubles of the outside world, if only for a little while.

As Alba slowly stirred her coffee, her gaze rested on Cassielle with a quiet intensity. "Have ya talked to Nicholas lately?"

The question lingered between them like a heavy fog over their conversation. Cassielle could feel its weight pressing on her.

Cassielle sighed, "No, not since our fight." She stared at her coffee, lost in thought. Losing him felt like the greatest mistake of her life, a pang of regret she couldn't shake.

As Alba's gaze bore into her, Cassielle's mind raced, searching for the right words to say. She wanted to push back, to tell Alba to mind her own business. But even the thought of disappointing the woman who had become a surrogate mother to her was enough to silence the words before they could leave her lips.

With a sigh, Cassielle shifted uncomfortably in her seat, looking down at her hands, avoiding Alba's probing stare.

She knew Alba cared about her, that her question came from a place of genuine concern. And yet, the weight of it all felt suffocating, like a tight knot constricting her chest.

Cassielle was saved from answering as their food arrived: a bowl of gumbo for Cassielle and a plate of fried catfish for Alba. The delicious aroma momentarily distracted Cassielle from the probing question hovering in the background.

Cassielle dug into her meal, savoring the rich flavors and hearty warmth of the gumbo. Each spoonful eased the tension in her muscles.

But Alba continued to watch Cassielle. Finally, unable to resist the silent inquiry any longer, Cassielle let out a sigh and speared a sausage with her fork.

"No, I haven't," Her voice tightened, the edges of her words sharp, as if each syllable was a small shield raised to protect herself.

Alba's expression softened, and the sides of her lips lifted slightly. "It's never too late to reach out, sugar."

But Cassielle shook her head, "I don't need to reach out to him," she insisted, her tone firm. "I'm doing fine. We're both moving on. It's fine."

Alba nodded in understanding, though Cassielle could sense the lingering worry in her gaze.

"We both agreed to separate." Cassielle hated herself for feeling the need to elaborate.

"So ya said," Alba took a sip of her coffee.

"I've moved on. I'm focusing on my work." Cassielle pushed the remnants of her food away, her hunger evaporating as anxiety twisted her stomach into uncomfortable knots. Alba raised an eyebrow at her, and Cassielle pulled the food back, pushing the contents around with her fork. "My business is new. I don't have time for a relationship."

Alba nodded again. She speared a piece of her fish and took a bite. After swallowing, she set her fork down gently on her plate. "How 'bout Brittany? Did ya have a fall-out with her?"

Cassielle felt a pang of guilt settle in her stomach like a heavy stone.

"Brittany texted me. I've been meaning to get back to her..."

"Think of good friends like the sturdy branches of a tree," Alba said, her voice soft and reassuring. "They stay steadfast and unwavering, providin' cover and support even when we wander off into the storm. They're always here for ya, dear, waitin' with open arms whenever ya ready to come back."

Alba's wise words resonated deeply with Cassielle. After a brief pause, Alba continued more directly, "So, if she texted ya, it means she's still willing to be ya friend, even though you've been dodging her."

Cassielle's gaze drifted to her coffee, the swirls of steam rising from its surface mesmerizing her for a moment. She hoped the change in subject would come naturally, without the need for words. True to form, Alba sensed her silent plea and gracefully shifted the conversation, seamlessly gliding into a new topic.

"How's ya business? Do ya need any help? If ya do, I can..."

"I'm doing fine, Alba." Cassielle interrupted. She reached out and placed her hand on top of the older woman's hand. "Please, don't worry about me."

Alba smiled and patted Cassielle's hand before giving it a squeeze, "Aight. You're like my child. I always worry. It's my job."

As they ate, Cassielle couldn't shake the feeling there was something she was missing, something important she hadn't uncovered in her cases. It niggled at the back of her mind, elusive yet insistent. "It's different working cases by myself. I'm used to having someone to bounce ideas off of." Cassielle chewed on her lower lip for a moment before adding, "But it's not like I can't do it myself. I've solved dozens of cases on my own. These aren't as hard as homicide cases."

Alba must have noticed the furrow of Cassielle's brow because she reached across the table and squeezed her hand reassuringly.

"Hey, don't worry 'bout nuttin, child," Alba said, her voice soft but firm. "You're one of the best. I know ya will figure it out."

Cassielle mustered a weak smile. Beneath the facade of reassurance, however, a sense of urgency simmered, driving her to maintain her vigilance. With clients waiting in the wings and bills looming overhead, she couldn't afford to falter. Each misstep threatened to unravel her carefully constructed facade of success, jeopardizing her livelihood. The specter of failure loomed large, a constant reminder of the high stakes at play. Without a steady stream of clients, Cassielle risked tumbling into the abyss of obscurity, her reputation hanging precariously in the balance.

As they finished their meal, Cassielle's gaze drifted to the front window, where the stranger once again stood across the street. His reappearance startled her, disrupting the calm of the moment. Before she could fully comprehend his sudden presence, a passing car obscured her view. When it moved on, he had vanished. Uncertainty clouded her thoughts as she grappled with the perplexing recurrence.

Alba's voice drew Cassielle back to the present moment. She furrowed her brow, realizing she hadn't quite caught what was said. Alba chuckled softly, her island accent adding warmth to her words. "Easy, dear," she said. "No need to fret. Staying in the past ain't gonna help. Just focus on the now, your friends, and what ya can control."

"Thank you, Alba," Cassielle expressed, her gratitude genuine as she met Alba's understanding gaze. "For everything."

With a reassuring smile, Alba nodded, her unwavering support a beacon of strength for Cassielle. "Anytime, child. Ya know where to find me."

Cassielle rose from her seat, bid Alba goodbye, and made her way to the door. The puzzle of the stranger lingered in her mind, igniting a spark of curiosity propelling her forward. With each step, she felt the weight of uncertainty lift. Maybe there was something to what Alba had said about Baron Samedi. Maybe that stranger thought he was Baron Samedi. Maybe the random person on the street knew him and had seen him with her. She needed to get to the bottom of who he was and why he kept showing up. If he had been so intent on speaking with her, why had he run away? She needed to find him and get some answers. Curiosity may have killed the cat, but people say cats have nine lives, so perhaps she did, too. Maybe curiosity made her stronger and she was a different kind altogether.

CHAPTER FIVE

The pounding on the door grew louder, each rap echoing through Cassielle's skull like a relentless drumbeat. The reverberation knotted her stomach, punctuating the silence of the early morning hours with an urgent and fierce insistence.

Cassielle squeezed her eyes shut, desperately clinging to the hope the noise was nothing more than a cruel trick of her overtaxed mind, a manifestation of her restless slumber. But the pounding persisted, each successive knock tearing through the remnants of her sleep like a hurricane through flimsy plywood, refusing to be ignored or dismissed.

"Cassielle!" The voice outside sliced through the thick walls of her apartment with frantic desperation, laden with fear and desperation.

"Go away!" she yelled back, her voice muffled by the pillow pressed tightly over her ears, a feeble attempt to drown out the unwelcome intrusion.

With a frustrated curse, she flung the pillow aside and stumbled to the floor, her limbs heavy with exhaustion and irritation. Disentangling herself from the twisted sheets ensnaring her legs, she groaned in protest, her body Resisting every movement as if rebelling against the intrusion on her much-needed rest.

"Someone better be dying, or I'll make sure they are!" she threatened, a futile attempt to ward off the unwelcome visitor.

"Come on, Cass, let me in!" The voice on the other side of the door sounded strained, on the verge of tears, its desperation seeping through the cracks in Cassielle's resolve like water through a leaky dam.

With a resigned sigh, Cassielle trudged to the door. Each step felt like a Herculean effort, dragging her closer to the inevitable confrontation awaiting her on the other side. With a sigh, she swung the door open, revealing a disheveled figure standing on her doorstep.

Brittany stood there, her usually vibrant demeanor subdued by an air of frantic urgency. Her clothes were wrinkled, her raven hair a tangled mess. Tear tracks marred her brown cheeks, and her rich mahogany eyes were red-rimmed and swollen. All-in-all, not the normal perfectly put together woman Cassielle knew so well.

"B-Brittany?" Cassielle's confusion mingled with concern as she stepped back to let her friend inside.

Brittany threw herself at Cassielle, her arms wrapping around her and her face burrowing into her shoulder, tears staining Cassielle's sleep shirt. "He's dead, Cass," she blurted out, her voice trembling with grief. "Michael's dead!"

Cassielle's heart clenched at the raw emotion in her friend's voice, her tough exterior momentarily cracked by the vulnerability on display.

"What...?" The news hit her like a sucker punch, her mind struggling to process the sudden onslaught of information.

Brittany slumped into Cassielle, shoulders shaking with silent sobs. Cassielle's irritation evaporated in the face of her friend's anguish, replaced by a deep sense of empathy and compassion.

"C'mon," she said gently, guiding Brittany to the couch.

Once Brittany was seated, Cassielle headed across the small room towards the kitchenette. With purposeful strides, she reached for a glass and filled it with water from the tap. The steady stream of water filled the glass with a comforting hum.

Returning to the living room, she offered the glass

to Brittany, who accepted it with trembling hands. "Okay, start from the beginning." Cassielle sat beside her, her gaze softening as she watched her friend struggle to find the words. Brittany took a shaky sip before beginning.

"Well... I went out with some friends last night... and I saw Michael with..." Brittany's voice faltered, tears welling up in her eyes. "They were..."

Cassielle's heart went out to her. She reached out, placing a comforting hand on her friend's shoulder.

"You saw him..." she prompted gently, her voice a soothing balm to Brittany's frayed nerves.

"H-he was kissing some woman," Brittany's tears flowed freely now.

"Okay, so you caught him cheating. But how did he end up dead?"

"I... I don't remember... I woke up, and... and he wasn't moving..." Brittany turned and collapsed into Cassielle's arms, sobbing uncontrollably.

Cassielle held her friend, patting her back awkwardly. She wasn't skilled at comforting crying people. She'd always tried to avoid being the one to comfort victims.

"Did you call the police?" Cassielle inquired. Brittany shook her head.

"Brittany, we need to call the police." Cassielle started to get up, wondering where she had left her cell phone.

"No!" Brittany cried, grabbing Cassielle's arm. "I can't go to prison! I... I didn't do it!"

"If we don't involve the police, you'll appear more guilty. Now, come on." Cassielle freed her arm and walked toward her bed, searching for her phone.

"Cassielle..."

She paused and looked back at Brittany, who seemed fragile and helpless. It broke Cassielle's heart.

"Please... you have to help me. You know I would never do anything to hurt anyone. Something must have happened. I just... I don't know why I can't remember!"

As Cassielle sat on her bed in her cramped apartment, her gaze shifting from the disheveled figure of her friend to the cluttered kitchenette, a whirlwind of conflicting emotions churned within her. Despite the pounding headache and the remnants of sleep clinging to her like cobwebs, her concern for Brittany's well-being overrode her initial annoyance. If Michael was actually dead and Brittany was the only one there, then it didn't look good. Her strange amnesia wasn't like her, either. Brittany had an incredible memory for odd details. It was what made her such a good investigative reporter.

Doubt lingered in the recesses of her mind, casting a shadow over the situation. Could Brittany truly be guilty of the crime she alluded to? The thought seemed inconceivable. Cassielle had known Brittany for years, had witnessed her kindness, her compassion, her unwavering loyalty. She couldn't fathom her friend capable of such a heinous act.

Brittany had been the one friend to stick around when Cassielle's mother was murdered. She had been the only one to be able to see past Cassielle's broken spirit to the girl she had once been. Now it was Cassielle's turn to step up. She wouldn't fail Brittany.

Protective instincts surged to the forefront of Cassielle's mind as she watched Brittany collapse onto the couch, her usually vibrant personality eclipsed by grief and despair. Despite her usual guarded demeanor, Cassielle felt a fierce determination to shield her friend from further harm or distress. She sensed the weight of responsibility settling on her shoulders, the unspoken understanding she would go to great lengths to help Brittany navigate this crisis. There was a line, she knew, but in this moment of urgency and desperation, Cassielle was prepared to walk dangerously close to its edge.

But personal convictions gnawed at Cassielle's conscience, injecting a note of uncertainty into the tumultuous mix of emotions. She believed in justice, in fairness, in the inherent goodness of people. And yet, as Brittany pleaded for her help, Cassielle couldn't shake the nagging feeling there was more to the story than met the eye. She refused to pass judgment without all the facts, recognizing the possibility of extenuating circumstances or foul play.

With a heavy sigh, she turned to her friend, ready to offer comfort, assistance, and unwavering support in the tumultuous days to come.

Without hesitation, Cassielle's mind clicked into action, her instincts taking over like a well-oiled machine. She didn't need to ponder her next move; it came to her naturally, as if she were born for moments like these.

She leaned forward, her gaze focused and determined, and gently placed a hand on Brittany's trembling shoulder. "Okay, I'll take a look at your apartment, but I need you to tell me everything you remember. Did anyone see you leave? Do you know if anyone heard anything?" Cassielle watched her friend, noting her reactions to the question. Surprise hit her when she realized she was analyzing her like she would a suspect. Old habits die hard.

Brittany's voice trembled as she spoke, her eyes glistening with unshed tears. She hastily wiped at them with a crumpled piece of toilet paper, revealing her lip subtly quivered.

"Did you notice anything out of the ordinary before you left?" Cassielle's inquiry was gentle, yet probing, her brows furrowed.

Brittany shook her head, her voice thick with emotion. "No, everything seemed normal. No one was outside, and I didn't see anyone as I left."

"Well, that's something, at least," Cassielle remarked, her attempt at solace fragile yet sincere. "You said you can't remember what happened. Tell me what you do remember from before you found Michael dead."

Brittany's voice quivered as she recounted the events. "I-I went home, trying to distract myself, you know?" Her hands trembled as she twisted the toilet paper in her grasp, the fibers threatening to tear under the strain. "When Michael came back, I couldn't hold it in anymore. I confronted him, and it was like a dam burst inside me." Tears welled in her eyes, threatening to spill over at any moment. "We argued... I-I threw things, I don't even remember what." Her voice cracked, a jagged edge of guilt lacing her words. "And then... it's like everything just... stopped. When I came to, I was standing in the kitchen, and Michael... he was..." She couldn't bring herself to say the words, the weight of the truth too heavy to bear.

Cassielle listened intently, her heart aching for her friend. She reached out, gently resting a hand on Brittany's shoulder, offering silent support in the face of overwhelming guilt and grief. "It's okay," she murmured, her voice a soothing balm to her friend's shattered nerves. "We'll figure this out together. You're not alone in this." She thought for a moment. "Why don't you stay here while I take a quick look around your house. I'll see if anything stands out."

Brittany's eyes widened with alarm, a fresh wave of panic seizing her. "No, you can't go there! What if they think you did it?"

Cassielle shook her head. "I'll be careful," she stayed firm yet reassuring. "I won't leave any trace of my presence, and I'll keep a low profile. But I need to gather any clues or evidence that might help us figure out what happened."

She extended her hand, "Can I have your keys?"

CHAPTER SIX

As Cassielle drove down the sun-drenched streets of New Orleans, the midmorning heat of summer surrounded her, turning the air thick and heavy. Beads of sweat formed on her brow despite the cool air conditioning inside her Dodge Charger. The vibrant colors of the city seemed to shimmer in the intense sunlight.

As she turned onto Esplanade Avenue, the historic buildings loomed tall and majestic, their wrought iron balconies casting intricate shadows on the sunlit sidewalks below. The air was alive with the buzz of cicadas, their rhythmic chirping adding to the symphony of city sounds.

Approaching 1014 Esplanade Ave, Cassielle noticed the ornate details of the townhouses lining the street, their pastel facades glowing in the bright sunlight. The scent of magnolia blossoms hung heavy in the air, mingling with the aroma of freshly brewed coffee wafting from nearby cafes.

Parking her car by the curb, Cassielle stepped out into the sweltering heat, feeling the warmth envelop her like a heavy blanket. The asphalt radiated heat waves, distorting the horizon in the distance. Despite the oppressive weather, the city pulsed with life and energy, beckoning Cassielle to uncover the secrets hidden within its sun-soaked streets.

Cassielle's gaze swept over the building's elegant architecture, tracing the intricate details of its weathered exterior. The soft pink siding, tinged with age, mirrored the faded hue of the white columns and trim. Tall, slender windows punctuated the facade, their delicate lace curtains whispering secrets to the passing breeze.

Veering off the well-trodden path, Cassielle made her way towards the wrought iron gate to the left of the building.

As she approached the gate, a knot tightened in Cassielle's stomach, a familiar pang of anxiety clawing at her insides. She recognized the sensation all too well-the thrill of the unknown, the intoxicating lure of chaos. It was a feeling she had tried to outrun, to bury beneath layers of routine and normalcy. But today, standing on the threshold of uncertainty, it surged back with renewed intensity.

The prospect of stepping into the chaos of a murder scene was disquieting for her. It was a sensation she knew all too well, a peculiar blend of dread and exhilaration. Yet, as she stood at the gate, poised on the brink of the unknown, she couldn't deny the pull of the darkness awaiting beyond. She pulled on a pair of plastic gloves and booties on her shoes and moved forward.

Fear crept over her, its icy fingers tightening around her heart with each step closer to the crime scene. It wasn't just any fear-it was a primal, gut-wrenching trepidation born from past encounters with the darkest corners of humanity.

As she approached the back door, a wave of memories crashed over her, each one a stark reminder of the addictive allure crime scenes held for her. It was a dangerous addiction, one which had previously left her teetering on the edge of sanity.

Crime scenes were a potent cocktail of fear, adrenaline, and raw emotion threatening to engulf her at every turn. She craved the rush of darkness, the intoxicating thrill of unraveling the mysteries hidden within. But she knew all too well the dangers lurking beneath the surface.

With a heavy heart, Cassielle had made the agonizing decision to walk away from it all, to leave behind the twisted labyrinth of violence and despair. It had been a painful sacrifice, a cold turkey withdrawal from the chaos that had captured her. As Cassielle took a tentative step forward, she couldn't help but wonder what demons she might unleash if she dared to indulge her cravings once more.

The keys jangled as Cassielle unlocked the door and pushed it open. The air was heavy with a sickening odor that assaulted her senses upon entering the room. The acrid scent of bodily fluids filled her nostrils, mingling with the faint but unmistakable stench of urine and feces. The atmosphere was tense, charged with a strange energy. It was the energy she found intoxicating. She could have done without the smell. As she moved closer to the source of the scent, the room seemed to close in around her, the oppressive smell clinging to her clothing like a suffocating shroud.

As she breathed through her mouth, closing her eyes, Cassielle felt herself transported. When she opened her eyes, in the doorway to the bedroom, a chilling tableau unfolded before her. It was an altercation between Brittany and Michael, playing out like an old black-and-white film with muted colors, but also a cacophony of noise. Michael threw his hands in the air in frustration, his voice rising in exasperation. As he turned away from Brittany, she seemed to freeze, her movements becoming unnaturally still. A peculiar calm settled over her, casting an eerie aura around her figure.

Cassielle watched in growing alarm as Brittany's posture stiffened, her usual animated demeanor giving way to an unsettling rigidity. It was as if a veil had fallen over her friend, obscuring her true self and replacing it with something foreign and unsettling. The air seemed to crackle with tension, and Cassielle felt a chill as she realized something was deeply wrong. Brittany moved almost mechanically towards the white dresser in the corner and pulled upon each drawer, moving from the bottom to the top, stopping when she reached the top drawer. She pulled out a pair of panty hose and turned back around.

"Hmm... these will work," Brittany mused. Michael had gone into the bathroom and was still muttering and cursing.

Something was off- this Brittany gave off a darkness that was unlike the Brittany she knew.

Brittany's voice, usually warm and imbued with a Southern cadence, now struck Cassielle as unsettlingly cold, devoid of its usual charm. "Mmm... I've always wondered what it would feel like to be a woman," she remarked, her accent oddly reminiscent of something out of a Law-and-Order episode-distinctly New York.

Cassielle froze at Brittany's words. The sudden change in accent and the cryptic remark sent a wave of unease through her. It was as if she was a stranger inhabiting Brittany's body.

As Brittany had rifled through the dresser drawers, her movements seemed disjointed, almost frantic. She watched her friend's typically organized demeanor give way to a sense of disorientation. It was unlike Brittany to act this way, and Cassielle couldn't help but wonder what had brought about such a drastic change in her behavior.

As Cassielle moved to get a better look at Brittany's face, she felt a wave of dread wash over her. Something was off-this wasn't her friend. Though the face was familiar, the eyes were cold and void of emotion, emanating a dark energy that could freeze anyone in their tracks.

Brittany stealthily approached Michael; stockings clenched tightly in her grasp. With a calculated swiftness, she lunged forward, the stockings becoming a deadly noose in her hands.

Michael's eyes widened in terror as he felt the fabric tighten around his neck, his hands instinctively reaching up to claw at the constricting material. With a guttural cry, he kicked out at the wall, trying to use his weight to leverage Brittany and throw her off. But her grip remained unnervingly firm, her unnatural strength overpowering his desperate attempts to break free.

Despite his frantic struggles and the sickening sound of his gasps for air, Brittany's expression remained chillingly composed, her laughter echoing through the room like a twisted symphony of madness. With each futile kick and gasp, Michael's movements grew weaker, his body gradually succumbing to the relentless pressure of Brittany's deadly grip.

As Cassielle stood frozen in shock, her mind reeling with disbelief, Brittany's actions unfolded with disturbing precision. With a final, chilling twist, Michael's body went limp in her grasp, his futile struggles silenced as the life drained from his eyes. In the following silence, the weight of what had transpired hung heavy in the air, casting a pallor of dread over the once-familiar surroundings.

"Now that this is done, can I go?" Brittany's voice sliced through the tense silence, prompting Cassielle to whirl around. There was someone else there. An unsettling figure lurking nearby-a shape cloaked in pure darkness. She could feel the hairs on her arms rise. Something about this figure was unnatural aside from the fact he seemed to lack features. With a subtle gesture, the figure signaled, and Cassielle caught the sound of Brittany drawing in a deep breath. Without another word, the figure turned and strode out of the apartment, allowing the door to swing shut behind them. Cassielle moved to follow, but as she yanked open the door, she found herself abruptly yanking back to the present, gazing out at the sunlit courtyard below the balcony entrance. She stepped back into the apartment.

Michael's body remained on the stool, draped over the newspaper. Cassielle approached him and glanced at the headline over his shoulder. "'New Orleans Gripped by Terror: String of Strangulations Leaves City on Edge.'"

Returning to the hallway where the murder occurred, Cassielle surveyed the scene, distancing herself emotionally from the perpetrator and victim. A shattered lamp littered the floor, along with various other objects hurled in the altercation. The dresser drawers lay ajar, a silent witness to the night's events.

She noticed a smudge of soot on the kitchen counter, resembling the residue left behind by an incense burner. Cassielle made a mental note and then dismissed it, attributing it to Brittany's habit of using incense burners during times of stress. It was plausible she had relocated it elsewhere in the apartment after lighting it.

Cassielle meticulously combed through the apartment, her trained eye scanning every corner as if she were reliving the crime scene itself. With each pass, the vision of the murder played out in her mind, the details unfolding like scenes in a movie. Yet, despite her intense focus, the elusive third person remained a shadowy enigma, slipping through the seams of her mental reconstruction. Frustration gnawed at her; a sensation unfamiliar to a detective accustomed to piecing together even the most intricate puzzles.

She turned her focus to the figure. He or she didn't say anything, but instead moved his or her hands about. She couldn't get a distinct look to see what the gestures were. It was as if he were nothing but a black misty blob with the center darker and the outer edge wispy. She could only tell they were moving their hands because every so often a limb would extend. She noticed the figure bend over before leaving the apartment through the front door. Finally, with a heavy sigh, she conceded defeat, her visions fading as she reluctantly left the apartment, the unanswered questions lingering like ghosts in her mind.

Cassielle crossed the street, digging out her car keys from one pocket as she tucked her gloves into her other pocket. Opening her car door and sliding in, she was about to close it when someone caught the door, preventing her from doing so.

CHAPTER SEVEN

She looked up to find a woman holding the door. Cassielle didn't recognize her. The woman wore a headscarf, a long white peasant top over a patterned blue skirt and had a cane in one hand. She stood without the support of the cane, her hand resting on the car door. Cassielle couldn't fathom how the woman had approached her without notice. Her face displayed age marks, yet her dark eyes seemed timeless. Something about her exuded the same darkness Cassielle had felt inside the house, causing her heart to quicken with alarm.

The woman's voice, low and smooth, didn't quite match her appearance. "You need to stay out of this, Cassielle," she warned. "If you don't, we'll keep coming for everyone you love. One by one."

Cassielle frowned. "What?"

The woman smiled, turned, and began walking away.

"Stay out of what?" Cassielle called after her, but the woman continued walking, paying no heed to the question.

"Hey!" Cassielle pulled herself out of the car and hurried after the surprisingly fast elderly woman. "Who are you?"

The woman was using her cane to walk slowly when Cassielle caught up with her. Cassielle reached out and grabbed her by the shoulder. The woman let out a surprised squeal and turned unsteadily to face Cassielle. Cassielle was taken aback by the change in the woman's eyes. They were no longer as dark and deep. One eye had a slight cataract, and the other appeared light blue.

"Can I help you?" The woman's voice sounded different, too. It wavered in a way it hadn't before and had a higher pitch.

She seemed puzzled and alarmed.

"You just..." Cassielle's words trailed off. She no longer felt the darkness. It was as if the ground beneath her had shifted.

"Who are you?" the woman asked, her voice filled with alarm.

"Is there a problem here?" A man approached holding a tiny rat dog who was barking and struggling as if it would have loved nothing more than to take a bite out of Cassielle or the older woman while simultaneously looking terrified. The man glanced between Cassielle and the older woman.

"No... I just thought..." The woman's eyes darted between Cassielle and the man as she slowly moved away from them. Cassielle shook her head. "I'm sorry. I thought I knew her." She turned, walking back to her car in disbelief.

As Cassielle reached for her car door handle, her eyes scanned the street, only to freeze upon the sight of the mysterious man from the day before. He leaned against a magnolia tree, his silhouette blending with the dappling sunlight. His dark clothing seemed to absorb the light, casting him as a shadow amidst the morning glow. With a blink, he vanished.

Heart pounding, she slid into the driver's seat and turned to grab her purse, her breath caught in her throat.

"Hello," he said, his voice cutting through the silence like a knife.

Instinct seized Cassielle as she froze, her fingers of one hand hovering inches from the steering wheel and the other held up awkwardly as she'd been about to reach for her purse. Panic tightened her chest as she fought to maintain composure, her pulse thundering in her ears.

"What are you doing here, and why are you following me?" Her voice quivered with tension as she spoke, cautiously avoiding sudden movements. She felt uncomfortable in his presence, uncertain of his intentions.

The stranger's gaze bore into her, his eyes seemingly

delving into her soul as he spoke. "I'm not following you, Cassielle. I'm here to seek your help," he stated calmly, insistent yet composed. "I'm afraid I failed to properly introduce myself." With a gesture, he extended his hand towards her. "Baron Samedi."

Ignoring his outstretched hand, Cassielle's brows furrowed in disbelief. The amalgam of confusion and fear within her was unsettling. She leaned back, furrowing her brows. "You expect me to believe that?" Her words dripped with skepticism, laced with incredulity. "You're out of your mind." She shook her head. "Also, you're not following me? Let's not play games. Let's agree you've been stalking me. It's an odd way to seek help," she retorted, her voice tinged with a vulnerability she despised. She had never been one to easily fear others, but in his presence, an unspoken dread crept over her.

The stranger chuckled softly, his amusement unsettling her. "Believe what you will, Cassielle. But the truth reveals itself in time," he replied cryptically. "There are evil spirits loose in this city causing chaos. I and some of the other Loa are trying to round them up while LaCroix, Plumaj, and Kriminel are doing their best to watch the gates. At the same time, Cimitiere and Babaco are busy retrieving lost souls and guiding them back to where they belong." His voice softened, a gentleness emerging. "You'll be fine. I promise. But I need your help." His intense gaze left her breathless, conflicting emotions stirring within her.

Growing impatient, Cassielle's voice took on a steely edge. "If I didn't think you were out of your mind, I'd assume you had something to do with these murders. Evil spirits loose in New Orleans? What, do you expect me to think they're the reasons why the murders are happening?" She narrowed her eyes at him.

Before Cassielle could say more, her phone rang, breaking the tense silence of the car. Startled, she glanced down at the screen, only to see it was a call from Brittany. "I need you to get out."

"You're making a mistake, Cassielle," he said softly. "I understand your reluctance to trust me, but there are forces at play here that you can't begin to comprehend. Whether you realize it or not, you need me."

Cassielle's pulse quickened at his words, a rush of adrenaline coursing through her veins. The air in the car felt charged, as if a storm were brewing beneath the surface.

"Get out," she said, her voice trembling despite her efforts to sound firm. "I want nothing to do with you... if you come near me again, I'll—"

"I understand it's hard for you to believe me," Samedi interrupted, his gaze drifting momentarily out her front window. When he looked back, his eyes bore into hers with an intensity she couldn't decipher. "What if I told you something about you and your mother that no one else could possibly know?"

Cassielle shook her head. "I can't imagine you'd know anything, so go ahead. Give it your best try. Even a charlatan fortune teller could be right sometimes. This could be interesting."

"Your mother loved you deeply. She was disappointed when you stopped following Voodoo, but she understood your fear of your growing powers," Samedi continued. Cassielle grumbled but stopped, remembering she had told him to try. "The song she sang to you as a child, 'La Berceuse des Esprits,' wasn't just a lullaby. It was a prayer—a protective spell to keep you safe from harm."

Encouraged by her reaction, Samedi leaned back slightly, his voice softening as he began to sing in a deep, resonant tone:

"Dors, mon enfant, la nuit est douce,
Les esprits veillent sur ta douce.
Sous la lune, les étoiles brillent,
Protège ton cœur, là où ils filent."

His melodic voice filled the car, the French lyrics flowing effortlessly. After singing a few lines, he hummed the rest of the melody gently, the tranquil notes easing the tension.

The tune carried Cassielle back to a time when everything felt safe and clear. Tears pricked at her eyes. She hadn't heard the song in so long. It felt as if her mother were there, her voice in the melody, wrapping her tightly like she used to do with the warmed towel after a bath.

She swallowed, trying to push down the emotions.

"Perhaps that's not enough?" Samedi raised an eyebrow. "How about your recurring dream?"

Cassielle folded her arms. "Everyone has recurring dreams."

"They do," Samedi acknowledged, his voice taking on a thoughtful cadence. "Yours may be a combination of comfort, preparation, and prophecy. Let me continue."

He smiled wryly. "You're in a mist-shrouded cemetery. Stepping through the mist, you reach the first Gate of Guinee and meet Papa Legba. He warns you of dangers ahead, but you insist on entering to find him before it's too late. He draws his Veve on the door, saying you're destined for greatness, Daughter of Marie and Heylel."

Looking out the window, Samedi's gaze returned to her, her anxiety palpable. The world outside seemed to blur, the car becoming a cocoon of uncertainty and revelation. "Running through the Gate and mist, you search endlessly. Unsure if you find what you seek, you meet your mother who says, 'Je t'aime, ma fille. You have a great purpose if only you would trust.' Then you wake."

Cassielle realized she hadn't breathed while he spoke. Could he know about her dream? She racked her mind. Did she tell Nick? Brittany? Alba? Maybe her mother long ago?

"You need to go," she said softly, trying to stifle her fear.

"If that would ease your mind," Samedi sighed, his

voice a soothing contrast to the turmoil inside her. "I'll return after you've had time to think." With a mischievous smile, he tipped his hat and vanished.

With panic rising within her, she looked around the interior of her car as if he could have somehow dropped into a crevice. She climbed out and circled it, looking everywhere for him, trying to figure out where he could have gone and how he could have gone. She had forgotten she had her phone in her hand until it rang again. The door hadn't opened. It hadn't opened for him to get in or to get out. Indeed, she was losing her mind. Seeking therapy again might not be such a bad idea after all. Brittany and Alba would be happy. The phone rang again. Cassielle answered swiftly, her thoughts racing.

"Brittany, what's happening?" Cassielle's breaths came fast, her heart pounding in her chest.

"That's what I called you to ask!" Brittany's voice quivered. Cassielle could hear she was on the verge of unraveling. Cassielle cursed herself for asking such a foolish question. Amidst the tension with the stranger, the murder investigation had almost slipped her mind. "What did you find at the apartment?"

Cassie straightened her posture, her jaw set as she attempted to banish thoughts of the stranger from her mind. The idea of someone repeatedly appearing and vanishing defied all logic. Yet, the nagging doubt lingered, planting seeds of uncertainty in her thoughts. Was she losing her grip on reality? She silently resolved to schedule an appointment with her therapist, hoping to find clarity amid the confusion.

As she pushed the troubling thoughts away, a flicker of memory stirred in the depths of her mind. It was something her mother had once mentioned about Voodoo. The stranger bore a resemblance to one of the Loa, a figure from the spiritual traditions her mother had shared with her. The unsettling connection added another layer of discomfort to her already troubled mind. She pulled herself back to reality. He wasn't a Loa any more than were the Loa he'd listed real. She'd never met a Loa. Though she had seen Voodoo's power, this felt like a step too far. Like saying someone was God.

"Brittany, we need to call the police," she said firmly, her voice tinged with urgency. "I know you're scared, but I really believe there was someone else there. You didn't do this. You couldn't have done this. It doesn't add up." She paused, waiting for Brittany's response, her mind racing with possibilities and unanswered questions. With a few buttons pressed, the air conditioner kicked on, blowing sweet, blessed, cool air on her. Cassielle started drumming her fingers on the steering wheel as she waited for Brittany's answer.

"Can you call Nick?" Brittany's voice sounded calmer than she had a couple of hours ago. "I know you, and you work so well together. If there was someone else there, the two of you will prove it. I won't have to worry if I know you're working together on this."

"Britt, I'm sure he'll be assigned to the case. I don't work for the precinct anymore. There's no way that I would work with him on this anyway. I don't need to -"

"Call him," Brittany pressed.

Cassielle's grip tightened on the steering wheel as Brittany's request echoed in her mind. Memories of cruel words and slammed doors flooded her mind. She hadn't spoken to him since that rainy January night. The wounds were still fresh, the scars of their breakup raw and tender.

With a resigned sigh, she relented; arguing was futile. "Alright," Cassielle acquiesced, her voice betraying her anxiety. "I'll call Nick." She hung up and took a steadying breath.

With practiced ease and precision, she located his number amidst the digital sea of names and numbers. As she pressed the call button, her mind raced. If he didn't answer, she'd have to tell Brittany to do it. She wouldn't blame him if he ignored her call.

The line rang once, twice, before a smooth but clipped voice answered. "Nick speaking."

"Nick, it's Cassielle." She took a steady breath. "I need

your help with something."

There was a pause on the other end, a moment of silence that spoke volumes. Cassielle could almost hear the tension crackling in the air, the unspoken questions lingering between them like ghosts of their past.

"Cass," Nick replied, his voice guarded yet tinged with a hint of curiosity. "It's been a while."

She hadn't realized she was holding her breath. Cassielle took a deep breath, steeling herself for the conversation ahead. "It's about Brittany," she began, her voice steady despite the turmoil raging within her. Her heart pounded against her chest; each beat a reminder of the unresolved emotions stirring within her. Talking to Nick after months of silence felt like tiptoeing through a minefield of memories, each step laden with the weight of their past. But for Brittany's sake, she pushed aside her apprehension, her determination to seek justice overriding her personal discomfort. "Something's happened."

CHAPTER EIGHT

Twenty minutes later, Cassielle found herself perched on the bumper of her car, the warm metal pressing against her thighs as she waited for Nick to arrive. The familiar growl of his Ford Mustang GT's V8 engine reached her ears before she caught sight of the sleek black vehicle rounding the corner. The sound triggered a flood of memories she had suppressed— the Sunday afternoon drive to the beach, the wind in her hair, and Nick's infectious laughter barely audible over the wind roaring in her ears. But she moved those thoughts aside, focusing on the task at hand as she slid off the car to her feet and watched him park behind her car.

As he emerged from his Mustang, Cassielle was unpleasantly surprised to feel a familiar flutter in her stomach. She couldn't help but admire the rugged charm he exuded, a quality she'd often found herself drawn to over the years. His approach was marked by an unreadable expression. Tall and sturdy, with a chiseled and handsome visage, he possessed an effortless charisma that had always seemed to command attention wherever he went. Cassielle's look lingered on him, a silent acknowledgment of the attraction she had long harbored for him, tinged with a sense of inadequacy she couldn't shake.

"Hola, where's Brittany?" His voice sliced through her thoughts, its sharpness snapping her back to reality. Despite his attempt to maintain a stoic facade, his concern for Brittany was palpable. Cassielle noticed a guardedness in his deep brown eyes, a departure from their usual warmth.

It's your fault. The thought made her heart sink. He was

right. It was her fault. She had been the ruin of everything. She forced herself back to the present with a sigh.

"She's at my place. She's rattled," Cassielle's hands found refuge in the pockets of her denim shorts. The months of avoiding Nick, the guilt of their unresolved past weighed heavily on her as she steeled herself for the conversation ahead.

Nick's gaze bore into her, his eyes searching for answers she wasn't ready to give. "You didn't go inside, no?" His words carried a faint, melodious Puerto Rican accent softened by years in New Orleans. His tone was accusatory, tinged with a hint of disappointment.

Cassielle met his gaze head-on, refusing to falter under his scrutiny. "Yes, but I didn't touch anything," she admitted, raising her hand in a gesture of surrender. "She said she didn't remember anything, so I wanted to verify before calling you. I've had the same training as you. The scene is uncontaminated."

Nick's expression softened slightly, but she could still sense his lingering disapproval. "Okay, well, I called in backup, so you can go. Do me a favor and bring Brittany by the station, alright?"

Relief washed over Cassielle as she nodded her agreement. She was grateful Nick didn't push the issue further, allowing her to escape the uncomfortable confrontation unscathed-for now.

Nick started to walk away. Cassielle couldn't help herself. She jogged after him. "Can I give you my impressions of the scene?"

Nick stopped and fixed her with a look she couldn't quite decipher. "You're not a homicide detective anymore, Cass." His voice was gentle, but firm. She bristled at the pity in his face.

"Yes, but I haven't forgotten my training, and I may have noticed details you'll miss. I'll wait for you here." She moved to lean against the old magnolia tree in front of

Brittany's house. He wasn't going to be able to go back to his car without passing her. She could practically hear Nick's annoyance as he shook his head.

"¡Ay, bendito! You could just tell me now," he was pulling on plastic gloves and peering down the road looking for the back-up he had called.

His use of Spanish, the familiar phrase he'd once used when she exasperated him, made something flutter unexpectedly in her chest. The way he said it triggered a memory of those playful arguments that often ended in good times. She pushed the thought from her mind, focusing on the present moment.

"I could... but I'd rather you be able to form your own opinion first." She shrugged and smiled. "Come on, you used to love this game." A shadow passed over his features and he frowned.

"I used to love a lot of things, Cass." He turned and paused to look back at her. "Si, that game was an amusing tease. You made me work for every piece of info." He gave a small, nostalgic smile before looking back towards the house. "Está bien. We can talk after I've looked around." He turned back and walked through the gate, his words landing like a heavy blow to her gut. She had messed up. It was a truth she couldn't escape, even as she tried to bury it beneath layers of regret.

"Hey," Nick's voice brought her back to the present, his expression grim as he returned. "I don't see any evidence of a break-in. There's no way Brittany could have done it, though. Sure, there's stuff thrown about and a boot scuff mark on the wall like he tried to use it to brace himself against it to push away whoever was strangling him. We'll need to compare it to his boots. That's my best guess for now. She weighs what, like 110? 115? And he's, what, 250? No way she could've stopped him from breaking free if he was pushing against the wall."

Cassielle exhaled a breath she hadn't realized she was holding; relieved Nick had reached the same conclusion. Yet, beneath her relief lingered an unsettling truth she couldn't ignore-the image of Brittany with supernatural strength and a chilling demeanor.

"But who could have done it, then?" Cassielle pushed off from the tree, her movements driven by the urgency of her thoughts. Unanswered questions raced through her mind, each one tightening a knot of uncertainty in her chest. The image of the stranger lingered at the forefront of her thoughts, his perplexing presence like a specter. Yet, she hesitated to mention him, a flicker of doubt whispering he might be nothing more than a product of her imagination.

"You said she doesn't remember what happened, ¿no?" Nick had removed his gloves and his fingers moved swiftly over his phone screen as he spoke.

"Right," Cassielle confirmed, squinting against the glare of the sun on approaching vehicles. "She said the last thing she remembered, she threw a lamp at him and missed. She said after that she was standing in the kitchen with no idea what happened in between."

As Nick continued typing on his phone, Cassielle's gaze followed the arriving vehicles-a procession of law enforcement and forensic units converging on the scene. Patrol cars, the distinctive CSI van, and an unfamiliar vehicle she assumed belonged to Nick's new partner. Her attention snapped back to Nick.

"She hasn't lost time like this before? From what I remember, she's not much of a drinker."

Cassielle shook her head, grappling with the unsettling implications of the crime scene. The shadow figure, the altered voice-signs of something beyond her understanding, something dark and inexplicable. She suppressed a shiver, unwilling to entertain the implications lurking in the depths of her mind.

"Not as far as I know, but she and I haven't really talked much recently," she admitted, her voice tinged with uncertainty. "Nick, what do I tell her?"

A look crossed Nick's face and he opened his mouth to say something but was interrupted by some people approaching them. She turned to look as Nick directed the CSI crew, his movements purposeful as he orchestrated the beginning stages of the investigation. "Give me a second, ¿okay?" he requested, before striding off to coordinate with the uniformed officers, who were already unfurling yellow police tape to cordon off the crime scene.

While he was gone, she took the opportunity to look around at the people starting to gather and observe the unfolding scene. Statistically speaking, criminals often return to the scene of the crime to relive the moment or satisfy some psychological need. Perhaps among the onlookers, she might spot the dark figure she encountered earlier and somehow recognize them. They had emitted a distinct aura that had left an impression on her. Though she never fully relied on her instincts, Cassielle had a knack for reading people. This skill could prove enough to identify the elusive third person involved in the mysterious events. She scanned the growing crowd, her gaze lingering on each face, searching for any hint of familiarity or suspicious behavior that might lead her closer to the truth. Mostly it seemed to be your average looking people. No one seemed especially suspicious.

"Hey Cassielle! Thinking of jumping back in the game?" Cassielle turned towards the approaching figure, her eyes narrowing slightly against the sunlight. A smile crossed her face. Ah, Marcus Fontenot and his infamous sports analogy.

Marcus cut an imposing figure as he strode closer. He stood well over six feet tall, his frame solid and broad beneath a tailored charcoal suit straining slightly at the shoulders. His dark hair, peppered liberally with gray at the temples, was neatly cropped. The lines etched around his hazel eyes spoke of years spent studying faces, piecing together truths from lies.

Approaching her with long strides. His smile was easy, his handshake firm as he clasped her hand. "Long time no see," he greeted.

"Just dropping by," Cassielle replied, noting the hint of disappointment in Fontenot's expression.

"Ah, just a spectator then. Well, if you ever decide to rotate in, you know where to find us," Fontenot flashed a brief smile before nodding to Nick who had returned. He nodded at Cassielle before departing to continue his rounds.

"I'll swing by with Brittany later. Shoot me a text when you're back at the station. She'll prefer talking to you," Cassielle said, retrieving her keys and heading off.

"Hey Cassielle?" Nick's voice stopped her in her tracks.

"Yeah?" She turned back, uncertain of what she expected to hear, but feeling a faint flutter of anticipation, nonetheless. It was a sensation she hadn't experienced in ages, the eager anticipation of a sweet word she'd almost forgotten.

"It was good seeing you. You look like you're doing well." Nick said, his voice carrying an unmistakable warmth. He paused, as if weighing his next words carefully. His gaze lingered on her, sending a flush through her. He opened his mouth, but closed it without saying another word. A familiar gesture that once had set her heart aflutter but now left her feeling hollow and yearning for what once was.

Cassielle's heart skipped a beat at his hesitance. Her mind drifted to their past intimate moments, a burning longing she'd tried to bury. "It was good to see you, too," she replied, her voice strained. "Thank you."

"For what?" Nick's face shifted to a look of bewilderment.

"For coming. I mean, for answering the phone and then also coming to help. You didn't have to. You could have ignored my call..." Her cheeks flushed, and she hoped he didn't notice her blush. "You're a good man."

Nick's eyes softened and a small smile crossed his face, "Some things will never change."

Cassielle felt a pang of something she hadn't allowed herself to feel in a long time. "Yeah," she whispered, "I guess some things don't." As she turned away, embarking on what felt like the longest short walk ever, the weight of their shared history lingered, bittersweet and undeniable.

The next couple of hours were a blur for Cassielle. After driving back to her apartment to pick up Brittany, she intended to drop her off at the police station. However, Brittany insisted Cassielle accompany her inside for "moral support." Cassielle, unable to refuse her friend's plea, found herself reluctantly agreeing.

Now, Cassielle sat perched on the edge of Nick's desk, patiently waiting. Although Cassielle was allowed access to the back area, she was confined to sitting near Nick's desk and not permitted in the room where Nick and his current partner, Marcus, were questioning Brittany. The bustling sounds of the New Orleans police department filled her ears-ringing phones, clicking computer keys, and overlapping voices. She found herself missing the lively atmosphere, contrasting with her quiet office space on Bourbon Street. Occasionally, on warm days with her window open, she could hear children's laughter from the nearby playground on Saint Philip Street. Yet perhaps it was better this way.

Finding a stress ball on Nick's desk, she idly played with it, her legs crossed. No one paid her much attention. Having been a competent detective who left on good terms, most assumed she had fallen out with Nick and couldn't bear to work with him any longer. It was the usual assumption when a woman left a job where she had been dating a coworker. Although it wasn't the case in this instance-they broke up after she left-Cassielle chose not to argue. She didn't want people asking questions she couldn't or wouldn't answer.

Her gaze fixed on the door through which Nick had taken Brittany. The drawn shades prevented anyone from peeking inside to witness the proceedings. She was familiar with that room-a table with two chairs on one side, one chair on the other-and it lacked the single dangling light bulb depicted in movies. Instead, fluorescent lights illuminated the space like the rest of the building. Nick and his partner were probably seated at the table, trying to put Brittany at ease. They wouldn't resort to good cop, bad cop tactics since she wasn't a hostile witness. However, her memory lapse would undoubtedly complicate matters.

Time dragged on until Nick emerged from the room, accompanied by Marcus. Marcus conversed with several uniformed officers while Nick made a beeline for his desk where Cassielle was waiting. Frustration etched across his face, a look she knew all too well. He ran a hand through his short hair as he stopped before her.

"Any luck?" she inquired.

"None," Nick replied, his tone filled with exasperation. "She insists she remembers nothing beyond shouting at him in their bedroom. Claims to have no recollection of anyone else in the apartment and she doesn't remember seeing Michael being choked. He pulled out his chair and slumped heavily into it.

"It's weird," Cassielle remarked, tossing the stress ball between her hands, lost in thought. "She has an excellent memory. Why would she not remember this? She's been through stuff before and never blacked out. Maybe she was drugged?" She saw a look on his face. "What are you thinking?'

Nick hesitated, locking eyes with her. "Look, if she had been there during the strangulation, why wouldn't she try to stop the perpetrator? There should be some kind of wounds or marks on her, ¿no?"

Cassielle's mind raced with explanations she couldn't say. She understood Nick's logical questions, but they only deepened the mystery. How had Brittany transformed into someone unrecognizable?

"Maybe not if she was drugged. She might have been out cold during the whole thing." She knew it wasn't true, but had to sound convincing so Nick wouldn't detect the lie in her tone. She needed to figure out who the third person was. Even if they hadn't explicitly caused the murder, they were clearly involved. She'd feel no guilt pinning it on them if it meant saving Brittany. She needed to figure out how.

She bit her lip, knowing she couldn't discuss the real mystery with him without sounding like a lunatic. Yet, she longed to confide in him about the unsettling encounters with the stranger and what she had seen in Brittany's house. She'd had to keep secrets before, unable to fully share her world with him. So many fights and slammed doors could have been avoided if she'd had the guts to lay her truth on the line. The realization weighed on her, a stark reminder of why their relationship could never have succeeded under the weight of her hidden truths. This was further evidence that leaving had been the right choice.

"So, are you going to detain her?" Cassielle's stomach twisted into knots as she held her breath, waiting for his response. The thought of her gentle friend facing jail time made her heart race with worry. Brittany had struggled to endure even a brief detention back in high school-it was hard to imagine her coping with anything more serious.

Nick shook his head. "Marcus and I talked about it. We're thinking no. I mean; we don't have enough to prove it was her and I don't think she did it. She's not physically capable of it. But I don't see evidence of someone else." He sighed. "This is an ongoing investigation. I really shouldn't be discussing it with you," Nick added, grabbing a pen from his desk drawer. "I have a lot of work to do, and you probably shouldn't be here."

"Oh, come on," she coaxed, leaning forward and placing her hands on either side of her legs, drawing closer to him. With the top she was wearing, she had no doubt she could recapture his attention and perhaps convince him to involve her in the case, at least while she was within his line of sight. But did she really want to use 'feminine wiles' to inch her way into the investigation? "You know you could benefit from my unique skill set."

He glanced down before meeting her gaze squarely, "Even if I wanted to, I don't know any more than you do at this point. Forensics hasn't come back with their report and the coroner, as far as I know, hasn't examined the body yet."

Cassielle's eyes lifted just as Brittany came out of the interrogation room. Her eyes were still red and puffy, but she didn't appear to be crying anymore.

"We must have overlooked something," Cassielle hopped off the desk. "There had to have been someone else there."

"Possibly. We'll have to keep digging." Nick was already starting up his computer to begin the inevitable slog of paperwork. His gaze fixed on the computer screen as he waited for the case management system to boot up. Nick's phone buzzed and he pulled it out of his pocket. A smile came across his face as he looked at the screen. It seemed out of place for this particular moment. She wasn't sure she wanted to know, but she needed to ask.

"You're hiding something," Cassielle stated, crossing her arms over her chest. "What aren't you telling me?"

"This isn't the time, Cass."

"You don't usually hide stuff from me," Cassielle said softly, feeling a catch in her throat.

"You mean like you do?" The look crossing his face was enough. She knew he instantly regretted what he said. "Dios, I'm sorry. I didn't mean to-"

"No," Cassielle's voice trembled slightly, "It's okay. I get it." She chewed on her lip, considering her words carefully. She kept her voice low, mindful of the people around them. "You're right. I wasn't always honest with you." She took a deep breath before speaking, "I really want to tell you everything. I should have been more up front with you about my feelings... I don't know if I'm ready yet." Her eyes met his, an ache spreading through her heart, "Not when I see you looking at me like you used to. Looking like you want to be a part of everything."

Nick ran a hand through his hair, glancing past her. Cassielle glanced behind her. Fontenot was speaking with Brittany outside of the interrogation room. "You don't have to." Cassielle turned her attention back to Nick as he continued,

"We've moved on. Maybe... maybe one day we can get past this and be friends."

Cassielle nodded, though her heart felt heavy. "Yeah, maybe. But today's not that day, is it?"

"Not today. But I hope we get there." Nick sighed. "I do need to tell you something... This isn't the time or place, but you'll likely find out eventually and I'd rather tell you, first." He paused and put his phone away, "I'm seeing someone."

Cassielle struggled to gather her thoughts. She hadn't expected Nick to remain single forever. Who could he be involved with, and how had he managed to move on? Some in the precinct called her a workaholic, but compared to him, she was a novice. He was married to his work, determined to become a captain by age 40. If anyone could achieve it, he could. Always by-the-book and impeccably skilled-his relationship status now felt like an unexpected twist in their conversation.

"Felicidades," she replied, uncertain of the appropriate response or even if her congratulations came off as sincere. Something in her tone must have alarmed him because he finally tore his eyes away from the computer screen and focused on her.

"I didn't want you to find out from someone else. Okay?" He watched her intently. She shrugged noncommittally and started to walk away.

As she moved toward the exit, Nick called out from behind her. Without breaking her stride, Cassielle felt a sudden, electrifying grip on her arm. Nick's touch lingered a heartbeat longer than necessary, sending a jolt through her body she couldn't ignore.

"Cassielle, wait," Nick's voice was a low, intense murmur. His fingers brushed against her skin, leaving a trail of heat.

She turned to face him, her breath hitching at their proximity. She was grateful that Brittany had gone out to the lobby and the hallway they were in was empty save for them. "I understand, but this isn't the time to discuss it," she said firmly, trying to maintain composure despite the way his touch stirred something inside her. She flicked her gaze toward Brittany, who stood by the door, then gently but decisively pulled away from Nick's grasp.

"I know you don't want me to get involved," Cassielle continued, her voice steady, "but I can't sit back. She didn't do this. She couldn't have." Her resolve hardened as she moved toward the lobby, her steps quick and purposeful.

"¡Coño, Cassielle!" Nick persisted; his tone urgent. She turned to face him; arms folded defensively. "You don't want to be charged with obstruction of justice," he slipped his hands into his pockets.

"I won't obstruct anything," she shot back, her gaze unwavering. "I'll make sure you don't overlook anything crucial, like evidence proving her innocence."

"Querida, you're too close to this. You know that." Nick reasoned, his expression searching. "Please. I'm concerned for your well-being in this. You don't need to have a criminal record tarnishing your name. It wouldn't be good for your business." He shuffled his feet a moment before continuing, "I want what's best for you and Brittany. I want to find out what really happened as much as you do." His eyes searched for something in her face. "You know that, right?"

The look he was giving her made her heart pound as if it were trying to burst out of her chest and cross the divide between them. She couldn't let herself be pulled into his orbit. It wasn't good for him. "You do what you do, and I'll do what I do." With that, Cassielle pivoted on her heel and gently escorted Brittany out of the station, leaving Nick's words hanging in the air behind her.

As she guided Brittany through the station's lobby, her mind raced with conflicting thoughts. Nick's warning echoed in her ears-obstruction of justice was a serious charge, one that could jeopardize everything she had worked for. Yet, the thought of Brittany facing accusations she couldn't possibly be guilty of gnawed at Cassielle's conscience.

What if Nick was right? What if her involvement did more harm than good? But then again, what if she stayed silent and they couldn't prove someone else was there? They'd have to rely on making sure there's enough doubt so they couldn't possibly charge Brittany. It wouldn't be a clear exoneration, but it might be the best they could manage.

Cassielle took a deep breath as they stepped into the sunlight, her gaze fixed on Brittany's weary face. She couldn't ignore the look in her friend's eyes-the silent plea for someone to believe in her innocence.

As they walked down the street towards her car, Cassielle's thoughts swirled with uncertainty. She couldn't turn her back on Brittany, but the consequences of getting involved weighed heavily on her mind. Cassielle resolved to tread carefully, unsure of whether to assist behind the scenes or maintain her distance. If Nick wanted to keep her at arm's length, so be it. Cassielle grappled with the uncertainty, feeling the weight of her decision and unsure of which path to take.

CHAPTER NINE

The Lafitte's Blacksmith Shop Bar stood at the intersection of Saint Philip Street and Bourbon Street. Its quaint one-story structure punctuated by two dormer windows peered out over the bustling street. Cassielle maneuvered her car into the slender sliver of shade cast by a tree across the street. With the afternoon sun beating down relentlessly on the streets below, it was a common custom to take shade when you could find it.

Inside the car, a heavy silence enveloped them, broken only by the hum of the engine and the occasional murmur of passersby on the sidewalk. Brittany had remained quiet throughout the drive, lost in her own thoughts, and Cassielle respected her need for solitude. She wasn't sure what she would say anyway. Brittany and Nick would be the first people to say Cassielle was terrible at small talk and even worse at comforting words. Alba often found herself puzzled by the notion, especially considering how Cassielle's mother, Seraphina, seemed to possess an innate talent for comforting others and making friends wherever she went. Seraphina's warm embraces and timely words of wisdom were like a soothing balm to those in need.

As they sat parked on the quiet street, Cassielle's mind buzzed with unanswered questions, each one a puzzle piece in the enigma of Brittany's sudden transformation and Michael's tragic demise. Brittany was not the type of person to harm a fly, let alone someone she loved as dearly as she loved Michael. They had been discussing weddings last week. Even if she'd been angered and shocked to find him cheating, her instinct would never have been to actually hurt him. Break his stuff, yes. But kill him, no.

So, if she didn't do it, perhaps she had been under the influence of drugs. This would perhaps explain the strange behavior she'd shown in Cassielle's vision. Cassielle would have to get some hair from her and see if she could arrange for a test. She wasn't sure if she had enough pull to get someone to conduct a blood or hair test for her down at the lab. An at-home test might not cover everything. Maybe if she leaned on Nick, he would share the results of the test they likely performed when they took Brittany into the back at the station. Brittany hadn't divulged what happened during the two hours she'd spent in the room with them. But what was with the strange figure there? Had she imagined them? If not, were they the stranger who kept following her?

Brittany turned her gaze toward the window, her voice breaking the silence. "LaFitte's?"

Cassielle shut off the engine, meeting Brittany's gaze with a sympathetic smile. "Well, for one, you can't go back to your house. Two, I don't want to leave you alone at my apartment, and three, I think you and I could use a drink. I know Alba has the space and will be more than happy to take you in."

The air clung thick with humidity, smothering the car's windows and embracing Cassielle and Brittany in a stifling grip. Each breath felt like wading through molasses, a physical echo of the morning's weighty events. Beads of sweat began to gather on their brows, a testament to the oppressive atmosphere both inside and outside the car.

Despite the weather's grip, a serene calmness blanketed the streets, a stark juxtaposition to the usual fervor of Mardi Gras or the lively festivities of St. John's Eve. Cassielle savored these tranquil moments, finding solace in the quietude of the off-season. It was during these rare respites that she felt a deep connection to the pulse of the city, immersing herself in its rhythm and forging genuine bonds with its inhabitants on the rare occasions she chose to do so.

LaFitte's wasn't Cassielle's preferred spot for a drink, its storied past often casting a shadow over her visits. Despite this, she found herself drawn there often, compelled by the allure of familiar faces and the nostalgia of good times from her childhood. While Brittany favored their Daiquiris, Cassielle's visits were more to see Alba and to feel a sense of home. The bar's proximity to her office made it a convenient choice, especially when Alba's maternal instincts compelled her to ensure Cassielle took breaks amidst her workload. Plus Alba would be apoplectic if Cassielle didn't come to eat at least a few times a week. Usually she was there daily for lunch.

As Brittany stepped out of the car with a hesitant stride, her eyes distant as she looked around, Cassielle followed closely behind. The familiar creak of the car door punctuated the stillness of the street. Cassielle reached back to grab her messenger bag from the back seat before joining Brittany on the sun-drenched pavement. Distant echoes of cars drifted through the sultry atmosphere.

Pushing open the door of Lafitte's, they were greeted by a wave of cool air tinged with the aroma of aged wood and spilled drinks. As Cassielle glanced around the dimly lit room, her eyes followed Brittany's gaze as it swept over the few eclectic individuals scattered throughout the space. Each patron seemed immersed in their own conversations or lost in contemplation over their drinks. Cassielle noticed a couple of regulars-the middle-aged man with the salt-and-pepper beard nursing a whiskey and the young artist sketching in a corner booth.

The bar was quiet, the mid-afternoon lull offering a brief reprieve. Cassielle knew it would pick up in an hour or two, but she didn't plan to stay long. She had work piling up-a daunting list including figuring out what to do about the mysterious stranger, proving Brittany's innocence, and wrapping up some paid jobs.

Out of habit, they settled at an empty table toward the

back of the bar. Cassielle couldn't help but notice the worn leather seats and the rustic charm permeating the space.

Cassielle felt a comforting reassurance wash over her that she had come to associate with this beloved establishment. Despite the weight of unanswered questions lingering in her mind, there was a sense of peace settling over her sitting there with Brittany. She could see Brittany's eyes staring unfocused at the door. She could practically hear her wishing Michael would walk in and everything had just been a bad dream. Boisterous and happy as ever. Cassielle's heart broke for her friend. She opened her mouth to say something comforting, but was spared the struggle by someone walking up to their table.

"Oh girls!" Alba's accent carried the melodic rhythm of Barbados, each word a gentle sway in the island's gentle cadence. "Lawd have mercy! I heard what happened to Michael. Brittany, my dearheart, how are ya doing?"

Brittany's face twisted with emotion, tears threatening to spill from her eyes, as Alba enveloped her in a comforting embrace. Alba lowered herself to Brittany's level, their bodies drawing close, offering solace in their shared embrace. Alba whispered softly, her words a soothing murmur barely audible above Brittany's sobs. Cassielle watched silently, struck by Alba's ability to provide comfort. Perhaps this was another thing to talk to her therapist about. How does one learn how to comfort others?

"Alba, I really hate to intrude, but would you by chance be able to keep Brittany in your apartment for a few days?" Cassielle's voice was tentative, but Alba's response was swift.

"Of course! Dearheart, ya can stay with me as long as you'd like." Alba released Brittany gently, sensing her regained composure. "Come, let me take ya upstairs and get ya settled in. I feel a good cup of tea would do ya well."

Cassielle waited patiently as Alba took Brittany upstairs and returned a short while later. She looked surprised to see Cassielle still sitting and waiting for her.

Cassielle rose from her seat. "Could I talk to you in private?" Her words were soft, but the urgency was clear. Alba nodded and led them behind the bar, into the cramped kitchen.

There, Alba's nephew Jamal worked diligently, plating fish cakes with practiced skill. Alba caught his eye and deftly signed to him in American Sign Language, prompting him to take a break. Jamal nodded in understanding, moving to leave them in privacy. Alba grabbed the plate and disappeared through the doors to the main dining room.

Cassielle's fingers moved fluidly and precisely as she signed a greeting to Jamal.

He glanced at her, his eyes widening with concern, his hands moving quickly.

"What's wrong?"

Cassielle offered a gentle smile, "Nothing serious. Just hoping to have a private conversation with your aunt. But before you go, were you here last night?"

Alba returned and started dealing with the dishes in the sink.

Jamal hesitated, his eyes darting away as he reached into his pocket and pulled out a cigarette. Cassielle's brow furrowed, puzzled by his sudden nervousness. "No, sorry," his movements were tense. With a quick, uneasy wave, he turned and hurried out. Alba's disapproving "tsk" echoed after him, the unlit cigarette trembling between his fingers as he disappeared through the door.

"Dat ain't right," Cassielle could feel Alba's disappointment deep in her soul and breathed a sigh of relief it wasn't directed at her. She'd had enough of it when she was in high school.

Returning her attention to Cassielle, Alba wiped her hands on her apron before pushing a strand of hair out of her face. Her mane of lustrous dark curls were braided down her back with strands escaping here and there thanks to the humidity. She looked over at Cassielle with her striking blue eyes.

"What are ya thinking?"

Cassielle joined Alba at the sink. She knew better than to stand idly by while someone else worked.

"I need to know what happened here last night when Brittany and Michael were here. Did you see anything?" Cassielle dried the dish Alba handed her.

"It was so busy I didn't even notice Michael was here 'til I see Brittany come in." She rested her hands on the counter, looking down and shaking her head. "I see that poor girl's face looking so hurt, and then I look and see Michael sitting with some other woman at their table. I remember thinking, 'Dat don't make no sense.' I've never seen him act so lewd. Not even with Brittany." She "tsk, tsked" like she had with Jamal. "I thought for sure she would have blista him. Rather, cursed him. But no. She didn't so much as utter a single word. I had half a mind to cuff him myself. What a goathead." Her face changed as if she had just remembered Michael was dead. "Lawd forgive me."

The idea of Alba hitting Michael was amusing, but Cassielle refrained from smiling. Instead, she focused on what Alba had said. Michael wasn't acting like himself and Brittany wasn't acting like herself. Cassielle leaned forward, her brow furrowed with concern. "Was there anything else off about him?"

Alba shook her head.

"Was there anyone else there who seemed... different?" She struggled to find the right words to describe the unsettling figure from her vision.

Alba shook her head slowly. "No, I don't think so," she replied, her expression thoughtful. She added, "Well, actually, there was a man who walked in and then right back out. I couldn't get a good look at him. He had his hood up over his face. I remember worrying maybe he was here to cause trouble. I was about to greet him when he turned and left in a real hurry," Alba continued with a shrug. "He never came back in. After that, I saw Brittany come in with that blonde woman and the redhead who never has enough clothes on, Cuh Dear. I saw her notice Michael, and then she run right out. Her friends run after her." Alba frowned; her tone turned disapproving. "I had half a mind to go give that boy a piece of my mind, but I decided to talk to JJ and let him handle it."

Alba's voice caught, and she sniffled as she pulled a tissue from her pocket, dabbing at her eyes. "I was so sure they were gonna get married," she said, her words thick with emotion. "They were so sweet to each other. What happened?"

Cassielle felt a pang of helplessness. She wanted desperately to comfort Alba but found herself at a loss for words once again.

"That stranger, can you give me a description of what you did notice?" Cassielle hesitated, her hand hovering over her bag as she considered asking for more details.

Alba glanced up, catching the pause in Cassielle's movement. "Well, he was tall," Alba began, leaning against the counter. "He wore a black sweatshirt of some sort and black pants. Oh, it was a black hoodie with the hood up, not a sweatshirt. I couldn't get a good look at his face. It was dim here. Ya know how it does get in here at night."

Cassielle nodded slowly, absorbing the details while her thoughts raced. The urge to delve deeper battled with her growing reluctance to get involved further. This wasn't her case to solve, and the risks of interference weighed heavily on her mind. She wasn't even sure why she was questioning Alba.

"Thank you," Cassielle finally said with regret. "I appreciate your help."

Alba nodded in understanding. "Anytime, dearheart. Ya know where to find me if ya need anything else."

Cassielle managed a small smile, hiding her inner conflict behind a mask of gratitude. "Of course."

As Alba picked up a tray of glasses, Cassielle's thoughts churned with conflicting emotions. She yearned to uncover the truth and assist her friend, but uncertainty clouded her determination. Resigned to her current state of indecision, she took the tray from Alba and followed her back into the main area of Lafitte's, the tray weighed nothing in comparison to her thoughts.

Cassielle set the tray of glasses on the counter and began stacking them on the shelves while Alba went over to a man at the bar, inquiring if he desired another drink. As Cassielle finished, a familiar sensation gripped her-a feeling akin to being doused with ice water.

Suddenly, a smooth, low purr broke the quiet ambiance of the bar. "Bonjour, ma belle."

CHAPTER TEN

She turned slowly, her pulse quickening, to confront the source of the seductive voice. As her gaze met his, her eyes widened imperceptibly, caught in the mesmerizing stare, pulling at her like a tide. Pushing aside her conflicted thoughts, she reminded herself this man was stalking her-a dangerous presence not to be swayed by. Yet, she couldn't help but admire his visage.

"Pardon the intrusion, but I couldn't help but be drawn to your captivating presence. Mind if I join you ladies?" His words cut through the ambient chatter of the bar, causing Cassielle's heart to skip a beat.

Cassielle found herself locked in a stare with the dark, magnetic eyes of the enigmatic figure that had crept through her thoughts for the past 36 hours or so. He leaned confidently against the bar, his hat and coat adding an aura of mystery to his presence.

"Cassielle, who's that handsome man?" Alba whispered loudly. Her Bajan accent always seemed to thicken when she saw a man she found attractive.

Cassielle rolled her eyes. "No idea."

"Samuel Baron, mademoiselle," he introduced himself, extending his hand to Alba. "But you may call me Sam." Alba was a sucker for a gentleman, especially one who exuded this much charm. Alba giggled and took his hand. He leaned in to kiss the back of her hand before releasing it. She was as giddy as a schoolgirl.

"Oh, Cassielle, I did like Nicholas, but this man..." Alba made a sultry noise. "He's a real gentleman. Where do you come from, Monsieur Baron?"

He chuckled. "Down south of here," he replied, winking at her. Alba giggled again. Cassielle could feel the warmth of a blush rising to her cheeks.

"So, Empire?" Alba guessed as Cassielle settled on a barstool next to an older man, placing her laptop on the bar in front of her. She hoped her stalker would take the hint and sit farther away. He chose to occupy the stool one seat away, as she had made a point of putting her bag on the vacant seat next to her. Cassielle couldn't fathom what was up with this guy.

Cassielle's pulse quickened, a cocktail of fear and attraction swirled within her. His proximity brought thoughts of her dream of him as well as their conversation in the car. She tried to focus on the screen of her laptop, her fingers trembling slightly as she typed. His presence caused her to feel a warm buzz surge through her body. It was like his presence caused every bit of her to come alive. She could practically feel his eyes on her. She glanced over at him as he spoke.

"Further south," Sam said, leaning against the bar, his gaze fixed on Cassielle.

"Mysterious... I like dat," Alba winked. "What can I get ya, handsome?"

"El Diablo, please," Sam replied, turning his attention back to Cassielle.

"Sure thing, sugar," Alba said, turning to Cassielle, "How 'bout I get something for ya? I bet you're ready for a lil' break." She smiled warmly. "The usual?"

"Yes, please," Cassielle responded, pulling out her laptop and hoping appearing busy would give the guy a hint to leave.

"If you're seeking assistance in liberating your friend from charges, all you have to do is inquire," he remarked, his eyes fixed on her. She stared at him for a moment. His odd way of speaking added to his unnerving presence. Was it an air he liked to put on? He exuded a dark energy that was both disturbing and intriguing. She couldn't pinpoint exactly why she felt like this. Maybe it was a combination of his stalker vibe-a person you look at and think, 'Huh, wouldn't be surprised if I see you outside my window at 3 am creeping around in my bushes' and how incredibly attractive he was. When he looked at her, she felt as if he was looking into her soul. "I'm also available for other kinds of interactions." He winked at her and took a sip of his drink, making her heart race. The warmth flooding her face was unmistakable. Why did he make her blush so easily? Maybe she really needed to get laid.

"Good to know," she answered, quickly turning her attention to her computer and opening her email account. They sat silently before Cassielle sang softly, "Row, Row, row your boat, gently away from me. Merrily, merrily, merrily, please just fucking leave."

"I want to help you," he said as Alba returned with their drinks. She placed a fruity red cocktail before Sam and a cold beer for Cassielle. He was still facing her, and she was trying hard to ignore him, but with little success.

"Listen," she turned to face him, attempting to keep her irritation in check since they were in public, and Alba didn't like brawls in her bar. "If you have something to say that's of use, please just say it. Drop the flirting. Just be straight with me." She turned, grabbed her glass, and had a long drink. If this guy stuck around much longer, she would need more of these to keep her temper in check.

"As you wish," he replied, and she watched out of the corner of her eye as he took a long sip of his drink, reached into his pocket, and pulled out cash. He set the cash on the bar and slid it towards Alba. "For both drinks, please." He smiled before looking back at Cassielle. "You know, you're a lot like your father... he can get quite terse when he feels like he's being unnecessarily bothered, too." Cassielle nearly choked on her drink.

"My father?" She turned to look incredulously at him. "Now you're claiming to know my father. That's particularly impressive, considering there isn't anyone written on my birth certificate for that role, so I'm not sure how you would know anything. You don't look old enough to have been hanging around with my parents at the time of my birth."

"I'm older than you think," he chuckled. "Also, I'm not surprised your mother didn't put him on that. He didn't exactly give her his real name."

She wasn't sure if he didn't understand what she had said, or if he was being purposefully dense.

"Then how the hell would you know who my father is?" She took another drink of her beer. This guy was certifiable.

He laughed again, and she couldn't understand why he found everything she said so amusing. Even his laugh was starting to annoy her.

"He's kept tabs on you–"

"That's not creepy at all," she took another drink. She needed more alcohol to cope with him, hoping the drink would make him disappear like it buried the dark feelings inside her.

"He would have stuck around, but he's a very busy man," he continued, sipping his drink. "He's hoping that you can help him out."

"You know, you sound like one of those scam artists who send those emails. You know the ones I'm talking about? Are you going to tell me that he's the prince of Nigeria and if I don't send him money soon, he will be in great trouble?"

Alba was hovering nearby, cleaning, but Cassielle knew she was eavesdropping. She was one of the most nosey people Cassielle knew, which was partly why she had come over. If anyone had noticed something, Alba would have.

"No, nothing like that. What he needs and what you're after are very much in line with one another. He is just as interested in stopping the murderer as you are."

"This is the second time you've said something about the murders. What do you know?" She turned to face him fully.

"I'm afraid I'm not at liberty to tell you everything I know here," he glanced over his shoulder at Alba, before looking back at Cassielle. "All I can say is you're right. It wasn't your friend Brittany. There was someone else there." He paused. "A couple of someone's, to be precise." He leaned closer to her. "Now, if we could go somewhere a little more private to continue this conversation..."

She finished her drink and slid the glass away from her before speaking again.

"You have to be kidding me," she said, running a hand through her curly hair, trying to find her words. If the humidity didn't set her hair to frizz, this man would. "If you had wanted to talk to me in private, you could have done so when I followed you into that alley. I don't know what your angle is-"

"What alley?" He furrowed his brow.

She ignored him and continued, "-and I honestly don't care. I am not now or ever going to go anywhere with you." Lowering her volume to avoid being overheard, she said, "And if you follow me and don't back off, I can't guarantee you'll get to live to regret it." Sam's brows lifted and a smirk crossed his face as he listened to her. Cassielle closed and slid her laptop into her bag before standing up. "Don't follow me."

It irritated her to see how amused he seemed. Maybe she would need to kick his ass to teach him a lesson. She hadn't beaten anyone up in a couple of weeks. She could use the workout.

"Don't tease," he grinned, his eyes gleaming with mischief. "But out of respect for you, I'll grant you some room to ponder. However, I would like to talk to you about what you meant by the alley. I don't recall going into any alley with you following me." A smirk crossed his face, "Had I been alone with you in some darkened place, I'd remember every detail." He tilted his head slightly. "And given the opportunity, I'd make sure you did, too." She opened her mouth and he held his hand up stopping her, "When you call upon me, just glance my way, and I'll be by your side. I'm more than ready to divulge what I possess."

"Don't hold your breath," she thought for a moment. "On second thought, please do. Hold your breath until you black out."

He laughed again and stood up. "You don't need to leave, dawlin'. I will go." He finished his drink. "Have a good evening, Madame Alba." He winked at her, earning another giggle. Then he looked back at Cassielle, smiling. "Until we meet again, Cassielle." He bowed slightly before turning and heading to the exit.

"What the hell was that?" Cassielle wondered out loud once he was out the door. She sank back onto her bar stool.

"He got a lil' bit ah madness, that one." Alba sidled back up to stand across from Cassielle.

"You think?" Cassielle couldn't stop the sarcasm from slipping out. Alba chuckled and busied herself with some bar tasks, wiping the counter with a damp cloth and adjusting a few glasses.

"They're real lively, those wild men," Alba grinned mischievously. "Real good in bed... always up for some fun." She winked, and Cassielle shook her head.

"I'm not that desperate, Alba," Cassielle shot back, setting her bag back down. "He seems like the kinda guy who'd turn a night out into a scene from a horror flick, pigs blood and all, rather than having 'some fun.'"

"It ain't about desperation, dearheart. We all got our needs." Cassielle could feel her cheeks heating up at the implications. She couldn't quite decipher her feelings about Sam. He scared her - was she afraid he might physically harm her, or that he had done something terrible to others, or was it something else? Perhaps she was scared she might be physically attracted to him. He wasn't unattractive, and if her dream meant anything... No, she wasn't going to let herself think that way, but as usual, her mind wasn't going to let the thoughts go.

Cassielle couldn't help but compare this uneasy attraction to her prior feelings for Nicholas. Nicholas had been safety - a steady port in the storm of uncertainty. A gentleman who had been patient and kind to her. But Sam, he made her feel unsteady and excited, a mix of fear and exhilaration she hadn't experienced before. She must be out of her mind to even acknowledge attraction to a stalker.

Cassielle was brought back to the present when Alba's playful demeanor shifted, her expression growing serious. Cassielle sensed if she didn't change the conversation now, she would never get to what she wanted to talk to Alba about, and she would learn far more than she ever wanted to know about Alba.

Cassielle heard the door to the bar open and close. She had a momentary dread that it was the stranger again, but the look on Alba's face told her exactly who had entered. Her face lit up like a child on Christmas morning. Cassielle glanced up at the mirror across the bar to see who it was.

"Nicholas!" Alba's accent seemed to thicken whenever she addressed him. Alba hurried around the counter to give him a hug.

"Alba, ¿cómo estás?" His words cut through the kitchen noise.

As Nick settled onto the neighboring stool, Cassielle felt a subtle shift in the air, an unspoken tension hanging between them. Alba's warm greeting to him, tinged with a not entirely platonic fondness, only accentuated the charged atmosphere.

"Estoy bien, gracias. ¿Y tú? Ya want the usual, love?" Alba said warmly, her eyes brightening at Nicholas's presence. Cassielle couldn't help but notice Alba's excitement, a contrast to her own conflicted emotions stirred by Nicholas's arrival.

"Bien, gracias. No, just water, please," Nicholas replied smoothly, his order sparking a noticeable spring in Alba's step as she moved away to fetch his drink.

"Cassielle," he greeted cheerily, the familiar warmth in his voice made her heart skip a beat. "I should have known I'd run into you here. I remember you were always a fan of day drinking. Though, usually not when working on a case."

"A little late on following this lead, aren't you?" Cassielle countered, her tone measured but the underlying tension palpable. Despite her attempt to appear unaffected, her heart raced a bit faster in his presence, the chemistry between them crackling like electricity waiting to blow. "You're fashionably late, I suppose."

He laughed, a genuine sound that made the air around them feel lighter. "Hey, better late than never, right? Besides, I wouldn't miss a chance to catch up with you, even if it's just for a drink."

Cassielle's composure relaxed slightly, a smile playing on her lips. "Well, aren't you charming. You won't be able to keep up with me by drinking water. Though, you've never been able to keep up with me before."

"Alright, dearheart, what brings ya down here? Long time no see!" Alba leaned against the bar.

"Unfortunately, Alba, I'm on official business," Nicholas said, pulling a notepad and pen from his pocket.

"Oh, not you, too!" Alba lamented. "I talked with Cassielle already. Ya can get the info from her."

"Cassielle isn't a detective with the force anymore. I need to talk to you. In fact," he paused, "She shouldn't even be working on this. I didn't ask her for a consultation; this isn't a missing person or lost animal situation. It's a murder. She needs to stay out of this." He hesitated, then added, a bit softer, "for her own good."

Alba's expression turned grave, her eyes flickering with concern as she glanced at Cassielle. "Cassielle, maybe ya should listen to Nicholas," she interjected with worry lacing her words. "This sounds serious. Ya don't want to get in trouble."

Cassielle shook her head, her resolve hardening. "Brittany asked for my help, so I'm working for her, whether you or he like it or not," she met Nick's gaze.

"Can't you bring Cassielle on as a consultant or somethin', Nicholas?" Alba's tone carried a hint of urgency as she turned to Nicholas. "That way, she won't get in trouble, and she can still help with the case." Alba looked at Nicholas with wide, innocent eyes, trying to use her charm to convince him. Cassielle doubted she would succeed. "Ya two always made such a good team. Why wouldn't ya want to help each other figure out what happened to poor Michael?"

"Alba, lo siento, I truly value your judgment and opinión, but I'm not sure if you realize how serious this situation is," Nicholas said gently, his expression sympathetic. "Cassielle's involvement could potentially be seen as obstruction of justice, you know? I'm sorry, but I need to speak with you about last night without Cassielle being here," he explained firmly.

Alba frowned, standing up straighter and grabbing a rag to toss it onto the counter. "Alright then. Ask ya questions," she said, beginning to wash the counter. Cassielle could tell by Alba's body language she wasn't interested in answering any of Nicholas' questions and she was miserable. When Alba was unhappy, finding another place to get drinks was best, as she tended to water down beverages for those who had irked her. Cassielle knew from experience, having taken a break from coming here after her breakup with Nick. Alba had been just as upset about their split as she was when her most minor favorite contestant won on a reality dating show or was unhappy with the direction of her soap operas.

"On that note... I'm leaving," Cassielle declared, standing up and slinging her bag over her shoulder, the strap secured across her chest.

"Love, I'm going to be praying ya find the truth," Alba bowed her head slightly to Cassielle. "Lord Jesus will provide!"

"I'm sure he will, Alba. Have a good rest of your day," Cassielle responded, her eyes lingering momentarily on Nicholas before she turned to leave. "I'm sure I'll see you at some point."

Nicholas caught Cassielle's gaze, his expression softening as he held it for a beat longer than necessary.

"Seems to be what's happening," he said, his voice carrying a warmth seemingly directed more at Cassielle than at Alba. Despite the seriousness of their circumstances, an unspoken connection existed between them. No matter how much she tried, Cassielle couldn't deny.

She offered a small, almost imperceptible smile in response, the corners of her lips tugging slightly upwards. Her gaze softened momentarily before she turned and stepped out into the warm afternoon sun, leaving Nicholas behind but carrying with her a lingering sense of their shared history and the unresolved tension seemed to spark between them with every encounter.

Cassielle pushed those thoughts aside and refocused on what she needed to do next. She needed to talk to Brittany's friends and gather more information. Maybe they'd seen the stranger that had piqued Alba's interest. Maybe they'd taken Brittany home and witnessed something important.

She pulled out her worn leather notebook from her bag, flipping to a fresh page. With a sense of purpose, Cassielle jotted down key points from her conversation with Alba, drawing lines and arrows to connect the stranger in the hoodie to Michael's murder scene. She wrote the names of Brittany's friends, Taylor Parker and Avery Bennett, labeling them as people to speak with. The pen scratched against the paper as she recorded her thoughts, mapping out her plan of action.

Cassielle pulled out her phone and opened VibraLink, a social media app she rarely used for posting. Her name and profile picture weren't authentic, but she was adept at gathering information by quietly observing others' online activity.

She navigated to Brittany's profile and quickly found a post from the previous night where Brittany had tagged Taylor Parker and Avery Bennett. After a swift scroll through their profiles, Cassielle noted Taylor's job as a barista at a nearby coffee shop and Avery's role as a receptionist at a doctor's office.

Decision made, Cassielle prepared to head to the coffee shop first. Maybe she'd get lucky and Taylor would be working there, providing another piece to the puzzle she was determined to solve.

CHAPTER ELEVEN

The bell above the door chimed as Cassielle stepped into the cozy coffee shop. She took a deep breath of the scent of coffee and chicory. The familiar smell mingled with the faint echo of whispers. Her senses heightened, Cassielle glanced around, trying to ground herself in the present moment.

This sensation wasn't new to her-it had plagued her since puberty, a ghostly presence lurking at the edge of her consciousness, ready to pull her into visions of times long past. Over the years, Cassielle had learned to build mental barriers, shielding herself from the unsettling echoes of history seeming to resonate in certain places. However sometimes she'd forget when in a new place and it would take her some time to put those barriers back up.

Amidst the bustling atmosphere of the coffee shop, she caught a glimpse-a fleeting image superimposed over the modern scene. A spectral vision materialized briefly before her eyes: the dark interior of a dimly lit room, the air heavy with tension and fear. A black man in worn clothes stood frozen, his eyes wide with terror, captured in a moment of agony and despair. The scene dissolved as quickly as it had appeared, leaving Cassielle deeply unsettled and reflective.

Shaking off the phantom remnants of a distant time, Cassielle focused on the present. Taylor Parker, the barista Cassielle had seen tagged in Brittany's post, worked diligently behind the counter, expertly crafting drinks with focused precision. Cassielle joined the line, patiently waiting her turn behind a young woman who approached the counter with confidence.

When the woman placed her order, Taylor leaned forward with a friendly smile. "Just a plain Matcha? It's going to be a bit more bitter and earthy."

The girl's eyes sparkled with playful enthusiasm. "I like earthy. The more dirt taste, the better."

Cassielle couldn't help but stifle a chuckle, her lips curling into a smile. *Oh, so she was that kid on the playground,* she mused.

Finally, it was Cassielle's moment to order. Taylor turned towards her with a warm smile. "Good afternoon! What can I get started for you?"

"Hi, could I get a medium Vanilla cold brew?" As Taylor began working on the order, Cassielle asked, "Hey, also, I'm looking for Taylor Parker. Are you Taylor?"

Taylor's smile faltered slightly, and she paused in what she was doing, her brow furrowing in curiosity. "Yes, that's me. How can I help you?"

"I'm Cassielle. I saw you were out with Brittany last night. I was hoping we could talk for a moment," Cassielle kept her voice low and respectful.

Taylor's expression shifted, her eyes narrowing slightly with a touch of apprehension. "Um, sure. Let me finish up with your order and these customers," she replied, glancing back towards the espresso machine.

Cassielle stepped aside, allowing Taylor to complete the order. She watched as Taylor efficiently served the remaining customers before motioning towards a quieter corner of the shop. "Let's talk over there," Taylor suggested. "Joe, I'm taking a break," she called to the other barista who was cleaning tables, before leading the way.

As they settled into a small booth tucked away from the busy counter, Cassielle began, "I'm investigating something important related to last night. Can you tell me about your evening with Brittany?"

"Sure," Taylor replied, adjusting her apron as she leaned forward. "Is this about Michael's death?" Before Cassielle could answer she added, "my boyfriend works with him, and they always carpool. When he got to the house, he saw it blocked off. After talking to the neighbors, he found out Michael was murdered..." She chewed on her lip, glancing around, before adding, "You don't think Brittany did it, do you?"

Cassielle shook her head, "I don't know what happened. I just want to see if I can find out whatever I can to help figure it out."

Taylor looked like she wanted to ask more, but didn't and said, "Brittany, Avery, and I went to LaFitte's. We wanted to unwind a bit; you know? Grab a few drinks and chat. As soon as we walked in, we saw Michael."

"Michael, Brittany's boyfriend?" Cassielle clarified.

"Yeah, we spotted him right away," Taylor explained, her expression turning solemn. "We weren't surprised to see him. He'd told Brittany he would be there with his friends. But we didn't expect to see him with some other woman."

"Did Michael seem to be acting unlike himself?" Cassielle asked, observing Taylor's body language for subtle cues.

Taylor shook her head, her brow furrowing. "I mean, Michael making out with some random girl was completely out of character. He never did dirty PDA with Brittany when they were out together, as far as I know, and he never seemed the type to cheat."

Cassielle nodded. "That does sound unusual. Did Brittany seem off that night, too? Aside from her reaction to what happened with Michael?"

Taylor paused, contemplating her response. "Brittany was really excited to hang out. She seemed upbeat, but she also mentioned she was worried about you. She was completely normal until that happened."

Cassielle arched an eyebrow, intrigued by this unexpected turn. "Worried about me? Why would she be worried about me?"

Taylor shifted in her seat, as if deliberating whether to

share more. "She mentioned that you haven't been returning her calls or texts lately. She thought maybe something was wrong between you."

Cassielle felt a pang of guilt gnawing at her, but she composed her features into a neutral mask, hiding her inner turmoil. Cassielle consciously set aside her feelings of guilt and concern about her strained relationship with Brittany, refocusing her attention on the matter at hand.

"Going back to last night, did Brittany react when she saw him?" Cassielle asked, observing Taylor's body language for subtle cues.

Taylor shook her head. "Kind of? I mean, she turned and left pretty quickly. We followed her outside to see if she was okay. She was hysterically crying by the time we caught up to her."

"What was it that he was doing when y'all saw him?"

"He was making out with some girl. Like, I'm talking full on get a room type of making out." Taylor made a face, her shoulders tensing. "I didn't recognize her. She looked like some tourist."

Cassielle made a quick note in her notebook, her pen scratching against the paper. "What did Brittany say after you joined her outside?"

Taylor hesitated, "Well, like I said, she was hysterical..."

Cassielle waited, observing Taylor's demeanor and movements, picking up on the tension in her body language.

"I mean, we all say things when we're upset, you know? It doesn't mean we mean them. It's just words. You know Brittany pretty well, right? You were college roommates, so you have to know she would never do anything really violent..."

"What did she say?" Cassielle pressed gently, her gaze steady.

Taylor's lower lip quivvered as she spoke. "She said she was going to kill him," Taylor whispered, her eyes welling with tears. "She loved him... She wouldn't have... she couldn't..."

Seeing Taylor on the verge of tears, Cassielle reached for a napkin from the table and offered it to her. "Here," Cassielle said softly.

"Thank you," Taylor murmured, her voice catching with emotion as she accepted the napkin.

Cassielle discreetly turned her attention to her notes, giving Taylor a moment to compose herself. She pretended to review her writing, offering Taylor some privacy to collect her thoughts.

After a brief pause, Cassielle looked up from her notes, sensing movement from the corner of her eye. Taylor had set down the napkin, and looked like she was ready to continue their conversation.

"Did you notice anything else unusual that night? Anyone out of the ordinary?" Cassielle watched her.

Taylor hesitated, tapping her fingers lightly on the table. "Well, there was this guy who passed us as we were standing outside. He seemed a bit out of place. I didn't think much of it at the time, but now that you mention it..."

Cassielle's mind raced with possibilities. "What do you mean by out of place? Can you describe him?"

"I mean, he wasn't dressed for the weather. He was tall, wore all black with a hoodie pulled up," Taylor recalled, her voice lowering slightly. "I only saw him for a moment before he left in a hurry. Who wears a hoodie in the summer?"

Cassielle thanked Taylor for her information and jotted a few more notes. "This is helpful. If you remember anything else, please let me know." She handed her a copy of her card with her contact information. "Would you, by chance, have Avery's contact information? I'd like to speak with her as well if I could."

"Hold on, let me text her to see if she's okay with me giving you her number." Cassielle watched as Taylor typed quickly on her phone. The amount she was typing had to mean she was doing more than asking for permission to share her number. The speed with which she receive a response made

Cassielle wonder if Avery was the type to spend a lot of time on her phone. "She says yes, and she thinks she got a pretty good look at the guy's face. Here's her number. She typically gets off work at 4."

Cassielle copied the number from the screen of Taylor's phone onto her notepad and thanked her again.

Taylor nodded, offering a reassuring smile. "Of course. I hope you can figure this out."

"Me too," Cassielle replied, her mind already planning her next steps in the investigation. As she sat and finished her coffee, she pushed aside the lingering sensation threatening to pull her into darker thoughts, focusing instead on the facts she had gathered and the path ahead. She didn't want to see the vision again. Not now. Not ever.

She sent a text to Avery to see when she'd be available to meet her and Avery agreed to meet her at LaFitte's when she got out of work, so about 4:30. Cassielle decided to stay a bit longer, nursing her coffee and jotting down notes in her notebook. The bell above the door chimed occasionally as more customers entered, but Cassielle remained focused on her task.

Cassielle heard the bell chime and then felt a presence slide into the seat across from her. She looked up and saw a woman with striking features, her dark hair cascading over her shoulders like a curtain of shadows. The woman's eyes were unsettling-completely black, devoid of any iris or sclera. It was as if the darkness of the night had taken residence within her gaze.

Cassielle's heart skipped a beat as she felt the energy emanating off the woman, sending a wave of unease through her.

"You're meddling in things you don't understand," the woman spoke, low and chilling. "Leave this alone, or you'll regret it."

Cassielle's instincts screamed at her to flee, but she held her ground, her gaze locked with the woman's unnerving black eyes.

"Who are you?" Cassielle demanded, trying to keep her voice steady despite the rising fear within her.

The woman's lips curled into a menacing smile. "I'm no one you want to trifle with. Consider this your last warning."

The woman stood up abruptly, her dark eyes boring into Cassielle's soul before she turned and swiftly exited the coffee shop. Without hesitation, Cassielle sprang from her seat and hurried after her, determined to get answers from her.

She caught up to the woman outside the shop, her breath coming in quick bursts. "Wait!" Cassielle called out.

The woman turned around, her expression one of genuine confusion. "Can I help you?" she asked, her eyes now a normal shade or gray green, devoid of any darkness or menace.

Cassielle paused, taken aback by the sudden change. "I... I'm sorry," she stammered, her mind reeling. "I thought... Never mind."

The woman raised an eyebrow, clearly perplexed by Cassielle's behavior. "Is everything okay?" she inquired with genuine concern.

Cassielle nodded slowly, her confusion mounting. "Yes, I... I apologize. It's nothing." She turned away, feeling a mix of embarrassment and disbelief.

As she returned to the coffee shop, Cassielle scanned her surroundings for any sign of the stranger described by Alba and Taylor, but she didn't spot anyone matching the description.

Back at her table, Cassielle sank into her seat, attempting to make sense of the unsettling encounter. The memory left her feeling more bewildered than before. Had she truly seen the woman's dark eyes? It felt so vivid in the moment, yet now it seemed like a distant dream, shrouded in uncertainty.

"Good afternoon, Cassielle," she choked on the coffee she had sipped. She hadn't noticed Sam slide into the seat across from her, but there he was. She hadn't heard the doorbell ring to signal someone having entered, and glancing around, no one else seemed to notice he'd appeared across from her.

"Do I know you? Is that why you keep coming back like a bad penny?" She leaned back as if putting physical distance between them would help. She felt an inexplicable magnetic pull towards him, which made no sense. Even as she grappled with solving the mystery at hand, his lingering presence persisted in her mind.

"Yes and no," he replied with a wry smile. His deep and resonant voice was reminiscent of James Earl Jones, but somehow more attractive. He would have made a good voice actor. If he wasn't already, he really should consider it.

"Okay... do you have a reason for being here? I'm not really in a chatty mood," she grumbled.

He chuckled. "Are you ever?"

She shot him a look and glanced down at her coffee, wishing it were spiked.

"Do you mind me joining you?" He smiled, leaning forward slightly. She avoided looking into his eyes. She felt like whenever she looked into his eyes, she started to get sucked into whatever he was. He was an enigma.

"I do, in fact, so, if you don't mind..." She slid out of her seat and grabbed her bag.

"You know your friend isn't responsible for what happened to Michael," he said as he slid out of his seat, causing Cassielle to pause as he stood between her and the door.

"Who are you really, and what do you know that you aren't saying?" she demanded, her frustration evident.

He reached out and gently touched her arm. "Let's continue this conversation over a drink, shall we?"

The unexpected contact was both unnerving and oddly intimate. She stopped, her heart racing as she turned to face him, her eyes flashing with a mix of anger and confusion.

"Do. Not. Touch. Me," she said, her voice sharp and deliberate, each word coming out through her gritted teeth. Her look bore into him, trying to convey the seriousness of her command.

His hold was firm; his thumb brushed against her skin in an uncomfortably deliberate way. He met her eyes with a look seeming to be reading her like a book. She could feel the heat from his body even in the sweltering sun. The way he looked at her quickened her pulse, the tension between them growing thicker than the heat around them. His touch wasn't threatening. That would have been easier for her to extricate herself. She tried to ignore the part of her wanting to melt into him.

"I can't seem to stay away from you," he said softly, both alluring and unsettling. His eyes searched hers as if trying to dig through her layers of fear and defiance to get to her very core. She feared what he would do if he got there.

She tried to pull away, but his grip remained, and the proximity only heightened her awareness of him.

"Just stay away," she said, her voice trembling despite her attempts to stay firm. The heat of the day felt like nothing compared to the heat coming off of him, and she could feel her resolve wavering under the weight of his intense stare.

As he finally let go, the brief contact lingered, and she found herself struggling to regain her composure. The air around them was charged with a strange energy, making it harder for her to breathe and think. She was being smothered by the blend of fear and attraction that was beginning to surface.

A car honked at them, and she glared at the driver before resuming her walk across the street. Once on the sidewalk, she turned to face him again, trying to stand tall at her 5'5" height to appear more intimidating. Her annoyance matched the scorching heat of the afternoon sun, which only added to her temper.

"Bien sur! Of course," he said, raising his hands in surrender. "I meant no offense, dahlin'." She glared at him before turning to continue her walk.

A part of her wondered if this guy had any involvement

in this whole mess. Maybe he had used Voodoo and wanted her help in undoing his actions. People often dismissed Voodoo but living in New Orleans long enough taught you there was some truth to it. Or he was somehow connected some other way. Maybe he'd been involved in some sort of gang initiation. But that wouldn't explain the eerie feeling she got from him. Maybe he was the dark shape she'd seen in the vision and the guy in the hoodie Alba and Taylor had noticed and he had been dabbling in things he ought to have left alone.

"Okay, since you are dead set and determined to follow me and show up everywhere somehow. What do you want?" She folded her arms over her chest and met his stare with as much confidence she could muster.

"As I've said before," He said slowly, "I want to help you."

Cassielle eyed him suspiciously, the midday sun casting sharp shadows around them. "Help me? With what, exactly?" She paused before adding, "and if you say something sexual, I'm out of here."

He regarded her with a solemn expression, as if choosing his words carefully. "I'm here because you're in danger. There are forces at play you can't comprehend yet."

Cassielle scoffed. "Danger? Look, I appreciate the concern, but I've been handling myself just fine."

The stranger's eyes narrowed slightly, a glint of frustration beneath his calm demeanor. "You're more connected to this than you realize. Your mother's legacy, your bloodline-it's entwined with the spirit world."

Cassielle's skepticism returned in full force. "Spirit world? I get it, people believe in spirits. Especially those who follow Voodoo. But to go so far as to say my heritage is entwined with the 'spirit world'? It's a bit much. What's your angle here?"

He sighed, seemingly resigned to her disbelief. "I've told you what I can for now. But mark my words, Cassielle-this is bigger than you or me."

She studied him for a moment, weighing her options.

"Fine. If you're so determined to be involved, then prove it. Show me something that makes sense."

His expression softened, a flicker of resolve in his gaze. "Meet me tonight in the City of the Dead. Midnight. I'll show you."

Cassielle hesitated, her logical mind warring with a strange curiosity. "St. Louis Cemetery? And what will I find there? My own murder? Or is this your attempt at getting some sort of kinky hook-up? No thanks."

He offered a faint smile. "Answers. That's all I can offer for now. But if you're open to it, in the future, we could have more... But, be careful, Cassielle. The shadows run deep in this city, and not all secrets are meant to be uncovered."

After his cryptic warning, a car backfired. Cassielle looked behind her, and when she turned back, he had disappeared, leaving her to grapple with the strange encounter and the unsettling truths it hinted at.

CHAPTER TWELVE

Cassielle went to LaFitte's to wait for Avery. She hoped the woman would have something useful to share. If she could find out who the stranger in the hoodie was, she could speak with them and see if they had something to do with Michael's death. If they did, she could turn them in and help clear Brittany's name and be done with this whole thing. If not, well then back to the drawing board.

When 5 o'clock came and went, and she still hadn't heard from Avery, she sent her a text. She waited another half hour before calling her and hung up after leaving a message when the call went straight to voice mail. She wasn't going to let herself worry. Witnesses flake. She'd have to track her down at her office tomorrow.

Giving up on waiting, Cassielle headed upstairs. She found Brittany curled up under a blanket on Alba's couch, Jamal's arm draped protectively around her shoulders. The air in the room felt stifling despite the little air conditioner humming away in the window.

The darkness descended upon her suddenly, swallowing her senses whole. It was as if she had been thrust into a void, her surroundings blurring into a murky abyss. Panic gripped her, suffocating her in its grasp, rendering her unable to move or speak. A silent scream echoed in her mind, but she couldn't find her voice to release it.

Just as swiftly as it had enveloped her, the darkness dissipated, leaving Cassielle gasping for air, her chest heaving with the effort to fill her lungs.

The door creaked open behind her, jolting her back to

reality. She whirled around to see Jamal leaving. Her mind struggled to regain focus, to remember why she had come here in the first place. But the lingering remnants of oppressive darkness made it difficult to shake off the feeling of unease.

When she moved in with Alba, the visions of past occurrences had seemed clear and vivid. But this felt different. Her mind went back to Brittany's blackouts. Was this from her traumatic experience? Then again, Jamal had seemed dodgy earlier. She'd have to figure it out later.

With a determined exhale, she pushed aside her disorientation, forcing herself to focus on the task at hand. She made a mental note to confront Jamal later, to uncover the secrets he was hiding. But for now, she had to gather her wits and piece together the puzzle before her.

Brittany's eyes were red and puffy, her gaze fixed on the flickering TV screen with a vacant stare. Cassielle doubted Brittany could even tell her what show was on if asked.

Cassielle sank onto the couch next to her, the heavy weight of worry settling in her chest.

"Hey," Cassielle said gently, her voice a soft interruption in the somber atmosphere.

Brittany murmured a barely audible greeting in response, her eyes still distant and rimmed with red. Cassielle hesitated, unsure of how to approach her friend's evident pain.

They sat side by side in silence for several minutes, Cassielle respecting Brittany's need for space. She couldn't imagine the depth of Brittany's grief and confusion, but she was determined to offer support however she could.

Finally, Cassielle ventured, "Do you want to talk?"

Brittany shifted slightly, her gaze flickering towards Cassielle before returning to the television screen. "I... I don't know," she replied, her voice hollow and strained.

Cassielle reached out and placed a comforting hand on Brittany's arm. "I'm here for you, whatever you need."

Brittany took a deep breath, her shoulders trembling slightly. "It's just... so hard. I can't believe he's gone."

Cassielle nodded empathetically, her heart aching for her friend. "I know."

Tears welled up in Brittany's eyes, and she finally turned to face Cassielle. "I keep replaying everything in my head... wondering if there was something I could have done and trying to remember what happened, but it's this hole in my memory. I might as well have been sleeping for all that I remember."

Cassielle squeezed Brittany's hand gently. She stayed silent, offering a comforting presence as Brittany processed her grief. They sat together, enveloped in shared sorrow and unspoken understanding.

After a while, Brittany spoke again, her voice barely above a whisper. "Thanks for being here. I don't know what I'd do without you."

Cassielle smiled softly. "Anytime. We'll get through this together."

As if the week couldn't get any stranger, the soap opera murmuring from the TV abruptly cut to a breaking news report. Cassielle's attention snapped to the screen, her heart sinking as she watched the scene unfolding.

"A hit-and-run occurred on 5th Avenue at 4:05 PM," the reporter's voice droned solemnly. Cassielle recognized the business front. The reporter was outside Dr. Johnson's office- a location all too familiar to her from her childhood. "The victim, a young woman in her twenties, was pronounced dead at the scene."

Brittany's shocked gasp drew Cassielle's gaze. She noticed Brittany's eyes fixated on something behind the reporter-a colorful purse lying discarded on the pavement.

"Wait... that's Avery's purse," Brittany muttered, her voice trembling with disbelief.

Cassielle's stomach twisted into knots. She followed Brittany's gaze, her mind reeling with the implications. Avery, the one person who might have seen the stranger stalking Cassielle, was now gone.

"Are you sure?" Cassielle asked, her voice heavy with sorrow.

Brittany nodded, tears welling up in her eyes. "Yeah... I recognize it. Avery was working on those designs for weeks. She was going to make me one next." Her voice cracked, and she looked down, biting her lip to hold back the sobs threatening to escape.

Cassielle sat there, frozen. She wanted to say something, anything, to ease Brittany's pain, but no words came. The weight of the recent deaths hung heavily between them, making the silence feel like a leaden shroud.

As Brittany's tears began to fall silently, Cassielle's mind raced. Avery's death wasn't just a loss; it was a missed opportunity. The stranger at LaFitte's could have been the key to everything, and now her chance seemed lost. Guilt churned in her stomach. Here she was, prioritizing the case over Avery's life. What kind of person did that make her?

After a long moment of shared grief, Cassielle finally broke the silence, her voice laced with urgency. "Please, Brittany, stay here. Don't go anywhere or let anyone in that you don't know. If the person from Michael's murder scene is involved in this, you could be in danger too."

Brittany's eyes widened, the realization dawning on her. "You think Avery saw something?"

Cassielle nodded solemnly. "It's possible. And if whoever harmed Avery thinks you know anything, they might come after you."

Brittany looked torn, her face a mix of fear and determination, but she nodded in agreement. "Okay, but please, be careful."

Cassielle reached out and squeezed Brittany's hand. She knew she had to uncover the truth about Avery's death and find any clues that could lead to the stranger. But first, she needed to confront the man who had been occupying her thoughts. He might be the only lead she had left.

CHAPTER THIRTEEN

As the evening stretched on, Cassielle found herself unable to shake the accident at the doctor's office and the encounters with the stranger. She paced around her apartment, her mind replaying Sam's words and the bizarre events of the day.

By the time midnight approached, curiosity outweighed her skepticism. Dressed in a jacket against the nighttime chill, she navigated the streets of New Orleans, guided by a sense of unease and reluctant anticipation.

The City of the Dead, known to visitors as St. Louis Cemetery No. 1, loomed ahead-a striking labyrinthine architectural landscape of aboveground tombs and mausoleums beneath the moon's faint glow. Cassielle stood at the threshold, her heart pounding with a mix of apprehension and determination.

It was midnight, and the streets were unusually quiet, with sporadic tourist traffic dwindling. The ghost walking tours were long gone by this hour. Cassielle couldn't quite understand why she had agreed to meet him in the middle of the night in such a deserted location. It felt insane. But there was something about his presence she found disturbing and frustrating. She was not one of those girls.

A thunderous bang jolted her from her thoughts. She spun around, her eyes widening as she caught sight of an Uber car hurtling down the street. Chaos erupted as a few passing cars swerved and honked, desperately avoiding the rogue vehicle careening through their midst.

On the other side of the street, cars turned sharply onto

City Park Avenue, creating a temporary gap in the traffic. Soon, it was hurtling toward her on the sidewalk, its tires screeching in protest. In a split second, her instincts kicked in, and she knew she had to run for her life.

Cassielle's heart pounded as she sprinted down the sidewalk, her mind racing. The Maze Cocktail Lounge was a three-minute walk away. She could maybe find help there. Her college years of bar hopping were finally proving useful.

Adrenaline surged through her as she tore down the sidewalk, wind whipping through her hair. The sporadic honking and screeching of tires fueled her urgency.

She quickly turned onto Canal Boulevard. Reality crashed on Cassielle-she wouldn't reach the bar, and even if she did, she could see people milling outside.

She couldn't be responsible for others getting struck by a car. The situation was spiraling into a nightmare, and she needed an escape. In her periphery, she spotted Greenwood Cemetery to her left across the street, beckoning like a sanctuary.

Without hesitation, she veered towards it, pushing herself to the limit and so thankful the other car was having to dodge cars and things to get to her.

The wrought iron fence of Greenwood Cemetery loomed ahead, a barrier between her and safety. Without breaking stride, Cassielle summoned her remaining strength, leaping towards the fence.

Her hands grasped the cold metal, fingers wrapping around the ornate spikes as she pulled herself upward. With a surge of effort, she hoisted herself over the top, the sharp points of the fence scraping against her palms.

Just as Cassielle landed on the other side and stumbled forward, a sharp, searing pain shot through Cassielle's ankle, accompanied by the unmistakable sound of a bone cracking. Before she could fully process the pain, the crash of the pursuing car smashing into the fence reverberated through the air, followed by the explosive pop of a radiator.

Cassielle wasted no time, her body propelled deeper into Greenwood Cemetery. With each step on her injured ankle, searing pain shot through her, causing her to wince and grit her teeth. She made it to the first mausoleum and threw herself on the ground behind it, gasping in pain.

She couldn't stop moving now. She pressed on, crawling on her hands and knees as quickly and quietly as she could. Her movements slowed by the injury, her movement uneven and labored. Sticks and rocks tore into her knees and hands, but she didn't stop. The chaotic sounds of her pursuer's rampage faded gradually into the distance as she crawled deeper into the cemetery, her eyes scanning for a potential hiding spot to catch her breath and assess her situation.

The moonlight cast eerie shadows among the tombstones and mausoleums looming ominously in the darkness. Breathless and trembling, Cassielle sought cover amongst the tombs, her senses on high alert, knowing she had only moments before her pursuer closed in.

A voice rang out followed by a gunshot piercing the air with deadly intent. The bullet buried itself into an angel statue in front of her. Fear coursed through her veins as she realized her pursuer was armed.

Cassielle's mind raced, searching for a way to survive. The pain from her ankle was overwhelming, threatening to cloud her senses. Still, she fought against it, knowing succumbing to the weakness meant certain doom.

She moved as fast as she could on her hands and knees, staying hidden in the shadows to stay ahead of her pursuer. Refusing to give up without a fight, she paused behind a large statue to catch her breath and figure out her next move. She needed to call for help, but could she risk him possibly seeing the light from the phone?

Her trembling fingers reached for her gun, fumbling to pull it out. As she struggled, she took a deep breath to steady herself. A chilling voice cut through the chaos of her thoughts, oozing with malice and arrogance.

"Ah, Cassielle," the man sneered, his voice carrying a twisted sense of delight. "You thought you could escape, didn't you? But you see, I always get what I want. Tonight, Vito DeLuca will learn he's not the true master of this city. It's time for me to take my rightful place at the top, and you... you're a pawn in my game."

His words dripped with contempt, each syllable laced with venom as he continued, relishing the terror he instilled.

"You should be honored. You're about to become a part of my legacy-the legacy that will surpass even the great Vittorio DeLuca. Tom Horn will at long last be at the top of everyone's list for the greatest Serial Killer who ever existed! But first, let's have a little fun, shall we?"

Confusion clouded her thoughts. Vittorio DeLuca? The Butcher? He'd died decades ago. Was this guy delusional? She pushed aside her doubts and let her police training kick in. Instinctively, she assessed the situation, evaluating her surroundings and calculating her options. She focused on maintaining calm, trying to anticipate her assailant's next move while keeping herself ready to react. She didn't dare speak lest she give away her position.

A mirthless chuckle filled the air as the man's voice drew closer. He was toying with her, reveling in her fear and vulnerability. "Oh where, oh where has my Cassielle gone? Oh where, oh where can she be?"

Silence enveloped them momentarily, broken only by Cassielle's labored breaths. She glanced to her right and jumped in surprise.

Samedi or Samuel or whatever his name was standing there calm as could be.

Cassielle's mind spun with questions. How was it he kept appearing seemingly out of nowhere? Was he exceptionally skilled at stealth. Had he been watching her from the cemetery, witnessing her escape from the dangerous man claiming to be Tom Horn? How had he managed to get in past Horn?

"Need some help?" Samedi asked with a wry smile.

"You think?" Cassielle was tempted to tell him off, but she could take whatever help he could give her now. If he had some sort of Voodoo magic-and that was a big if-now would be the perfect time for him to show her.

As Cassielle watched, a strange sensation washed over her, accompanied by a subtle shift in the air. She blinked, momentarily disoriented, as Baron Samedi's grin seemed to widen, his form blurring before her eyes. It was as if the shadows themselves reached out to wrap him, enveloping him in their dark embrace.

Then, in an instant, he was gone.

The space where Samedi had stood moments before now felt oddly vacant, the lingering impression of his presence fading like a dissipating fog. Cassielle's heart raced as she tried to comprehend what she had witnessed. It was as though he had melted into the night, leaving behind only the echo of his mischievous smile.

She couldn't rely on him to get her out of this mess, not with his parlor tricks. The eerie silence enveloping the cemetery heightened her senses. The usual sounds of nocturnal life were conspicuously absent, as if even the creatures of the night sensed the looming danger and had gone into hiding. Cassielle strained to hear any sign of Horn, but the night remained unsettlingly still and quiet.

Her thoughts wrestled with the urgency of the moment. She weighed the risk of exposure against the need to locate her pursuer. With a deep breath to steady herself, Cassielle made a split-second decision. Gathering her resolve, she braced herself and cautiously peered around the moss-covered statue.

A bullet ricocheted off the stone monument above her head, prompting her to recoil instinctively. The close call reinforced her need to act swiftly. Ignoring the pounding of her heart, she scanned the moonlit cemetery, her senses sharpened by the urgency of the hunt. She needed to keep moving.

Cassielle prepared to move, her eyes darting, searching for any sign of movement or shadow that might betray Horn's location. She needed to get the upper hand.

Just as she was about to dart to another spot across the broken path, Samedi appeared again.

One second he wasn't there. The next, he stood dead center in the path.

"Hello, Tom," Samedi's voice floated from the darkness, laced with a mysterious calmness contrasting sharply with the chaos of the moment. Horn responded with another gunshot, the bullet passing through Samedi as if he were a wisp of smoke. Samedi laughed, unfazed by the futile attack.

Cassielle's breath caught in her throat, torn between awe and fear at the supernatural display unfolding before her.

Samedi vanished again. A thump echoed from the direction where Horn had been standing. Peering around the statue, Cassielle saw Horn sprawled on the ground in a heap, stunned and disoriented. Samedi stood nearby, his hands enveloping a dark, writhing mist. Before him, a rip opened in the fabric of existence-a large, dark opening that defied explanation.

With swift and decisive motion, Samedi shoved the mist inside, and the opening swallowed it whole, snapping shut without a sound. Cassielle stood frozen, watching in awe as the supernatural drama unfolded before her eyes, leaving her to grapple with the unsettling truth of the world beyond her mortal comprehension.

Samedi pivoted toward her, his eyes locking onto hers. "Are you ready to talk?"

CHAPTER FOURTEEN

Cassielle felt the urge to retort with something clever, but after Samedi had essentially saved her life and demonstrated he was far from human, she decided to take the situation more seriously.

"Yes, but can I start with a question?" Samedi seemed to have forgotten about the man behind him, but Cassielle hadn't. Limping past Samedi, she carefully kicked the man's gun away before gingerly kneeling down to check for a pulse.

The shadows of the cemetery cast unsettling shapes in the dim moonlight, adding to the eerie atmosphere.

"Of course - and so you know, he's fine. His possession is over." Samedi's intense gaze followed her every move. When she glanced up at him, she couldn't decipher his expression.

"What did you do just now?" She slowly stood up, looking around for something to bind the man's wrists. She wasn't going to give him the opportunity to attack her.

Samedi smiled his charming smile, leaving Cassielle uncertain whether he was bored or simply toying with her. "I extracted the soul of Tom Horn from his body and returned it to Limbo where it belongs. This man," he tapped the man with his foot, "is Joseph Banks. A decent man who unfortunately found himself vulnerable enough for possession."

Cassielle furrowed her brow. "What made him vulnerable to possession?"

Samedi's smile widened. "A person's emotional state can make them susceptible to certain influences. Negative emotions or vulnerabilities can attract unwanted energies or entities seeking to take advantage."

Cassielle, frustrated with the lack of suitable tools, resorted to quick thinking and resourcefulness. Her eyes scanned the surroundings, and they landed on a bouquet adorning a nearby statue, its ribbon fluttering gently in the night breeze. Ignoring the pain in her injured ankle, she hurried over to the statue.

Grasping the ribbon, Cassielle returned to the man, Joseph Banks, her heart quickening as he stirred and began to groan and mumble. Adrenaline surged through her veins, urging her to act swiftly. With practiced precision, she maneuvered behind him, pulling his arms into position with careful urgency.

The ribbon was slender but strong enough, a makeshift binding she wrapped around Joseph's wrists. Her fingers moved deftly, tying the ribbon into a secure knot. As she finished, Cassielle cast a glance at her handiwork, hoping against hope the impromptu restraint would hold.

Samedi's drawl carried a lazy reassurance. "That's really not necessary. He'll be fine when he wakes up. Maybe a bit confused, but nothing serious."

Cassielle narrowed her eyes skeptically as she rose to her feet.

"Better safe than sorry," she cautioned.

Samedi responded with a slight, conceding bow, silently acknowledging her decision despite any doubts he harbored. In the distance, the wail of approaching police sirens intensified, cutting through the solemn silence of the graveyard like a piercing lamentation.

Samedi's gaze flickered anxiously across the graveyard, his body poised as if ready to depart. "Let's get out of here," he urged.

"Not a chance," she responded, patting down the man's pockets to ensure he didn't have any other weapons. The pain in her ankle flared with each movement. "I'm not going to flee from a crime scene, innocent or not."

"You're injured," Samedi began to move towards her,

but she held up a hand. Surprisingly, he stopped.

"I appreciate you saving me. However, after everything I just witnessed, I'm going to need at least a good four feet between us," she paused, then added, "and yes, I realize distance clearly means nothing to someone who can disappear and reappear somewhere else on a whim, but at least give me the illusion of a safety bubble, okay? Just while I process this?"

Samedi's once playful and flirty demeanor shifted into seriousness, his smirk replaced by a focused expression. "As you wish. But we don't have time to play games with the police," he stated firmly. He gestured towards Joseph on the ground, who was moaning and slowly starting to come to.

"As you can tell, the spirits are upping their game. They know about you. Whoever freed them knows about you. You aren't safe," Samedi continued, his tone grave. "All they need to do is find one disgruntled person, and they can easily go in and try to harm you again. You won't know who it is. There's no way you could predict it."

The gravity of Samedi's words slammed into Cassielle like a Mack truck, leaving her momentarily stunned. Cassielle's mind raced with worry and realization. What Samedi was saying sounded insane, but something inside of her said it could be true, and she felt a chill of fear creeping up her spine. As she watched Joseph stirring, she understood the urgency of the situation. Whatever she'd seen Samedi do, it had seemed to work on this guy. If what he was saying was true, then nowhere would be safe. She realized the magnitude of the danger she was facing.

"However, if I'm around, they'll be a bit less likely to do so. Or, they'll gather more allies, and it could lead to a concentrated and larger attack," Samedi explained, watching Cassielle closely for her reaction before continuing. "Would you like to take that chance?"

Cassielle's thoughts raced as she absorbed Samedi's words. Fear and uncertainty mingled with a growing sense of reliance on Samedi's protection. She knew she was vulnerable, and the idea of facing spirits alone was terrifying. But so was he.

Her gaze met Samedi's, and in that moment, she made her decision.

"The guy had a gun, Samedi, and tried to run me over with a car. Yes, I know you're saying he was possessed, but there were witnesses on the road who saw me running. If I leave, there will be more questions." She took a breath before continuing, "I get it, you want me to believe there's Limbo and Loa and all of this Voodoo nonsense. I loved my mom, and she believed so deeply in it. I don't know what I really think, but I don't think that's going to fly with the police when they come knocking on my door to ask why I was being chased by the guy in the car and why I didn't stick around to talk to them."

In an instant, Samedi's whole demeanor changed. A grotesque image flashed across his face. His skin appeared ashen and gaunt, resembling a skull. Hollow eyes stared back, and where his nose should have been, there were only two dark slits.

With a menacing growl, Samedi advanced towards Cassielle, his transformed appearance bearing down on her.

Cassielle's heart raced as she stared back at Samedi's horrifying transformation. Fear and shock washed over her, her injured ankle throbbing with pain as she took a small step back.

Her jaw clenched with determination, and she gritted her teeth against the rising panic. Despite the fear gripping her, Cassielle stood her ground, refusing to yield to Samedi's intimidation. She locked eyes with him, hoping her face didn't give away her terror.

Samedi's expression shifted from menacing to conflicted. The intensity in his eyes softened slightly, revealing a hint of regret beneath the eerie facade.

As if he realized the impact of his actions on Cassielle, Samedi paused in his advance. His features began to revert to their normal state, the grotesque image fading away like a fleeting nightmare.

"I'm sorry," Samedi murmured, his voice carrying genuine remorse. "I didn't mean to scare you. But we must go. It's not safe here."

Despite his earlier aggression, Samedi's tone now held a note of concern, almost pleading. He extended a hand toward her. Still wary and shaken by Samedi's sudden transformation, she met his apology with a mixture of apprehension and resolve. She took a deep breath to steady herself before responding.

"I appreciate your concern, but I need to stay," Cassielle said firmly, her voice tinged with determination despite her lingering fear. "I really should talk to the police about what happened here. They need to know..." She hesitated a moment.

"Are you sure you want to do that?" Samedi eyed her for a moment.

"No, I don't ever want to deal with them in this type of situation, but I think I'd have more trouble if I ran..."

As she spoke, the distant chatter of police radios grew louder, signaling the approaching law enforcement. Cassielle's gaze flickered toward the sound.

Samedi's expression tightened with frustration, torn between concern for Cassielle's safety and his own duties. "Fine," he relented, his tone clipped. "But be careful. I'll be nearby and when you're done, we can talk."

As Samedi spoke, his eyes softened slightly, lingering on Cassielle for a moment longer than necessary. Cassielle sensed a vulnerability beneath his supernatural facade-a flicker of emotion she found intriguing, despite her wariness.

In that fleeting moment, Cassielle felt a shift in the air between them, an unspoken tension she couldn't quite decipher. Samedi's hesitation hinted at something more, but Cassielle's thoughts were muddled with uncertainty.

Caught off guard by the intensity of Samedi's gaze, Cassielle's heart fluttered. She found herself drawn to him again, even as she tried to maintain a facade of indifference.

As the sounds of approaching authorities disrupted their exchange, Cassielle's mind raced with questions. Despite her attempts to resist, she couldn't shake the lingering desire to unravel the mysteries surrounding Samedi-an attraction she was reluctant to acknowledge, yet unable to ignore.

With that, Samedi turned and disappeared into the shadows, leaving Cassielle to face the police on her own. Gone. Again. Cassielle couldn't resist an annoyed eye roll. The disappearing act was getting old.

As the police arrived, the scene in the cemetery crackled with tension and urgency. Flashing blue and red lights illuminated the headstones from a distance, casting eerie shadows across the grassy expanse. Officers approached on foot, their figures silhouetted against the pulsating lights of their parked vehicles.

Cassielle, heart racing, watched as the officers fanned out, their movements purposeful and determined. Some approached with caution, hands resting on their holstered firearms, while others engaged in urgent radio communication.

She raised her hands slowly as instructed by the approaching officers, her palms open in a gesture of compliance amidst the unfolding chaos. The harsh commands and urgent radio chatter filled the air, amplifying the sense of urgency and gravity of the moment.

Surrounded by law enforcement, Cassielle felt a surge of adrenaline as she recounted the strange events leading to this surreal confrontation. Despite the pain throbbing in her ankle, she answered their questions as best she could, her voice steady amidst the flurry of activity.

Meanwhile, paramedics swarmed around the unconscious man on the ground, carefully assessing his condition and preparing him for transport. The steady drone of the ambulance's engine provided a constant backdrop to the unfolding scene.

One of the officers, noticing Cassielle's injured state,

approached with a concerned expression. Gently guiding her towards another waiting ambulance, he emphasized the need for immediate medical attention. Reluctantly, she allowed herself to be assisted into the vehicle, the antiseptic smell triggering memories she fought to suppress.

At the hospital, the harsh fluorescent lights overhead flickered relentlessly, casting stark flashes across the sterile corridors. The antiseptic scent consumed Cassielle as she underwent tests and consultations for her injured ankle, the memories of her mother's final moments following her like specters in the clinical surroundings.

Despite the emotional triggers, Cassielle remained resolute, determined to keep moving forward. With the fractured ankle diagnosis, cast in place, and crutches in hand, she eagerly departed the hospital, ready to leave the sterile environment behind and return to the familiar comfort of her own space.

CHAPTER FIFTEEN

Cassielle gingerly pushed open the door to her apartment, the weight of her cast on her leg making each step a deliberate effort. The familiar scent of her home greeted her-slightly musty with a hint of lavender air freshener. She maneuvered carefully through the doorway, her crutches echoing softly on the hardwood floor.

The layout of her apartment unfolded before her tired eyes. To the right, the bathroom door stood ajar, offering a glimpse of the tiled floor and the edge of the sink within. A short hallway beckoned her toward the main room, where her life seemed to converge within the confines of one open space.

Directly across from the kitchenette was her modest living area. The couch, worn but welcoming, faced the television mounted on the opposite wall. A scattering of books as well as the TV remote lay haphazardly on the coffee table, remnants of late-night distractions during quieter times.

At the far end of the room, Cassielle's sleeping area beckoned-a makeshift bedroom defined by a stand-up bureau doubling as her clothes storage. The unmade bed, a tangle of sheets and pillows, awaited her return like a silent promise of rest.

The soft glow of lamplight bathed the space in a warm ambiance, casting gentle shadows dancing across the walls. Despite the clutter and disarray, Cassielle found solace in the familiarity of her surroundings. This was her sanctuary, her haven in a city that felt too chaotic.

Cassielle navigated toward the kitchenette. The island, cluttered yet functional, presented a challenge to get around.

She leaned against it for support, her gaze fixed on the task at hand. Retrieving a mug from a nearby drawer, she carefully positioned it on the counter, her movements deliberate despite the ache in her limbs.

The next hurdle-the stove-loomed ahead. Cassielle approached it with a mix of apprehension and resolve. Gripping the crutches tightly, she filled the kettle with water from the sink, the steady flow echoing in the quietude of the apartment.

As she waited for the water to heat, Cassielle's eyes wandered to the couch and the television beyond. The thought of sinking into the cushions and losing herself in mindless distraction was tempting, but she knew her mind wouldn't allow it. Sleep seemed elusive tonight, her thoughts consumed by the recent events.

Finally, the whistle of the kettle broke the silence. Cassielle poured the hot water into the waiting mug, the steam rising like wisps of comfort. She dipped a tea bag into the water, watching as the liquid slowly transformed into a soothing brew.

Returning to the couch in an awkward juggling act of walking with a crutch while carrying her warm mug, Cassielle settled into its embrace. The television remained dark, a silent companion in the stillness of the room. Smelling the fragrant tea, she closed her eyes briefly, allowing herself a moment of respite amidst the chaos that threatened to overwhelm her.

As Cassielle savored the first sip of her tea, a sense of calm began to settle over her weary frame. The warmth of the mug seeped into her hands, providing a comforting contrast to the lingering ache in her ankle. She let out a soft sigh, relishing the tranquility of the moment.

But just as her mind started to drift, a rustle of movement caught her attention. Startled, she opened her eyes and glanced toward the kitchenette, her heart skipping a beat. There, sitting casually on a bar stool, was Samedi.

He lounged with the ease of someone who belonged,

his expression unreadable. His attire was changed into a crisp black suit, impeccably tailored-but the setting felt incongruous, as if reality itself had been temporarily suspended.

Cassielle blinked, willing her beating heart to slow down and hoping her face wasn't giving away her not entirely pure thoughts. She didn't know why she was so attracted to him, but she wished she wasn't. She resorted to her usual defense mechanism. Sarcasm.

"Oh, fantastic! Just what I needed: a surprise cardiac event courtesy of your sudden appearing act. Next time, I'll be sure to have a CPR buddy on standby. Maybe you should be a magician since you seem to enjoy pulling disappearing tricks."

He smiled, his dark eyes glinting with mischief. "Ah, Cassielle, your wit strikes again," he remarked, his tone casual as if they were meeting for a scheduled appointment.

Cassielle's mind raced, a million questions fighting for dominance. She decided to start with the easiest one, "How did you get here like that?" she demanded, setting her tea on the coffee table with more force than intended.

Samedi's smile widened. "It's what we do," he replied cryptically, as if it explained everything. "I wanted to make sure you were okay."

The sentiment was touching.

Despite her lingering discomfort, Cassielle found herself drawn into his presence, but she wasn't going to let him know. "You mean how I'm doing after nearly dying when I was attacked because I had gone out to meet you?" she retorted.

Samedi's expression shifted slightly, a flicker of contrition crossing his features. "Ah, I'm afraid you can't blame me for that. Or, rather, you can for that it happened then, but something akin to it would have likely happened eventually anyway."

Cassielle eyed him warily, her mind still reeling from the day's events. With a resigned shrug, Cassielle settled back into the couch, her tea forgotten for the moment.

Samedi's presence, though unconventional, offered a welcome distraction from the turmoil of her thoughts. As they sat in companionable silence, Cassielle couldn't help but wonder what other mysteries awaited in the company of this being.

"Alright, Samedi... or Sam-" Cassielle started.

"Baron Samedi is my true name," he admitted, his tone measured. "But among the living, I often use the name Sam to remain somewhat undercover."

Cassielle's brow raised, "Undercover?"

Sam's lips curved into a wry smile. "As a Loa who governs over the dead, my interactions with the living are not strictly permitted," he explained. "However, your father, recognizing the need for intervention, instructed me to seek you out. Using the name Sam allowed me to maintain a level of discretion so that I could talk to you." His smile broadened, his teeth extraordinarily white against the contrast of his dark skin, "Although, I suppose, I could have just kept myself hidden from the humans, but then they might have thought you insane for speaking to yourself. We could speak that way when in public if you'd prefer?"

Cassielle narrowed her eyes. "No, I think I'd rather be seen talking to a person than to thin air, thanks. I have enough problems feeling like I need psychiatric help; I don't need you to add to it, too." She reached for her tea and took a breath. "So, you're saying you are Baron Samedi?"

Samedi inclined his head slightly. "Indeed. You may continue to call me Sam when we are out and about and Samedi, when it's the two of us," he offered, his gaze unwavering. The sly smile crossed his face again and she braced for whatever flirtatious remark he may have up his sleeve, "Or, if you'd prefer, you could call me cheri mwen?"

Cassielle nearly choked on her tea.

He chuckled and then added, "What's most important is you know I am Baron Samedi, guardian of the dead and keeper of the gates."

Cassielle composed herself, "Okay, Samedi." She leaned

forward a little, looking him in the eyes. "Can we speak plainly?"

He spread his hands out before him in an encouraging gesture.

"Why do you keep playing with me? If you have come to me for help with some grave issue, what benefit is this cat and mouse game with then?" The way he looked at her unarmed her, and she didn't like it.

He continued to watch her like a cougar stalking it's prey. She wasn't sure if he was going to try to eat her, or ravage her, but either way, she found it both unsettling and alluring. He leaned forward, resting his elbows on his knees and wrapping his hands around his walking stick.

"I like you," he said simply. "You are, truly, one of a kind." He sat back again, "But, you are right. There will be plenty of time for flirting, or more amusing ventures once we have finished our duties."

Cassielle could feel her cheeks burning. His flirting was affecting her in ways she wished she could just turn off. In an attempt to stop her feelings, she allowed her mind to wander back to the lessons her mother had imparted to her about the Loa-the mystical spirits of Voodoo, also known as "mysteres" or "the invisibles." Her mother had spoken of them with reverence, describing them as intermediaries between Bondye, or the "good God," and humanity.

She remembered her mother's voice, filled with a mixture of awe and respect, as she explained the Loa were not merely abstract concepts but entities with distinct personalities, preferences, and rituals. Each Loa had their own likes and dislikes, songs, dances, and special symbols called Veve used in ritual practices.

Cassielle recalled the stories her mother shared about the unique modes of service to different Loa-how offerings of specific foods, drinks, or rituals were performed to honor and appease them. The Veve symbols, drawn on the ground during ceremonies, were said to invite the presence of the Loa, bridging the gap between the earthly realm and the spiritual world.

As Samedi sat before her, the supposed embodiment of one of these revered spirits, Cassielle couldn't help but feel a sense of wonder mingled with trepidation. Her mother's teachings had always seemed like folklore, distant and mystical. Here she was, supposedly face-to-face with a guardian of the dead, a Loa in the flesh.

Yet, deep down, she knew her encounter with Samedi transcended mere folklore-it was a confrontation with the supernatural, a convergence of her disbelief and tangible proof she was wrong. With proof came a pang of guilt. A memory of cruel words shouted at her mother in frustrated anger. After her mother's death, the fight had seemed so petty. A friend's party hardly seemed more important than spending time practicing with her mother. She'd give anything to spend more time with her mother now. She swallowed the lump forming in her throat.

As she sat in her small apartment, her gaze fixed on the Loa before her, Cassielle mustered the courage to voice her inner conflict. "Samedi," she began, hesitating slightly before continuing, "I'm struggling to understand... If you are a Loa, and you're able to come into our world, why haven't you before?" Her voice carried a blend of curiosity and awe, tinged with a hint of skepticism. "I remember my mother asking for intervention and it wasn't like one of you popped up to give her what she was asking for."

Samedi regarded her with his characteristic smile, his eyes twinkling with ancient knowledge. "Ah," he replied, his voice resonating with a deep, melodic timbre, "the boundary between our worlds is not as rigid as it may seem, however, we are bound by rules set by your father and Bondye. The Loa, like myself, have the ability to transcend the spiritual and physical realms, manifesting where and when we are required by them."

Cassielle listened intently, her mind absorbing his

words with a mixture of wonder and uncertainty. All of this felt like a dream. She kept thinking she should pinch herself to make sure she was truly awake.

"If I may," Cassielle continued, her tone earnest, "You said you came to me because of escaped souls?"

Samedi regarded her with an intensity piercing through the air, his gaze unwavering. "Ah," he began, his voice low and melodious. "It all began with a misguided attempt to breach the boundary between the living and the dead."

Cassielle's brow furrowed as she listened, her mind racing to grasp what he meant. The way he spoke was making her head hurt. "A ritual to speak to the dead?" she guessed.

Samedi nodded solemnly. "Indeed. Someone sought to commune with the spirits beyond the veil, but they lacked the understanding of the delicate balance governing such matters. We are working on righting the error." Samedi sighed, frustration seeping into his words. "This is what happens when people disregard the rules. If it weren't for the person who attempted to connect with the other side but botched the process..."

As Samedi spoke, Cassielle's thoughts swirled with questions, her skepticism giving way to a growing sense of unease as her thoughts touched on what her mother had taught her. "Which Loa were they trying to talk to? Are you saying they messed up the ritual and then the souls escaped?"

Samedi's expression darkened slightly, a pall passing over his features. "They weren't seeking to talk to or gain something from a specific Loa. They were trying to commune with someone who has passed from your world. The ritual required offerings to each of the Loa guarding the seven gates to allow them to request someone in particular," he explained, his words carrying a weight of ancient knowledge. "But when the first ritual was performed incorrectly, it triggered a catastrophic chain of events."

Cassielle's eyes widened. Her mother had always warned her about this. Especially to the seven Loa who guarded the gates of Guinee. Those, if offended, would open all of the gates and allow the evil contained to spill out into our world.

Samedi's gaze held a haunted quality as he nodded gravely. "Yes, all seven gates were breached," he confirmed, his tone somber. "Evil spirits and dark souls, once bound within the depths of the spirit world, were unleashed upon the living."

Cassielle's mind raced with the implications of Samedi's words, her surroundings momentarily fading into the background. She thought back to their previous conversations. "And these spirits... they're possessing people?" she ventured, struggling to comprehend the magnitude of the supernatural forces at play.

Samedi's gaze bore into hers, his eyes gleaming with an unsettling mixture of solemnity and resolve. "Yes," he replied. "The dark souls of the departed, twisted by malevolent energies, seek vessels to inhabit and wreak havoc upon the living."

Cassielle processed this information, her thoughts whirling with a mix of fascination and apprehension. "If what you're saying is true," she began slowly, "perhaps we should locate the person who opened the gates, right?"

"I fail to see what difference that would make," Samedi mused, watching Cassielle with a look she couldn't decipher.

"I want to know if they messed up on purpose or by accident. Because if it was intentional, we need to know why and what this person hoped to achieve," Cassielle explained.

"That's only if this person is still alive. They may have been one of the first victims," Samedi pondered.

"Wouldn't you know? Didn't you see who was opening the gates?" Cassielle picked up her tea and took another sip.

"No. I was otherwise occupied. The person never reached my gate; they didn't need to. As soon as they performed the incantations and offerings incorrectly, the gates opened wide and released the evil inside," Samedi repeated.

"Wouldn't the person have been left at the gates though, if they were the first victim?" She rose from her seat to take her now empty tea cup to sink. Samedi moved quickly to take it from her and gestured for her to sit back down. She didn't need to be told twice. Her ankle was throbbing in spite of the medication she'd been given at the hospital.

"Not if they were the first possessed person," Samedi moved his free hand in a strange fluid gesture and her tea cup vanished. He grinned at her, "Don't worry, that cup will be safely where it belongs, cleaned and dried." He moved to sit beside her on the couch draping and arm across the back, uncomfortably close to her.

Cassielle adjusted her foot propped up on her coffee table and tried to act like his proximity to her didn't cause her heart to start beating faster. She adjusted the pillow she leaned against before asking her next question. "I have another question - "

"Just one?" Samedi grinned. Cassielle ignored him and continued.

"Why didn't any good spirits escape? Aren't they the gates to the underworld?"

"The 'good' spirits," Samedi said with air quotes, "pass through the gates quickly, and I escort them to the underworld, where they reunite with their loved ones, or, if they decide they'd like to try the whole living thing again, they're moved on to begin the process of reincarnation. However, the malevolent ones, along with the evil spirits banished from this world by God, remain in limbo. They never find their way through the gates to the other side, except if they earn their passage through various means, which I won't delve into," Samedi twirled his walking stick as he observed Cassielle. "A few of the good spirits who were in the process of passing through did accidentally slip out, but we were able to round them up more easily as they did not wander far."

Cassielle leaned back to process his words and figure out the next steps. "So, it's not just dark souls that escaped...

the malevolent spirits, or demons, banished from this world could have also crossed over," she paraphrased, trying to grasp the implications. The idea made her blanch. A world filled with demons was terrifying. "If they're out, how come we haven't seen more problems? All I've heard about were the murders which you're saying were caused by human spirits possessing people? Or were they the demons?"

Samedi's face grew grim, "Luckily, it's just been the evil human souls. I suspect the malevolent spirits, or demons as you called them, are coming up with a strategy before they attack. They don't want to be banished again. You've been lucky thus far you have only encountered the souls of departed humans. I and the other Loa have been working hard trying to track down the malevolent spirits as well. They're trickier and unfortunately for you, and us, God does not get involved so much as he once did."

"Okay, so priority number one would be..." Cassielle's voice drifted off as she tried to think. This was a lot to take in. What would be more pressing? Evil souls possessing people and killing other people or Malevolent spirits may eventually be causing havoc? Plus there was still the whole issue of Michael was dead and the only suspect the police had was Brittany. Her head was now starting to hurt along with her ankle.

"For me, priority one is healing you. I sent for Maman Briggitte. I wanted to talk to you before she came so as to not alarm you further. I wouldn't want you to expire from shock."

Cassielle fixed him with what she hoped was a withering stare. "Expire?" She ground her teeth before continuing, "For one, I am not some delicate flower. You didn't seem too worried about scaring me to death when you showed me your true form, and two, why can't you talk like a normal person? Your flowery language is tedious."

He chuckled and shrugged, "Fair enough." Cassielle became aware of him playing with a strand of her hair, twisting it around his finger as if he were flirting with her. She swatted his hand away. "I will do my best to stop using 'flowery language'."

"May I remind you I had requested four feet of space, which you seem to have already forgotten?" Samedi laughed and vanished only to reappear standing what Cassielle could only guess was exactly four feet away.

"My apologies, ma cherie," he said with a slight bow. His theatrics were something else. Cassielle wasn't quite sure how she felt about them. "Maman Briggite should be here soon. And then, rest for you."

CHAPTER SIXTEEN

From out of nowhere, a figure emerged, standing just in front of the glass door to her balcony. The air shifted subtly as Maman Brigitte gracefully made her way towards Cassielle. Each step seemed to resonate with purpose, the faintest hint of a delicate fragrance trailing in her wake. Cassielle watched, captivated, as Maman Brigitte approached.

Maman Brigitte walked with her head held high with relaxed and easy movement. She practically floated across the floor towards her. Dressed in a flowing dress the color of midnight, with intricate patterns of white and gold adorning the fabric, she moved with effortless grace. Her long, ebony hair cascaded in loose curls down her back, intertwined with delicate white feathers swaying with each movement. Around her neck, a necklace of bones and beads clinked softly, a testament to her connection with the spirits of the departed.

As Maman Brigitte stood before Cassielle, her eyes gleamed with wisdom, reflecting the underworld's secrets. The deep, dark hue of her gaze seemed to hold a thousand untold stories. She spoke, her voice both soothing and authoritative. "Child, fear not. I shall aid you in mending your wounded leg. Let my touch be the balm that accelerates healing and restores your strength."

Cassielle felt a surge of reassurance wash over her as Maman Brigitte knelt before her, extending her hand. A sense of otherworldly energy radiated from Maman Brigitte's touch, enveloping Cassielle in its warmth. It was as if the essence of healing was summoned into the air around them, casting a faint, ethereal glow.

As Maman Brigitte's hand touched the cast on Cassielle's injured ankle, a wave of energy pulsed through her body. Cassielle's senses were heightened-the air seemed to shimmer with the energy of the Loa, and a gentle current of life flowed into her, revitalizing every cell. The lingering pain in her ankle dissipated, replaced by a comforting sensation of relief. A soft, luminescent glow emanated from inside her cast, a visible manifestation of Maman Brigitte's healing powers at work.

Cassielle's eyes widened in amazement as she felt her ankle growing stronger with each passing second. She imagined muscles, tendons, and ligaments repairing themselves with remarkable precision. The passage of time condensed into mere moments, accelerating the natural healing process to an extraordinary degree.

Cassielle smiled with gratitude and awe as she realized the extent of Maman Brigitte's abilities. The Loa's healing touch had far surpassed any conventional means, erasing the physical damage and residual discomfort. Samedi's hand waved, and Cassielle's cast vanished.

Expressing her heartfelt appreciation, Cassielle extended her gratitude to Maman Brigitte. She smiled warmly at Cassielle, her gaze filled with compassion. With a gentle tone, she spoke, "You're welcome, dear Cassielle. May the blessings of healing guide your path." Her words carried a soothing undertone, resonating with the power of the Loa.

Turning her attention to Samedi, Maman Brigitte's eyes lit up with affection and familiarity. Rising gracefully, she strode across the room to him and reached out, gently caressing Samedi's cheek with the back of her hand-a tender gesture that spoke volumes of their deep connection. "Take care, my beloved Samedi," she murmured softly, her voice laced with love and concern. They exchanged a meaningful glance, a silent understanding passing between them.

As swiftly as she had emerged, Maman Brigitte gracefully disappeared into thin air, her presence fading as if she had never been there. Yet, Cassielle realized she could still sense Maman Brigitte's influence lingering, leaving an indelible mark on her soul.

Cassielle stood up from the couch, her mind buzzing with newfound purpose. As she paced, forcing down her swirling emotions, she focused on the problem at hand.

"Next," Samedi spoke as if there had been no interruption to their discussion of what needed to be done, "We need to train you."

Cassielle halted her pacing, fixing Samedi with a look. "Train me?"

"Yes," Samedi replied, smiling as he moved and settled back on the couch, twirling his staff above himself like an elegant fidget toy. "Heylel explicitly tasked me with training you."

Cassielle's mind raced as she tried to recall the significance of the name Heylel. Memories hovered out of reach, obscured by time and deliberate forgetfulness. Voodoo had been a part of her past she had hoped to forget, but now, confronted with these names, the pain of those memories resurfaced, unwelcome yet insistent.

Samedi must have recognized her struggle because he added, "Your father."

The revelation sent a ripple of shock through Cassielle's body. How had she forgotten he'd mentioned knowing her father? Her father's identity had always been shrouded in mystery, his absence a constant void in her life.

"Heylel?" Cassielle repeated, the name foreign yet strangely familiar. It carried weight and significance within the realm of Voodoo.

Samedi's eyes held a knowing glint as he watched Cassielle process the revelation. "Your father," he repeated solemnly.

Cassielle's thoughts whirled, trying to reconcile this newfound information with her childhood memories. "Heylel... my father?" Her voice tinged with disbelief.

Samedi nodded gently. "Your father is Heylel, a revered figure within our realm," he explained. "He sought to protect you from the complexities of our world, but now, as the balance falters, it is time for you to understand."

"You said you'd stop speaking cryptically, remember?" Cassielle urged, her eyes locked on his face. "Why do I recognize his name?"

"He has many names. Heylel, Lucifer, Satan... But we mainly call him Heylel," Samedi replied with a smile.

Cassie stared at him in disbelief. "You must be joking..."

"Ah, I never joke about the boss, dawlin'. I'm sure it must be a bit of a surprise..." Amusement tinged Samedi's voice.

"Understatement of the century." Cassielle took a moment to collect herself before continuing. "So... you're saying my father is the devil?"

"That is correct. He chose your mother because of her excellent bloodline," Samedi explained matter-of-factly.

"If you are telling me the the Vodouisants believe in actually do guard the gates, then how is there a Devil?" Cassie asked, seeking clarification.

"No religion is entirely correct, Cherie," Samedi replied, resting his hands on his walking stick. "Each touches on something that is, or is close to, the truth. There is indeed a devil. God, or Bondye, is the great creator of Earth, while Heylel is the creator of Vilokan, where the dead go. He is remote from Vilokan, just as God is separate from Earth. We, the Loa, are responsible for keeping the two worlds separate. We have failed in this."

A rush of emotions swept over Cassielle-confusion, curiosity, and a profound sense of loss. "Why was I kept in the dark about him?" she asked, her voice wavering.

Samedi regarded her with compassion. "Your father believed ignorance would shield you from danger," he replied gently. "But now, with the gates breached and dark forces unleashed, it is imperative you embrace your heritage."

Cassielle's thoughts whirled with unanswered questions, her heart heavy with the weight of her father's legacy. "What does this mean for me?" she asked, her voice barely above a whisper.

Samedi's expression softened. "It means you carry a lineage of protectors, those who stand between the worlds," he explained. "You have a role to play in restoring the balance and safeguarding both realms."

Cassielle's mind raced, trying to grasp the magnitude of her destiny. "And I'm... meant to continue this legacy?" she ventured, her voice filled with uncertainty.

Samedi's eyes sparkled with affirmation. "Yes, you have been chosen to carry the essence of Heylel," he replied, his tone filled with conviction. "With training and guidance, you will fulfill your destiny as a guardian."

"Wait... so does this mean..." Cassielle's lips curved into a wry smile. "Does this mean I'm like Jesus, but the devil's daughter instead?"

Samedi laughed warmly. "How astute of you. Yes. Bondye was Jesus's father. Like you, he had abilities. He was more of the giving life type. Yours are the opposite. He helped usher people to Heaven. He was able to forgive them so they could go. You, however, could damn people if you so chose." He smirked. "Though, knowing you, I don't think you'd do that to someone who didn't deserve it."

Samedi rose from the couch, gesturing towards Cassielle's bed. "I must keep reminding myself that though you are Heylel's daughter, you do have human needs. Sleep first, then food, then we can continue our discussion."

Cassielle nodded slowly, her mind buzzing with newfound purpose. "I still have so many questions," she admitted, her gaze searching Samedi's for answers.

Samedi's smile was reassuring. "And you will find the answers in due time," he assured her. "For now, let us focus on awakening your abilities and preparing you for the challenges ahead... after you rest."

CHAPTER SEVENTEEN

Cassielle didn't remember how she wound up in her bed, but she awoke to the sound of birds chirping, cars passing, and coffee brewing. The air was infused with a rich, intoxicating aroma dancing delicately upon her senses. With each inhalation, the scent of freshly brewed coffee mingled seamlessly with the earthy notes of chicory, creating a symphony of fragrance enveloping the room in warmth and comfort.

As she rolled over, her eyes fluttered open to find Samedi standing beside her, a tray balanced delicately in his hands. On it sat a spread of Eggs Sardou, a quintessential New Orleans breakfast dish, accompanied by a steaming cup of coffee and a small vase of vibrant flowers.

The sight filled Cassielle with a sense of warmth and comfort, a feeling akin to being wrapped in a familiar embrace. The aroma of the food teased her senses, evoking memories of lazy Sunday mornings spent indulging in hearty Creole fare.

But it wasn't only the food stirring something within her-it was the gesture itself. The thoughtful act of Samedi preparing breakfast. She wouldn't have thought him capable, being a Loa and not human.

As Cassielle sat up, a smile tugged at the corners of her lips. She felt a surge of appreciation for the simple yet meaningful gesture, a reminder how even amidst the chaos of their current situation, there could be moments of kindness and connection to be found.

Reaching out, she accepted the tray from Samedi, her fingers brushing briefly against his as she did so. In that fleeting touch, she felt a spark of something she couldn't name. She did her best to ignore it and set the tray on her lap.

Taking a sip of the fragrant coffee, Cassielle savored the rich, bold flavor, letting it warm her from the inside out. With each bite of the Eggs Sardou, she felt a sense of contentment wash over her, a feeling of being grounded in the present moment.

As she ate, Cassielle couldn't help but marvel at the beauty of the flowers sitting beside her, their vibrant colors a stark contrast to the muted tones of the room. They seemed to radiate a sense of hope and renewal, a reminder that even in the darkest of times, beauty could be found. That thought made her feel like some sentimental schmuck.

"What do we do now?" Cassielle set her napkin on the tray.

With a subtle gesture from Samedi, the tray, now empty, vanished into thin air, leaving only the lingering scent of coffee in its wake. Cassielle watched in awe as the remnants of her breakfast disappeared.

Samedi regarded her with a steady gaze, his expression solemn. "Now, we begin your training,"

Cassielle nodded, her mind buzzing with anticipation and apprehension. Based on the struggles she'd had controlling what she knew how to do now, she suspected unlocking the full extent of her powers would be no easy feat. But she was ready to face the challenges ahead.

With a subtle gesture, Samedi extended his hand towards her. Without hesitation, Cassielle reached out, her fingers intertwining with his in a gesture of trust and solidarity. In that fleeting moment of connection, Cassielle couldn't help but feel a stirring deep within her soul.

In an instant, the world around them seemed to blur and fade away, replaced by swirling darkness. The sensation was disorienting yet exhilarating.

As they emerged on the other side, Cassielle found herself standing in a clearing bathed in the soft light of dawn.

The gentle rays of the sun filtered through the canopy of trees, casting dappled shadows on the forest floor.

Recognition washed over Cassielle as she surveyed the familiar terrain. This was the place where her mother had once trained her, where she had learned about Voodoo and its sacred rituals. It was a place of memories and revelations, a sanctuary resonating with the echoes of generations past. Cassielle closed her eyes and took a deep breath, allowing the energy of the Bayou to envelop her like a warm embrace.

Samedi released her hand.

"Did your mother ever tell you the true extent of your abilities?" He crossed the clearing to brush his fingers against the weathered bark of a cypress tree. He gazed up into the canopy as if he were having a deep conversation with the tree.

"No..." She allowed her mind to drift back, sorting through her memories of her training with her mother. She'd shown her rituals and spells. Nothing else. "No," she said more definitively. "She didn't show me anything about myself. It was all the normal training and teaching of a Voodoo queen... at least I presume it was the normal training. I'm not sure I'd know what was normal or not. It's not like I've watched people be trained." She moved to stand near him, pulled to him like a magnet. "I stopped training when I was 14." Regret flooded her mind. "Maybe she would have eventually gotten there, but I was foolish..."

"Your mother loved you," Samedi moved towards her, his hand grasping her chin and lifting her eyes to meet his. "You weren't foolish. You were young. Naive. She understood."

Cassielle's gaze met Samedi's, and for a moment, time seemed to stand still. In the depths of his eyes, she saw a warmth and understanding washing away the doubt and regret clouding her mind.

"She did," Samedi murmured, his voice a soothing balm to her troubled soul. "And she would have wanted nothing more than to see you embrace your true potential."

Her breath caught at the gentle touch of his hand on

her chin, sending a jolt of electricity coursing through her veins. In that moment, she felt an inexplicable connection to Samedi, a bond transcending the boundaries of time and space. She should move away, but she wasn't sure why she wasn't moving.

"I was foolish," she admitted, her voice barely above a whisper. "I let fear and doubt cloud my judgment, and now... I'm not sure if I'll ever be able to make up for lost time."

Samedi's expression softened, his thumb tracing a gentle arc along the curve of her cheek. "You're not alone," he reassured her. "I'm here for you every step of the way."

His words filled her with a sense of comfort and reassurance, dispelling the lingering doubts plaguing her mind. Cassielle wondered if she had found a kindred spirit in Samedi, someone who understood her in a way no one else ever could. He knew her dark side and was okay with it.

Without another word, Samedi pulled her into his embrace, wrapping her in a cocoon of warmth and protection. She stiffened, suddenly alarmed at the closeness, her heart racing with a mix of nerves and attraction. His scent of sandalwood and spice filled her senses, both unsettling and oddly comforting. Cassielle hesitated, then slowly buried her face in the crook of his neck, feeling her tension begin to melt away despite her lingering discomfort.

She started to feel she had found her anchor in the storm, a beacon of light in the darkness threatening to consume her. As they stood together, locked in each other's arms, Cassielle felt a glimmer of hope ignite within her heart, illuminating the path ahead with newfound purpose and determination.

"Now, let's begin," Samedi declared, his voice firm yet encouraging as he stepped back from her. She half expected him to say something flirty about their moment, but he didn't. He was focused on the task at hand. "First, we'll work on your ability to teleport."

Cassielle nodded, her heart racing with anticipation.

When people talked about superpowers they could have, she had always liked the idea of teleportation. It provided a sort of freedom, the ability to traverse vast distances in the blink of an eye. It was a power she had only dreamed of possessing, and now, with Samedi's guidance, it was within her grasp.

Samedi stepped forward. "Focus your energy," he instructed. "Picture your destination in your mind's eye, and let the magic flow through you."

Closing her eyes, Cassielle took a deep breath, centering herself amidst the pulsing energy of the Bayou. She pictured a familiar street corner in the heart of New Orleans, the bustling crowds and vibrant energy calling out to her.

It felt like several minutes passed. When she opened her eyes, she was disappointed to see nothing had happened. She looked over at Samedi, who shook his head. "Let loose the block you have up here." He tapped her forehead.

She closed her eyes and tried again, imagining the wall she had built disintegrating. Reaching for the well of energy in her chest, she focused intently.

With a surge of concentration, Cassielle felt the magic begin to stir within her, coursing through her veins like a torrential river. She focused on the image in her mind, willing herself to become one with the magic surrounding her.

And then, with a sudden rush of exhilaration, she felt herself being torn from the fabric of reality, hurtling through the void of space and time. It was a sensation unlike anything she had ever experienced, both terrifying and exhilarating in equal measure.

When she opened her eyes, Cassielle found herself standing on the familiar street corner, the sights and sounds of New Orleans bustling around her. She couldn't help but grin in awe and wonder, exhilarated by her newfound ability.

Samedi's voice echoed in her mind. "Well done, Cassielle," he said, his tone filled with admiration. "You've taken your first step into a larger world."

But their training was far from over. With each passing

moment, Cassielle felt herself growing more attuned to the magic coursing through her veins. Under Samedi's patient guidance, she learned to control her powers with precision and finesse, honing her abilities until they became second nature.

Together, they delved into the darkest recesses of her mind, confronting the shadows of her past with courage and determination. Cassielle learned to relive dark scenes from her memories, facing her fears head-on and emerging stronger with each passing trial.

She discovered the power of her aura sight, seeing the world in vibrant hues of light and darkness. With a single glance, she could discern the true nature of those around her, sensing the darkness that lurked within their souls.

And perhaps most unsettling of all, Cassielle learned to harness the power of her touch, delving into the minds of others with a single caress. She saw their darkest deeds laid bare before her, the sins of their pasts laid bare for all to see. They practiced by having her walk through a busy mall, 'accidentally' bumping into people.

The experience left Cassielle completely overwhelmed. Each 'accidental' touch brought her a torrent of thoughts and memories crashing into her mind. Most were dark and unsettling. People were darker than many thought. Everyone has dark thoughts. Some are worse than others. She struggled to maintain her composure as she navigated through the crowd, her senses bombarded with a mix of emotions from strangers' lives. She felt their pain, guilt, and fear, all swirling together in a chaotic storm.

Samedi's voice was a constant in her ear, guiding her through the turmoil. "Focus, Cassielle," he instructed, his tone calm but firm. "You need to learn how to filter through the noise and find the clarity within the chaos. You need to learn how to keep your mind open and not take in all of the thoughts and feelings of those around you. Let your senses guide you to only the ones that are important."

It was easier said than done. With every touch,

Cassielle felt her control slipping. She saw not just the flashes of betrayal, whispering secrets, and the weight of regrets of the people there, but she started to see things, too. Things that had happened in that place before. Dark things. Things best forgotten. Her head started to throb with the effort of keeping it all at bay.

"Again," Samedi urged, as she staggered back from yet another encounter, her breathing labored. "You must master this, or it will consume you."

People were starting to look at her. Cassielle clenched her fists, willing herself to push through the discomfort. She had to do this. She could not fail. She ducked into a bathroom stall to recenter herself. She took deep breaths, focusing on her breathing and pushing all other thoughts from her mind. She then re-emerged and resumed her training, working on controlling what she allowed herself to feel and see. She was in control of her own mind. She had to be.

As the sun dipped below the horizon, casting long shadows across the clearing, Cassielle and Samedi emerged from their intense day of training. The air hummed with residual energy, crackling with the promise of newfound strength and resilience.

With a sense of accomplishment tingling in her veins, Cassielle took a moment to savor the stillness of the bayou. The tranquility of the natural world offered a stark contrast to the chaos of their training. She felt a newfound sense of clarity and purpose, a determination to embrace her destiny. For the first time, she felt comfortable in her own skin. Maybe with more practice, she could learn to control her dark side and not worry about the lust for experiencing the darkness in the world.

Turning to Samedi, she offered him a small smile. "Thank you," she said softly. "For everything."

Samedi returned her smile, his eyes alight with pride. "You did well, Cassielle," he replied warmly. "But remember, this is just the beginning. There's still much left for you to learn."

Cassielle nodded in understanding and focused her mind on her apartment, envisioning its familiar surroundings. With a surge of energy, she and Samedi disappeared from the clearing, reappearing in the comfort of her home.

Cassielle moved across the floor, flicking on the scanner with a click. The soft hum of the machine filled the room, its steady rhythm a comforting backdrop to her thoughts. She wondered if by listening, she could learn about more murders than the media or public were aware of. If they could catch word of it, she could check the crime scenes for more clues. Maybe she'd see the figure again.

She sank onto the worn cushions of her couch, discarding her bag on the coffee table. The clatter of her belongings echoed in the quiet space. Seeking a moment of respite, she closed her eyes and listened to the radio chatter. Amidst the stream of reports, one transmission caught her attention-a distressing report emerged: 10-31E, a murder on the corner of Bourbon Street and Saint Philip Street.

Panic surged as she reached for her phone, dialing Alba's number and pacing anxiously until Alba answered.

"Cassielle!" Alba's voice resonated loudly, carrying an evident strain. "It's awful! There's a body outside my door!"

"Take a breath, Alba. What happened? Is Brittany okay?" Cassielle grabbed her jacket and bag, ready to head out. She had a terrible sinking feeling. If the person who opened the gates knew her favorite haunts and where she lived, they probably knew who she cared about. This put Alba, Brittany, and Nick in grave danger. She pushed these worries from her mind for now.

"It all happened so quickly..." Alba's voice quivered with sadness. "Armand Roich... He's been working for me for years!" It took only a moment for Cassielle to remember him. Armand, a bouncer at Lafitte's, was known for he gentle nature, though he could handle rowdy crowds when necessary. A big teddy bear.

"Did he get into a scuffle with a customer?"

"No, it wasn't with a customer. He was escorting a man out who was causing trouble. The guy was too drunk to resist much, so Armand had an easy time of it. But as soon as they step outside, somethin' change. He started choking the guy. Martin tried to intervene, but Armand was much larger. He punched him, knocked him to de ground and broke his nose," Alba explained, her voice cracking with emotion. "He killed Martin!"

"I'm on my way, Alba." Cassielle's heart ached. Martin was a genuinely good person, with a wife and child waiting for him at home. The news of his untimely death would devastate Janice. Delivering such heartbreaking news was a task Cassielle had unfortunately faced many times before, and she knew it was never easy.

"Oh, darlin'," Alba sniffled, her voice filled with sadness. "You don't have to come here... Nick is already here, and I'm going to close the bar for the night once everythin's done."

"It's going to take a while, Alba. I'm already on my way," Cassielle insisted, determined to be there for her friend and provide whatever support she could.

Cassielle turned to Samedi, who lay on her bed twirling his staff over him. If she didn't know any better, she'd think he wasn't paying attention to her conversation. His response proved otherwise.

"There's no point going there right now, Cherie. The spirit will likely be gone, and you won't be able to scry to see what happened with all the people there," Samedi said quietly. Cassielle pressed the mute button on her phone.

"Here's where you're wrong. If someone guided the spirit to commit the murder, they'll likely want to watch the chaos unfolding. You said they thrive off chaos and fear. What better opportunity than to stand at the sidelines, unnoticed, and just drink it all up?"

Samedi slowly smiled and nodded. "Touche."

Without another moment to waste, Cassielle and

Samedi stepped into the shadows and reappeared in Cassielle's office. Once in her office, she unmuted her phone.

"I'm almost there."

"Thank you," Alba sniffled.

Cassielle and Samedi quickly exited the building to see the chaos of a crime scene in a public place.

Cassielle's thoughts drifted to Martin. He was a regular at Lafitte's, a quiet man with a quick smile and a ready laugh. Nick was probably dealing with the chaos outside the bar, and Cassielle's stomach flipped with anticipation.

"Oh, Cassielle, what am I going to do? Will they draw the chalk outlines on the sidewalk? I can't have that!" Alba's voice trembled over the phone. There was a brief pause before she continued, "Oh, I'm terrible for worrying 'bout chalk lines when Martin is dead!"

Cassielle swiftly maneuvered through the gathering of onlookers. The sinister magnetism of the crime scene pulled at her, her heart raced and an unsettling hunger stirred in her belly. It wasn't actual hunger but a morbid desire for death, blood, and chaos. Determined, she pushed her way to the front of the crowd. Caution tape cordoned off the crime scene, and as she approached, one of the officers halted her progress.

Cassielle's vision blurred as she gazed at the body bag. "Not now," she thought, realizing the crowded setting prevented her from succumbing to her visions.

"Cassielle, what are you doing here?" Nick's voice pierced the air. Strangely, she was grateful for his presence, as his voice seemed to restore clarity to her vision. Nevertheless, the lingering scent of blood remained.

"Alba called me," Cassielle replied.

"Cassielle!" She turned to see Alba rushing toward her, her makeup smudged and her tear-filled eyes a testament to her grief. Before Cassielle could react, Alba enveloped her in a tight and slightly suffocating hug. She managed to extricate herself.

"So... what have you got?" Cassielle watched Nick who

was jotting down some notes in his notebook.

"Nothing to share with you." Nick snapped his notebook shut and faced her. "Go home."

"Well, since you asked so nicely," Cassielle grumbled. She turned to Alba. "Do you want me to go up with you?"

"No, love. I'll be alright. I told Brittany to take a nice long bubble bath and don't fret over this. I'll go check on her." Alba forced her into another bear hug, though she released her much more quickly this time.

Cassielle watched as Alba entered the bar. Glancing in Samedi's direction, she confirmed he was still watching her. With the crowd dispersing now that the coroner had taken the body and the suspect had been taken to the precinct, Cassielle realized she wouldn't gather any information from the onlookers. She turned and spotted someone in a dark hoodie. After a beat where she was sure they'd seen her, they turned and bolted.

"*This will be fun,*" Cassielle thought. Samedi and Cassielle shared a smile before running after him. They followed him around a corner. Seeing there was no one else on this street, they stepped into the shadows and stepped out in front of the figure, causing him to collide with them and stumble back. When Samedi grabbed him by the shoulders, his hoodie fell off. Cassielle felt as if her heart had stopped.

"Jamal?"

CHAPTER EIGHTEEN

Cassielle stared at Jamal in shock. There was no way. There was no way he was the person who had been showing up at the scenes where there were possessions. Samedi didn't seem to notice or care that Cassielle had frozen.

"He's not possessed," Samedi almost sounded surprised.

"Thanks, Captain Obvious." Cassielle pulled herself together and raised her hands. "Jamal, what the hell?"

He sighed and looked down for a moment before looking back up at her. "I'm sorry, I'm so sorry, Cassielle!"

"Sorry for what, Jamal? What have you done?" Cassielle crossed her arms, her eyes narrowing.

Jamal's shoulders slumped, and he looked like he was about to collapse under the weight of his guilt. "I agreed to help someone," his hands heavy in his response.

"In exchange, they promised to help me have a relationship with Brittany. I didn't know Michael would end up dead. I was told I only had to help with a ritual, and that was it. But after that, I started losing time, blacking out, and then waking up in different places, always wearing this hoodie." He tugged at the garment.

"It felt like a deep, dark hole where I couldn't get out."

Cassielle's shock deepened. "You... you agreed to a ritual?" She felt a cold dread creeping over her.

"I didn't know, Cassielle!" Jamal's eyes were wide and desperate. "I thought it was harmless, just some weird ceremony. You know I never followed Voodoo with Aunt Alba. But then everything went wrong. I started waking up with no memory of what I'd done, and I kept finding myself at those crime scenes. I don't know why I was there. I swear!"

Samedi observed him with an unusual seriousness, and, to Cassielle's surprise, he started signing. "It sounds like you were manipulated, Jamal. Someone used you as a puppet."

Jamal nodded frantically. "Maybe... I can't remember. Please, you have to believe me."

Cassielle took a deep breath, trying to process what Jamal was saying. "Who was it? Who made you do this?"

Jamal hesitated, his eyes filled with fear. "I... I don't know their name. They approached me, said they could help me be with Brittany. I wasn't thinking. I've liked her for so long. I don't know why I went along with it. Aunt Alba is always saying people shouldn't mess with things they don't understand."

Cassielle exchanged a glance with Samedi, who gave her a subtle nod. She looked back at Jamal, her expression softening slightly. "We believe you, Jamal. But we need to find out who did this and stop them. Can you remember anything about them?"

Jamal closed his eyes. "I couldn't make out their features. I was enthralled because they had this swirling black mist surrounding them. I couldn't see through it. But I did see something on their hand during the ritual I helped them with. It was on St. John's Eve, in the cemetery."

Cassielle waited expectantly, and after a brief pause, Jamal motioned for a pen and paper. Cassielle pulled her notebook out of her bag along with a pen. Jamal then began to sketch a complex geometric design.

Intrigued, Cassielle observed as Jamal meticulously drew a circle. At the top, he inscribed the letter B, followed by U on the right, E at the bottom, and R on the left, all neatly positioned within the outer circle. Another circle, slightly smaller, enclosed these letters, creating a layered effect.

Within the inner circle, Jamal intricately detailed a series of smaller circles and intersecting lines. The arrangement vaguely resembled a ladybug, with a crudely drawn trumpet pointing downward. A line extended from the trumpet, leading to the letter S, intersected by another line.

Cassielle's heart skipped a beat. She recognized the symbol.

"Buer," Cassielle and Samedi simultaneously uttered before sharing a meaningful glance. Jamal looked between Cassielle and Samedi as their lips moved and signed, "What?" prompting Cassielle to explain how Buer is a demon often depicted with a lion's head and five or six goat legs arranged around the head in a wheel-like formation, allowing it to move swiftly and effortlessly.

"If I had to choose the most troublesome demon to deal with, it would undoubtedly be him," Samedi grumbled, his irritation palpable. Cassielle interpreted this to Jamal, who observed with a mix of concern and curiosity.

"Before you go, I have a couple more questions," Cassielle's hands moved with urgency.

"Was the ritual you were involved in messed up on purpose?"

Jamal furrowed his brow, shaking his head. "I don't know. They just told me it was a ritual to help with something, but I didn't understand what it was for. If I helped them, they'd help me." His hands lingered a moment.

"They asked me to call them the 'Shadow Master.'"

Cassielle's brow furrowed with frustration. "Do you know where you first met with this person? This Shadow Master?"

Jamal hesitated, his gaze dropping to the ground. "I... I'm not sure. I don't remember. I think it was outside of LaFitte's. My memories are all a blur. It's like I'm in a dream between the times I black out and then wake up in different places, wearing this hoodie. I don't feel like myself anymore."

"Do you know why Avery was killed?" With this question, Jamal's shoulders began to shake as he let out a horrendous sob, tears running down his face.

"I saw you talking to Brittany's friend at the coffee shop and remembered she and Avery had been at the bar that night with Brittany. I then worried her friend Avery may have seen my face at the bar the night Michael died. I panicked. I went home and prayed she hadn't seen my face. The Shadow Master showed up and I told them..." his hands shaking. "I don't know what I thought they would do-"

"You had to know they would kill her. Haven't enough people died that you could piece that together?" Cassielle felt her anger rising.

"We should go," Samedi offered, resting his hand on Cassielle's shoulder. She took deep breaths to calm herself.

She sighed, realizing they had hit a dead end for now. "Alright, go home and stay safe. We'll figure this out."

"Jamal, you've provided us with valuable information," Samedi signed.

Cassielle nodded. "We'll uncover the truth behind this. But for now, you must keep yourself safe and remain out of sight. Go to Alba's. Tell her you've gotten into a bit of trouble and you need a protective spell. She'll take care of you. Those responsible will probably look for you now. The spell should help, right?" She looked to Samedi, who nodded.

With a nod of understanding, Jamal expressed his gratitude, tears of relief tracing down his cheeks. "Thank you, Cassielle. I will."

Cassielle softened, looking into his face and remembering the kid with whom she used to make mud pies. He'd gone away to a school for the Deaf, but they'd spent holidays together. He was the closest thing she had to a brother. She took a deep breath and offered a reassuring squeeze to his shoulder. "We're in this together, Jamal. We'll find a way through."

As Jamal hurried off into the night, Cassielle pivoted towards Samedi, her eyes ablaze with determination. "We need to find Buer and stop him now that we know he's involved."

Samedi's nod conveyed his solemn agreement, his

features etched with a steely resolve. "I suspect he's utilizing the Shadow Master as his conduit, tapping into the darkness for power. Jamal's unwitting presence at the crime scenes may have served as Buer's means to harvest dark energy without direct involvement. I wouldn't be surprised if Jamal bears the sigil as well."

Cassielle's heart plummeted. "How can we save him, Samedi? Once Buer learns he's spoken to us-"

"He'll eliminate him," Samedi interjected, his gaze piercing through the night with a chilling intensity mirroring Cassielle's dread.

"Isn't there anything I can do?" Cassielle wrapped her arms around herself, the warmth of the night failing to dispel the chill creeping into her bones.

"Your abilities thrive on darkness and death. You're an enforcer, not a savior," Samedi murmured. "But Alba's Voodoo should help."

Samedi looked at her, and she must have looked worried, for he moved towards her, drawing her into an embrace that offered solace as tangible as it was comforting. In his arms, she found refuge, a fleeting sense of belonging reminiscent of home - a feeling she hadn't experienced since her mother's passing.

As the weight of their conversation hung heavy in the air, Cassielle found herself again drawn to Samedi. His dark allure, the aura of mystery surrounding him, seemed to offer an escape from the turmoil of their reality.

In a moment of vulnerability, Cassielle leaned in, her lips seeking his in a desperate bid for distraction. Samedi hesitated for a fraction of a second before yielding to the kiss, his turmoil momentarily forgotten in the heat of the moment.

Their lips met with a hunger born of shared sorrow and uncertainty. Each sought solace in the other's embrace. The warmth of Samedi's touch enveloped Cassielle, driving away the cold grip of fear threatening to consume her.

For a fleeting instant, they were lost in each other,

the world around them fading into insignificance. But as the kiss deepened, a nagging voice in the back of Cassielle's mind reminded her of the dangers lurking in the shadows, of the darkness threatening to consume them both.

Reluctantly, she pulled away, her breath coming in ragged gasps as she met Samedi's gaze. A mixture of longing and regret was reflected in his eyes.

"We can't," she whispered, her voice barely more than a breathless murmur. "Not now."

Samedi nodded, a flicker of understanding passing between them as they reluctantly let go of each other, the moment of intimacy shattered by the harsh reality of their situation.

But even as they parted, the memory of their kiss lingered, a bittersweet reminder of the fragile bond forming between them-a bond that, for better or worse, could shape the path they would tread in the days to come. Without another word, they stepped into the shadows to return to her apartment.

CHAPTER NINETEEN

Time passed in a blur as Cassielle drifted in and out of restless sleep, her dreams haunted by visions of darkness and despair. When she finally awoke, the morning sun cast its golden rays through the window, bathing the room in a warm, comforting glow.

With a deep breath, Cassielle rolled over in bed to face the light pouring in. Despite the weight of uncertainty hanging heavy in her heart, she knew she couldn't afford to dwell on the past. There was work to be done. There was a lot of work to be done if she even considered her work before this mess. But, she was ready to face this fiasco head-on so that she could maybe, eventually, get back to her real life.

Her conversation with Jamal rolled around in her brain like a mime trapped in an invisible box. She knew there was something there, but she was missing it. She needed to think everything through. Samedi agreed to go with her to her office, though he was anxious about capturing the escaped spirits. His presence was making it difficult for her to think as well. She felt drawn to him in a way she'd never felt with Nick. Nick had been safe, comfortable. Samedi was intense, dangerous even. She felt like her dark side was obsessed with him in an unhealthy way. Almost as if there were two of her. She wasn't sure which one would win out.

Cassielle was pulled from her thoughts when Samedi spoke. "While you slept, I was notified the other Loa are doing pretty well at capturing the escaped human souls. But we really need you to collect the escaped malevolent spirits. They have been especially evasive and Heylel is losing his patience."

Cassielle rolled over to face him standing beside her bed holding a tray of food and a fresh coffee. She noted a sweet aroma, tinged with a hint of bitterness, enveloping the room like a warm embrace. Cassielle sat up and Samedi set the tray over her lap with a dramatic flourish. She glanced behind him at the kitchen for the telltale mess of flour-dusted bowls or a tray of cooling beignets. The counters, however, remained untouched by any sign of baking.

"Magic," He grinned.

Cassielle raised an eyebrow, "If you have magic, why can't you all do it?" Cassielle was slowly savoring the beignets Samedi had acquired for her. If there was a way to her heart, these beignets might be it. "I thought I was just helping."

"Our powers are limited. We can grab human souls, but our skills are fairly limited when it comes to malevolent spirits. We throw barriers up to keep them where they are. Heylel can do it, but he's busy getting the underworld back in order and can't do them all himself. So, we have you-his right hand, shall we say?"

"What about Bondye?"

"It's best to keep him out of it," Samedi grimaced.

Cassielle's fingers lingered on the delicate, powdered surface of the beignets, relishing the sweet aroma. Each bite was a symphony of flavors, the crispy exterior giving way to a soft, pillowy center. She closed her eyes, momentarily lost in the simple pleasure of the moment.

As she chewed thoughtfully, Cassielle mulled over Samedi's words. Being Heylel's right must mean more than just carrying out tasks; it was a position of trust and authority, one with its own set of challenges and expectations. She couldn't afford to falter, not when so much depended on her abilities.

She told Samedi why she needed to go to her office - so she could outline events and figure out the connections. She needed to see everything to piece it together. There were too many details to try and do it in her brain. She needed to look for patterns in the deaths. Cassielle had decided to borrow from Jamal and call the shadowy figure she'd seen "The Shadow Master" to clarify the difference between him and any other mysterious characters who may or may not pop-up.

Once she finished eating, they made their way to her office, the familiar surroundings offering a sense of order amidst the chaos that surrounded her. As she settled into her desk, she couldn't shake the feeling the calm was merely a facade, a fleeting respite from the storm raging outside.

It was a quiet Saturday morning in the heart of summer, devoid of the bustling activity typically seen during February's Mardi Gras or in the fall when tourists sought to avoid the Mardi Gras chaos while still enjoying New Orleans.

Cassielle relished the summers in New Orleans. With fewer tourists and more locals, it provided a quieter atmosphere. Yes, the heat was unbearable, but it was worth it. Cassielle had more clients in the off-season as the crowded streets did not deter them. While she momentarily contemplated going to Lafitte's for a drink, she felt the pressing need to delve into the case before the district attorney could seal Brittany's fate and before Buer could do anything else.

As she glanced out the window, a horse-drawn carriage passed outside. Samedi switched on the light, causing the overhead fan to whir to life, illuminating her small office. She rose from her chair to go turn the little window air conditioner on. It was too hot to go without it.

Approaching the corkboard on the left side of her desk, Cassielle began removing the pictures and strings adorning it. She had wrapped up a case last week where she'd used the board to organize her thoughts with, but hadn't gotten around to taking down the photos of the unfaithful wife and her boyfriend in various locations. The husband had been far from pleased, but he had generously compensated Cassielle for the evidence proving his wife had violated their prenuptial agreement and had been stealing from his company—no money for you, Madame Gerou. A job well done deserved a fat paycheck and several shots of tequila.

Cassielle settled into her chair behind the desk and powered up her laptop. Working on Brittany's case was going to be challenging. The police, rather Nick, was unwilling to share his findings, so she would have to rely on her observations and, perhaps, find a way to access the other crime scenes without being noticed. As she waited for her computer to load, she pulled out some note cards and started to scrawl on them:

> Michael dies (Shadow Master present?)
> Gates Opened
> Vittorio "The Butcher" DeLuca
> Shadow Master (what do they want?)
> Jamal memory lapses - possession/control
> Armand death
> Avery death
> Brittany memory loss
> Tom Horn

She then proceeded to pin them to her bulletin board. Shadow Figure in the center, string connecting outward to Vittorio DeLuca, string connecting to Michael's and Armand's deaths, and then Gates Opened, Brittany and Jamal memory lapses, and Avery's death out on their own, not connected to anything. She went back and attached Jamal memory lapses to the Shadow figure and made a note that he was "hoodie guy."

Samedi sat in one of the chairs across from her desk, watching her as one might watch a cute puppy playing.

"It's fascinating watching how your mind works," he said.

Cassielle looked over to see him lean forward, hands folded atop his cane and chin resting on top of his hands as he gazed at her in a manner that set her heart fluttering in her chest like a bird eager to escape its cage. Warmth spread through her body.

She pushed impure thoughts from her mind and turned back to the board. There had to be a connection between all of it. Maybe she needed to see the other crime scenes. She moved to her chair and signed into her computer. It wouldn't be too hard to find the news about them.

Out of habit, she scanned her emails. As expected, she found multiple requests for meetings regarding potential cases. She ignored them for now. There was a response from the mother, Adrianna, who's daughter, Sarah, had gone missing. She fired a quick response that she unfortunately did not have time at this moment to assist, but she would connect her with one of her old colleagues at the precinct. She then emailed Detective Shafer in the missing person's unit with the mother's contact information and asked her to please follow up. She chewed on her lip, guilt gnawed at her for not helping that mother, but she couldn't. It would be unfair for her to agree to a case she didn't have the time to handle.

She turned her thoughts back to the possession cases. It may be time to shift her focus onto something else. Sometimes, the solution presents itself when you stop fixating on a problem. But before delving into another task, she quickly emailed her lawyer friend, Pierre Augustin Charles VI. Pierre loved to regale people with stories of how he was the sixth great-grandson of the original Pierre Augustin Charles, who had served as the sixth governor of Louisiana. He often joked he should have become a doctor instead of a lawyer to avoid the question of when he would run for governor. Pierre was the finest defense attorney Cassielle knew. Their relationship had begun with him defending the criminals she arrested. Still, they had become friends after she left the force. He was an incredibly kind-hearted guy. If anyone could provide legal assistance to help clear Brittany's name, it was Pierre. If she wasn't able to find better proof, Brittany was going to need him.

Having finished, she opened an email titled "Please help - Murders."

Dear Ms. Madison,

I was informed you are renowned as the best private investigator in New Orleans...

Starting with a compliment. It was a good strategy, as far as Cassielle was concerned. But a bit on the nose.

I understand your usual cases involve lost animals, cheating spouses, or missing children. However, I've heard you were an exceptional homicide detective. This is precisely why I am reaching out to you.

Cassielle would have stopped reading, but a glimpse of the following sentence caught her attention, prompting her to continue.

I do not intend to interfere with any ongoing murder investigations. Instead, I am a journalist for the Journal Gazette and have stumbled upon some intriguing cases that I would like your assistance with. I have uncovered a series of rapes, murders, and other violent crimes committed by individuals who seem unlikely to be involved in such acts.

One specific case involves Sister Mary Joseph, who is accused of murdering a child during a disciplinary meeting before taking her own life by hanging. Sister Mary Joseph was a teacher at Cathedral Academy in the French Quarter. It is highly unusual for a nun to commit such a heinous act, especially against a child. Both murder and suicide are mortal sins.

Moreover, my editor refuses to publish anything about this case, deeming it "unnewsworthy." None of my colleagues seem to find it essential either. It feels as if I'm trapped in the twilight zone. The police refuse to answer my questions, which doesn't surprise me.

In addition to the nun's case, there have been several incidents of rape and assault committed by individuals who don't fit the profile of perpetrators of such crimes and have no memory of having done it.

I would greatly appreciate any help you can provide in obtaining more information about what is happening in our city. I have examined crime statistics and noticed a sudden surge in violent crimes starting on the night of St. John's Eve.

Although I am not superstitious or religious, I can't shake the feeling something beyond our understanding is at play here. I know you are rational and level-headed, so I hope you will assist me in uncovering the harsh truth behind these cases.

Thank you for your time.

Please email me back.

I want to meet with you soon to discuss this matter further.

Sincerely,
Rebecca Tyler
Reporter at the Journal Gazette

Cassielle recognized the name. Rebecca Tyler was infamous for prying into ongoing cases, always hungry for more information from the precinct. She was a serious reporter, not given to flights of fancy, and her reports could be brutally frank. Cassielle had heard from her colleagues Rebecca Tyler was the last person you wanted to see at a crime scene or press conference. Once she latched onto a story, she wouldn't let go until she had every last detail. Why was she seeking Cassielle's help? If the case she mentioned was genuine, why wouldn't her editor jump at the chance to publish it?

Cassielle opened her web browser and did a quick search on the Cathedral Academy. The search yielded nothing about Sister Mary Joseph or any such incidents. She found a few articles on the school's history and recent events, but nothing related to the murder or the nun.

"Interesting," she murmured, leaning back in her chair and tapping her chin thoughtfully.

Samedi's eyes followed her every movement, a spark of curiosity in his gaze. "What's interesting?"

Cassielle glanced at him and recounted what she had read.

Samedi straightened up, his expression turning serious. "If Rebecca is digging into this, she needs to be cautious. She might wind up like Avery, who obviously knew too much."

Cassielle frowned, her fingers pausing mid-tap. "We don't know that for sure," she argued, though she didn't say her gut agreed with him. Avery's death had always felt off to her, like there was something more beneath the surface. Speaking with Jamal had confirmed it.

Cassielle's fingers hovered over the keyboard, her mind a whirlwind of possibilities. Each click of the keys felt like a heartbeat, echoing her own rapid pulse. She typed out a brief message to Rebecca, her words precise and cautious. As she hit send, she could almost feel the weight of the decision settling on her shoulders.

She had chosen a secluded spot, one shrouded in the shadows of the city: Jackson Square Water Fountain, 11 PM. Cassielle added a final note of caution, her fingers trembling slightly: "Be careful not to be followed."

She leaned back in her chair, eyes flicking to the window, the gravity of her choice sinking in. This meeting could unravel the mystery-or entangle them both in a web of danger.

CHAPTER TWENTY

Cassielle sat by her open window, letting the street sounds drift up from below-laughter, distant jazz, the hum of traffic. From her third-story vantage point, St. Louis Cathedral's spire and clock stood like silent sentinels against the twilight sky. She had come home to rest, knowing it would be another late night. Samedi had insisted on a brief training session first, so she had returned sweaty and exhausted. Now, freshly showered, she would have enjoyed a breeze to break the oppressive heat that felt heavier than a sauna. Some people hated the heat. Her hair sure did. But she loved it. Maybe it was her ancestry. Being half devil had to account for something, right?

Samedi had stepped out briefly to "handle a few matters," leaving her on her own for the moment. He assured her he wouldn't be gone long enough for anything to happen. She wrapped her hands around her coffee mug, letting its warmth seep into her fingers, and let her thoughts wander. If she still worked for the precinct, accessing the recent reports and investigating the murders would be straightforward-no need to deal with a persistent reporter.

Thinking of Rebecca, Cassielle reached for her tablet and checked her email. Rebecca had replied, confirming she would meet with Cassielle at the location and time she'd suggested. Cassielle then opened nola.com and began scrolling through the news section, taking occasional sips of her coffee. To her surprise, there was no mention of the murder at LaFitte's. With witnesses and the location in front of one of New Orleans' most renowned bars, she had expected headlines.

"You won't find anything in there." The deep voice from behind startled her. Cassielle jumped, knocking over the small table beside her. She managed to hold onto her tablet but dropped her coffee mug, which shattered on the floor, splattering its contents.

Samedi lounged on her couch, his top hat tilted down, ankles crossed, and a cigarette smoldering in his hand. She hadn't realized he was there. He could be so still and quiet... like the dead.

Cassielle set her tablet on the chair and knelt to clean up the broken shards of her coffee mug. "Please don't startle me like that," she muttered, walking past him toward the kitchen to dispose of the broken pieces and fetch a towel.

"Bien sur, ma cherie. Whatever you need," Samedi replied, his voice laced with amusement. "I noticed you looking at the news, so I wanted to tell you you won't find anything in there. It's a waste of time."

As she cleaned up the spilled coffee, curiosity nagged at her. "Why do you say that?" she asked, rinsing the towel in the sink and picking up her tablet again.

"Because your father has been working to cover up this calamity. We can't afford humans panicking and running amok in the streets."

"And how is he covering it up?"

"Oh, you know... calling in favors, good old-fashioned possession," he said, taking another drag from his cigarette.

"Possession?!" Cassielle exclaimed, setting the table back on its feet and placing the tablet on top. "Seriously? How does that make him any better than the spirits we're supposed to catch?"

"Because he isn't killing people when he's in control. He influences them not to publish certain things or makes them forget what they've seen... things like that." He shrugged, "I'd bet that's why Rebecca's editor wouldn't publish her story."

"You mentioned he called in favors?" Cassielle moved to

sit at the end of her bed, facing him.

"You'd be surprised how many people are willing to sell their souls to the devil for various things," Samedi replied, sitting up and adjusting his top hat.

"I really wouldn't," she muttered.

Samedi laughed. "I do enjoy your cynicism." Chuckling, he stood up. "Before you meet with Rebecca, we're going to visit a friend."

"You have friends?"

Samedi's lip twitched, suppressing a smile.

"Now, some have approached me properly, seeking to connect with the other side. This particular person has been respectful and a devoted servant. Queen Sabine Mahalia."

"I thought you said you weren't supposed to see humans?" She narrowed her eyes. It seemed odd to her; Samedi would visit another Queen despite thinking so highly of her own mother, who had prayed to him, yet he had never visited her.

"Things have changed recently..." Samedi waved his hand dismissively. "Anyway, we'll find her at Voodoo Authentica."

"Seriously? At that tourist trap?" Cassielle raised an eyebrow.

"Just because she makes a living selling to tourists doesn't make her any less devoted," Samedi snapped, his mood shifting suddenly. His gaze hardened, a volatile edge in his eyes. Apparently he was mercurial about some things. Good to know that was true.

"Sorry. I didn't mean any offense. I just thought true practitioners would be more private about Voodoo and not into selling books about it," Cassielle said cautiously, gauging his reaction.

"You have much to learn," he replied, turning and heading toward the door.

Cassielle went to the safe beside her bed, entered the combination, and retrieved her gun and holster. She secured them to her belt and grabbed a light jacket to conceal her weapon. After grabbing her phone and car keys, she followed Samedi out the door and down the street. Her apartment's proximity to St. Louis Cathedral's gardens made it a short walk to the church.

As she stepped outside, the wailing sirens of approaching police cars reached her ears. She watched as they pulled up in front of her building, officers swiftly emerging, some directing traffic while others shouted at people to leave the cathedral gardens.

She recognized one of the uniformed officers directing traffic and jogged over to him.

"Jim, hi!" Cassielle called out. The large man glanced at her before returning his attention to the traffic, his lips set in a grim line.

"Hello Cassielle, long time no see," Jim-James Denaud-replied in his endearing Haitian accent. Like a giant teddy bear, he was fun to go to bars with. Whenever creeps started bothering her, Jim would walk over and stand there with his arms crossed until the creeps ran away. Not that she needed him to. He liked to watch them squirm. "I hope you weren't planning on attending that funeral for the sister. We're evacuating the cathedral."

"Why?" Cassielle looked back toward her building and noticed Samedi watching her. She quickly shifted her gaze back to Jim.

"Somebody's inside with a machine gun, holding everyone hostage. I have no idea why they're doing it or who it is, but it's not looking good. The negotiators are on their way," Jim gestured for a car to turn and stepped aside to allow the police barrier to be set up. "You should probably go home, Cassielle."

"Thank you," Cassielle patted his arm before jogging back to where Samedi stood. She turned to watch the police running around and getting into position. Police cars were parked haphazardly, Jim directing the traffic away from this section of the street. The scene was quickly becoming more chaotic with curious onlookers being kept back by officers and barricades. It was only a matter of time before SWAT and the news arrived. "Looks like we wouldn't be attending the funeral even if we wanted to. We'll also have to go around to get to Voodoo Authentica."

She started walking but noticed Samedi wasn't following. Turning back, she saw him heading across the street towards the Cathedral. She hurried to catch up. "Didn't you hear me? I thought we were going to see your friend."

"He's in there." Samedi's face wore an inscrutable look. "We need to get in."

"We can't, Samed... Sam. There's an armed madman inside..." Cassielle began, her voice filled with concern.

"That's one of them." Samedi turned and started walking toward Pirate Alley. "We're going in."

"We can't!" Cassielle jogged after him. "If we did, what are you going to do? If there's a dark human soul inhabiting the person with the gun, don't you think it would just jump?"

"If it jumps, I'll catch it." Samedi continued walking, picking up the pace to cross the street.

"Well, great. You go right ahead and shadow walk right in there. I'll join the crowd watching the commotion and skip being shot at," Cassielle retorted, keeping up with him until he stopped in the shade of the cathedral.

"We'll go in through the shadows together," Samedi said before Cassielle could respond. He grabbed her hand, and her vision went black. She felt a force pulling her toward the building, surrounded by darkness. A faint scent of sulfur filled her nostrils, and Samedi's hand was chillingly cold. When her vision cleared, she felt as if she had abruptly stopped. Samedi released her hand, and she looked around, realizing they were in clear view at the front left of the church. The man with the gun stood in front of the pulpit, scanning the seated people.

Cassielle swiftly darted behind one of the columns, pressing her back against it and quietly withdrawing her gun.

She cursed mentally, between frustration at Samedi and shock at what had happened. Why had he brought them inside? Glancing over, she saw Samedi wasn't hiding. She opened her mouth to say something but hesitated, not wanting to make a sound.

"Hey!" Samedi called out, grabbing the gunman's attention. The man turned, pointing his gun at Samedi. Cassielle had a sinking feeling he knew how to handle the light machine gun he held.

"What are you doing here?" The man's voice sent a shiver through her. While she couldn't quite place it, it had a strange quality reminiscent of the homeless man's voice from the previous day. It was slow and deliberate, tinged with malice.

"Just enjoying the sights," Samedi replied, twirling his walking cane as he moved closer to the man. Cassielle closed her eyes momentarily. If Samedi was going to be reckless, she needed to make sure none of the people in the church got hurt. The last thing they needed was for the man to open fire. If it happened, the police would have to storm the building, resulting in a potential shootout and more casualties.

"Don't you have a gate to watch, Guardian?" the man sneered.

"Unfortunately, I have no reason to be there with you and your little friends roaming free. But I'd gladly return to my post once you all return to Hell, where you belong. You know the Master won't be pleased about your escapades and what you've been doing," Samedi retorted.

Cassielle could hear quiet sobs coming from the pews. She glanced over and saw the man watching Samedi intently as he circled the back of the pulpit. If Samedi could distract him, she might have a chance to take a shot. Just one shot was all she needed.

"Master? He's not my Master. I belong here. This world is ours. It's time for you to go, Baron Samedi. You and your kind have overstayed your welcome." The man raised his gun, and

Cassielle moved into position to take her shot. Cassielle aimed, held her breath, and squeezed the trigger before the man fired. Her bullet struck him in the left shoulder, causing him to stagger back and drop his gun. He clutched his wounded shoulder, his gaze shifting toward her in surprise.

Cassielle caught the metallic scent of blood in the air and was momentarily stunned by the sudden change in the room. People screamed and rushed toward the front doors, but the dark aura previously emanating from the man was no longer there. She noticed black tendrils moving away from him in the opposite direction.

"Oh, no, you don't!" Samedi called out. He appeared in front of the dissipating vapor, which halted and abruptly changed direction. Samedi removed his hat and stabbed it with his walking stick. The vapor seemed to adhere to the stick's end, and he lifted it, sliding his hand toward the tip. Placing the top hat over the end, he enclosed the vapor within it, then swiftly removed it and placed it back on his head.

Cassielle stood rooted to the spot, her gun still aimed. The man she had shot staggered, his eyes wide with shock, before collapsing to his knees. His face paled, sweat beading on his forehead. Cassielle's heart pounded in her chest, the weight of the moment pressing down on her.

Holstering her gun, she rushed over to him as the sanctuary filled with the sound of police officers pouring in. She knelt beside him, her hands steady despite the adrenaline coursing through her veins. With a swift motion, she pulled off her tee-shirt, revealing the white tank-top underneath, and pressed her grey tee-shirt against his bleeding shoulder.

"Stay with me," she murmured, applying firm pressure to stem the bleeding. The man winced, his breathing ragged, but she kept his focus by talking to him, her eyes locked on the wound as she worked to control the blood flow.

Samedi strolled over, his gaze falling on Cassielle and the injured man. "Nice shot," he remarked casually.

Cassielle didn't look up, her attention fixed on the man.

"Sir, what's your name?" she asked, her voice steady but urgent.

"Steve..." he murmured, his face contorted with pain as he tried to move.

"Stay still, Steve," she instructed, pressing her tee-shirt more firmly against his wound. "You're at St. Louis Cathedral in the French Quarter. How did you get here?"

Steve's eyes darted around, pain and confusion etched across his face. "Why am I here? I was at home..."

Cassielle glanced up at Samedi, searching for answers. His serious gaze met hers. "He was possessed, not sure how we can prove it, though," he murmured.

An officer appeared at her side, his presence solid and reassuring. "What happened here?" he demanded, his eyes darting between Cassielle, Samedi, and Steve.

Cassielle nodded toward the discarded machine gun. "I found this man in the sanctuary with a gun. He had it pointed at the people in the pews." She hesitated, then added, "Based on his behavior, I think he might have been on drugs or having a psychotic break. He seems to have come out of it now."

The officer's brow furrowed. "So you shot him?" he asked, his voice tinged with disbelief.

"Well, yes, but I waited until I had no choice because he was about to shoot. Sam here decided to draw attention to himself, and I took my shot when it was clear the man intended to shoot him," Cassielle clarified, nodding towards Samedi. She looked over her left shoulder towards the pulpit. Turning back to Samedi, she noticed he showed no signs of injury. She'd shot at just the right time.

"Are you injured, sir?" the officer asked Samedi.

"No, I'm just dandy," Samedi replied with a smile, casually leaning against the pulpit.

Meanwhile, EMS personnel flooded the scene, efficiently taking over. Cassielle stood up, leaving her blood-stained shirt behind. The officer, who had been kneeling beside her, now stood before her, his hands resting on his belt.

"Do you have a permit?" he asked, his tone direct.

"Yes, of course." Cassielle reached into her pocket for her wallet. She pulled out her permit card and handed it to the officer, who glanced at it before handing it back.

"We'll need your gun for ballistics," the officer continued, his gaze steady.

"Sure," Cassielle agreed, spotting a familiar face approaching.

"Parker, how's it going?" She greeted the forensic specialist as she safely removed her gun and handed it to him. Parker, wearing gloves, accepted the weapon and placed it into a plastic evidence bag with practiced precision.

"Not bad at all. Seems like you've found yourself in a bit of a pickle, eh?" Parker smiled, glancing briefly at Samedi before focusing back on her.

Cassielle sighed, a hint of sarcasm in her voice. "Yes, trouble always seems to find me."

"Cassielle!" a voice called out, causing her to wince. She recognized that voice all too well.

She turned, pasting on a bright smile. "Oh, hi, Nick! Fancy meeting you here!"

Nick stormed over, his expression a mix of anger and worry. "¡Dios mío! ¿Qué demonios están ustedes aquí?" he demanded, his eyes narrowing as he looked around. He always slipped in to Spanish when he was mad. "Who let her in?"

Cassielle noticed the tightness in his jaw and the furrow in his brow-classic signs of his concern masquerading as frustration.

"No one let her in, Rush. She shot the suspect," the officer explained. "I'll take her to the precinct for questioning."

Nick's expression shifted from anger to confusion. "What are you even doing here? Why were you at this funeral?" His voice hardened.

"If you recall, I live across the street," Cassielle shoved her hands into her pockets, considering her response. Instead of concocting a lie, she chose honesty. "This one," she pointed over her shoulder at Samedi with her thumb, "Even though he knew there was an active shooter situation going on. I went in after him to make sure he didn't get shot."

"¡Ay! You're lucky you weren't killed. Both of you. I mean it," he sighed in frustration. "If I catch you near any more crime scenes or interfering with investigations, I will arrest you," Nick warned, looking directly at her, his eyes filled with worry. He then turned to the officer. "Take Ms. Madison to the precinct, get her statement, and escort her to a holding room. Fontenot and I will speak with her."

Nick looked at Samedi. "And what's your story?"

"Ms. Madison said the shooter turned his gun on Mr..." the officer referenced his notepad, "Samuel Baron."

"Mr. Baron, come with me. I'll take your statement, and then you'll be free to go," Nick directed, gesturing towards the pews. Samedi followed him, bidding Cassielle a cheerful farewell.

Anger swelled within her as she was escorted out. Why did she need to wait at the precinct for Nick and Fontenot to question her? She could give another detective her statement and then be gone. He was wasting her time. She knew he was doing it on purpose. During the ride to the police precinct, annoyance replaced anger. If Cassielle hadn't allowed Samedi to drag her into the church, she wouldn't have had to shoot the man, and she wouldn't be in this predicament. Her annoyance was then replaced with concern. Samedi had said the souls could possess anyone. She was going into a Police Precinct full of people with guns. And she was unarmed. She contemplated vanishing from the back of the car but decided against it. She'd do it if she needed to. But not yet.

The questioning at the station was straightforward, but waiting to speak with Nick and his partner seemed to take an eternity. Cassielle paced back and forth in the interrogation room, growing increasingly impatient. She believed Nick was punishing her for meddling in things she shouldn't have. But she didn't feel deserving of any punishment. She hadn't asked to get involved, and she would have been perfectly content staying out of it, except for helping Brittany... and then there was the whole escaped spirits possessing people thing going on.

After what felt like the sixtieth pass of the table, the door finally opened, and Nick entered with Fontenot.

"Please siéntate. Sit," Nick motioned towards the chair. She sat across from the two detectives, observing their calm demeanor. Sitting on this side of the table felt strange. She should have been nervous, but she wasn't. She hadn't done anything wrong-she had prevented a potential massacre. They should be thanking her. But she knew they wouldn't.

"Start from the beginning, Cassielle. Why were you at Sister Mary Joseph's funeral?" Fontenot inquired, his soothing voice putting her at ease. "Did you know her?"

"No." She proceeded to recount everything except for the entering via the shadows, Samuel Baron's true identity, and the fact she's the daughter of the devil. That all seemed a bit much to tell them.

Nick seized upon the fact Cassielle hadn't provided much information about Samedi.

"Samuel Baron. How do you know him?" Nick's voice was cold and distant as if he were treating Cassielle like a criminal. She narrowed her eyes at him. Was he jealous?

"He came to my office two days ago wanting my help," Cassielle explained.

"Help with what? Finding a lost cat?" Nick's voice dripped with sarcasm, eliciting her glare.

"No. He wanted my help in solving the mysterious, violent crimes that have been happening. He believes..." Cassielle hesitated, unsure how to continue.

"He believes what?" Fontenot asked gently.

"He believes someone attempted to open the Gates of Guinee but failed, resulting in evil spirits escaping and running rampant in our city and spreading into the rest of the world," Cassielle prepared herself for Nick's skeptical response.

"The Gates of Guinee?" Fontenot looked confused.

"It's related to Voodoo," Nick interjected, dismissing the concept. "Eso es ridículo. Why haven't you taken him to get help? He needs it. ¡Qué estúpido!"

He was angry. She couldn't quite figure out why. Was he worried about her? He never spoke this much Spanish at work, unless he was speaking with a Spanish speaking suspect or victim. Fontenot was also looking at Nick with concern. He'd worked with him long enough to notice this as unusual behavior.

They were interrupted by a buzzing sound. Nick reached into his pocket and withdrew his phone. After reading the screen, he grabbed Fontenot by the arm and leaned in to whisper before looking back to Cassielle, "Excuse us for a moment."

Nick and Fontenot exited into the hallway, the door shutting behind them. Through the small window, Cassielle could see their heated argument, their gestures animated but their words inaudible.

"Ready to go?"

Cassielle nearly fell out of her chair at the sound of Samedi's voice. He was leaning against the wall behind her, a mischievous glint in his eyes.

Before she could respond, he said, "What better way to show them something unnatural is afoot than to vanish from a room with one way in and one way out?"

Cassielle considered his suggestion, glancing from Samedi to the small window in the door and back. After several moments, she nodded. She pulled out her notebook and ripped out the page with the image Jamal had drawn last night and set it on the table before standing and pushing her chair in. She joined Samedi, and together they stepped into the shadows. The room's dim corners swallowed them whole, leaving no trace behind.

When Fontenot and Nick would return, they'd find the room empty, the air thick with an unsettling quiet, and a piece of paper with the Sigil of Buer on it.

CHAPTER TWENTY-ONE

Cassielle made her way to Jackson Square, the weight of recent events pressing heavily on her mind. The night sky above was a canvas of deep indigo, dotted with a handful of stars peeking through the city's light pollution. A crescent moon hung low, casting a silvery glow over the iconic square. The air was thick with humidity, the remnants of the day's oppressive heat lingering even as a faint breeze tried to stir.

The centerpiece of Jackson Square, the water fountain, stood serenely amidst the manicured greenery. Under the moonlight, the water sparkled and danced, creating a mesmerizing display of ripples and reflections. The sound of the fountain's gentle splashing provided a soothing backdrop, contrasting sharply with the tension clinging to the square.

In stark contrast to the tranquil fountain, the cathedral behind it was cordoned off with bright yellow crime scene tape, fluttering slightly in the breeze. The usually welcoming steps of St. Louis Cathedral were now a solemn reminder of the earlier chaos. Police barricades and the occasional glint of an officer's badge were visible in the dim light, ensuring no one crossed into the restricted area.

Cassielle spotted Rebecca near the fountain, her silhouette barely discernible against the darkened landscape. The clock on the nearby spire chimed eleven times, each toll resonating through the night and amplifying the eerie quiet that had settled over the square. Cassielle quickened her pace, her footsteps barely audible on the paved path.

Rebecca stood with her arms wrapped around herself, glancing nervously at the cathedral and then back at the fountain. The shadows cast by the nearby lampposts added an air of mystery, their golden halos unable to fully pierce the darkness.

As Cassielle approached, the water's murmurs grew louder, and she could see the weariness etched into Rebecca's face. In the dim light, Rebecca's silhouette was defined by the contours of her tight red pencil skirt and cap-sleeved white blouse. Her blonde hair, artfully pinned up with a pencil, caught the faint glimmer of the nearby lampposts. As she stood near the fountain's edge, her exact features remained shrouded in darkness, leaving only the outline of her figure and a faint look of the colors of her hair and clothing visible in the night.

Across from her, Samedi made his way to the fountain's edge and settled on the edge. His presence loomed in the shadows, his form blending seamlessly with the darkness around him. Cassielle could feel his gaze fixed on Rebecca, but his face remained obscured, leaving his expression a mystery in the depths of the night.

"Rebecca Tyler?" Cassielle inquired.

Samedi hissed but stopped when Cassielle shot him a quick glare before returning her attention to Rebecca.

"Yes, you must be Cassielle. It's nice to meet you!" Rebecca stepped forward, extending her hand. Cassielle shook it briefly before they started to walk, moving away from the officers and deeper into the darkened grounds. Samedi followed, his dark glare fixed on Rebecca. Cassielle sighed, dismissing his mood.

"You mentioned having some information about the strange crimes," Cassielle said, folding her hands on the bar.

Rebecca reached into her bag and retrieved a green folder, offering it to Cassielle. "All my notes and information are in there. I can't understand why my editor won't publish any of it. I've even tried submitting my articles to other outlets, but no one seems interested. It's baffling."

Cassielle moved to stand beneath a lamp and opened the folder skimming through the pages. It contained copies of police reports documenting various crimes occurring at night since St. John's Eve which she had noted on a piece of paper.

"How did you get these?" Cassielle stared at Rebecca in surprise. She smiled shyly and shook her head. She wasn't going to say.

"It's difficult to see how these crimes are connected, but there must be something," Rebecca commented. Samedi remained silent, glaring at Rebecca, who seemed unfazed.

"Well," Cassielle began, trying to gather her thoughts, and figure out how much to share. She glanced at Samedi who subtly shook his head. He'd been very clear he didn't want Rebecca involved in this. However, Cassielle knew how investigative reporters were. Brittany had previously worked as an investigative reporter, but was now an editor for the Jambalaya News - a Spanish only paper.

Rebecca leaned forward, her brow furrowing as she studied the papers Cassielle held. "It's hard to wrap my head around the idea that all these individuals are somehow connected to a cult or gang. I'd have to delve deeper into their backgrounds to be sure. At first glance, there doesn't seem to be a clear pattern, except for the fact these incidents all occur at night, the perpetrators have no recollection of their actions, and many of them display unusually heightened strength and behavior that's out of character," she mused, her voice tinged with skepticism. Then, with a thoughtful pause, she added, "I did notice mentions of soot at the crime scenes, but it was just a passing remark. I'm not even sure if the police paid much attention to that detail."

Cassielle closed the folder containing the papers and locked eyes with Rebecca. "How familiar are you with Voodoo?"

As Cassielle felt Samedi's presence behind her, his breath tickled her ear. "I hope you're not considering what it seems like you're considering," he murmured.

She turned slightly toward him, their faces inches apart. "She needs to understand, so she doesn't continue to dig," she whispered back.

"What do I need to understand?" Rebecca's voice cut through their hushed exchange, her curiosity evident in her gaze.

Samedi's eyes remained fixed on Rebecca as he spoke to Cassielle, his tone carrying a hint of warning. "She's dabbling in matters beyond her understanding."

Cassielle sighed and redirected her attention to Rebecca. "Please excuse his temperament."

Her mother's words echoed in her mind-Samedi was known for his unpredictable moods. If he sought her aid, he would have to tolerate her efforts to seek assistance and information without stirring up trouble.

"Okay..." Rebecca eyed Samedi once more before returning her attention to Cassielle. "What does this all have to do with Voodoo?"

Cassielle brushed off Samedi's discontented murmurs and proceeded to recount the events of the past few days, carefully skimming over her upbringing and training without delving into the more fantastical aspects. She knew mentioning her lineage as the daughter of the devil would only lead to disbelief and skepticism, so she kept it to herself.

Rebecca's expression shifted from curiosity to incredulity as Cassielle laid out the extraordinary sequence of events. The skepticism in Rebecca's eyes cut deep, almost like a physical blow. Cassielle couldn't blame her; if roles were reversed, she'd probably react the same way to such outlandish claims.

"You really expect me to believe all of that?" Rebecca's disappointment was palpable, and Cassielle felt a pang of regret for even broaching the subject. "I tried getting information from Nick; he's quite tight-lipped about his work, but at least he didn't start spinning ridiculous tales."

The mention of Nick caught Cassielle off guard. Her narrowed eyes betrayed her confusion.

"Detective Nicholas Rush? You worked with him before, right?" Rebecca watched her.

"Yes... but I'm pretty sure he's never permitted a reporter to be so casual with his name. He's not the type to befriend them," Cassielle replied.

"Well, we've been dating for some time now, so I don't think I need to be formal about him." Her words hit Cassielle harder than expected. Was Nick dating a reporter? How did that happen? And why? He preferred dating a reporter over trying to mend things with her? Though, to be fair, she hadn't even given him a fair chance at that.

Cassielle mentally shook herself, reminding herself she had ended the relationship. Even if it was an intrusive reporter, Nick was free to date whoever he pleased. He had always been private about his love life, making it difficult for her to fathom how he managed to date someone whose job involved prying into others' lives. Had he given her this information? That was even more difficult to believe.

"Oh," Cassielle responded, her words lacking enthusiasm.

Rebecca looked past Cassielle. "Listen, I should be going. Please see if you can find anything about those cases that don't have to do with the supernatural. Maybe we can have a chance at figuring out why our city is actually descending into chaos. Maybe there's some drug in the water, or something." She glanced at Samedi, then back to Cassielle. "Thank you again for meeting me, and I look forward to working with you." She extended her hand to Cassielle, who hesitated momentarily before finally shaking it.

"Yeah... sure thing. I'll email you if I come across anything." Rebecca withdrew her hand, adjusted her bag, and seemed to want to say more but decided against it, heading towards the exit.

"Ms. Tyler," Samedi interjected. Rebecca stopped and

turned to face him. "You would be wise to distance yourself from this. It's not safe."

"If that's the case, maybe your girlfriend shouldn't be involved either," Rebecca retorted. "But from what I've heard, good luck trying to tell her not to." She turned away and left.

"I'm not his girlfriend!" Cassielle's voice echoed after Rebecca, but the words fell on deaf ears as she disappeared into the night. Frustration boiled inside Cassielle as she closed her eyes and massaged her temples. This week seemed determined to heap more troubles upon her already overburdened shoulders. Would Rebecca become another casualty in the chaos enveloping New Orleans? Cassielle couldn't shake the sinking feeling gnawing in her gut.

Pulling out her phone, Cassielle hastily composed a text to Nick. She hesitated before hitting send. She wouldn't bring up her 'supernatural tales' again. Instead, she focused on the immediate concern: Rebecca's safety. With a few taps, she sent a message expressing her worry about Rebecca's well-being, omitting any mention of the otherworldly dangers lurking in the shadows and instead focusing on 'if there is some connection, she shouldn't get involved.'

"Okay..." Cassielle glanced over to find Samedi still standing beside her. "Now what?" Her head was spinning. The thought of Rebecca possibly going home to Nick caused her to feel some sort of way.

"Now it's time to refresh your memory of Voodoo," his voice was gentle. "Embracing your lineage fully will enable you to protect yourself from others who might seek to harm you. It wouldn't surprise me if the dark souls and evil spirits who have escaped are gathering followers. There are even Satanists who could easily be deceived into believing a dark soul is Satan himself. Of course, this would greatly anger him. Still, humans aren't always discerning when it comes to recognizing true deities," Samedi's tone was now more cheerful than it had been when addressing Rebecca.

Cassielle rolled her eyes. "Alright then, let's go see your

friend, and then you can show me where the gates are so I can investigate who was there on St. John's Eve."

"I'm glad you're embracing this, Cassielle," Samedi said, sounding genuinely pleased. "Your father, I'm sure, is equally proud."

"Well, good to hear I'm making at least one parent proud," Cassielle muttered, allowing Samedi to lead the way to his liaison.

"Your mother is proud, Cassielle," Samedi's voice softened. "When she passed through the gates upon her death, she passed straight through and now resides in the underworld. Your father visits her from time to time. She intended for you to be the next Voodoo Queen. She had begun the process." He watched her as they walked back towards the gates leading to the street. "You still can fulfill your role."

"I don't know about that. Let's focus on what we must do to deal with these dark souls, okay?" Cassielle replied, unsure of the weight of such a responsibility. They returned to Cassielle's apartment so she could get a few hours of sleep before going to see Samedi's friend.

CHAPTER TWENTY-TWO

Voodoo Authentica was about five blocks away from her apartment, so the next morning, Cassielle and Samedi decided to walk. The oppressive heat of the sun weighed down on them, even at this early hour, and upon arrival at Voodoo Authentica, Cassielle found herself drenched in sweat and feeling irritable. On the other hand, Samedi seemed unfazed, as if the heat didn't bother him at all.

Noticing Cassielle's glare, he smiled warmly. "I'm from a much hotter place than this. It's nice and balmy here," he remarked. He gestured toward the tan building with pink doors. "Here we are."

A brown sign hung overhead, displaying "Voodoo Authentica" in orange and red lettering. Beneath it, in red lettering, it read "Cultural Center and Collection." Like many buildings in New Orleans, there was a second-floor balcony adorned with chairs and potted plants. Hanging flower pots decorated the edge of the railing, and several people mingled outside. A woman secured her bicycle to a short pole in front of the building.

Samedi's excitement was palpable as they reached the store. Cassielle, however, felt far from enthusiastic. She was hot and tired, and all she wanted was to go home, grab an ice-cold drink, and delve into the notes Rebecca had given her. The prospect of Voodoo lessons or whatever awaited her at Voodoo Authentica did not ignite her excitement. Samedi was correct.

She needed to learn to embrace who she was to succeed, which also meant confronting her past. She'd started to learn to control her dark powers, but through that she was still able to push her past from her memory. She knew she needed to face those painful memories, but she wasn't sure she was ready for that yet.

The bell above the door jingled as Samedi and Cassielle entered the brightly lit shop. Harsh fluorescent track lighting illuminated the space, showcasing a variety of neon signs on the walls. Some signs displayed the shop's name and available items like potions and dolls. In contrast, others advertised services such as tours and rituals. A young Hispanic woman sat behind the counter near the entrance, engrossed in a paperback novel without looking up.

Samedi approached the counter and leaned jauntily against it, one hand resting lazily on his walking stick. "Bonjour, ma cherie. Is Sabine around?" he inquired.

The woman barely glanced up from her book and gestured toward the back of the store. She then resumed reading, disregarding them. Cassielle glanced at the book's title, "Taken by the Viking." She noticed the half naked man leaning over a dark haired woman on the bed and struggled to stifle laughter. The woman caught her eye, and they exchanged a sly smile before Cassielle followed Samedi toward the back of the shop.

Navigating the aisles as directed, they eventually arrived at a door in the back left corner. Without hesitation, Samedi opened it and stepped through, with Cassielle following suit. They found themselves at the base of a staircase, and Samedi wasted no time ascending the steps.

"Shouldn't we check if they're expecting us? Maybe she meant for us to wait here," Cassielle hesitated, remaining at the bottom of the stairs. Samedi paused and looked down at her.

"Since when did you become so cautious?" he teased.

"When you told me I had to meet a Voodoo Queen..."

Cassielle muttered, reluctantly making her way up the stairs. Samedi chuckled at her remark and continued to the top. Two potted plants flanked the door at the landing, which resembled her third-floor apartment's landing, and a summer wreath adorned it. Across from the door was another entrance, painted deep purple with intricate designs carved into its facade. Samedi knocked sharply on the door and stepped back, resting both hands on his walking stick.

"Don't worry, Cassielle. I'm confident you'll pick it up quickly," Samedi assured her.

"That's what I'm worried about," Cassielle mumbled. The door swung open then, revealing a stunning woman on the other side. Her hair was wrapped in a red cloth, and she wore a floor-length white sundress that contrasted with her dark skin. A red shawl draped over her shoulders. Her eyes briefly scanned Cassielle, giving her little attention before settling on Samedi. Surprise registered on her face as she recognized him.

"Baron Samedi! This is quite unexpected. Come inside," she exclaimed, stepping back allowing them entry. Samedi hung his top hat and cane on a hook by the door and proceeded further into the apartment. Sabine's place was quaint, with antique furniture, wingback chairs, and old-fashioned settees. Deep mahogany and marble end tables matched the coffee table in the center of the living room. Dimly lit by scattered lamps, the room had a cozy ambiance. A small sleeping area occupied the far wall to the right, while a cooking and dining area sat on the left. Storm windows kept the space darker, shielding it from the bright sunshine outside. The air conditioner worked tirelessly to combat the New Orleans summer heat.

"Please, have a seat. Can I offer you anything? Sweet tea, perhaps?" Sabine offered as she closed the door behind them. She guided them to the sitting area.

"No, thank you," Samedi declined, and Cassielle followed suit.

"So, Baron Samedi, what can I do for you?" Sabine sat on one of the wingback chairs across from them; her gaze focused on Samedi.

"I'm sure you've noticed the imbalance that has occurred since St. John's Eve," Samedi began, leaning back and crossing one leg over the other.

"Yes, of course. I've performed protection spells for myself and my followers to ward off the growing darkness," Sabine replied, leaning forward with her hands resting on her thighs. "What is the cause of it? Your presence here concerns me. Who is guarding the gates?"

"The gates were opened," Samedi revealed, his expression grim.

Sabine paled, clutching her skirt tightly. "No," she whispered. "Was it a failed ritual? Or something more nefarious?"

"It appears someone did fail a ritual. However, whether it was on purpose or not, we don't know," Samedi confirmed with a severe tone.

"Well, how can I assist?" Sabine asked, her concern evident.

"Cassielle here would benefit from your guidance and assistance in performing the spells, incantations, or prayers necessary to protect herself and track down and recapture the malevolent sprits," Samedi explained, leaning forward. "I need not emphasize the urgency of dealing with this matter promptly."

Sabine fell silent, her hands still gripping her skirt tightly. She shifted her gaze between Samedi and Cassielle, contemplating their request. Finally, she spoke slowly and deliberately, "Yes... Yes, I understand. However, I'm concerned about how quickly I can educate this young woman if she hasn't practiced Voodoo in years. Will she be able to contribute effectively?"

"Of course, you would think that," Samedi responded, leaning back again with a sly smile. "You don't know who she is."

"No... should I?" Sabine asked, her curiosity piqued.

"She is the great-great-great-granddaughter of the Voodoo Queen Marie Laveau. Voodoo runs in her blood," Samedi revealed.

Sabine blinked, then focused her intense gaze on Cassielle as if studying a specimen in a lab. She narrowed her eyes, leaning forward until her eyes widened, and she sat back. "Mon Dieu..." she exclaimed, shaking her head. "I knew your mother well."

"Oh?" Cassielle glanced at the clock on the wall, wondering how long it would take to escape this meeting.

"Yes, she taught me everything she knew about Voodoo. She intended for you to become the Queen of New Orleans, not me," Sabine said, leaning back and narrowing her eyes as she studied Cassielle. "I will help you, Baron Samedi, but only to clear out the dark spirits. I will not train her to replace me. I have worked hard to reach where I am, and my followers love and trust me."

Samedi's face suddenly changed, his amusement replaced by a dark, murderous look. Cassielle saw his skull-like face, but it was only fleeting. Sabine paled and sat back, her face drained of color.

"It is not for you to decide who is or is not the Queen of New Orleans. It is her birthright, not yours. You acted as a placeholder until she was ready to take her rightful place. You will do as your lord commands," Samedi's voice rumbled deeply, shaking the furniture. Cassielle could feel the darkness emanating from him. His temper was volatile. Sabine bit her lower lip and lowered her eyes in deference.

"My apologies, Baron Samedi. I had no right to speak that way and believing I could hold onto my position when it is not mine to keep," Sabine said, folding her hands in her lap and bowing her head. "I beg your forgiveness and pray our Lord God forgives me for my arrogance and selfishness."

Samedi's demeanor shifted again, and the heat that

had crept into the room dissipated. Cassielle found all of this pointless. She had no desire to return to practicing Voodoo. She had no positive memories of it. Her mother had been devoted, and Cassielle remembered attending all her ceremonies. She remembered the feeling of power and the connection to the spirit. It should have been comforting like it was for others, but it made her nervous and disconcerted. It was the first time she had felt that way. This feeling, although not as intense, was similar to what she experienced at murders and particularly dark crime scenes. If she had known there was something even more terrifying and thrilling, perhaps the ceremonies wouldn't have scared her as much. Truly understanding herself may have helped, too.

"You really shouldn't worry about losing your place," Cassielle said, knowing Samedi wouldn't appreciate what she had to say, but it was her life and her choice. "I have no desire to be the Queen of New Orleans. I will do all that I can to help restore the balance of life and death, but hear this, Baron Samedi: I will not be bullied into devoting my life to a religion I feel no love for. Voodoo has a place in the world, but that doesn't mean I have to have a place in Voodoo."

Samedi's face started to darken again, and Cassielle held up her hand.

"I know what you'll say, so save your breath. This isn't important to argue about right now. I'm sure there is something we should be doing. Shouldn't we be planning how to round up and get rid of the dark souls?" She stared Samedi down, refusing to look away. His face remained dark, and he looked like he would love nothing more than to slap her for her impudence. "The training you provided me should be enough, no? Why do I need to re-learn all of the old Voodoo practices?"

"You are correct," he said slowly. "We should focus on what we need to do next. But know this, Cassielle Madison-Heylel: You have a greater purpose in this world. Your parents have high hopes for you, and I will not be blamed for not doing everything within my power to help you fulfill your purpose."

Sabine watched the exchange, her eyes widening again when Samedi said "Heylel." Samedi glanced at her.

"That is her second last name. Cassielle's mother refused to include it on her birth certificate, much to her father's displeasure." He looked back to Cassielle, "You have your mother's stubbornness and strength. Though infuriating, you will need both qualities to survive what will come next."

"Heylel is another name for..." Sabine began, her face turning ashen.

"Satan, yes," Samedi confirmed.

Sabine crossed herself and whispered a prayer. "And you would have her be the Queen of New Orleans?"

"Yes. Remember, Heylel is the keeper of the underworld. He brings death and keeps the evil spirits on the other side as long as we keep the gates. He decides where you go when you die. He is typically jovial, but we, Loa, who guard the gates of Guinee, have failed him, and it is up to all of us to make it right." Samedi appeared bored with the conversation, his anger dissipating as he studied the nails on his right hand.

"But... how... why would Heylel create a child with a human?" Sabine wondered aloud, her gaze still fixed on Cassielle. Cassielle was growing tired of being scrutinized like some specimen.

"That is not for you to know," Samedi snapped, clenching his fist and glaring at Sabine again.

"But I think I have a right to know," Cassielle said. "You said he wanted help on Earth... how am I supposed to help? Did he know this would happen? Or is there something else he had in mind?"

"That is not important now," Samedi declared, standing up. "Begin your lessons. I have somewhere to be." And with that, he vanished. Cassielle looked over to where he had hung his top hat and cane, but they were also gone. A part of her felt the void he'd left behind.

"Shit... he has a worse temper than I do," Cassielle

muttered.

"They all do," Sabine said quietly. "All the Loas have very short tempers. This is why we must show them respect. They have the power to retaliate in ways you can't imagine." She sighed and stood. "Well, we don't have much time to work. Come with me."

CHAPTER TWENTY-THREE

Sabine led the way back to the door, and they crossed the landing to the room on the other side. Cassielle had noticed the door when they first ascended the stairs. Still, now she noticed what she had initially thought were designs were symbols related to Voodoo. Veves, she recalled. A chill ran down her spine, and she hesitated at the door. The closer they got to her practicing Voodoo, the more apprehensive she felt. She wasn't exactly sure why she was so uncomfortable with it. Perhaps it was because it had been so long since she had participated, or maybe it was because she was well acquainted with its power. Or, more likely, it brought a deep sorrow back to her. A void her mother once filled. She'd broken her mother's heart by abandoning Voodoo as a rebellious pre-teen. To come back after her mother's death felt almost sacrilegious.

Sabine entered the room, and Cassielle slowly followed. Sabine turned on the overhead light and moved to the center of the room. The light barely illuminated the area. It was an open space with minimal furniture. A table displayed various items-pictures of Catholic saints, ceremonial rattles, drums, bells, flags, sacred stones, knives, and more. Cassielle recognized some of them from her past experiences with Voodoo. There were candles, plates for offerings, money, amulets, and ritual necklaces.

In front of her table, on the floor, stood an Altar. The altar was structured in three tiers, each level meticulously arranged to showcase its array of sacred artifacts. At the heart of the altar stood a square stone post, an imposing centerpiece that Cassielle recognized from her childhood. It was used for sacrifices, a conduit her mother had said "reached to the center of the sky" to allow the Loas to descend. The post was adorned with a spiral design, depicting the two snake Loas, their entwined forms wrapping around the stone in a serpentine embrace.

"As you can see, this is where I practice," she said, gesturing towards the cluttered table. "We must perform spells to protect ourselves from the dark souls. The inhuman malevolent spirits are too powerful for these to work. Perhaps we can help send some of the human ones back to where they belong. We will prepare ourselves by casting a protection spell to prevent the dark souls from entering either of us while we work," Sabine paused, "Should he return, Samedi, of course, would be safe. He's too powerful for us to affect or influence."

Sabine began arranging candles in a circular pattern and gathering the necessary items-stones, amulets adorned with saint images, ceremonial rattles, a feather, a knife, and a small bowl filled with what appeared to be dirt. As she collected these objects, she explained, "We must protect both parts of our soul-the ti-bon-ange and the gros-bon-ange." She moved across the room to a small chest of drawers Cassielle had overlooked during her initial survey. Cassielle thought for a moment to translate. The little good angel and the great good angel.

"We will call upon the Loa, the natural forces, our ancestors, and spirits to help us foresee what lies ahead, identify the paths of the evil spirits, and safeguard us from possession and harm."

Cautious and curious, Cassielle watched as Sabine positioned the dirt bowl on one side of the circle, followed by the feather on the other, the rum at the top, and the knife at the bottom. "If you call upon spirits, how can you ensure only benevolent ones respond?" she inquired.

Sabine remained silent as she lit each candle. Once they were all aflame, she turned off the overhead light. "Step inside the circle, Cassielle," she beckoned.

She cautiously did as she was told and entered the circle formed by the flickering candles. As she passed the flames, they surged upward as if stirred by an unseen wind. Sabine gestured for Cassielle to sit at the center of the circle. At the same time, she picked up one of the ceremonial rattles and began circling.

"I call upon the spirits of my elders to come to our aid," Sabine chanted, her words rapid and urgent. "I summon the spirits of those who have walked this Earth before me and those who are yet to come. We beseech your protection and blessings in our time of need. I invoke the Voodoo Queens and Kings who have come before..."

"Cassielle..."

Startled, Cassielle turned, but no one was there. The room beyond the candles remained dark and motionless, the flickering light of the candles could not penetrate it. She glanced back at Sabine, who appeared unaware of the voice, and was continuing her rapid incantation.

"Papa Legba, we implore your protection against the malevolent spirits that roam freely through our world. Come to our aid!"

"Be cautious, Cassielle," the voice echoed again, more precise this time. "Things are not always as they seem."

Cassielle spun around once more, not expecting to see anyone, yet a woman stood outside the circle of candles. The woman wore a large head wrap and a wrap around her shoulders, the faint colors of tan and a red fabric with an indistinguishable pattern catching Cassielle's attention.

As Cassielle looked back at Sabine, she realized Sabine was still engrossed in her ritual, oblivious to the woman's presence or the voice Cassielle was hearing. Turning her focus back to the woman, Cassielle opened her mouth to speak, but the woman gently placed a finger over her lips.

"Hush, cherie. It's best not to inform her that I am here," she whispered.

Cassielle peered past the woman, scanning the area to see if Samedi had returned. Indeed, if this woman were a spirit, he would be aware of her presence. Yet, Cassielle could discern nothing beyond the candlelit circle except for this mysterious figure. Only her shoulders, neck, and head were visible, while the rest of her gradually faded away into the darkness.

"I am Marie Laveau, your great-great-great grandmother," she revealed, her face instantly recognizable to Cassielle. Resembling Cassielle's mother and grandmother, the connection was undeniable, causing the hair on her arms to stand on end.

"They know where you are, Cherie. They sense the power within you, and they are furious-so furious," Marie warned.

Cassielle wanted to inquire further, but she heeded Marie's earlier advice and kept silent, focusing on her ancestor as the woman continued speaking.

"They despise your father for creating Vilokan. He created two realms-one for the spirits of light and another for those of darkness, those who will never be redeemed and able to pass through the labyrinth to sanctuary. The dark spirits suffer torment, while the light spirits enjoy a peaceful existence in Vilokan. You are his vulnerability, Cassielle. I I don't know why he lay with your mother, but I fear there is a purpose, and you will soon discover it."

Marie Laveau's image began to fade, and Cassielle yearned to hold onto her presence, to prolong their conversation. However, spirits were not meant to linger on Earth. Marie Laveau would need to return to where she came from. As did the evil spirits who were breaking the rules by remaining.

"The figure you followed in the rain was not Samedi," she spoke quickly now. "You must be careful. I will do my best. You will be safe, Cassielle. As safe as I can make you," her ancestor reassured before disappearing. The sound in the room seemed to return all at once. Sabine's voice became audible again, and the area beyond the candles brightened.

"We thank you, spirits, for blessing and protecting us on our quest. Thank you for infusing these amulets with your power. Go in peace," Sabine concluded her words, and the candles appeared to dim slightly. Cassielle stared at Sabine as she held out one of the amulets to her. She couldn't quite piece her thoughts together after her encounter.

"Cassielle?" Sabine furrowed her brows as she watched her.

"Sorry," Cassielle accepted the amulet and then a chain. She carefully threaded the chain through the hole in the top of the amulet and slipped it over her head, expecting the cool touch of metal. To her surprise, warmth spread through her body. She lifted the amulet to examine it-an intricate white design etched on a black surface, resembling a heart with symbols and lines.

"Now," Sabine began, "I will try to scry and look for their next destination. Maybe you can be there to catch the spirits before they act."

"I don't think that's a good idea," Cassielle said, recalling her conversation with Marie LaVeau.

"Why do you say that?" Sabine asked, folding her arms across her chest. She, too, wore an amulet-deep red with gold lining and symbols matching Cassielle's. Cassielle looked away from the amulet and met Sabine's gaze.

"I have a feeling," Cassielle replied, refraining from mentioning Marie LaVeau. Uncertain if she had indeed seen her or merely hallucinated, she hesitated.

"To be certain, let us proceed," Sabine insisted, arranging the necessary items for the ritual. Cassielle had a pit in her stomach again.

Sabine closed her eyes, clutching her ceremonial rattle, and began to shake it, speaking as she paused its motion. "We summon the spirits, seeking your guidance and wisdom." The rattle shook once more. "We call upon the spirits of the earth, our ancestors..." She continued invoking any spirits who would provide the guidance they sought.

Cassielle's stomach clenched, and the surroundings grew darker beyond the candlelight. But this darkness felt deeper, heavier, and more oppressive. The circle they had formed no longer brought comfort. Cassielle felt the urge to leave, about to voice her concerns, when another voice interrupted her. This voice lacked warmth and comfort, sounding grave and unsettling.

"We've found you, Cassielle Madison - Heylel..."

Cassielle's breath turned frigid, forming visible clouds with each exhale. Goosebumps pricked her arms.

"Who's there?" Cassielle demanded, rising to her feet. Simultaneously, Samedi appeared by her side.

"Do not stop," he commanded Sabine, who resumed her ritual. Cassielle hadn't realized she had paused in alarm.

"Tell us who you are!" Cassielle scanned her surroundings, sensing someone watching them.

"Hush," Samedi whispered, causing Cassielle to practically leap out of her skin. She looked to see him behind her, leaning closer. "I see him. Be silent."

"Baron Samedi, you may see us but cannot stop us. I have triumphed. We are free, forever released from the darkness," the voice taunted, accompanied by a gleeful cackle.

"Are you Buer?" Cassielle persisted, disregarding the spirit's provocations.

"Inquisitive, aren't you? You shall soon discover our identity. It's a pity your father was so careless in his affair with the human woman you call your mother. He should never have created you," the voice laughed. "We almost had you, and you didn't even know it. Your beloved Loa couldn't have saved you."

"You have no power here," Cassielle refused to yield. "You answered our summons, and now you must answer our questions."

"Such demands," the voice chuckled. "Neither I nor my

brethren will comply. We are coming, and no amulets shall protect you. We will get you the next time we come."

Before Cassielle could respond, the voice interrupted her again. "Do not act superior, Daughter of Heylel. You revel in the carnage I caused-the blood, death, and terror. Your soul yearns for more. You are as dark as Heylel. He imprisoned us to safeguard others, but we are his favorites. He adores the darkness, only keeping us confined out of fear of his brother. You offer him true chaos."

Cassielle winced, waves of emotions overwhelming her. The scent of blood filled her nostrils, and the heat of chaos enveloped her soul. Her cheeks flushed with desire. He wasn't entirely wrong. A part of her cherished this darkness, and it terrified her.

"Ah, yes. Heylel's daughter revels in death and torment, just like him."

Shaking her head, Cassielle resisted. She bit her tongue, dispelling the fog threatening to consume her mind and plunge her into desire. She fought against her longing, regaining her senses. Once she felt in control again, she spoke.

"You're mistaken. I will eliminate you and your kind. I'll send you back where you belong, and you'll regret ever escaping."

A deep, mocking laugh greeted her words. "You're a feisty denier, my love. Have you ever wondered why the devil would descend to Earth and indulge with a human? Why choose the descendant of Voodoo Queens as the vessel for his child?"

Cassielle grew tired of this topic repeatedly resurfacing. Although she should have wondered and cared, she was weary of the game. She wanted nothing more than to rid herself of the dark souls, Baron Samedi, Sabine, and everyone involved.

"Marbas," Samedi whispered. Cassielle recognized the name and knew he'd said it because he needed her to catch him. She recalled their training on how to capture the more powerful malevolent spirits.

Cassielle's heart raced as she faced Marbas. With a deep breath, she tapped into the wellspring of power within her, her connection to the spirits and the ancient magic coursing through her veins. Her eyes glowed with an otherworldly light as she extended her hands, fingers trembling with the weight of the magic she was about to unleash.

The air crackled with energy as Cassielle focused her will, feeling the raw power of the spirits responding to her call. With a swift motion, she reached out with invisible tendrils of energy, grasping hold of Marbas's essence. At first, he appeared as a man, his form twisted and contorted with malevolence. But as Cassielle tightened her grip, Marbas's shape shifted, morphing into a great lion, its eyes burning with fury and malice.

With a primal roar, Marbas lashed out, attempting to break free from Cassielle's grasp. But she held firm, channeling all her strength and willpower into her magic. She could feel the strain of the effort, the weight of Marbas's dark presence threatening to overwhelm her. But she refused to yield, her determination steeling her resolve.

With a final surge of power, Cassielle unleashed her magic, Samedi had opened a portal akin to the one he'd used against Tom Horn and she cast Marbas back into the depths of hell where he belonged. The air shimmered with the remnants of her spell, the echoes of her power reverberating through the night. As the last traces of Marbas's essence faded away, Cassielle felt a sense of relief wash over her.

A look crossed Sabine's face that she couldn't quite read. It was a mixture of fear and confusion, a shadow of something darker lurking beneath the surface. Cassielle attributed it to the residual effects of the confrontation with Marbas, the lingering tendrils of his malevolent presence still clinging to the room like a sinister fog.

"Are you alright, Queen Sabine?" Cassielle asked, her voice laced with concern as she approached the older woman.

"It's over now. Marbas has been banished back to the depths of hell where he belongs."

Sabine's eyes darted nervously around the room, her hands trembling ever so slightly. "Yes, yes, of course," she replied, her voice strained. "I... I just need a moment to collect myself."

Cassielle exchanged a glance with Samedi, a flicker of unease passing between them. Something wasn't right. Despite Marbas's banishment, the air still hummed with an undercurrent of darkness, a lingering malevolence clinging to the space like a parasite.

CHAPTER TWENTY-FOUR

Cassielle's confrontation with the demon left her trembling. She stated she needed some fresh air and left the room, down the stairs, through the store, and out the heavy wooden door of the Voodoo shop. She felt Samedi following her, but didn't stop.

Outside, the air felt tense, the faint scent of incense lingering on her clothes. Cassielle's steps were quick and purposeful, her mind racing with a torrent of emotions. She refused to let fear paralyze her.

She was about to go back inside when her phone rang. She picked it up when she saw it was Nick.

"Nick? What's up?" She couldn't fathom why he would be calling. He didn't want her involved in the investigation, and he was seeing someone else. Ice slid through her veins as those thoughts ran through her mind. The laugh at the other end of the line stopped her heart.

"Not Nick, doll face. The name's Vittorio DeLuca, but you can call me Vito. You've probably heard of me, right? I've gone by a bunch of names. The Puppeteer Killer. Some called me the Stagecraft Killer. My first and favorite nickname was The Butcher. But that was back in the day. I'm sure you noticed I had a lot more finesse toward the end? Personally, I think Stagecraft Killer suited me better when I was in New York. Maybe now they should start calling me the Voodoo Doll Killer here?" He spoke quickly, laughing at the end. Even though it was Nick's voice, it didn't sound like Nick's voice. The accent was strange, identical to the accent Brittany had used when she was murdering Michael. Cassielle was finding it hard to breathe.

"Now listen carefully, doll. You're going to help us to help yourself and your little boyfriend, kapish?"

"What do you want?" Cassielle steeled herself. She had to remove her emotions from this situation. Emotions wouldn't help anyone. Samedi moved to stand in front of her, watching her face. She turned on the speaker phone.

"Get yourself away from that Loa, and come to LaFitte's at midnight. Come alone or we'll make sure tonight's sunset will be the last one your precious Nick breathes through, got it?" Cassielle was sure he meant it. He had nothing to lose since he was dead already.

"Okay, I'll try to make it, but first I want to know why you're doing this. As far as I knew, I thought Vittorio DeLuca was smart enough he didn't need to work with someone else? Now all of a sudden he's someone else's puppet?" Maybe she could get him to reveal something as well as play to his ego and convince him to stop helping whoever it was who had freed him. Then perhaps he'd leave her friends alone.

Before she could continue, a chill descended upon her. The line went silent for a moment, then Nick's voice returned, but it was colder, devoid of any amusement.

"You don't get to ask questions, doll. You just do as you're told. Time's ticking. Don't keep us waiting or your Nick will have a nice pair of cement shoes." The call ended abruptly.

Cassielle stood there, her mind racing. She needed to act, but she also needed a plan.

The unforgiving July sun beat down on them as they stood, the air thick with humidity and the distant strains of jazz adding to the city's lively atmosphere. Despite the brightness of the day, shadows lingered in the alleyways and beneath the canopies of towering buildings, a reminder of the spreading darkness.

Cassielle's voice wavered with desperation as she turned to Samedi, her eyes pleading for reassurance amidst the chaos threatening to consume them. "What do we do, Samedi?"

A heavy silence hung in the air, suffused with the weight of their predicament. Cassielle felt as if someone had reached into her chest and clenched her heart in a vise-like grip, each beat a painful reminder of the danger looming over them.

"We will meet him," Samedi replied, his voice low and resonant, echoing with a solemn resolve. "And we will pull him out of Nick, casting him back to the depths from whence he came. That's what we'll do."

Cassielle swallowed hard, her gaze fixed on Samedi's dark countenance, the shadow of his hat obscuring his features, lending an air of menace to his already formidable presence. His words offered a glimmer of hope amidst the encroaching darkness, but she couldn't shake the nagging fear lingering in the depths of her mind.

"Samedi," she implored, her voice tinged with desperation, "please tell me it's possible to extract the evil souls without causing harm to the host. The last two we had to hurt. I couldn't bear to do that to Nick... Not like that." Each word carried the weight of her anguish, a plea for mercy in the face of an uncertain fate.

Samedi pulled her into an embrace, his voice rumbled in his chest against her cheek as he spoke, "Of course it is possible. However, we must hurry. The longer Nick is possessed, the harder it will be to bring him back. Up to now, the people you've encountered were possessed for minutes, maybe hours. When the evil soul leaves the body within that time frame, the soul of the person has not wandered too far and are able to find their way back. The longer it goes, the harder it is for them to find their way back. If Nick is possessed for long enough, we may never be able to get him back to his body."

Cassielle's heart sank into her stomach. "What do you mean? Where does the person's soul go?" She felt cold in spite of the summer heat. The thought of losing Nick forever hurt more than she could have ever imagined it would. She hadn't relished breaking up with him, but she also hadn't considered losing him for forever. She'd known he would still be alive and would move on and be okay - at least she'd hoped he would. The idea of him being dead and gone was unbearable.

"They go to limbo. They're lost because they aren't supposed to be dead. They wander until one of us Loa find them and help them to the other side, but that can take some time as we are often busy." He sighed. "Luckily possession doesn't happen often. We do pretty well containing souls in Limbo, but your Catholic church tells stories of people possessed and I wish I could say they were wrong."

Cassielle began pacing the sidewalk trying to sort out this knowledge. "But you said evil souls and malevolent spirits were kept in Limbo. How is it they can get out to possess people?" She stopped to turn and face him head on. "It's your job, isn't it? To make sure they stay in? Sounds like if they're getting out often enough to possess people and have the Catholic Church dealing with it y'all aren't doing too bang-up of a job."

Samedi's face shifted, the skull flashing once again as he scowled down at her. Cassielle froze, her breath catching as she met Samedi's gaze, the flash of his skull-like visage a stark reminder of the power he wielded. The air between them crackled with tension.

"It's not that simple," he said, his voice a low growl. "I hadn't told you this before, because I didn't want to alarm you. The barrier between the worlds is weakening. Forces are at work even the Loa struggle to contain. It has been getting worse as the centuries go on." He let out a sigh and rubbed his forehead in frustration. "This is why your father created you." He lowered his hand to study her. "He had not anticipated someone opening the gates and causing this chaos.

He thought..." He shook his head, "No, I won't speculate on what Heylel and Bondye think. We must prepare to face him. We have until Midnight, so rest for you and then it's high time you met your father."

CHAPTER TWENTY-FIVE

Cassielle slowly opened her eyes, her gaze landing on an unfamiliar man at the stove. His back was turned, but he moved with a practiced ease, stirring and flipping ingredients in a skillet. The stress of the day still weighed on her, but waking to a stranger cooking in her apartment didn't alarm her as much as it should have. Samedi was lounging on the couch watching the man cook which offered an odd sense of reassurance.

"Good morning, sunshine!" The man's cheerful voice broke the silence.

"It's afternoon," Samedi mumbled.

The stranger turned, revealing a plate piled with a mouthwatering breakfast, a cup of orange juice, and neatly arranged utensils. He set salt and pepper shakers on the counter, ready for use. Was this man her father? He looked young.

"Time is an illusion," the stranger grinned.

"Don't stay in bed forever. Come on over and eat. We must discuss your plans," Samedi said, rising and walking to sit on one of the stools. He glanced at the man cooking. "Must you cook? We have magic for that."

The man shrugged, waved his hand, and the dirty cooking implements vanished. "I like cooking."

"We don't eat," Samedi reminded him.

"I did once," the man responded casually. He turned to

Cassielle, who was now standing by her bed, watching their exchange. With a dramatic bow and a flourish of his hand, he said, "Allow me to introduce myself-Ghede Nibo, at your service."

Cassielle sighed, frustration mounting. Not her father. She knew a little about Ghede Nibo from her readings but kept her distance.

"Ghede Nibo, the guardian of the second gate, isn't it?" she recalled, a touch of weariness coloring her voice.

"You may call me Nibo." Cassielle noticed a faint hint of cigar smoke floating about her apartment. Looking back to Nibo, she saw he now held a cigar. "Do you mind?"

She narrowed her eyes at the audacity of the Loa and moved around her bed to the terrace doors. She propped one open before turning back to him, "I do mind, actually."

He shrugged, and with a flourish, the cigar vanished in a puff of smoke.

"My apologies," he said, moving to sit on the couch. Cassielle decided to make the most of the opportunity and sat at the counter to eat the breakfast Nibo had provided. She studied him quietly for a moment.

Nibo's eyes, deep and expressive, held a certain allure, his gaze carrying a hint of mystery. His features possessed a subtle androgyny, blurring the lines between masculine and feminine, lending him an ethereal quality as captivating as it was intriguing. A mischievous smile played upon his lips, suggesting a playful nature lurking beneath the surface.

"You said something about having once eaten?" She took her plate and spun on the stool so she could face him.

"Samedi told me of your mission to rescue your Nicholas," Nibo said, propping his feet up on her coffee table. "It reminds me of a love story from long ago. A tale of a handsome young man, much like myself, who was enslaved in the Nubian civilization known as the Ta Seti kingdom. Our kings ruled Egypt during the 25th dynasty under the reign of the first Nubian King, Sabacus. I - he, lived in the southern region of Egypt, now known as Sudan."

Cassielle's curiosity piqued, and she glanced at Nibo, his features momentarily betraying a sense of reflection. With a quiet sigh, she allowed his words to weave through her thoughts.

"He was compelled to toil in the trade of precious commodities like gold, ivory, and ebony. Days turned into weeks and weeks into months as he navigated the vast expanse of the Nile River on a boat. Despite the hardships, he found solace and freedom in the water. He worked diligently, keeping his head down, and he found love in one of the port towns they stopped at."

Nibo's voice grew softer, as if immersed in memories. Cassielle couldn't help but be captivated by the tale, her imagination painting vivid images of a life long gone.

"There was a girl, an enslaved person like him, held captive in the home of his master, serving his wife. Their hearts entwined, and against all odds, they were allowed to court and be wed before his fateful final journey. He was loyal to his master, devoted to his wife, but such loyalty couldn't shield him from the resentment of those who desired what he had."

Nibo's words were tinged with sadness, his voice carrying the weight of a tragic fate. Cassielle empathized deeply with the handsome man's struggle.

"One of the other enslaved people, consumed by jealousy, believed the girl should belong to him. He fostered a friendship with her brother, both harboring a disdain for the handsome man's love. One night, as he lay vulnerable in slumber, they attacked him. Their rage knew no bounds, beating him mercilessly until he teetered on the precipice of death. And in a final act of cruelty, they thrust a blade through his heart and cast his lifeless body into the river."

Cassielle winced, the graphic imagery searing her imagination. She wondered what became of the girl, left to navigate a world without her beloved, and whether the bonds of love could withstand such cruelty.

Nibo's voice trailed off momentarily, the story's weight hanging in the air. Cassielle's gaze shifted to his enigmatic figure, her curiosity demanding answers to unspoken questions.

"Did she find happiness, Nibo?" she asked softly, her voice filled with empathy.

A fleeting melancholy shadow crossed Nibo's face before he met her gaze with a wistful smile. "Ah, dear Cassielle, the path of love is often tangled and fraught with pain. But remember, love has a way of transcending time and even death itself."

"So you were human once?"

Nibo placed a finger to his lips and winked. Cassielle turned back to set the plate on the counter and continued to eat. Nibo watched her as she devoured the food, savoring every delectable bite. It was clear Nibo's culinary skills remained unmatched despite his abstention.

With her hunger satiated and the empty glass of orange juice marking her contentment, Cassielle leaned back, relishing the pleasant sensation of a well-fed belly. As she contemplated making coffee, Nibo approached, placing a steaming mug of the aromatic brew in front of her. The rich scent enveloped her senses, the fragrance providing a comforting embrace.

"Has anyone ever told you that you make a mean breakfast?" Cassie asked, a warm smile gracing her lips as she sipped her cup.

Nibo beamed with pride, his eyes twinkling. "Why, thank you! I do enjoy watching those cooking shows. If circumstances were different in my time, perhaps I would have pursued a career as a chef."

A tinge of disappointment flickered across Cassie's expression as the reality of Nibo's limitations resurfaced. "I suppose that's not an option for you now, is it?" she asked.

Nibo's smile waned, his gaze momentarily distant. "No,

not at all," he replied softly, his words carrying the weight of unattainable dreams.

Just as the conversation began to settle into a comfortable lull, Samedi's voice resonated through the room, interrupting their reverie. Cassie's senses tingled with the presence of the Loa behind her, their connection growing increasingly natural and effortless.

"Now that you're done," Samedi's voice rang out. Cassie refrained from jumping, having already sensed his arrival. The development of her abilities brought a sense of both pride and trepidation. "It's time to go see your father."

"Before that. I wanted to tell you my plan," Cassie replied, facing Samedi directly while cradling her cup of coffee. The room fell into a momentary silence as Samedi remained uncharacteristically stoic. Undeterred, she continued, "Well, the plan is simple. We meet DeLuca, rescue Nick, then go after Buer. By taking out his main follower, we'll show him that his time is running out."

Samedi shook his head, his expression a mix of skepticism and conviction. "Heylel is getting frustrated. I'm worried he won't agree with wasting your time on DeLuca. Let the Loa take him out."

"You heard him. If someone else shows up to meet him, he's going to kill Nick," she set her mug down.

"He's playing you," Samedi retorted, his voice laden with certainty. "He knows you'll never sacrifice your friend. He's wasting your time. We will have to do it. You need to focus on getting Buer."

Cassielle's glare bore into Samedi, a fiery determination burning within her. "You won't have to. I will save Nick and then take out Buer," she declared defiantly. "Where is this even coming from? You didn't seem to be against the idea when we got the call."

A flicker of irritation crossed Samedi's features as he met her gaze. "You can try it your way, but your focus should be on getting Buer."

"You didn't answer my question," she sighed, momentarily deflated, and sipped her coffee, the bitter taste mirroring the unresolved conflict between them. Her gaze shifted to Nibo, who suddenly appeared engrossed in washing the dishes, offering no solace in this brewing dispute.

"We'll cross that bridge when we come to it," she continued. "For now, let's focus on the task at hand. It's time for me to get dressed and for us to get moving."

Collecting her chosen attire-a pair of jeans, a t-shirt, undergarments, and a lone pair of socks-Cassielle made her way into the bathroom, preparing herself for the night ahead. Uncertain about how her meeting with Nick would go, she knew they would find a way, step by step. Knowledge could be their guiding light, enabling them to uncover patterns leading to each malevolent soul.

Emerging from the bathroom, She discovered Nibo waiting at the end of her bed, he was wringing his hands. Sensing his underlying concern, she prepared to inquire but was preempted by his words.

"We are meeting with the rest of the Loa now," Nibo began, his eyes fixed intently on her.

"Okay," she responded calmly, reaching up to braid her hair and securing it with a tie.

"I don't know if Heylel will be there," Nibo added, his watchful gaze never wavering.

"Okay," Cassielle echoed, sitting on the couch and lacing her boots.

"I thought you might be nervous or something, meeting your father," Nibo ventured, his curiosity evident.

"Not particularly," she replied, her voice betraying her true feelings on the matter. She finished tying her bootlaces and rose to her feet, attempting to exude an air of detatchment. "Where are we meeting them and how long do you think it'll take?" She inquired, ready to go rescue Nick.

"In the cemetery, by Marie Laveau's grave," Nibo explained, his voice echoing in the quiet surroundings.

Cassielle raised an eyebrow. "Any particular reason why they're meeting there? Seems like an odd place for a reunion."

Nibo chuckled softly. "We often meet in cemeteries. This one, in particular, is favored due to the protective spells surrounding the grounds. It's unlikely an evil soul would find its way in while we gather there." He paused, "Of course whatever opened the gates happened there, so they're not one hundred percent impenetrable. With help they can do it."

"Well, it sounds like a plan," Cassielle said, rising from her seat. "But I have a meeting with Nicholas." She reached for her phone. "I think I'll call Alba and see if she can keep the bar quieter than usual. I don't want to raise his suspicion, but I also don't want too many people around that he could hurt."

Nibo stretched, a grin spreading across his face. "Good idea. Let's get to it!"

Cassielle returned the smile and glanced at Samedi, who stood silently by the window.

"I already informed Heylel," he said, offering his arm. "We'll free your Nicholas and then meet with him. Shall we?"

CHAPTER TWENTY-SIX

They slipped through the shadows, emerging into a narrow alley two blocks from LaFitte's. Samedi and Nibo disappeared into the darkness, their presence fading as they moved to their positions. Their task was to keep watch over the exits, ensuring no one slipped away unnoticed. Cassielle, however, made her way into LaFitte's.

She navigated through the dimly lit room, the soft hum of conversation drifting toward her on waves of cigar smoke. Though not as bustling as the lively evenings at LaFitte's, a few patrons scattered about added a quiet buzz of activity. She scanned the room, noting a couple of animated patrons in the corner and a small group of men huddled over drinks at one end of the bar. She made her way to the other end, where a row of stools offered a quiet sanctuary away from the other patrons.

Alba, ever the caretaker, approached her and slid a drink her way. "Oh, mon coeur! I'm so happy to see you."

Cassielle tried to put on a normal smile, but she wasn't sure she succeeded based on the look Alba gave her. "Is everything okay?"

Cassielle sighed, "Just a lot to deal with right now... work." This was the safest explanation. She hadn't told her much over the phone, but Alba had reassured her this time of night there usually weren't many patrons, but she'd make sure they didn't have a surprise crowd. She hadn't asked for more details, for which Cassielle was grateful.

"Something non-alcoholic but fizzy, then? For focus?" Alba plucked a glass from a pile and used the sprayer to fill the glass before sliding it across the bar to Cassielle.

Cassielle frowned but understood Alba's intentions. She picked up the fizzy clear drink, identified it as seltzer water, and took a sip. She scanned the crowd, observing the patrons. The men at the other end fixed their gaze on the game playing on the TV, and a group of girls appeared to be finishing a lively night, one of them wore a "bride" sash and tiara, albeit with an excess of makeup and a shortage of clothing. They were heading out the door.

Returning to her drink, Cassielle peered into the mirror behind the bar, discreetly surveying the room. Everything seemed ordinary, lacking the sense of evil accompanying DeLuca's presence. Another sip of seltzer water passed her lips, causing her to wince at the taste she had never particularly enjoyed.

Suddenly, Cassielle saw him in the mirror above the bar as he entered with a woman. They made their way to a secluded table in the unoccupied section of the bar. From her vantage point, it appeared as though Nick was skillfully playing the part of a man interested in taking her home, and the woman was undeniably drawn to his charm. How could she resist? Nick's tall, muscular frame, snazzy fedora, button-up shirt, suspenders, loosened tie, and form-fitting pants showcased his attractive assets. It was easy to understand why anyone would be captivated by him. The attire, however, was odd for him. He looked like he had stepped out of a turn of the century Mafia movie.

She shook her head and rose from her stool. With a few steps she stood behind the redhead, facing Nick (DeLuca).

"Hello, sweetheart," he greeted, his voice carrying an eerie quality. He stood up, "Excuse me, doll," he winked to the redhead and moved around her, stepping towards Cassielle. He leaned in, his chest brushing against her side, while his hand found its way to her lower back, resting possessively. His breath tickled her cheek, and his words dripped with a sinister undertone. "Miss me?"

Cassielle's eyes shifted beyond him, and she noticed Nibo watching them disapprovingly. It made her feel better to see him there. Cassielle stepped back from Nick, collecting her thoughts.

"What's wrong, doll?" Nick (DeLuca) whispered in her ear. "Don't ya like me like this?"

"Get the hell out of him," Cassielle hissed, her voice low but laced with a seriousness that left no room for misinterpretation.

"Oh, but this one is so fun!" he exclaimed, leaning back slightly, his smile morphing into a frown. "Turns out I can hold on to a body for quite a while." He grinned, his eyes roaming over her body before returning to meet her gaze. The predatory look might have once thrilled, and surprised, her coming from the honest Nick, now made her stomach churn with disgust. "Much better than the Deaf chap."

Cassielle wrestled with her predicament. She needed to get DeLuca out of Nick. Her plan had been for Nibo to enter the bar through the kitchen and Samedi to step out of the shadows behind Nick. However, she hadn't counted on the woman. Who was she? What if she tried to get involved? The other patrons were drinking and distracted. She wasn't sure they'd notice anything. The redhead, however, was paying close attention to her and Nick (DeLuca).

Her mind raced, desperately searching for a solution. Could she convince him to go outside with her? She knew all too well he would see through her ruse. The weight of worry and guilt settled like a heavy stone in the pit of her stomach.

"Oh... I can see I've displeased you," he remarked, leaning back in, a frown marring his face. "Were you planning something? Have I messed it up?" A smile played across his lips. "You know, this could all be so much easier for you. Just come with me as I travel the world. We could have so much fun." He leaned closer, his mouth hovering inches from hers. "You like the blood and death. I saw it on your face. At your friend's house... outside of this bar. We could have so much fun," he repeated, his words a chilling proposition hanging in the air.

"No," she protested, attempting to shift away from him, but his hand moved to her wrist, his firm grip prevented her escape, pulling her closer. His words dripped with a twisted charm, patronizing her resistance. "Now, darling, don't worry. I understand your hesitation. You've spent your whole life being told how to behave, what's right and wrong." He drew imaginary parentheses with his free fingers before trailing them down her face, cupping her cheek, and then gripping her chin, keeping her face close to his. The rest of the bar faded from her view, obscured by his dominating presence. She strained to catch a glimpse of Nibo or Samedi, desperate for their intervention. Why weren't they doing something? Didn't they possess a means to expel him from Nick's body without the patrons noticing? Maybe not.

"What the fuck?!" A voice cut through the tension, causing both Cassielle and Nick to turn. Over his shoulder, Cassielle spotted Rebecca, her countenance transformed from cheerful to furious. Blonde locks cascaded in disarray around her shoulders, framing her face with wild intensity. Her once warm blue eyes now glimmered with anger and hurt, fuelled by the sight of Nick engaging in flirtatious banter with Cassielle. Rebecca's purposeful strides conveyed her annoyance, each step brimming with fury. She adjusted the strap of her bag impatiently.

Rebecca approached the bar, her gaze locked onto them. "When Nina texted me a picture of the two of you and said where you were, I thought she must be wrong. It couldn't be," Rebecca seethed, folding her arms across her chest. "So this is what you mean by being 'over her'? I should have known you could never be over her!" In a fit of anger, she snatched the forgotten glass of seltzer and hurled it at Nick, the water splashing onto both him and Cassielle. Cassielle instinctively recoiled from the spray. Nick had never seemed like the type to be attracted to blondes, but Rebecca possessed a commendable figure. Perhaps she had been a successful rebound.

Nick (DeLuca) glowered at Rebecca, his voice dripping with hostility. "Go away," he snarled, redirecting his attention back to Cassielle. He showed no signs of loosening his grip despite the interruption.

"Like fuck I'm going away!" Rebecca exclaimed, determined to pry them apart.

Cassielle seized this opportunity, freeing herself from Nick (DeLuca)'s grasp with a twisting motion forcing his hand to release.

Rebecca retreated a few steps keeping a safe distance. "We had a good thing going, Rush, and you've fucked it up royally."

Nick (DeLuca) turned to face Rebecca, his rage emanating like molten lava, filling the space around him. Past DeLuca and Rebecca, Cassielle caught a glimpse of Nibo inching closer, pausing just a short distance away. Samedi stood beside him, gesturing towards Nick (DeLuca) and Rebecca as they faced off.

"Who the hell are you and who do you think you are interrupting us?" Nick (DeLuca) snarled at Rebecca. A hush fell over the bar as the few people turned their attention to the unfolding drama. Even the patrons engrossed in the game couldn't resist the allure of this spectacle. People always craved a dramatic showdown. Lovers quarrels especially.

"Are you kidding me?" Rebecca snapped back, her voice seething with anger. "Just yesterday morning, you were moaning my name, and now you're pretending like you don't even know me?"

Cassielle's mind raced, searching for a plan. She couldn't bear the torment of Nick's possession any longer. Perhaps she could abduct him, tie him up, and extract this spirit. It seemed like a viable option. She needed...

Nick (DeLuca) seized Rebecca's wrist, gripping it tightly as he pulled her closer, his face contorted with rage. "Get lost. I couldn't care less about you. I probably never cared about you in the first place. How about that, you slut?"

With surprising agility, Rebecca executed a swift self-defense maneuver, freeing her arm from Nick's grasp. It was evident possessing Nick didn't grant DeLuca the same martial arts prowess. If he had been proficient, their encounter would have escalated into a full-blown scuffle rather than an instant escape.

"What the hell is wrong with you?" Rebecca retorted, her voice dripping with contempt. "I worried about you and your relationship with this bitch. I thought things would be fine since she no longer works at your precinct. But you have some serious commitment issues!" With that, she turned and stormed out of the bar.

Cassielle was taken aback by Rebecca's insult. She had only met her a few times, and now she was being called a bitch? Shaking off her offense, Cassielle refocused on the situation at hand. She had a bigger problem to deal with-Nick's possession.

Seemingly recovered from his irritation, Nick (DeLuca) shifted his attention back to Cassielle, inching closer to her. His smile returned as if the previous confrontation had never happened. Cassielle glared at him.

"We were at the part where you were going to do this the easy way and vacate my friend's body," she hissed, keeping her voice low. The bar was still abuzz with the lingering attention.

"I don't recall agreeing to that," Nick (DeLuca) responded, stepping closer to her, causing her to back up until she bumped into a nearby stool. "I thought we were discussing a different arrangement-something more enjoyable than swapping bodies but still involving you and me." He grinned. Cassielle could have sworn bile rose at the thought.

"I'm afraid that's not going to happen," Nibo interjected from Cassielle's right, inserting himself into the conversation.

Cassielle felt a wave of relief wash over her.

"No one asked for your opinion, Loa," Nick (DeLuca) hissed, reaching out to grab Cassielle's wrist again. "If you don't mind, we'll be leaving."

Cassielle grabbed his wrist with her other hand and twisted his arm behind his back in what was likely a painful contortion causing Nick (DeLuca) to yelp. "Do. Not. Touch. Me." She hissed, shoving him down into the table, and then regretting it since Nick might feel that when he's no longer possessed.

"We do mind," Samedi's voice boomed from behind Nick (DeLuca). "Now that you're listening, let's go."

"I'm afraid I have no intention of leaving this body," Nick (DeLuca) replied defiantly. He pushed away from the table with preternatural strength, sending it crashing into the wall and causing Cassielle to fall back into Samedi, who stood behind her.

Nick (DeLuca) grabbed the woman he had entered with before they could react, pulling her close. He turned back to them, nonchalantly resting his hand on the gun holstered at his hip. "I'll be on my way now. I assume I don't need to list the things I will do if you try to stop me."

Samedi started to move, his hand going to his hat and Cassielle stopped him, "No, he could hurt her!" She hissed.

Samedi glared down at her, but before he could retort, Nick (DeLuca) spoke to the woman with him, "Think about my offer, yes?" The woman's face lit up, and she nodded eagerly. How did she not see everything that just happened? Why on earth would she agree to go home with him?

"We can't let him leave with her," Cassielle whispered urgently.

"When they leave the building, we'll make our move," Nibo whispered back, his voice barely audible amidst the bar's ambient noise.

Nick (DeLuca) and the redhead began walking toward the exit, their footsteps echoing through the room. DeLuca paused, facing the trio of Nibo, Samedi, and Cassielle.

"Hold on, love," he murmured to the woman, his voice dripping with charm. Then, he nodded to Nibo, Samedi, and Cassielle, his tone shifting to cold menace as a confident grin crossed his face. "Follow me, and I'll jump bodies, leaving this one lifeless. But if you back off, no harm will come to him." His chilling smile punctuated the threat. "You have my number."

Nick (DeLuca) slid his arm around the woman's waist, pulling her close as they walked out of Lafitte's, their silhouettes fading into the darkness beyond.

Cassielle exhaled sharply, her heart sinking as the gravity of the situation set in. "We can't go after him," she whispered, her voice trembling with fear.

"We have to," Samedi's voice was firm, unyielding.

"He'll kill Nick," she hissed, desperation edging her words.

"He's already dead if he stays possessed much longer," Samedi replied softly. "DeLuca has no control over whether Nick returns to his body or not."

"Besides that, he may kill that woman," Nibo whispered.

Cassielle's stomach clenched. They should have evicted DeLuca right here, gun or no gun. After all, Samedi had done it at the cathedral before and they'd manage to not have any casualties then. Though the people had all been ducking behind the pews, so they may have not seen anything, or if they did, they chalked it up to a trauma-induced hallucination. And it was probably by sheer luck no one was shot.

"You're right," she said softly. "We can't leave him with her."

Cassielle rushed out into the darkness, scanning the dimly lit streets for any sign of Nick and the red-headed woman. Her heart pounded in her chest as she hoped she wasn't too late.

"That guy's a real dick," came a woman's voice from her left, dripping with a deep Southern twang. Cassielle turned and with relief saw the redheaded woman. "He promised me a good time, but when I told him my price, he tried to hit me." She shook her head. "I don't put up with that." She must have mis-understood Cassielle's reaction because she added, "I didn't call the cops. I don't need that kinda shit, either."

Cassielle let out a breath. "Did you see which way he went?"

The woman shook her head. "He flagged down a taxi and it went that way, but after that, I don't know." She pointed down Bourbon Street.

"We have to go," Samedi said softly from behind her.

"I have to find him," Cassielle said firmly, turning to face Samedi and Nibo.

Nibo, pulled out a cigar and took a long puff, the smoke swirling around him as he muttered under his breath.

Samedi, however, regarded her with a look of concern. "We can't do that now," he said, leaning heavily on his walking stick. "We need to go."

Cassielle's gaze was unwavering as she met Samedi's eyes, her frustration evident in the tight set of her jaw. "I have to find him. We can't leave him like this. We need a plan to capture DeLuca end Nick's possession, and then I'll meet whoever you need me to meet."

"Had you not stopped me, we would have already done that. You blew your chance." Cassielle winced. He was right. She should have let him act. Her stomach churned with regret and guilt, a nauseous wave that made her feel sick. Samedi hesitated, his expression softening. "I get why you stopped me. We can't change that now. Our priority is to meet the Loa. They might know how to find him. Unless you already know where he went?"

Cassielle's shoulders slumped slightly under the weight of her decision. He was right. She didn't know where he was. "Fine. But we find out where he is from them, and then we focus on rescuing Nick. Agreed?"

Samedi nodded, a reluctant agreement in his eyes. He

gestured for her to follow, leading the way down the street. They stepped into the shadows, moving away from the lively chatter of the bar patrons, the air between them thick with unspoken promises and unresolved tension.

CHAPTER TWENTY-SEVEN

Nibo turned to Cassielle, raising an eyebrow. "Ready to meet everyone?"

Cassielle let out a breath, her shoulders felt tight. "As ready as I'll ever be." Since her tense interaction withDeLuca, she'd been on edge. Every moment spent here felt like wasted time when Nick needed rescuing.

Together, they set off toward Marie Laveau's tomb. The cemetery was quiet, their footsteps echoing off the old tombstones. Cassielle, Nibo, and Samedi were the first to arrive. Samedi glanced at her and Cassielle noticed a fleeting emotion on his face that she couldn't quite decipher.

"What?" she asked, trying to read his expression.

Samedi's eyes snapped back to hers, caught off guard. "What?"

"You gave me a look," she pressed.

Before he could respond, the other Loa began to arrive, materializing one by one. To Cassielle's surprise, they looked like ordinary people, their true forms hidden. She had half-expected skull faces and spectral appearances, but they remained in their human guise. The gathering swelled to nearly twenty individuals, each engaging in quiet conversations, yet giving Cassielle a respectful distance.

Leaning against a tomb beside Nibo, she observed the scene, her mind racing. She couldn't help but notice their reserved demeanor, the way they seemed to move with an unspoken understanding, creating a space for her in their midst.

To her left stood Marie LaVeau's tomb. Cassielle moved towards it to read the plaque inscribed: "This Greek revival tomb is the reputed burial place of this notorious 'Voodoo queen.' A mystic cult, Voodoism, of African origin, was brought to this city from Santo Domingo and flourished in the 19th century. Marie Laveau was the most widely known of many cult practitioners."

She could see X's all over the tomb. Visitors seeking Marie LaVeau's mystical intervention left X's covering the sides of the tomb and the plaque. Cassielle recalled her mother sharing the legend that one must obtain a brick from another tomb, spin around, and mark three Xs on the Laveau tomb to grant their wish. As she glanced at the kept Xs, Cassielle wondered if she dared make a wish to escape the danger and reclaim her everyday life. Would her ancestor heed her plea? Probably not based on her earlier encounter with her.

"I know you're worried about your friend," Nibo looked around at the crowd, keeping his voice low. Cassielle waited suspecting his nonchalant demeanor and speaking softly meant he had something to say he didn't want Samedi or the other Loa to know. "I didn't tell you this, but," he shifted, "You could go into limbo to fetch Nick's spirit." He looked at his nails absentmindedly.

"Wouldn't that be dangerous?" Cassielle kept her voice down too, watching the other Loa. Samedi was standing a ways away watching the gathering.

"Most definitely, but at this point, we have to try. You don't know where Nick's body is right now, and even if you did, there's no guarantee his spirit is still near him," Nibo pulled out another cigar and started smoking. After a few puffs he continued, "When we have a chance, I'll show you what you need to do."

Cassielle felt as if Nibo had thrown her a lifeline. The thought of going to Limbo made her nervous, but at least she could get Nick back. This would give them a little more time to findDeLuca.

Samedi glanced towards them. Nibo casually changed the topic.

"They don't know how to relate to you," Nibo observed the crowd.

Cassielle turned to him, a quizzical expression on her face. "Huh?"

Nibo clarified, "The Loa don't often interact with the living, so they're unsure what to say to you." Cassielle couldn't quite figure out why Nibo was saying this as it didn't seem to her they were behaving oddly. Though he knew them. She didn't.

Cassielle surveyed the crowd and noticed Samedi was now standing alone with another man. Neither of them engaged in conversation with each other or anyone else. Was that man Heylel? She considered asking Nibo, but a hush fell over the gathering. Unable to determine the cause, Cassielle patiently looked for what had captured their attention.

As the murmurs subsided, the crowd respectfully parted, creating a pathway for a commanding figure to stride toward Cassielle and Nibo. Dressed in a finely tailored suit, his form exuded an air of authority and mystery. A vibrant cravat adorned his neck, adding a touch of color to his ensemble, while a short top hat sat atop his head, decorated with a small skull. His hair, meticulously tied back, cascaded down his back in a mesmerizing display of intricate curls.

Behind a pair of dark glasses, one eye was concealed from view, but in the other his gaze held an enigmatic, captivating, and elusive quality. The presence he commanded was undeniable, radiating both power and, she imagined, a profound understanding of the intricate forces governing the realms beyond mortal comprehension.

"Cassiellelle, I am so happy to see that you are okay," his low and soothing voice rumbled. Cassielle's heart quickened, a mixture of anxiety and intrigue bubbling within her.

Something was unsettling about his calm demeanor.

"Um... thanks?" Cassielle replied, her gaze flickering to Samedi, who observed the encounter.

The man brought a glass to his lips, taking a leisurely sip. The aroma of rum wafted through the air. With a cigar between his fingers, he drew a slow drag. The entire interaction moved languidly as the assembled Loa stood silently, engrossed in the unfolding scene. It was odd to her, but the Loa didn't even blink.

"Thank you all for gathering here. I will keep this brief as we have much to do," The man's voice carried effortlessly over the hushed ambiance of the cemetery. He turned away from her to face the gathering. Cassielle wondered what an outsider stumbling upon them would perceive. Would they be able to see all the Loa or merely witness her standing alone? The mysteries of their world fascinated her.

"You have tirelessly worked to capture the escaped souls, for which I am grateful. I bring news that we are down to the final thirteen who remain unaccounted for. One of them, Vittorio DeLuca, has made himself quite conspicuous. Samedi has been leading the charge to apprehend him, but he has proven elusive," The man announced.

Cassielle's gaze shifted towards Samedi, observing his reaction. She noticed a slight flinch from him, drawing the attention of other Loa, who exchanged glances of surprise or amusement. Samedi's struggle with DeLuca did not bode well for him. But how was he supposed to capture him when he kept showing up in crowds?

The man continued, his voice carrying authority and an undercurrent of anger. "I understand you have an update for us?" he turned his attention to Samedi.

Stepping out from the shadows where he had been lurking, Samedi moved closer to the man, maintaining a respectful distance. "Yes, I do," he replied, his voice steady. "I started Cassielle down the path of training to be a Voodoo Queen. This has of course taken some time. We did findDeLuca, and we know who he is possessing..."

Interrupting Samedi, Heylel's voice rumbled angrily, cutting through the air. "Then why has he not been apprehended yet?"

Cassielle felt a surge of responsibility and spoke up. Heylel turned his attention towards her, a flicker of surprise crossing his face.

"That's my fault," she admitted, meeting his gaze head-on. Her nerves were momentarily gone, replaced by a strange confidence.

"Oh?" The man tilted his head and watched her.

"DeLuca has possessed a dear friend of mine, and I couldn't allow Samedi or Nibo to harm him. He's a good person," Cassielle explained, feeling the weight of the Loa's eyes on her. Their soft murmurs filled the air as they engaged in hushed discussions. "We haven't been able to get him alone..."

"If you were so worried about him being harmed, couldn't you have done it in a non-life-threatening way?" The man smirked. "Explain yourself," he commanded, his gaze unyielding.

"I think before I say anything else, I'd like you to tell me who you are," she folded her arms over her chest. She had a feeling who he was, but it was rude not to introduce oneself. She was feeling oddly brazen facing him down.

The man's lips twitched as if he wanted to smile. "My apologies for not introducing myself. I go by many names, but you may call me Father, if you'd like, as that is who I am to you."

Cassielle let out a breath she hadn't realized she'd been holding. She'd been right. She had half a mind to tell him off about the whole 'call me Father' nonsense. He'd never been around for her. That hardly made him Father material. She hoped she would get to face off with him another time. They had a lot to talk about. Now, she opted to stay on topic.

"Okay, then. Back onto your question, I don't think there's much to explain. DeLuca is occupying Nicholas because we couldn't get him out of Nick's body when we confronted him at the bar. He left with a woman and I was concerned because he threatened to abandon Nick's body if we followed which could have killed Nick since his spirit wasn't around. Nick hasn't done anything to deserve-"

"None of the unfortunate souls who perished in this chaos deserved their fate!" Heylel's eye flared with a fiery red hue as if fueled by oxygen. "By letting him live, you prioritize the life of one man while he continues to perpetrate rape and murder upon countless others."

Her anger surged, replacing any remaining nerves. "Really? You're placing the blame on me?" Cassielle's voice quivered with intensity. "I am not responsible for any of this! I had no part in opening the gates, and my friends have suffered enough. They don't need me to kill someone else they care about. I shouldn't have been dragged into this mess in the first place, except for my connection to you! If they weren't so bent on seeking revenge against you, my friends wouldn't have been targeted at all." She took a deep breath before continuing. "If you're going to point fingers and blame others, start by looking at yourself. Why did you have to engage with a human woman and bring me into this world?" The words tumbled out, her frustration and anger pouring forth like steam from a boiling kettle. "And why weren't any safeguards in place to prevent such a breach? It seems foolish to leave such a vulnerability in your system."

A stunned silence enveloped the gathered Loa. Cassielle was reasonably sure none of them had ever dared to speak to Heylel in such a manner, but she couldn't contain her anger any longer. If he wanted to blame her for this entire mess and the resulting deaths, he had another thing coming. Despite the guilt and fear gnawed at her, she stood her ground. She wouldn't sacrifice Nick. She needed to be sure Nick's soul would go back into his body.

"Are you finished?" Heylel's voice returned to its calm, even tone, devoid of warmth. She couldn't discern any emotion from his expression, and his cold composure unsettled her even more.

"For now," Cassielle replied, shifting her weight uneasily. The silence stretched on, and she felt his piercing gaze on her. As the awkwardness grew unbearable, he finally looked away from her.

"You're right. We should have been more diligent in securing the gates. However, they are meant to serve as a connection between this world and the afterlife. To ensure complete security, the link would have to be severed," Heylel explained, his eyes meeting hers again. "Both the living and the dead require connection for balance. It's a precarious tightrope act, but it is what it is." He studied her face intently. "I'm afraid the solution to dealing with DeLuca might require hurting your dear Nick." Without allowing her to argue, he turned to address the others, continuing his speech.

"Guede Doubye will handle it. Nicholas Rush, right?" Heylel asked.

Samedi nodded. Both scanned the crowd, eyes sharp and searching.

A figure emerged, moving with a purposeful stride. The crowd's murmurs fell silent, and the air grew thick with anticipation. Guede Doubye, the skeletal guardian of the afterlife, stepped forward. His presence commanded attention, an aura of solemnity and undeniable authority surrounding him.

Guede Doubye's cloak billowed around him like a wisp of smoke. The tattered funeral attire draped his skeletal frame, swaying gently with each deliberate step. The fabric, worn and faded, whispered stories of countless souls who had crossed his path.

As he neared Heylel, Guede Doubye's empty eye sockets glistened with an otherworldly gleam, seemingly illuminated from within. The intricate, ethereal, and translucent veil that covered his skull fluttered softly as if stirred by unseen forces. It whispered secrets of the realms beyond, hinting at his vast knowledge. She was relieved he hadn't approached her first. There had to be a reason he appeared in his full form instead of a human guise. His appearance was terrifying, causing her to feel chilled in spite of the heat of the night.

With reverence and humility, Guede Doubye inclined his head in a deep, graceful bow before Heylel. The moment hung in the air, charged with solemnity and purpose until Heylel interrupted it.

"You, Samedi, will be assigned a new spirit to hunt for since DeLuca seems to be so elusive for you and you're clearly incapable of completing your mission to train Cassielle. Nibo, you will remain with Cassielle. See to it she finishes her training and then starts after Buer. You are under no circumstances to leave Cassielle's side, no matter what happens with the other Loa or the outside world. If you fail at this, I may rethink your permanent duties."

An audible gasp came from the crowd. Cassielle felt her anger burning inside of her. How dare he lecture Samedi and Nibo in front of others? Did he know nothing about good leadership? Nibo and Samedi looked abashed and ashamed. It was her fault that DeLuca was not apprehended. She had half a mind to call him out on his terrible leadership, but glancing at Nibo caused her to keep her mouth shut. He didn't want her to say anything. So, she wouldn't.

The Loa slowly dispersed in puffs of black smoke as they were dismissed by Heylel to do their duties. Cassielle watched as one by one they vanished, each leaving a lingering wisp of darkness in their wake. The air grew still, and only Heylel, Samedi, and Nibo remained. Heylel gave Samedi a sharp look, and with a tip of his hat, Samedi too dissolved into smoke, his presence evaporating like smoke on a breeze.

Cassielle felt a sudden emptiness, a hollow ache as if a comforting quilt had been stripped away. She took a deep breath, trying to steady herself against the unexpected sense of loss.

"What now?" she asked, her voice barely above a

whisper, the weight of the moment pressing down on her.

Heylel's gaze softened, a rare glint of empathy in his eyes. "Now, you prepare," he said. "There is much to do and little time. Buer will not rest, and neither should we."

Cassielle swallowed her frustration. She wanted to go save Nick. She needed to clear Brittany's name. Buer was a problem, yes, but why did he have to be her problem? Heylel stepped closer, placing his hands on her shoulders and holding her at arm's length. She felt an uncomfortable fluttering in her stomach as he scrutinized her, his eyes intense and searching.

"You look so much like your mother," he murmured softly, a hint of nostalgia in his voice. He released her and turned to Nibo. "You have your instructions."

Nibo nodded solemnly. Without another word, Heylel vanished in the blink of an eye, leaving Cassie and Nibo alone in the dim light of the cemetery. Cassie stared at the spot where Heylel had stood, her mind racing with unspoken questions. She wasn't sure what she would have said if given the chance, but the moment had passed, leaving her with a lingering unease.

"Well, shall we?" Nibo offered her his hand. Cassielle wrapped her arms around herself as if she were able to hold herself together.

"Shall we what? Leave Nick to suffer in Limbo while I train to go after the Demons?" She pursed her lips and hugged herself tighter warding off the chill that the night seemed to be bringing.

"Not quite..." He looked around, "Just trust me, okay?" He gave her a small sly smile.

She took a deep breath before placing her hand in his. She was quickly overcome by that feeling of being sucked into the shadows. When she again felt solid ground under her feet she opened her eyes. Puzzled, Cassielle looked around herself. She could feel rain on her skin. It had started to rain wherever they were. She could smell the dampness and mildew, the solid concrete beneath her feet, and hear the sound of raindrops splashing against the stones. Her hair was quickly soaked with rainwater, her clothes becoming damp and clinging to her body. She looked around at the tombs surrounding her, the sporadic solar-powered lights casting haunting shadows.

Nibo produced a lantern, which ignited on its own, casting an ethereal glow. In the dim light, she observed the solemn tombs of the deceased surrounding them, with darkness enveloping the outskirts. In the darkness beyond the lantern's reach, the cemetery stretched into obscurity, its secrets hidden beneath layers of night. Yet intermittent light spots emerged, revealing solar-powered lamps scattered throughout the graveyard. Rather than dispelling the eeriness, these illuminations lent a spectral aura to the place, as if unseen spirits lingered just beyond the glow.

As raindrops cascaded upon her exposed skin, dampening her clothes and hair, Cassielle's breath mingled with the misty air, adding to the mystique of the cemetery. She couldn't help but feel a tingling on her skin, a palpable connection to the spirits that inhabited this hallowed ground. It was a place where history whispered in hushed tones, and the living trod softly, respectful of the dormant souls beneath the cold stone markers. Cassielle tightly wrapped her arms around herself.

She hadn't experienced the cold for long before she sensed someone standing behind her. She turned to see Samedi with an open umbrella and a dry coat. He handed them to her and then stepped to stand near Nibo, resting a hand upon the younger Loa's shoulder.

"Any trouble getting here?" Samedi asked, his deep voice resonating in the rain-soaked air.

"None at all," Nibo answered, a satisfied smile playing on his lips as he lit his cigar and took a long drag. "No one followed us, and no one seemed to notice."

He extended the cigar toward Cassielle, who shook her head, declining the offer. Zipping up the coat, she held the umbrella in one hand while the other found solace in the pocket.

"Can I now ask why we are here?" Cassielle asked..

Nibo paused for a moment, choosing his words carefully. "Well... we couldn't take you home," he began, his voice calm yet tinged with underlying concern. "And we aren't familiar with safe places in New Orleans to take you. We must be cautious since Buer and DeLuca know where you go. So, we needed a location to remain hidden, and you could be safe. And we needed to meet-up where the other Loa and Heylel wouldn't think to be."

Cassielle furrowed her brow, considering their predicament. "You're Loa, powerful beings with vast knowledge. Shouldn't you know safe places, secrets hidden from humans and be able to hide from each other in places other than cemeteries?"

"You'd think that, yes," Nibo shrugged. "But anyway, we are here because Samedi and I needed to swap places."

"You see," Samedi stepped closer to her, lifting her chin so that she was looking into his eyes, "I didn't want to entrust your safety to Nibo." He glanced over at the other Loa, who was now pretending to be interested in the fingernails of his right hand. "Not that I don't trust him, but... well, I..." He frowned. "It doesn't matter."

"Doesn't it?" Nibo asked, looking over at him sharply.

"I do trust you, Nibo," Samedi said softly. Nibo looked between Samedi and Cassielle. An expression crossed his face that Cassielle couldn't decipher in the dim light.

"I'm going to go do your job now, then, okay?" Nibo said lightly. "Unless you need or want me to stay?"

"You can go," Samedi nodded.

"Fabulous," with a step, Nibo was gone, leaving Cassielle and Samedi alone in the cemetery. Why did Cassielle's heart and body draw her towards him in such a betraying manner? She needed to rescue Nick. She needed to stop the demons. Yet right now, the only thought she had was of him. That magnet clinging to its mate.

Samedi's arms enveloped Cassielle, drawing her into a tight embrace. She melted against him, the warmth of his touch seeping into her skin, banishing the chill that had settled in her bones.

In the shelter of his embrace, Cassielle felt a sense of solace wash over her, a fleeting moment of respite amidst the turmoil that surrounded them. His closeness was both comforting and intoxicating, stirring a tumult of emotions within her.

She buried her face against his chest, breathing in the scent of him, a heady mixture of earthy musk and smoky incense that sent her senses reeling. With each beat of her heart, she felt the magnetic pull of his presence, drawing her ever closer.

Their bodies pressed together, igniting a spark of desire that crackled between them like electricity. In the soft embrace of the afternoon sunlight, their shared moment felt suspended in time, a stolen interlude in the midst of chaos.

Lost in the heat of the moment, Cassielle's fingers traced the contours of Samedi's back, feeling the firm muscles ripple beneath his clothes. Samedi's touch against her back sent waves of pleasure coursing through her veins, igniting a fire that blazed with a fierce intensity as his hands roamed over her back, tracing the curve of her spine with a tender reverence.

With a hunger born of longing, Samedi leaned his head down pressing his lips against hers, capturing them in a passionate kiss that stole her breath away. Their kiss was a symphony of desire, a melody of longing and yearning that echoed in the depths of her soul.

As their lips met in a fervent embrace, Cassielle felt herself falling deeper and deeper into the abyss of desire. With each caress, each unsaid word of longing, she felt herself losing herself in the intoxicating whirlwind of sensation.

With a sudden surge of passion, Samedi lifted Cassielle into his arms, carrying her with a strength that belied his ethereal form. He stepped into the shadows and emerged in a room she didn't recognize but vaguely resembled a hotel room, her arms and legs wrapped around him as he held her up, never breaking the kiss.

As they moved towards the bed, the world outside faded into obscurity, leaving only the two of them entwined in a dance of desire   . In the dim light, their love blazed like a beacon in the darkness, a testament to the bond that bound them together.

As they stood locked in each other's arms, Cassielle couldn't help but feel a flutter of anticipation, a longing that stirred deep within her soul. Samedi laid her on the bed, joining her, their connection deepening as they surrendered to the passion that consumed them.

CHAPTER TWENTY-EIGHT

Cassielle's eyes snapped open, the weight of realization settling heavily in her chest. The room was shrouded in darkness, the soft glow of moonlight casting long shadows across the floor. Beside her, Samedi lay in a state of quiet vigilance, his presence a comforting anchor in the night. The sight of him, even in the dim light, brought her a measure of peace, but it couldn't dispel the unease that gnawed at her.

As she lay there in the darkness, her mind raced with possibilities, going back to the room with Sabine after she'd removed the demon. What if the demon hadn't come alone? What if it had left behind a part of itself, a remnant of its dark energy that now lurked in the shadows, waiting to strike?

Her thoughts turned to Sabine, the unwitting host of their impromptu encounter with the forces of darkness. What if the lingering presence she felt wasn't confined to their circle but had taken root within Sabine herself? A cold dread settled in her stomach as she considered the implications.

"Cassielle?" Samedi sat up, his voice cutting through her spiraling thoughts. He looked down at her, his eyes filled with concern. "Everything okay?"

She took a moment to collect herself, to push aside the rising tide of panic. "Did you sense the lingering darkness after we banished Marbas?"

Samedi nodded, his expression grave. He waited for her to continue.

"Didn't you think it odd? I mean, usually when we get rid of the evil spirits, that feeling is just gone once they're gone." Her feet hit the floor as she slipped out of bed and began gathering her discarded clothing, needing something to do with her hands.

"This was an inhuman malevolent spirit, not an evil human soul. They're stronger," Samedi explained. In a blink, he vanished into the shadows, only to reappear in front of her, halting her as she pulled her shirt over her bra.

"I don't know... I have a feeling," Cassielle murmured, her voice trailing off. "She had this look of fear that didn't make sense. Wouldn't you feel relieved that a demon was removed? Why would you still be that afraid? Especially if you were in the presence of a Loa you trusted to protect you." She paused as Samedi cupped her chin in his hand, lifting her gaze to meet his. His touch was electric, setting her skin on fire.

"If she was involved in the ritual or has been influenced by one of the demons, we need to stop her," Samedi agreed, his tone firm but gentle. "That's what you think, right? That she was influenced?"

Cassielle's breath caught in her throat as Samedi drew nearer, his touch sending waves of heat coursing through her veins. The warmth of his skin against hers, his proximity, ignited a primal longing within her. It was hard to think with him touching her and being so close. With a hesitant sigh, she leaned into his embrace, her heart pounding in rhythm with the unspoken desire that pulsed between them.

"What do you want to do?" His voice, a husky whisper, sent another surge of heat through her as his hand slid to her lower back, drawing her closer still.

Cassielle's cheeks flushed crimson as she met Samedi's gaze, her breath hitching at the intensity in his eyes. "I'm not sure I could do that again right now," she admitted, her voice barely above a whisper. "Isn't three times enough for one night?"

Samedi's gaze intensified, his deep, dark eyes locking

onto hers with an intensity that sent shivers down her spine. "I could do that with you all day, every day, for the rest of eternity," he confessed, his voice a low, husky murmur, "and still want more." His words hung in the air, heavy with desire and a longing that echoed her own.

As she stood there, enveloped in the aftermath of their passionate encounters and the potential promise of another, Cassielle's mind drifted between conflicting emotions. She couldn't deny the intensity and bliss of her multiple rendezvous with Samedi, the way every touch and caress had ignited a fire within her. It had been a moment of respite, a release from the relentless stress and fear that had consumed her in recent days. It had felt like it went on for eternity yet was also done far too quickly.

Yet, beneath the surface of her euphoria, guilt gnawed at her conscience. Nick was in danger, held captive by forces beyond her understanding, and here she was, indulging in pleasure while he suffered. Brittany still hid at Alba's, worried that she would be arrested for a murder she didn't remember committing because she'd been possessed. Not that she knew that, of course. The weight of her responsibility pressed down on her, reminding her of the urgent need to keep moving forward.

Despite the guilt, Cassielle couldn't deny the truth of her feelings. Her encounter with Samedi had been more than just physical pleasure; it had been a connection unlike any she had ever experienced. But now, duty called, and she couldn't afford to let her personal desires overshadow her commitment to helping her friends.

Cassielle swallowed hard, forcing herself to extricate from his arms. The lingering warmth of his embrace left a tingling imprint on her skin. She took a deep breath, grounding herself in the urgency of their mission. "We have to stop DeLuca, and we have to capture Buer. I think Sabine knows more than she let on." Her voice was steady, but beneath it she could hear her anxiety poking through.

She resumed pulling her clothing on, her movements quick and efficient as she tried to avoid looking at Samedi's naked figure. The temptation was overwhelming, her more primal instincts threatening to take over. She focused on the task at hand, trying to suppress the desire that still simmered beneath the surface.

When she looked up at him again, he was fully dressed. He'd changed his look, and the transformation was striking. His attire exuded an air of dark mystique, befitting his role as a powerful Loa. He wore a tailored black suit adorned with intricate gold embroidery, each thread weaving a tale of ancient power and mystery. The lapels of his jacket were adorned with ornate skull motifs, a symbol of death and rebirth that echoed his divine nature.

Beneath the jacket, he wore a crisp white shirt, its collar open to reveal a hint of his muscled chest. Around his neck hung a string of dark beads, each bead imbued with spiritual significance, a testament to his connection to the spirit realm. His trousers were well tailored, falling in elegant lines to meet polished black shoes that gleamed in the dim light. Despite the formality of his attire, there was an undeniable aura of raw energy and primal force that surrounded him, a reminder of his divine nature and his dominion over life and death.

Cassielle glanced down at her casual attire, suddenly feeling a pang of self-consciousness. Her denim shorts and tee-shirt seemed woefully inadequate compared to Baron Samedi's suit. But this was what she had to work with, like it or not. She squared her shoulders, pushing aside the self-doubt.

"Before we confront Sabine, I want to make sure I'm right. I need a chance to look around her place." Cassielle grabbed her bag and slung it over her shoulder, the weight of it grounding her in reality.

Samedi's eyes sparkled with understanding and mischief as he extended his hand to her. "Say no more, Cherie," he winked. "Shall we?"

A smile tugged at her lips. Despite everything

happening around them, being with Samedi made her happy. She felt more comfortable and at ease with him than she ever had with anyone else. She could be herself, fully, without fear of hurting or scaring him. She didn't need to tread carefully around him; if she saw something, he did too.

Sure, it was strange to be involved with a deity older than time, but it had been exhilarating. The fun they had was undeniable, and she knew she would do it again in a heartbeat. The memory of their time together sent a warm flush through her, a secret thrill that bolstered her courage for what lay ahead.

"Let's go snooping." Cassielle smiled, taking his extended hand.

As they stepped into the shadows once more, a sense of familiarity washed over her. The inky darkness felt almost natural now, like a second skin. She barely had to think about it, her movements fluid and confident. The shadows swirled around them, cool and comforting, as she realized it wasn't just Samedi guiding her-it was her own powers, her own abilities, coming to life. She felt a surge of pride and strength, knowing she was no longer a passive participant but an active force.

The transition was seamless, and as they emerged from the shadows, the night air wrapped around them. Cassielle took a deep breath, her senses sharp and her mind clear. This time, she was ready for whatever awaited them.

The street was quiet, save for the symphony of nature. Crickets and cicadas created a rhythmic backdrop, their steady chorus filling the warm night air. The scent of magnolia and jasmine mingled, creating an intoxicating, heady atmosphere that enveloped the senses.

No cars drove down the empty streets, and the sidewalks were deserted-an unusual sight for summer nights when the temperatures were more tolerable and drinks flowed freely. But it was early in the morning. Most people would be home in bed, but the city seemed to lack the few that would have still been out. Cassielle was starting to notice a steady decline in the number of people out since the murders had started. No doubt, the city was worried. Rumors of cults and gangs had spread, causing people to avoid interacting with strangers, casting a pall of unease over the normally lively streets.

"I'll check to make sure she's asleep and stays asleep," Samedi said, his voice a low murmur.

Cassielle nodded as they stepped through the shadows. Emerging in Voodoo Authentica, she cast a quick glance around the store, her heart pounding in her chest. She hoped Samedi was upstairs, ensuring Sabine remained unconscious.

The store was eerily quiet, the darkness thick and oppressive. Cassielle moved cautiously across the floor, navigating the shadowy aisles toward the back. The space felt heavy, as if the air itself was thick with malevolence. She could sense the darkness lingering, a palpable presence that made her skin prickle. It was as if the building had absorbed years of hatred and malevolence, becoming a cesspool of dark energy.

Each step she took was deliberate, her breath shallow as she tried to make as little noise as possible. The old floorboards creaked beneath her weight, each sound echoing through the stillness like a gunshot. She winced with every creak, fearing it might awaken someone-or something-in the darkness.

Cassielle's mind raced, her thoughts a chaotic swirl of fear and exhilaration. She felt as though unseen eyes were watching her, the shadows themselves holding their breath. Every instinct screamed at her to turn back, but she forced herself to keep moving, her resolve steeled by the need to uncover the truth.

She reached the staircase and hesitated, her hand hovering over the banister. The steps loomed before her, dark and foreboding. She took a deep breath and began to ascend, each step a test of her nerve. The stairs groaned underfoot, the sound a haunting reminder of how vulnerable she was in this place.

As she climbed, she couldn't shake the feeling that something was lurking just out of sight, waiting for the right moment to strike. Her heart beat louder with each step, the oppressive atmosphere pressing down on her, making it difficult to breathe. She silently prayed that Samedi was keeping Sabine in a deep slumber, buying her the time she needed to uncover whatever dark secret lay hidden in Sabine's rooms.

She started in the ceremony room. Looking around, she saw a bookshelf along one wall. She used the flashlight from her phone to scan the titles. Most had nothing written on their spines. She pulled out a few and flipped through the pages. They appeared to be old journals. She didn't have time to go through all of them to see if there was anything useful in them.

She walked to the other side of the room to the table that held her Voodoo items. She reached for the peristyle and it was as if her hand had become one with it. Cassielle held the peristyle tightly, her knuckles white from the force of her grip that she was unable to let go. The room around her seemed to dissolve, replaced by a rapid, disorienting series of visions. It was as if she was watching Sabine's descent into darkness on fast forward.

In the vision, Sabine stood in a darkened room, her eyes gleaming with malevolent intent. She chanted fervently, invoking Met Kafou, the guardian of the crossroads. As her words echoed, the room filled with an eerie light, casting grotesque shadows that seemed to dance of their own accord. The air hummed with an oppressive energy, and Cassielle could almost feel the weight of the dark force pressing down on her.

Sabine's rituals grew more complex and dangerous. She inscribed intricate veves on the floor, the symbols glowing with a sinister light. Ceremonial items-rattles, knives, and amulets-were laid out with meticulous precision, each one charged with dark magic. Sabine's face twisted and manic, her eyes wide and unseeing, driven by an insatiable hunger.

Cassielle's heart pounded as she saw Buer, a terrifying presence lurking in the shadows. His form was monstrous, with the head of a lion and multiple legs, his eyes burning with a malevolent intelligence. He hovered near Sabine, whispering insidious thoughts into her ear, guiding her hand as she performed the rituals. Sabine seemed unaware of his influence, her focus entirely consumed by her ambition.

The scene shifted and she saw Alba and Sabine. They were sitting and Cassielle felt tears come to her eyes as she recognized her mother's ritual room. Sabine looked younger. She couldn't have been much older than Cassielle was now - roughly in her late 30s.

Cassielle watched in a trance as the scene unfolded before her. The air seemed to thicken with the weight of solemnity as Sabine and Alba commenced their ritual to invoke the loa Erzulie Danto. Each movement, each incantation, carried with it a sense of urgency and desperation, an unspoken plea for deliverance from the shackles of abuse.

It shifted again and her heart caught in her throat when she saw her mother. "Sabine, you must use caution," her mother's warm voice resonated in her mind. "Every request comes with a price. You don't get to choose the price."

Seraphina's words hung heavy in the air, a cautionary tale amidst the fervor of the ritual. Cassielle could see the concern etched in Seraphina's features, the furrow of her brow, the trembling of her hands as she clasped her tea cup.

"I understand, but she needs our help. If I do nothing, I worry she won't survive the abuse," Sabine's voice quivered with emotion, her eyes glistening with unshed tears.

"Alba is like a sister to me. I am worried about her, too. But this is not the way to free her. She needs to make the choice to leave," Seraphina's tone was gentle yet firm, her gaze unwavering.

"She has made that choice. Surely she's talked to you?" Sabine's voice was tinged with frustration, a hint of accusation in her words.

"Yes, she's spoken with me. I told her I would help her leave but she's convinced he won't leave her alone and the only way to make sure he goes away is to ask the Loa," Seraphina's voice was soft. "It's not the way to go about it, but as God gave us the freedom to make our own choices, I too must respect and accept the choices my loved ones make... it does not mean I have to agree with them."

The vision shifted seamlessly, transporting Cassielle to the heart of the ritual. Sabine and Alba were there again and stood side by side, their peristyles clutched tightly in their hands, their faces a mask of determination and resolve.

Cassielle felt a surge of apprehension as she watched the ritual unfold. The air crackled with energy, charged with the power of ancient forces. Symbols and sigils adorned the ground, drawn with painstaking precision, each one a conduit for the 's divine influence.

Sabine and Alba's voices rose in unison, their chants echoing through the night, a solemn invocation to the Erzulie Danto. The words seemed to hang in the air, shimmering with an otherworldly light, as if carrying the weight of centuries of tradition and belief.

As the ritual reached its climax, Cassielle felt a sense of foreboding wash over her. She could sense the presence of unseen forces, their eyes watching from the shadows, their whispers echoing in the darkness.

And then, as if in response to the summons, a figure materialized before them, bathed in a halo of ethereal light. It was Erzulie Danto herself, the of love and protection, her presence both awe-inspiring and terrifying in its intensity.

The 's voice reverberated through the night, her words a solemn promise and a dire warning. "I will grant your request, but know this: every boon comes with a price. You may seek freedom from your tormentor, but in exchange, a price will be paid. I cannot tell you what that price will be, but it may be dear to you."

Sabine and Alba exchanged a glance, their resolve unshaken. With a solemn nod, they accepted the 's terms, sealing their fate with a pact forged in blood and desperation.

And as the ritual drew to a close, Cassielle could feel the weight of their decision hanging heavy in the air, a silent reminder of the choices we make and the prices we pay.

The visions shifted and accelerated, showing Sabine summoning spirits and invoking powerful s, her voice rising in a fervent crescendo. Each ritual brought her closer to her goal, but also deeper into darkness. Cassielle could see the toll it was taking-Sabine's features grew gaunt, her skin pale and drawn. Her eyes, once filled with determination, now reflected a hollow madness.

Sabine's ultimate goal became clear-to become the next Voodoo Queen of New Orleans and, eventually, to extend her dominion over the world. Cassielle's breath caught in her throat as she saw glimpses of Buer, his form shifting and contorting, a dark presence influencing Sabine's every move. He was pushing her to open the gates, to unleash untold horrors upon the world. Cassielle could see the malevolent delight in his eyes as Sabine unknowingly played into his hands.

The vision shifted, transporting Cassielle to St. Louis Cemetery No. 1. The air felt humid and smelled of decaying flowers, mingling with the metallic tang of blood. Moonlight bathed the crumbling tombstones in an eerie glow, casting long, distorted shadows across the ground.

Sabine stood before the tomb of Queen Marie Laveau, the Voodoo Queen of New Orleans, her hands raised high as she chanted in a haunting, melodic tone. Her voice echoed through the graveyard, intertwining with the whispers of the spirits that lingered in the darkness. The tomb was adorned with offerings-candles, coins, and veves drawn in chalk-flickering and casting an unearthly light on Sabine's face.

Cassielle could see Jamal, his eyes wide with fear and determination, standing beside Sabine. He held a ceremonial knife in one hand and a bowl of blood in the other, as directed by Sabine. His hands shook as he traced the veves on the ground, the symbols glowing with an unnatural luminescence. The air crackled with energy, and Cassielle could feel the presence of the spirits growing stronger, drawn to the power of the ritual.

As Sabine's chants grew louder, the ground beneath the tomb began to tremble. Cracks appeared in the earth, and a swirling portal of chaotic energy started to form, its edges crackling with dark lightning. Cassielle's heart pounded in her chest as she watched in horror. The portal's vortex twisted and churned, a maelstrom of shadows and light, threatening to engulf everything in its path.

Buer's form materialized beside Sabine, his monstrous visage a grotesque mix of lion and man, his eyes burning with an insidious glee. He whispered into Sabine's ear, his voice a seductive hiss, urging her to continue. Sabine's face was a mask of frenzied devotion, her eyes glazed over as she surrendered herself entirely to the dark force guiding her.

Cassielle's pulse raced as she saw Buer's influence permeate the ritual. The symbols on the ground pulsed with a sickly green light, and the portal's energy grew more chaotic, more dangerous. The air was filled with a low, ominous hum, the sound of countless spirits stirring, ready to cross the threshold into the mortal realm.

Jamal's eyes held a silent plea for help in their depths. He was trapped, just as Sabine was, caught in the grip of a force far beyond his control. Cassielle's heart ached for him, for the danger he was in, and for the darkness that was about to be unleashed.

Buer's gaze shifted, locking onto Cassielle through the vision. A cruel smile spread across his face as he reached out, his clawed hand extending towards her. Cassielle felt a jolt of terror, the connection sending a freezing wave through her. She could feel his malevolent presence, cold and invasive, probing her mind.

With a gasp, Cassielle broke free from the vision's grip, stumbling backward. The room around her snapped back into focus, the oppressive darkness lifting slightly. Her heart raced as she struggled to regain her bearings, the remnants of the vision lingering in her mind.

She dropped the peristyle, her hands trembling. The weight of what she had seen pressed heavily on her. Sabine was falling deeper into darkness, her ambition blinding her to the malevolent force guiding her. Cassielle knew she had to act quickly, but the terror of Buer's gaze still lingered, a stark reminder of the danger they all faced.

Her resolve hardened. She had to stop Sabine, save Jamal and Nick, and send Buer back to hell. The fate of their world depended on it.

CHAPTER TWENTY-NINE

Samedi murmured behind Cassielle as she hammered on Lafitte's door. It was nearly 3 am, but her need for answers couldn't wait.

"Perhaps there are more urgent matters at hand," he suggested, his presence looming over her shoulder. Cassielle paused and shot him a pointed glance.

"Having sex with you wasn't exactly pressing either, but you didn't seem to mind," she retorted, her knuckles striking the door with renewed urgency.

"Who's makin' all dis noise?" Alba appeared in the doorway adorned in her floral nightgown and silk nightcap. She stood barefoot, pulling on a robe. "It's a wonder ya ain't waking the dead!"

"I'm sorry for the noise, but we need to talk," Cassielle said, brushing past her into the bar. Samedi followed, shrugging sheepishly.

"And it couldn't wait three more hours 'til my morning walk?" Alba closed and locked the door, folding her arms over her chest. Cassielle paced, trying to find the right words. Finally, she opted for bluntness.

"Did you and Sabine conduct a ritual to get rid of your ex-husband against my mother's advice?" Cassielle faced Alba, whose face paled in the dim light. "Please, tell me the truth."

Samedi took a seat at the bar, watching as Cassielle struggled to control her emotions. She teetered between wanting to yell and cry.

"What's going on down here?" Brittany's voice cut through the tension as she appeared in the stairwell doorway. Cassielle had forgotten Brittany was staying with Alba. Clad in a pink robe, Brittany looked at Cassielle and Samedi, then turned to Alba. "Who's he?" Concern etched her features as she looked back at Cassielle. "Cassielle, what's wrong?"

Ignoring Brittany's questions, Cassielle pressed on. "What was the price you paid to free yourself of him? He died a year before my mother, yes?" Alba nodded, momentarily mute.

"Yes," Alba began slowly, pulling a chair from a table and sitting on it. "Sabine helped me with a ritual to free myself from him. He was controlling and violent. I couldn't escape him - this bar was all I had and he knew it." Her eyes welled up. "If I went through a divorce, he woulda burried me in legal fees and mashed up my business. LaFitte's been in my family for generations. He told me he'd make sure I had no life if I left him." She shook her head. "I know it sounds dumb, but I believed him. I didn't know if he woulda killed me or Jamal, or burned this place down with us inside. I shoulda listen to your mother, but I was scared, and Sabine told me everything would be okay."

Cassielle's suspicion gnawed at her. "But what about my mother? What happened to her?"

Alba's face crumpled with guilt. "Before yuh mother pass, I had a dream. It was so vivid I remember it like it was yesterday," she said, her voice breaking. "In the dream, Erzulie Danto appear to me. She was furious, saying the balance been disturbed. She warned that a price must be paid for meddling with the dark forces."

She paused, tears streaming down her face. "I dismiss it at first, thinking it was just my fear tricking me. But Sabine and I completed the ritual, and a week later, Seraphina died. I felt like it was connected. Then, Sabine said there was a message in one of her visions-it said the debt had been paid. I knew it was my fault. Our plea for help cost Seraphina her life."

Cassielle felt a cold chill through her body. "You're saying the Loa took my mother as payment for freeing you from him?"

Alba nodded, sobbing. "Yes. I shoulda listened to Seraphina's warning. I was desperate, and now the guilt is unbearable. I never meant for this to happen."

Cassielle's heart ached with a mix of anger and sorrow. The pieces were finally falling into place, and the truth was more painful than she could have imagined. With a deep horror she turned to face Samedi. If this was true... no, she couldn't think that through. She just couldn't. "Did you know?"

Samedi's expression grew somber, his usual playful demeanor replaced with a grave seriousness. "Yes, I knew," he admitted quietly. "Your mother's death was a debt paid, but I had no control over it. It wasn't my bargain to make-and had it been, I would never have made it."

Cassielle's eyes widened. "Then who was behind it? Was it Erzulie Danto?"

Her mind flashed to the image of Erzulie Danto from her mother's old book. The Loa was fierce, holding a knife with an intense expression, embodying both protection and vengeance.

Samedi shook his head. "No, it wasn't Erzulie. Though the malevolent spirits are locked away, some can perform rituals to open small gateways, just enough for them to act. Many humans are tricked into thinking their prayers are being answered by the Loa, but we do not take lives. Those dark entities manipulate and deceive, leading people to believe they're making deals with the Loa when they're not."

Alba, still trembling, looked up. "So it was a bad spirit who answer our plea?"

Samedi nodded. "Yes. They exploit desperation and fear, disguising themselves as benevolent spirits to fulfill their own sinister purposes. They take advantage of those who are vulnerable, promising solutions but exacting terrible costs."

Cassielle clenched her fists, trying to steady herself. "So

my mother died because of a trick, a deception by demons?" For some reason, she found it hard to believe. Her mother had been shot in a bodega. It wasn't a malevolent spirit. It couldn't have been.

"Yes," Samedi confirmed, his voice filled with regret. "The balance was disturbed by Alba's plea, and the malevolent spirits took advantage. They influenced someone else to commit the murder. Unlike now, where they're free to do as they please. In limbo they are somewhat limited in their actions. They need people to unwittingly open doors." Samedi shifted on his stool. "But know this: had it been in my power, I would have protected Seraphina. We all would have. She was devoted and loving, embodying all that is good in this world." He looked at Alba. "While I understand your desire to free yourself, you were foolish. Seraphina was right - God does not interfere, and you should not seek out God or the spirits to change your life. You should do what you can, what is within your power." He leaned forward on his staff. "What is done is done, and you cannot change the past. But you should have told Cassielle sooner."

Cassielle studied a spot on the floor, gathering her thoughts. She remembered the night her mother died as if it were yesterday. She was having a sleepover at Alba's with Jamal. They'd rented several horror films around Fete Gede - Halloween. Determined to terrify themselves, they wanted to prove how 'cool' they were as teenagers. The whole night, she felt a dread she couldn't shake. She kept telling herself it was just nerves about the movies, even though she wasn't usually afraid of them. They were set up in Alba's living room, the air-conditioner humming away as it battled the heat. She'd fallen asleep at some point, and when she woke, the room was dark - the TV had turned off, and Jamal was sleeping on the floor next to her. She saw her mother sitting beside her. She later convincing herself it was a dream.

"Do not harbor anger in your heart, Cassielle," her mother said, reaching out and stroking black tendrils of hair out of Cassielle's face. "They knew not what they did. I am safe and at peace, and so you will be, too. I love you." She didn't remember anything else after that. The following day, the police came and delivered the news that destroyed Cassielle's world. Her mother was in a coma. Cassielle watched her die in the hospital.

She'd spent years returning to that bodega, replaying her mother's final moments over and over, trying to understand why. Now, her anger towards those spirits was fiercer than ever. She had wanted revenge on the person who had killed her mother. That revenge would now be exacted on the demons. But could she ever forgive Alba for making such a grave mistake that had cost her so much?

Alba sat crying softly, with Brittany beside her, offering comfort. Brittany glanced at Samedi, her voice trembling. "Is there any way to stop them? To prevent others from being tricked like this?"

Samedi's gaze was stern. "Yes, there is. Knowledge and vigilance are our best defenses. We need to educate others about the true nature of the Loa and the dangers of rituals they don't fully understand. Together, we can close these gateways and protect those seeking help."

Alba, tears streaming down her face, whispered, "I'm so sorry, Cassielle. If I had known..."

Cassielle shook her head, tears streaming down her cheeks. "But you did know. You understood the risks of turning to Voodoo for something like this. Did you even consult Papa Legba first? My mother always said he should be your first stop. That might have prevented this, and you know it." She wiped angrily at her tears. "You should have listened to my mother."

Alba's shoulders shook as she sobbed. Brittany glanced between Alba and Cassielle, clearly unsure of what to do. "Cass, I know you're upset..." Cassielle narrowed her eyes at her, making her fall silent.

Samedi cleared his throat and placed a reassuring hand on Alba's shoulder. "We can't change the past. But we can fight for the future. We need to ensure no one else suffers like this."

Samedi fixed Cassielle with a steady look, and she let out a resigned sigh. She didn't need to forgive Alba right now; they needed to focus on moving forward.

After a few minutes of heavy silence, they headed up to Alba's apartment. Their footsteps echoed faintly in the stairwell, each lost in their own thoughts. Alba took charge in the kitchen, the scent of pancake batter mingling with the aroma of brewing coffee, while Brittany expertly navigated the countertops, preparing the morning brew.

Alba's apartment exuded a sense of familiarity mixed with the passage of time. It offered a touch more space than Cassielle's, with two separate bedrooms branching off from the cozy living area and compact kitchenette. During her teenage years, Cassielle and Alba had shared one of the rooms, while Jamal had squeezed into the other, barely larger than a walk-in closet. The trio had felt cramped in those early months following her mother's passing.

The kitchenette, adorned in a cheerful yellow hue, boasted white lace curtains that had filtered the morning light through the dormer windows those years she lived there. The kitchen island, adorned with a mismatched set of stools, stood as a central hub for their shared meals. From the sink beneath the window, one could steal glances at the bustling street below, a silent observer of the outside world.

In the living area, an eclectic mix of furnishings painted a portrait of their shared history. An old floral couch, its fabric worn but comforting, sat opposite an antique coffee table that bore the scars of time. A well-loved brown corduroy recliner occupied a corner, its cushions worn with use. Against one wall, a dresser-turned-TV-stand proudly displayed Alba's modest flat-screen TV, a token of affection from Cassielle and Jamal.

As Brittany settled onto a stool next to Cassielle, her gaze shifted toward Samedi, who leaned casually against the wall, his fingers idly twirling his walking stick. Cassielle hesitated, casting a subtle glance in his direction before addressing Brittany's unspoken question.

"His name is Samuel Baron," she began, her voice steady as she observed Samedi's reaction. He ceased his twirling, his gaze fixating on Brittany with a piercing intensity.

"I sought Cassielle out when I noticed the strange murders," Samedi interjected, his voice carrying an undertone of urgency. "I'm glad we have met because I wanted to assure you there was a reason why you couldn't remember what happened the night your boyfriend died."

Cassielle subtly shook her head behind Brittany's back. Samedi paused before continuing, "I've been looking into it. You and the others who have been losing time during these murders may have been drugged so as to not remember what you saw."

Cassielle breathed out a sigh, silently grateful that Samedi refrained from divulging the full truth. She knew Brittany would struggle more with the idea of possession than with the notion of an external assailant.

"If that's the case, wouldn't it have shown up in a toxicology screening?" Brittany's arms folded defensively across her chest as she scrutinized Samedi, her expression a mix of skepticism and apprehension.

He hesitated, momentarily at a loss for words. "That report might not be back yet," he finally admitted, his gaze shifting to Cassielle before he pushed away from the wall. "I'll be right back."

With purposeful strides, Samedi exited the apartment, leaving Cassielle, Alba, and Brittany in a tense silence. The door clicked shut behind him, the faint sound punctuating the gravity of the moment.

"No offense," Brittany spoke up, turning her attention to Cassielle, "but he creeps me out."

Cassielle furrowed her brow, her thoughts momentarily consumed by Brittany's candid remark. "Why?"

"You don't find it creepy that he dresses up like Baron

Samedi?" Brittany shook her head incredulously. "Please tell me he isn't going to be your rebound."

"He's not my rebound," Cassielle asserted firmly, suppressing the memory of her recent encounter with Samedi.

"I'm hoping he's more than a rebound," Alba interjected, diverting the conversation as she set plates of pancakes, eggs, and bacon before them. "He's a charmer."

Cassielle's phone abruptly shattered the lingering silence, its ringtone jarring in the tranquil atmosphere. Startled, she retrieved the device from her pocket, her surprise deepening as she saw Marcus Fontenot's name displayed on the screen. She almost forgot he was still a contact.

With a mixture of apprehension and curiosity, Cassielle answered the call, her heart quickening with each passing moment as Fontenot's strained voice echoed through the receiver.

"Fontenot? Is everything okay?" she inquired, her gaze flickering between the phone and Brittany, who watched her with a mixture of concern and curiosity.

"Have you heard from Nick?" Fontenot's urgency was palpable, his tone tinged with desperation. Cassielle hesitated, grappling with the weight of his words.

"I have, but he didn't sound like himself," she replied cautiously, offering a half-truth to mask her own uncertainty.

"Did he say where he was? Rebecca wouldn't tell me the full story, but did say that he didn't come home. We got a call to another crime scene, and he's not answering dispatch or the captain. It's not like him," Fontenot explained, his voice laden with worry.

Cassielle's pulse quickened at the mention of Nick's disappearance, her mind racing to figure out what to tell him.

"How fast can you get here?" Fontenot's question hung in the air, punctuated by a heavy silence as Cassielle grappled with the implications of his request.

"What?" she stammered, her thoughts spinning as she tried to process the urgency of Fontenot's plea.

As Samedi re-entered the apartment, Cassielle's gaze darted towards the door, her curiosity piqued. His expression was inscrutable, his features masked in an enigmatic veil. She couldn't decipher the purpose of his brief absence. With a furrowed brow, she tore her gaze away from Samedi, returning her attention to the phone call, her mind buzzing.

"We're stuck with these murders, and you were the best detective we had," Fontenot continued, his voice growing more urgent with each passing moment. "No suspects blacked out this time. The room was locked from the inside, windows closed and locked. It's a classic locked room mystery. The captain agreed to bring you in-just don't mention the vanishing from the interrogation room. That shook us, so we kept it quiet."

Brittany leaned closer, her voice lowered to a whisper as she sought answers amidst the mounting tension. "What's going on?" she inquired, her fork still suspended mid-air.

Cassielle held up a finger, signaling for a moment of reprieve as she grappled with the weight of Fontenot's request. With trembling hands, she raised the phone to her ear once more.

"I can come now, where are you?" she managed to respond. He told her and she agreed before hanging up, her fingers trembling as she stared at the screen.

"What is it, cherie?" Alba's voice broke through her thoughts, concern etched on her face. Cassielle realized everyone in the room had been watching her intently, hanging on her every word during the conversation.

"There was a murder at Voodoo Authentica," Samedi's voice cut through the tense silence. Cassielle turned towards him, eyebrows furrowing in surprise.

"How did you know?" she asked, her voice tinged with disbelief.

"Sabine is dead," Samedi sighed heavily.

CHAPTER THIRTY

Cassielle paced Alba's apartment, chewing on her lip. "We need to find Nick," she insisted. "But Sabine has been murdered, and we need to find out who killed her."

Samedi intercepted her path, his presence commanding attention. "We know who killed her," he stated firmly, his gaze locking with Cassielle's. "It was Buer."

The name hung in the air, a heavy silence settling over the room. Brittany's brows furrowed as she glanced between Cassielle and Samedi, confusion etched into her features. "Who's Buer?" she asked, her voice tinged with apprehension.

Alba's voice trembled with uncertainty. "You mean the demon?" she questioned, her eyes wide with disbelief. "Is he who... who-"

Cassielle cut through the uncertainty with a soft but resolute tone. "We don't know for sure that he's the one who tricked you and Sabine," she explained, her words measured. "But, we suspect that he's behind a good portion of this."

Brittany's disbelief morphed into incredulity as she shook her head in denial. "You're joking?" she exclaimed, her eyes wide with disbelief. "You're saying you think demons are real? I mean, I was willing to accept that y'all think Voodoo had something to do with your mom's dying - everyone needs a reason behind stuff. But this stuff isn't real." She furrowed her brow, "I'm especially surprised you're suggesting this, Cass."

She rose from her seat, her movements filled with disbelief. "I refuse to believe this. I'll accept that someone drugged me somehow to black out during Michael's murder, but to say that demons and Voodoo are behind all this? That's ridiculous."

Cassielle met her gaze squarely, her expression unwavering. "I didn't say Voodoo was behind this," she clarified, her voice calm yet firm. "Voodoo is a peaceful religion. It doesn't condone murder and certainly doesn't encourage its followers to summon demons."

Samedi stepped forward, his demeanor grave. "Cassielle is right," he affirmed, adjusting his hat with a solemn gesture. "This is caused by people engaging in evil rituals that lead to connecting with demons and death. It has nothing to do with any religion."

He turned to Cassielle, his brows knit with concern, a flicker of urgency in his eyes. "I think it might be a good idea to make protection amulets for Brittany and Alba as well, Cassielle," he suggested, his tone carrying a weight of seriousness. "I wouldn't put it past Buer to go after everyone you care about. If he killed Sabine, then he knows how close you are getting to finding him."

"I have some Gris-Gris we could use?" Alba offered.

"No, we need amulets specifically made to protect you all from this. Gris-Gris are not powerful enough for this," Samedi looked between Cassielle and Alba. "I think–"

Just then, the shrill alert tones of Cassielle, Brittany, and Alba's phones pierced the air, a collective jolt of tension filling the room. Emergency warnings flashed on their screens, urging people to seek shelter and report any information about an active shooter or shooters in the French Quarter. Cassielle and Samedi exchanged a meaningful glance, a silent understanding passing between them.

Brittany's body slumped onto the couch, her eyes glued to the screen of her phone as if searching for answers within its glowing interface. A flicker of unease danced across her features, her gaze darting towards the entrance and windows of the apartment.

With a sudden surge, she sprang into action, her movements quick and purposeful. Rushing to the door, she fumbled with the lock, ensuring it was securely bolted shut. Her fingers then grasped the curtains, drawing them closed with a swift tug, shrouding the room in a veil of darkness.

Each action carried a sense of urgency, a silent testament to the gravity of the situation unfolding outside their sanctuary. As the curtains fell into place, Brittany's posture relaxed marginally, though the tension lingered in the air, palpable and unyielding.

Cassielle turned to Alba. "Do you have a peristyle I can borrow?" she asked, her voice steady.

Alba nodded, as she led Cassielle into the small room that had once belonged to Jamal. Transformed into a place of worship and meditation, it was adorned with various Voodoo artifacts and symbols, each holding a significance in their spiritual practices.

Cassielle wasted no time, her hands moving deftly as Alba guided her through the steps, their shared knowledge and memories serving as a guiding light in the dimly lit space. With each movement, she recalled the teachings of Sabine and her mother, her fingers tracing the intricate patterns etched into the black stones.

Finally, she held up two amulets, their dark surfaces gleaming in the dim light of the room. The intricate white designs adorned them, resembling a heart, each symbol and line bearing a significance known only to those initiated into their tradition.

Brittany's hand reached out, her fingers brushing against the warm surface of the amulet. With a sense of solemnity, she accepted it, draping the chain over her head and letting it rest against her chest. Alba followed suit, the weight of the amulet settling against her skin with a comforting familiarity.

Samedi looked at Alba and Brittany. He spoke with a tone that brooked no argument. "Stay here. Don't let anyone in, even if you know who they are. Do you understand me?" They nodded. Cassielle noted the fear in Brittany's eyes.

Cassielle gently pulled Brittany aside, her expression serious as she sought to convey the gravity of the situation. "I know you don't believe in this demon stuff," she began. "I know it all sounds crazy, and I get it. But you can't ignore how messed up things have become. It's not just about the shooters anymore. It's bigger than that."

She paused, her gaze searching Brittany's eyes for any flicker of understanding. "There have been too many murders, Brittany. Too many lives lost in such a short span of time. And it's not just random violence. A nun? Michael? It's insane," she continued, her voice barely above a whisper. "You've seen the news. You know what's been happening."

Brittany nodded slowly, her expression conflicted. Doubt lingered in her eyes, but beneath it lay an undeniable weight of unease. The darkness of the situation weighed heavily on her, casting a shadow over her skepticism. She wanted to dismiss Cassielle's words, to rationalize away the inexplicable, but the evidence of their reality was undeniable.

And then, unexpectedly, Brittany spoke, her voice trembling with emotion. "I wasn't drugged, was I?" she whispered, a single tear tracing its path down her cheek.

Cassielle's heart broke at the sound of Brittany's sob, her resolve hardening as she pulled her friend into a tight embrace. In that moment, she realized just how much she needed Brittany, the thought of anything bad happening to her was unbearable.

As they held each other, Cassielle's mind raced with a flurry of thoughts and emotions. She remembered the fear and uncertainty that had driven her to push Brittany away before, afraid that the darkness within her would somehow harm her friend. But now, she was feeling more in control. She wasn't like the demons and evil souls because she did still feel bad for those who were harmed. It was the energy that pulled her in. Not that she enjoyed what she saw. She didn't want to create that. In this moment of vulnerability and doubt, she understood that she couldn't face this alone.

With Brittany in her arms, Cassielle felt a sense of clarity wash over her. She had been wrong to shut her friend out, to deny herself the comfort and solace that Brittany offered. She had felt out of control, consumed by the darkness that lurked within her, but now she knew that she could control it, that she could harness its power for good.

And as she held Brittany close, Cassielle made a silent vow to never push her away again, to always stand by her side no matter what darkness may come.

Cassielle felt a surge of apprehension, her heart pounding in her chest as she contemplated leaving the safety of the apartment. The air seemed charged with uncertainty, a foreboding sense of danger looming on the horizon.

Samedi turned to Alba and Brittany, his voice steady as he explained the veves that needed to be drawn around the doors and windows to ensure Lafitte's protection. With a nod of understanding, they set about their task, their movements swift and purposeful.

As Cassielle and Samedi stepped through the front door, a chill settled over her, the darkness of the city enveloping them like a suffocating shroud. The air seemed to hum with an ominous energy, each step forward fraught with a sense of impending doom. Through the window, Cassielle watched as Alba hurried to draw the veves, a silent guardian against the encroaching darkness that threatened to consume them all.

"We should walk," Samedi suggested, his voice carrying a note of determination. His gaze met Cassielle's, a silent acknowledgment passing between them.

Cassie took a deep breath, the weight of their mission settling over her like a heavy shroud. With a nod, she reached out and clasped Samedi's hand in hers, the contact grounding her in the midst of uncertainty.

With each step they took through the dimly lit streets of the French Quarter, Cassielle's sense of urgency grew, her heart pounding with every footfall. She knew she needed to call Fontenot, to get a grasp on the situation unfolding at the crime scene before they arrived. Pulling out her phone, she dialed his number, her fingers trembling with anticipation.

As the line rang, each tone seemed to stretch on endlessly, amplifying her anxiety. Finally, Fontenot answered, but before she could even utter a word, the cacophony of gunfire erupted from the other end of the line. The sound froze her in her tracks.

"Now's not a good time," Fontenot's voice crackled over the line, strained and filled with tension. The chaos of the situation was palpable, even through the phone. "We're dealing with an unknown number of people shooting at us. Jesus fucking Christ!"

Cassielle's heart clenched at the desperation in Fontenot's voice, the gravity of the situation hitting her like a ton of bricks. She could hear the chaos unfolding in the background, the frantic shouts and bursts of gunfire echoing through the phone. She should have predicted this. Many in the south loved their guns and how many of those may be dealing with stuff that might make them susceptible to possession?

A surge of adrenaline coursed through her veins, driving her forward. She knew they were walking into a dangerous situation, but she also knew they had to press on. With a steely resolve, Cassielle pocketed her phone, her jaw set in determination as she forged ahead, her mind focused on the task at hand.

Samedi stopped her and pulled her into an alley.

"Hold on one second," Samedi pushed back a strand of her hair before looking down the alley. "Nibo, you can come out."

Nibo stepped out of the shadows, his gaze meeting hers with an intensity that made her heart skip a beat. His features were shrouded in shadow, his form draped in a long, flowing trench coat that billowed around him like a cloak of darkness.

"Cassielle," he remarked, his smooth and melodic voice

tinged with amusement. "Absence truly makes the heart grow fonder!"

"We don't have time for idle chit chat, Nibo. Are the others heading to Voodoo Authentica?" Samedi kept looking around as they talked. Cassielle felt as if her heart might burst from her chest.

In stark contrast to the darkness enveloping the day, Nibo sported a flamboyant white button-up blouse, its billowy fabric left deliberately unfastened, teasing at the sculpted contours of his chest beneath. With each graceful movement, the fabric swirled and fluttered, imbuing his presence with an aura of whimsicality and theatrics.

As he spoke, his voice carried a melodic cadence, tinged with a hint of amusement. "Yes, they are. However, I don't think Heylel will be pleased should he learn that you had me take over your duties so you could stay with her," he remarked, his tone laced with humor. "Although I really can't blame you. A woman as captivating as she should be kept close lest someone else sweep her off her feet."

Samedi stared at him, his face dark and imposing. Sensing the tension, Nibo quickly amended his statement. "Sorry, yes and no. It would appear that whoever is coordinating the human spirits has spread them out, so we're kind of scrambling right now."

His expression turned grave as he continued, furrowing his brow in concern. "Heylel has been busy trying to track down the inhuman spirits," he glanced at Cassielle, "The demons. There are too many out right now. He'd like to avoid reaching out to Bondye, but, you know, if things get much worse, Bondye's going to be angry. Is Cassielle ready to go after them? She took out one already."

Samedi's gaze shifted to Cassielle beside him. "One at a time for now," he replied, his voice measured. "Her power is still growing."

Her mind hummed with questions, each word spoken by Samedi echoing in her thoughts like an elusive melody.

Growing? The concept reverberated within her consciousness, stirring a potent mixture of curiosity and apprehension. Had she not reached the zenith of her abilities? Was there still untapped potential waiting to be unleashed?

With a shake of her head, she refocused her attention on the matter at hand. "We don't have time to waste. Samedi, are we certain that Sabine's death was orchestrated by Buer? If so, there's little use in venturing there. Send out some of the Loa to reclaim the human spirits causing trouble, while we prioritize locating Nick. We have to save him from Vittorio DeLuca's clutches before confronting Buer. We've let it go for far too long already."

Surveying the darkness shrouding their surroundings, Cassielle's unease intensified, the feeble glow of the streetlights struggling to ward off the encroaching shadows. Day had turned to night as if the evil itself had sucked all the light out of the city.

Anxiety gnawed at her nerves, urging her to get out of the open. "We can't stay here," she urged, a note of urgency tainting her words. "You two may be impervious to harm, but I, on the other hand, am not keen on becoming a target for stray bullets."

"Nick isn't our primary concern at this moment," he stated, his voice carrying the weight of urgency. Samedi raised his hand to halt Cassielle's protest, his expression firm with resolve.

Cassielle shook her head adamantly, ignoring his attempt to interject. "No, Samedi. Buer murdered Sabine. What's to stop him from harming Nick?" Her voice was edged with desperation. "Nick has been possessed for far too long. I refuse to believe it's too late to get him back into his body. Nibo mentioned that his spirit could be found..."

"By keeping Nick under his influence, Buer knows you'll go to great lengths to ensure his safety," Nibo interjected softly, his words somber. In the dim light, Cassielle saw a flicker of sympathy in Nibo's eyes, a stark contrast to Samedi's simmering fury.

"Nibo mentioned what?" Cassielle bit her lip, realizing she had let something slip. Nibo visibly cringed under Samedi's gaze.

"I should go," Nibo muttered, turning to step into the shadows. Samedi was quicker, grabbing him by the lapel and spinning him around.

"You told her, what, exactly?" Samedi snarled, lifting Nibo off the ground by his lapels, their faces inches apart.

Nibo's eyes widened in panic. "I merely explained that she could go to Limbo to get his spirit back," he stammered. "So, not as much hurry, though some hurry as he could lose his sanity there."

"Whatever we do, we can't stay here." Cassielle stepped forward, placing a hand on Samedi's arm. The tension in the alley could be cut with a knife, and she could feel her heartbeat thundering in her ears. Samedi released Nibo, who stumbled backward, catching his balance after a few unsteady steps. "If there are people out there with guns, we're sitting ducks standing here," she added, glancing around.

Samedi's eyes narrowed as he scanned the surroundings. "I'll handle the spirits harassing the police," he declared, his voice sharp and decisive. Before Cassielle could argue, he vanished into the shadows, his presence lingering only as a faint echo.

Nibo met her gaze, extending his arm in a gesture of polite invitation. "Shall we proceed with your training then?" he proposed, a hint of amusement dancing in his eyes as he offered her a charming smile. But Cassielle was in no mood for pleasantries.

"No, I'm finding Nick," she declared, creeping toward the alley's exit, every sense on high alert. Peering around the corner, she was met with an eerie stillness that made the hairs on the back of her neck stand on end. "You told me I could go into Limbo and that is what I will do. If I can fetch Nick, I can force Vittorio DeLuca out of his body and shove Nick back in, then I will give him one of the protection amulets to keep him safe." She turned to face Nibo, "You can either help me, or watch me get harmed when I fail to do it properly. Wouldn't it be better that I get in and get Nick safely than kill myself in the process of trying to go to Limbo?"

Nibo frowned at her, "You know, if I didn't know any better, I'd think you were trying to get me in trouble." He sighed, "but I agree with you. I think our best bet of saving your friend is getting him from Limbo and then we will defeat Buer and the rest of those damned, pardon my language, annoying demons." He smiled. "I suppose it's time I teach you how to cross over to the underworld."

CHAPTER THIRTY-ONE

The air in the bayou was thick with putrid humidity, clinging to her skin and making every breath feel labored. There was nothing worse than the humidity that followed a storm, but she needed to train, and this was the only place she was guaranteed not to be disturbed. Her phone lay abandoned in her bag, and she reclined on a red and white checkered blanket in a small clearing. With her eyes closed and hands folded on her stomach, she tried to focus.

"Now you're going to use visualization like you did before with shadow walking. This time, only your spirit will travel," Nibo instructed. He sat cross-legged beside her, his voice a steady anchor in the oppressive heat. "You have to spirit walk to get to Limbo."

Cassielle took slow, deep breaths, feeling her hands rise and fall with each inhale and exhale. She pushed all other thoughts from her mind, but worry for Nick kept creeping back in. A trickle of sweat ran down her temple, grounding her momentarily before she refocused on her breathing.

The sounds of the bayou surrounded her: the distant croak of frogs, the rustle of leaves as a light breeze stirred the air, and the occasional splash of something unseen in the water. She imagined her spirit drifting away from her body, rising above the blanket, above the humid, suffocating air.

Nibo's voice continued to guide her, low and rhythmic. "Visualize your spirit lifting, like a feather caught in an updraft. Feel the separation, but keep your connection strong. You are in control."

Her breathing steadied, her hands moving more rhythmically on her stomach. She pictured a thread of light connecting her spirit to her body, a lifeline ensuring her return. The world blurred around the edges as she focused inward, the noises of the bayou fading into the background.

But then, a flash of Nick's concerned face intruded, her concentration wavered, the connection flickering. She squeezed her eyes tighter, willing the image away, striving for the peace she needed to succeed.

Nibo noticed her struggle. "Let the thoughts come, acknowledge them, and then let them go. Don't fight them. They have no power unless you give it to them."

Cassielle exhaled slowly, releasing the tension in her shoulders. She acknowledged the worry for Nick and the uncertainty gnawing at her, then gently set it aside. The fear of the possessed people with guns in New Orleans crossed her thoughts. She acknowledged and pushed it away. Her spirit felt lighter, the separation more pronounced.

The bayou's dense air seemed to thin as she drifted, her spirit floating higher, guided by Nibo's calm, steady instructions. She felt the pull of the earth lessen, the freedom of her spirit exhilarating and terrifying all at once.

"You're doing well," Nibo's voice came through, clear and encouraging. "Just a little further now. Trust in yourself."

Cassielle's spirit soared, and for the first time, she felt peace amidst the humid chaos of the bayou. She was learning to let go, to trust in her abilities, and to navigate her complex emotions. She opened her eyes and saw her body beneath her. She was near the tops of the trees. If she went a little higher she might be able to see the city in the distance.

"Okay, now bring yourself back down," Nibo guided. Cassielle spotted something beyond the tree tops. Smoke was rising into the sky. Nibo's voice took on an edge of urgency. "Cassielle, focus. You need to come back now."

But Cassielle's spirit was drawn toward the smoke, an unseen force pulling her away from the safety of her body and Nibo's guidance. The smoke curled and twisted, an ethereal beacon beckoning her closer. She felt a compulsion to investigate, to see what lay beyond the trees.

"Cassielle, listen to me. You're drifting too far. You need to return now," Nibo commanded, his voice sharper, cutting through the trance-like state.

But the pull was too strong. Cassielle's spirit floated higher, the smoke becoming more distinct, forming shapes that danced and flickered with a life of their own. The faint glow of flames became visible, licking at the edges of her awareness. She could almost feel the heat, a distant warmth against her insubstantial form.

Panic set in as she realized she was losing control. "Nibo, I can't... it's pulling me."

Nibo's presence intensified, a grounding force against the invisible tether. "Cassielle, you must fight it. You're in control. Visualize your thread, your connection to your body. Strengthen it."

She tried to follow his instructions, but the fire's allure was overwhelming. It whispered promises and secrets, its crackling voice a siren call in the quiet of the bayou. Cassielle's spirit wavered, caught between the need to obey Nibo and the urge to succumb to the fire's enticement.

Nibo's voice grew louder, more insistent. "Cassielle, you must return. Now!"

Desperation tinged his words, and Cassielle felt a sudden, forceful tug. Nibo was trying to pull her back, but her spirit resisted, caught in the fiery attraction. The smoke was closer now, the flames vivid and consuming, almost within reach.

"Nibo, help!" Her cry was more a thought than a sound, but Nibo responded immediately. She felt his energy surge, a powerful force wrapping around her spirit, pulling with a strength she couldn't resist. His connection was a lifeline, yanking her away from the dangerous allure of the fire.

The world spun around her as she was dragged back, the flames receding, the smoke dissolving into the distance. Her spirit was yanked downwards, the bayou's familiar sights and sounds rushing back. The thread connecting her to her body thickened and solidified under Nibo's command.

With a sudden jolt, Cassielle's spirit slammed back into her body. She gasped, eyes flying open, her chest heaving from the journey. Nibo was there, his hands firm on her shoulders, grounding her.

"Breathe, Cassielle. You're back. Just breathe," he said, his voice a calming anchor.

Cassielle took several deep, shuddering breaths, her body trembling from the ordeal. The humid air felt heavy and thick, grounding her in the reality of the bayou. She looked at Nibo, his expression a mix of relief and concern.

"What happened?" she asked, her voice barely above a whisper.

"You started to drift too far. The smoke you saw was a distraction, a danger. If you had reached it, you might not have been able to return," Nibo explained, his tone grave. "But what you saw wasn't fire. It was the spreading darkness from Buer. Heylel is fairly certain the other malevolent spirits have gone elsewhere, but for some reason, Buer has taken it upon himself to focus on New Orleans. My suspicion," he said, gently placing a hand on her back and the other hand taking her hand closest to him, helping her sit up, "is that once he found out about you, he decided this was a great place to exact his revenge against Heylel."

Cassielle pulled her knees up to her chest, wrapping her arms around them. She shivered despite the oppressive humidity, the weight of Nibo's words settling over her like a dark cloud. "So it's my fault all those people have died in New Orleans?"

"No, not necessarily," Nibo reassured her, his voice softer now. "The evil human spirits would have likely still gone on their murdering sprees. But Buer has taken the opportunity to power up from all the horrific deaths and crimes they caused. He's feeding off the chaos."

Cassielle's mind raced, trying to process the enormity of the situation. Her presence had somehow exacerbated the malevolent forces at play in New Orleans. She felt a surge of guilt, her chest tightening as she thought of the innocent lives lost. But she also felt a flicker of determination. She couldn't let Buer continue his reign of terror.

"So, now that I can leave my body, how do I get into Limbo? And how do I prevent that from happening again?" she asked, pushing herself up with her hands and rising to her feet. Her legs wobbled slightly, but she steadied herself, locking eyes with Nibo.

Nibo stood as well, his gaze intense. "Entering Limbo is different from spirit walking. What you just did was the beginning of Spirit Walking. To enter Limbo, you will need to spirit walk through the gates of Guinee. It's a dangerous journey. Limbo is a place between worlds, filled with lost souls and dark entities. The gates are basically thin places where the veil between the living world and Limbo is weakest. We man those gates to protect them. There are some Loa temporarily guarding the gates while Samedi and I are out."

"How do I find one?" Cassielle asked, her curiosity piqued despite the lingering fear.

"There are several around New Orleans," Nibo replied. "Cemeteries, old churches, or other places where the spiritual energy is high. But finding a gate is only the beginning. You'll need to navigate through Limbo, avoid the malevolent spirits, and locate Nick's soul you're supposed to retrieve. But we will need to get Nick's body first. It wouldn't be good for him to spend too much time on this side without a body."

"What would happen then?" Cassielle reached up and tied her hair up with the hair-tie that she had around her wrist. The humidity was wreaking havoc on her curls and she couldn't stand the sweat on the back of her neck.

"It's best not to dwell on that, but if we get Nick, we have to make sure that DeLuca doesn't just abandon ship. A body without a soul doesn't do well, either," Nibo cringed at the thought. Cassielle didn't want to imagine that.

"Okay, so how do we keep DeLuca in Nick's body until we return with Nick's soul?"

"You will need Voodoo for that," Nibo said softly looking in the direction of the city.

"So I should go back to Sabine's place," Cassielle's stomach clenched at the thought. If the people were still there shooting, she would be a walking target, but perhaps she could shadow-walk in and out without anyone noticing? That was banking on nobody being inside. Nibo seemed to have had the same thought.

"Let me go and see if the coast is clear in her apartment," he didn't wait for her to respond and simply vanished in a puff of black smoke that smelled faintly of cigars.

Cassielle's heart was racing in her chest like a butterfly in a net. Her senses were heightened, listening for any sound of life beyond the clearing. The creatures of the Bayou were noisy, as if mother nature herself knew of the danger that lurked beyond the bayou.

Cassielle took a deep breath, the humid air filling her lungs. The bayou around them seemed to pulse with life, a reminder of the world she was fighting to protect. She squared her shoulders, ready to get going.

Nibo returned a few minutes later and nodded at her, "Coast is clear. Let's go."

Together, they gathered their things, the weight of their mission hanging heavy in the air. Cassielle felt a mix of fear and excitement, the gravity of her responsibility fueling her resolve. As they prepared to step into the shadows, she couldn't help but glance back in the direction where the fire had appeared to her. She couldn't see it now, but could imagine the large ploom reaching towards the heavens. The darkness was lurking, waiting for any chance to consume her. But she was ready to face it head-on, determined to protect her city and her friends.

The ceremony room was quiet as a tomb as Cassielle stepped out of the shadows. She had expected to hear gunfire or shouts from outside, but there was nothing. Pure silence enveloped the room, a stark contrast to the usual buzz of life in New Orleans. Nibo, creeping toward the window, seemed to notice it too.

Without waiting to hear from him, Cassielle moved swiftly to the table laden with ceremonial items. Everything was undisturbed, not a speck of dust displaced. The murder hadn't happened here. No traces of fingerprint powder or any sign of police presence suggested they had been interrupted before reaching this room. She found Sabine's current journal, sank to the floor, and turned on her phone's flashlight, keeping the beam as dim as possible. She wasn't sure what she was looking for, but she thought she'd recognize it when she found it.

"There's no one out there," Nibo whispered. "No police, no people, no spirits. Nothing. It's strange." He abandoned the window and moved to the bookshelves, pulling books off one by one, flipping through them rapidly in search of the spells they needed.

Cassielle continued leafing through the journal. Spells for love, protection, fertility, ceremonial activities for various holidays filled the pages. "What am I even looking for?" she muttered, glancing at Nibo, who had already gone through dozens of books.

"I believe the humans called the spells Infernal Binding and Ethereal Binding. The Infernal Binding is used to create a stone to cast demons or evil spirits out of bodies. With your power, you can not only use it to pull them out but also to trap them inside the stone. The other, Ethereal Binding, will create a Bindstone to trap a soul in a body. If you use that one on Nick, it will keep DeLuca from jumping out of the body, allowing you time to go to Limbo to fetch Nick's spirit. When you return, we can pull DeLuca out and cast him back to Limbo."

Cassielle's brow furrowed. "How does the Infernal Bindstone work? We've only faced human souls so far. I imagine malevolent spirits are more difficult to catch. Can they fight back? You haven't really explained what I'll be facing. I feel like the one I took care of here was kind of a fluke. We'd had a circle created already for some extra protection."

Nibo paused, pulling another book from the shelf. "Heylel would be the one to tell you precisely how a battle with a malevolent spirit goes, but I can tell you that you can do it. It's a battle of wills. You and Samedi were working on pushing with energy to force spirits out. You could use that same idea to push energy at them or pull energy from them. After all, that's basically what they are. Energy."

Cassielle nodded, squinting to decipher Sabine's cramped writing. The room's silence pressed in around her, amplifying the urgency of their task. She could feel a strange energy there. Where were the police? Even if the shooters had been taken care of, there should have been someone lingering taking notes on the evidence left behind.

"Look," Nibo's voice cut through the air, drawing her attention. He crouched before her, extending a weathered book toward her. It took her a moment in the dim light, but recognition surged through her like lightning. Her hands reached for it of their own volition, trembling slightly as Nibo passed it to her. She cradled it delicately, as if it were the most precious treasure in all the world - and to her, it was. It was her mother's journal.

She brought the book up to her nose, inhaling deeply, and closed her eyes. The scent of lavender, sage, and mint enveloped her senses, flooding her with memories and emotions. Tears welled up in her eyes as she was transported to another time and place.

When she opened her eyes, she found herself seated in her mother's ceremonial room. The room was suffused with warmth and the soft glow of candlelight. She sat on her mother's lap, feeling the comforting embrace of her arms around her. Her mother's journal lay open before them on the floor, its pages filled with wisdom and love.

"See here," Seraphina's gentle voice broke through the stillness, her finger tracing the lines of an open page. "Here is a good prayer for protection and comfort. You can say it any time you feel nervous, my petite ange." She wrapped Cassielle in a warm hug, the scent of lavender and sage mingling with the sweetness of her mother's presence.

"Cassielle?" Nibo's voice brought her back and she opened her eyes to see him watching her, his brows furrowed and concern reflecting in his eyes.

"I'm okay," She said softly, lowering the book. "It was just... After my mother died, when Alba and I were going through the house and boxing things up... I couldn't find this. I thought it had somehow gone missing and was gone forever." She flipped through the pages with more care than she had shown Sabine's notes. "Sabine must have nicked it at some point..."

She paused on a page bringing her flashlight closer to read her mother's neat, flowy writing. "Ethereal Binding," she read, skimming down through the ingredients needed and incantation. She turned the page to find "Infernal Binding" on the next page. "Here they are."

Nibo moved closer to Cassielle, his presence a reassuring anchor amidst the growing unease. Peering over her shoulder, he studied the pages she was scanning, his brows furrowing in concentration. "Sabine must have all of these things, right?" Nibo inquired, his gaze seeking confirmation from Cassielle.

Cassielle nodded, her finger trailing along the lists etched in Sabine's journal. "Yeah, I'd say they're pretty standard items for any Voodoo ritual or prayer," she murmured, her voice tinged with uncertainty. "Obsidian or black onyx, rue, sage, garlic, salt, holy water. I'm not sure if she'll have that labeled; we may be safer grabbing that from a church."

"Easy enough to do. What else?" Nibo prompted, his eyes scanning the room as if mentally cataloging their surroundings.

"Candles, and the usual items needed for incorporating the four elements," Cassielle continued, her gaze flitting between the journal and their surroundings. "Yeah, I'd say pretty much everything would be here. We may need to hit her kitchen for the garlic, salt, and sage, unless she keeps a stash in here... but I know my mom usually fetched those from our kitchen pantry since she could keep them nice and dry in there. You don't happen to know -"

Cassielle's words were abruptly cut off by a distant sound that shattered the silence like a thunderclap. A low rumble reverberated through the room, its ominous resonance freezing her In her place. She exchanged a glance with Nibo, the gravity of the situation weighing heavily upon them. Time was running out.

"What is that?" Cassielle whispered, her voice barely audible over the unsettling din that permeated the air. She strained to discern its origin, her senses on high alert. It was too prolonged to be a mere thunderstorm, yet it echoed like the primal roar of nature itself, stirring instincts deep within her.

The sound was soon followed by a sudden explosion, its shock wave rippling through the room like a seismic tremor. Jars rattled on the shelves, their contents clattering in protest against the violent upheaval. Cassielle's breath caught in her throat, her instinct urging her to rush to the window to investigate, but her rational mind cautioned against such recklessness.

Shouts erupted from outside, followed by the unmistakable crackle of gunfire. Her breath caught in her throat as fear clenched her heart in its icy grip. She heard screams and cries, a cacophony of terror that echoed through the room like a haunting melody. Every instinct screamed at her to flee, to escape the impending danger that loomed over them like a dark cloud, suffocating the air with its heavy presence.

Her heart hammered against her ribs, a desperate attempt to break free from its confining cage. Adrenaline surged through her veins, electrifying every nerve in her body with a sense of urgency. The hairs on the back of her neck stood on end, as if warning of the impending danger that lurked just beyond the shadows, waiting to pounce.

"Nothing good," Nibo's voice cut through the chaos, firm and resolute. "Let's get these things, then I'll stop at a church for the holy water."

He didn't wait for her agreement before he leaped to his feet, his movements swift and decisive, fueled by the urgency of the situation. Cassielle watched as he rushed from the room, returning moments later with a shopping bag he must have found somewhere in Sabine's apartment. Without another word, they scrambled to gather the ingredients listed in Seraphina's journal, their hands moving in a blur of motion as they hastily packed them into their bag.

The urgency of their mission propelled them into action, each movement fueled by the sense that something was approaching, something they couldn't afford to face unprepared. Cassielle made sure she had Sabine and Seraphina's journals in her hands, clutching them tightly to her chest as if they were talismans of protection against the encroaching darkness.

As they rushed to leave, Cassielle couldn't shake the feeling that they were being watched, that danger lurked just beyond the shadows, waiting to pounce. She took one last glance around the room, committing the scene to memory before stepping into the shadows, allowing their comforting embrace to whisk her away from the danger that lurked in the city of New Orleans.

CHAPTER THIRTY-TWO

Cassielle emerged from the shadows into the tranquil clearing of the Bayou, a stark contrast to the chaos engulfing the city. She braced herself for the sight of devastation, but the air was heavy with an eerie calmness. The damp grass underfoot whispered secrets of an imminent storm, yet the danger seemed distant, contained within the confines of the urban jungle. The usual symphony of chirping crickets and croaking frogs had dwindled to a hushed murmur, as if the natural world held its breath in anticipation.

Nibo emerged from the shadows, a jar of clear liquid in hand. "Holy water, my lady," he announced with a gallant flourish.

Cassielle nodded, her expression grave as she accepted the offering. "Okay, we don't have much time to do this."

With urgency driving their actions, Cassielle and Nibo set to work, their movements swift and purposeful. They laid out the necessary items for the rituals, arranging them meticulously upon the makeshift altar fashioned from fallen branches and moss-covered stones. On the first level, they placed a white uncooked egg on a mound of white flour as an offering for Damballah. The second level held an herbal pacquet and a Voodoo doll for Erzulie Red Eyes. Cassielle had packed the pacquet herself, its fragrant herbs emitting a calming scent. The third level was dedicated to Papa Legba, his simple yet significant offerings of peanuts and cigars placed with reverence. The air around them buzzed with anticipation as they prepared to summon the spirits.

Cassielle carefully lit the candles, their flickering flames casting dancing shadows across the clearing. Nibo arranged the herbs and crystals, their potent energies mingling with the whispers of the Bayou spirits. Each component held significance, imbued with the symbolic power to banish evil and protect the soul. Together, they recited the ancient incantations, their voices reverberating through the stillness of the night, a solemn plea for divine intervention.

As the rituals unfolded, a palpable shift occurred in the atmosphere, a subtle merging of the earthly and the ethereal. The air crackled with energy, charged with the promise of salvation and redemption. Cassielle felt a surge of strength coursing through her veins, fueled by the knowledge that they were not alone in their fight against the forces of darkness.

But even as they worked tirelessly to create the ethereal and the Infernal binding stones, a sense of foreboding lingered in the air. Time was a cruel mistress, and they knew that their window of opportunity was rapidly closing. With each passing moment, the shadows grew deeper, threatening to engulf them in darkness once more.

Cassielle lost track of time as they worked, the day slipping away unnoticed. By the time they finished, night had draped its dark mantle over the clearing. The dim glow of the candles flickered in the soft summer breeze, casting wavering shadows around their circle of light. Darkness seemed to hover just beyond, a silent, unseen watcher.

After their final incantation, they sat in silence. Cassielle's eyes were fixed on the two stones before her. One was obsidian, etched with a red rune of intricate curves and lines. The other was onyx, marked with a blue rune. Both stones glowed faintly in the dimness, their power palpable.

"Will DeLuca and Buer be able to feel that?" Cassielle finally broke the silence, glancing at Nibo. He lay on the ground, staring up at the stars, his thoughts seemingly far away.

"Hmm?" Nibo turned onto his side, propping his head up on one hand as he gazed at her with lazy curiosity.

"The stones," she gestured toward them, as if he hadn't been involved in their creation. "Will they sense the power in them?"

"Not if you keep them hidden until the last minute." He pushed himself up to a sitting position, crossing his legs. "You have power coming off of you, too, in case you didn't realize it."

"What?"

"You emanate power. It's been growing through your training. Anyone versed in Voodoo or with power of their own will be able to tell. There might be a way to hide it in the future, but I'm not sure how."

"You know," Cassielle began gathering the remnants of their ritual supplies, "it amazes me how much you and Samedi don't seem to know for how old you are."

"We're pretty specifically trained. Samedi knows more because his gate is the first, so he sees more of the human world. Centuries ago, I was the one who knew more, since I had been human at one time." Nibo joined her in clearing the items. "I think you should rest a bit before we go after DeLuca. You may not feel it yet, but you used a lot of your power, and going after DeLuca and Buer now might not lead to the best outcome."

Cassielle picked up the stones, marveling at their weight and the warmth they emanated. It was astounding how far she had come since meeting Samedi just days before. Had he asked her to do this then, she would have laughed him out of the room. Her initial fear of Voodoo had been slowly replaced with a sense of wonder and admiration for the skills she was learning.

Despite this, fear still lurked in her belly-fear of failing to save Nicholas, of not capturing DeLuca and Buer, of facing a demon, a malevolent spirit. And the thought of descending into the underworld to retrieve Nicholas's soul filled her with dread. What if she got lost there?

Cassielle realized she'd stopped listening to Nibo, who was still speaking. "Sorry?" she asked, blinking back to attention. Maybe she was more tired than she thought; her focus was slipping.

"I said, I think you're more than ready to do this, but it's probably best to get some rest first."

Cassielle shook her head, trying to hold off the rising panic she felt pounding in her chest. "Ready or not, I need to do this. I can't take more time to rest. I feel like that's all we do! We've already wasted so much time!"

Nibo shrugged, You're prepared. I was just worried you'd be tired. But you're not alone. If you're determined to push forward, I'll help."

"Ok, so where is the first Gate of Guinee," she took a steadying breath. "We don't have any more time to waste. As soon as we have Nick's body with DeLuca trapped inside, I need to go through that gate to fetch Nick's spirit."

Nibo nodded, his lips pressed in a firm line before he spoke. "We'll go back to Marie LaVeau's tomb. That is where Samedi's gate is. I hope that the fact that she is your ancestor means that you'll be able to find your way back more easily. Her tomb can act as an anchor for you. It happens to be one of the strongest portals to Limbo in the city. But be prepared. Once you enter, there's no turning back until you complete your mission." He paused. "I know I said you have us, but we cannot go in there with you. Heylel would obliterate us if he knew we were helping you with this. I will try to linger nearby in case you have any problems, but I may not be able to help you once you've gone in."

Cassielle nodded, ignoring the deep pit in her stomach.

"It'll be okay. I can do this. First step, lure in DeLuca, and I think I know exactly how to do it," Cassielle said, pulling out her phone and pressing the screen to go to her contacts. She selected Nick's number. "Wish me luck."

Nibo watched her intently as she composed the message, his eyes reflecting both hope and caution. Cassielle's fingers hovered over the keys for a moment before she started typing.

"DeLuca, it's Cassielle. I've done a lot of thinking since we last spoke. After dealing with the Loa and seeing how my father doesn't care about human life at all, I've realized something important. I do still want to get Nick back, but you are right to be upset the Loa kept you trapped in Limbo. It's wrong and I want to help you. Meet me at the old plantation house on the outskirts of the Bayou at midnight. Alone. We need to talk."

She read the message over, ensuring it conveyed the right mix of desperation and sincerity. Then, with a deep breath, she pressed send.

She turned to Nibo. "Now we wait. I'm sure he'll know I'm up to something, but he'll take the bait. He has to."

The minutes ticked by with agonizing slowness. The soft chirping of crickets filled the air, the only sound breaking the tense silence. Cassielle paced back and forth, her mind racing with the possibilities of what lay ahead.

Nibo remained seated, his eyes following her movements. Cassielle could practically hear the sound of the ticking clock.

Her phone buzzed, breaking the silence. She snatched it up, her heart pounding. The message from Nick's number was brief but to the point.

"Midnight. Don't be late."

She stared at the message for a moment, then looked up at Nibo. "He's coming. "

Nibo stood up, his expression serious. "Let's get ready."

"Get ready for what?"

Cassielle nearly leapt out of her skin, her heart racing as Baron Samedi stepped out of the shadows behind Nibo. His tall, imposing figure seemed to merge with the darkness, the flicker of candlelight catching the gleam of his piercing eyess.

"Samedi!" Cassielle exclaimed, struggling to steady her breath. "I didn't hear you."

Samedi's grin widened, revealing a row of sharp, white teeth. "That's the idea, my dear." His voice was smooth, laced with charm. He stepped closer, his eyes narrowing as he glanced at the items spread out before them.

"Looks like you've been busy," he remarked, gesturing toward the ritual setup. "But you didn't answer my question. Get ready for what?"

CHAPTER THIRTY-THREE

Her stomach churned at the thought of telling Samedi their plan. She chewed on her lip as she looked between him and Nibo. She was sure he'd be fine with using the two stones-that wasn't the problem. It was the spirit-walking part that worried her. She was fairly certain he would disapprove, mainly because it put her in danger. Though it probably wasn't any more or less dangerous than facing off with a demon, but it seemed like Samedi liked to be in charge.

"Well, we made the Ethereal and Infernal Binding stones, and I reached out to DeLuca," Cassielle began cautiously. "I'm going to meet with him and trap him in Nick's body."

Samedi's eyes narrowed slightly, his gaze piercing. "And you plan on getting close enough to him to use that stone how?" He leaned casually against a tree at the edge of the clearing, his posture relaxed but his eyes watchful.

Cassielle forced a grin, trying to ease the tension. "Using my feminine wiles," she said, with a playful tone.

Nibo snorted a laugh, breaking the heavy silence. Samedi raised an eyebrow, a faint smile tugging at the corners of his mouth. "Is that so? And what if your 'wiles' aren't enough?"

"I've got backup plans," Cassielle replied confidently, though her heart pounding in her chest must have given her nerves away. "I can handle it."

Samedi's gaze lingered on the stones, his expression thoughtful. "You've come a long way," he said finally.

"Thank you," she whispered, her voice barely audible over the crackle of the candles. Samedi glanced at her, his eyes twinkling with a mixture of amusement and pride.

"Don't thank me yet, my dear. The real battle is just beginning."

Together, they set to work. Cassielle gathered the two stones, carefully placing them in a small pouch she had taken from Sabine's. Nibo blew out the candles and packed them up, plunging them into darkness. They moved quickly, knowing that any mistake could be disastrous.

As the minutes passed, the anticipation grew. The night deepened, the sky a tapestry of stars twinkling above them. The Bayou remained eerily quiet, a stark contrast to the turmoil brewing in Cassielle's mind.

Finally, it was time. Cassielle, Nibo, and Samedi left the clearing, making their way through the dense foliage toward the old plantation house. The path was familiar yet haunting, shadows dancing in the moonlight as they crept through.

The plantation house loomed ahead, a ghostly silhouette against the night sky. Cassielle's heart raced as they approached, her grip tightening on the pouch containing the stones. This was it-the moment of truth.

They reached the entrance, and Cassielle paused, taking a deep breath to steady herself. "Stay close," she whispered to the Loa, who nodded in agreement before vanishing.

Pushing open the creaking door, she stepped inside. The air was thick with dust and memories of a bygone era. The interior was dimly lit by the moonlight streaming through broken windows, casting eerie patterns on the floor.

Cassielle moved to the center of the room, her eyes scanning the darkness for any sign of movement. She knew DeLuca would arrive soon, and she had to be ready. She put her hand in her pocket, finding comfort in the warmth emanating through the small pouch. She pulled out the one for trapping DeLuca and slipped it into her other pocket.

Minutes felt like hours as she waited. Finally, she heard a door creak open and shut. She listened carefully but couldn't hear approaching footsteps. Then, a shadow detached itself from the darkness at the far end of the room. Nick stepped into the dim light, his eyes gleaming with a mix of curiosity and suspicion.

"You came," he said, his voice smooth but edged with menace.

She hated how her heart flipped at the sight of Nick. She knew he wasn't the Nick she knew. Nick was lost in the darkness of Limbo and who stood before her was the evil and cunning serial killer Vittorio DeLuca. Yet somehow her body still had a physical reaction to Nick's presence in the room. She would have thought that would be gone considering the circumstances.

Cassielle straightened, meeting his gaze. "I did. And I'm ready to make a deal. But first, we need to talk."

He smiled, a wide, almost manic grin that reminded her of the Cheshire cat. His movements were deliberate as he sauntered across the room toward her, his hands hidden behind his back, clearly fiddling with something. The sight made her heart race, a pang of anxiety tightening in her chest. She took a steadying breath, maintaining her composure, even as unease prickled at the edges of her calm facade.

She quickly thought back to her knowledge of DeLuca when he was alive. He preferred strangulation. He'd once written to the news papers that he enjoyed it because it was close, personal, and he relished the feeling of his victim's life slowly leaving their body. She had no doubt that he had some sort of strangulation implement behind his back. She wasn't terribly worried about that. She knew how to get out of a situation like that, and she knew Nibo and Samedi were close by, so he wouldn't have the upper hand here.

"I'm all ears 'dahlin" as you southerners would say," he

stopped a few feet in front of her. She kept her eyes on him. She knew he'd have a tell if he were to move to attack, and she was ready.

"Well," she turned on her 'southern' charm as best as she could, "I had the delightful opportunity to finally meet my dear old father as well as the rest of the Loa, and wouldn't you know, that not a single one of them actually gives a shit about humans?" She shook her head in a 'what a pity' manner. "Samedi even took me into a Cathedral where I could have been shot by that maniac, Tom Horn. He wasn't nearly as clever as you were, though." She smirked, "holding a congregation hostage? Did he think the Loa wouldn't be able to catch him there?"

DeLuca chuckled, a low, menacing sound. "You think that was a dumb move on his part? Let me tell ya somethin', kid. You know how the coppers caught him? That fool was practically beggin' for it. Me? I was never caught. I lived out my days in style. But that knucklehead, he was leavin' breadcrumbs everywhere. Can you believe it took 'em so long to nab him? I remember readin' about it, back when I was outta the game. Real disappointment, that one. Pathetic."

Cassielle smiled sweetly, "Oh, I remember readin' about you. You were on the list of suspects, but they couldn't catch you, could they? No DNA testin' back then, and somehow you had alibis for some of 'em... How'd you manage that, anyway?" She knew stroking his ego would get her somewhere. Guys like him loved to talk about themselves, especially when it was all praise.

DeLuca laughed, a rough, guttural sound. "Oh, you flash enough dough, and folks will say whatever ya want 'em to. Helps when you're takin' out low-life hookers and junkies. Nobody misses 'em." He slowly looked her over, his gaze lingering in a way that made her skin crawl. She wanted to go home and shower in scalding hot water to wash off that look.

"Ya know, dames like you are a rare commodity," he continued, his voice dripping with sleaze. "I dunno why you even want that Nick back. He didn't treat ya right. He let ya go. See, I'd'a never let you go. Women these days have too much freedom. You'd have had a few of my kids by now."

What was he even talking about? It took a real effort on her part not to react. He clearly wasn't all there, but she had to play along.

"Oh, I'm sure. Times must be a lot different for you now," She slipped her right hand casually into her pocket. "I mean, things must be tough for you, what with men losing their rights and women taking their jobs." She shrugged, "But that probably compares to what you dealt with in Limbo, right? So, let's talk about how we get you a more permanent body so you don't have to go back? I really would like to get my friend back, you know."

Cassielle suppressed a shudder, maintaining her composure. "Maybe you're right," she said, forcing a coy smile. "Maybe Nick was never good enough for me. But he still has something I want."

DeLuca raised an eyebrow, intrigued. "Oh yeah? What's that, doll?"

"Closure," she said, taking a step closer to him. "And maybe a little revenge." She tilted her head, letting her hair fall to one side, revealing' the neckline of her shirt. "You know, you're right 'bout one thing: women do have too much freedom these days. Sometimes, I think it would be nice to have someone strong enough to take control."

DeLuca's eyes gleamed with a predatory light. "I knew you were a smart dame," he growled, advancing toward Cassielle, his intentions clear. She could sense the danger emanating from him, and her mind raced for a plan.

As he closed the distance between them, Cassielle kept her composure, her gaze fixed on his movements. She knew she had to act fast if she wanted to gain the upper hand. Her eyes seized upon the rope she had seen him concealing behind his back.

"First, I need to make sure you're really committed to

helping me," she said, her voice steady but her heart pounding with adrenaline. She took a cautious step backward, buying herself a fraction of a second to formulate her next move.

DeLuca chuckled, his grin widening as he closed in on her. "Oh, I'm committed," he replied, reaching out to grab her arm with a vice-like grip.

Cassielle winced at the pressure but maintained her focus, her eyes darting to where she had seen the rope tucked away. As DeLuca leaned in, his attention momentarily diverted, she seized the opportunity.

In one swift motion, Cassielle twisted out of his grasp, her hand darting toward his concealed weapon. With a deftness, she snatched the rope from his grip, her fingers closing around the coarse fibers.

DeLuca stumbled backward, taken off guard by her sudden maneuver. "Wha-what are you doing?" he stammered, his surprise giving way to anger as he realized he had been outmaneuvered.

Cassielle wasted no time, moving with the fluidity and precision of a trained martial artist. She swept DeLuca' legs out from under him, sending him crashing to the ground. He grunted and tried to roll away, but she was on him in an instant.

DeLuca fought back fiercely, swinging his fists and thrashing his legs. One wild punch grazed her cheek, but she shrugged it off, her focus unwavering. He reached for the gun holstered at his hip, but she was faster. With a quick, sharp twist, she wrenched the gun from his grip and tossed it across the room, where it skidded out of reach.

Undeterred, DeLuca bucked and twisted, trying to dislodge her. Cassielle countered his moves, locking her legs around his torso and using his momentum against him. She drove her elbow into his side, knocking the wind out of him. As he gasped for breath, she shifted her position, straddling his back and pinning him down with her weight.

With one arm twisted behind him in a textbook

armlock, DeLuca grunted in pain but still struggled, trying to break free. Cassielle kept her grip firm, using her free hand to loop the rope around his wrists. DeLuca thrashed harder, but she pulled the rope tight, binding his hands securely behind his back.

DeLuca yelped in surprise and outrage, struggling against his restraints, but Cassielle held firm, her grip steady as she took control of the situation.

She reached into her pocket and pulled out the onyx stone, its blue etchings glowing faintly in the dim light.

DeLuca frowned, suspicion clouding his features. "What's that for?"

"Insurance," she said smoothly. His eyes widened and she could see his spirit starting to escape. Before he could get out, she pressed the stone against his chest, chanting the binding incantation. DeLuca' eyes widened in realization, but it was too late.

The onyx stone glowed brighter, pulsing with energy. DeLuca struggled, trying to pull away, but the stone seemed to root him to the spot. His body convulsed as the binding spell took hold, locking his spirit into Nick's body.

"You... tricked me," he snarled, his voice distorted by the power of the spell.

Cassielle stepped back, her heart pounding in her chest. "Not any more than you were trying to do," she said, her voice steady. "You're not going anywhere. Not this time."

As the light from the stone dimmed, DeLuca' body slumped, his body restrained and spirit trapped. Cassielle took a moment to steady herself, then turned to Nibo, who had stepped from the shadows.

"It's done," she said, her voice barely above a whisper. "Now we just need to get Nick back."

"And how are you proposing you'll do that?" Samedi said as he stepped out of the shadows, folding his arms over his chest gazing down at her.

"I'm going through your gate." She looked between the

two Loa, "change in plans. Nibo, stay with DeLuca, Samedi, come with me or not. Your choice."

She didn't wait for Samedi to argue before she stepped into the shadows and emerged at Marie LaVeau's tomb. The ancient cemetery was cloaked in a somber silence, the air thick with the scent of damp earth and decaying leaves. Crumbling tombstones stood like silent sentinels, their surfaces weathered and etched with the passage of time. Vines crept along the ground, weaving through the wrought-iron fences that guarded the resting places of New Orleans' long-departed.

Samedi stepped out of the misty ink shadows just after her. She could tell by his expression that he did not approve of this plan. The moon cast a ghostly glow on the mausoleums, their marble facades gleaming under its pale light. Shadows danced among the graves, flickering like phantoms in the night.

Ignoring her nerves, Cassielle began setting up the blanket on the ground. She hoped the fabric would provide a small barrier between her and the cold, damp earth.

"I know it's useless to try to talk you out of this," Samedi watched her carefully as she lay out the red plaid picnic blanket and sat on it.

"Yup," she settled in, the chill seeped through despite her efforts to create a comfortable space. The tomb of Marie LaVeau loomed nearby, its presence both daunting and reassuring, a silent witness to the ritual she was about to perform.

The cemetery's stillness was occasionally broken by the distant hoot of an owl and the rustling of leaves in the gentle breeze. Cassielle's heart pounded as she prepared for the task ahead, the weight of the ancient spirits around her pressing in on all sides.

Samedi knelt beside her, his eyes now serious and filled with a depth of concern. He gently brushed a stray lock of hair from her face. "You know, Cassielle, this isn't just about bravery. Spirit walking is dangerous. There's no guarantee you'll come back."

Cassielle reached up and took his hand, giving it a reassuring squeeze. "I know the risks, Samedi. But I have to do this. For Nick. For myself."

He sighed, a heavy, resigned sound. "You're stubborn, just like your mother," he paused. "She would be proud of you."

A lump formed in Cassielle's throat at the mention of her mother. "Thanks. That means a lot." She closed her eyes, taking a deep breath to steady her nerves. "I need you to watch over me, okay? Make sure nothing happens to my body while I'm gone."

Samedi nodded, his expression softening with a touch of affection. "Of course, my dear. I'll protect you with everything I have."

She smiled up at him, the familiar lines of his face providing a strange comfort. "I know you will."

"Say hi to Papa Legba for me if you see him," Samedi said with a smile.

As the moments passed, the reality of what she was about to do settled over her like a heavy fog. The fear was there, lurking just beneath the surface, but she pushed it aside. This was for Nick. She had to be strong.

Samedi began to chant softly, his voice a low, melodic hum that resonated with the ancient energies of the cemetery. Cassielle closed her eyes again, focusing on his words, letting the rhythm of his voice guide her into a meditative state. The world around her began to fade, the boundaries between the physical and spiritual realms blurring.

She envisioned rising up out of her body, letting herself float up to her feet. No more feeling of the wind or the earth beneath her. She was as light as air itself. Gone would be her physical body. All that would remain would be her essence.

As Cassielle glanced downward, a gasp escaped her lips. She was still laying on the blanket, her physical body motionless. However, she had separated from it, now existing as a separate entity-a spectral apparition. Her spirit body shimmered with a faint, translucent glow while her physical form lay dormant below.

The sight of her disembodied state ignited a minor freak out in Cassielle. Panic fluttered in her chest, and her mind teetered on the edge of uncertainty. What had she gotten herself into? How would she navigate this foreign realm without losing herself entirely?

She felt a strange tugging sensation, as if her spirit were being gently pulled from her body. The fear bubbled up again, but she forced herself to remain calm, to trust in the process. The cemetery's cold, damp air seemed to disappear, replaced by a sensation of weightlessness.

Suddenly, she found herself standing on the threshold of the spirit world, a place where shadows and light intertwined in an ethereal dance. She glanced back at her physical form, lying motionless on the blanket, with Samedi's vigilant presence beside her.

Before her stood the first gate of Guinee, Samedi's, an imposing structure that seemed to pulsate with an otherworldly energy. The gate was made of wrought iron, intricate patterns of skulls and crossbones woven into its design, their eyes appearing to follow her every move. Vines of ghostly white flowers twisted around the bars, their blossoms emitting a soft, luminescent glow that cast eerie shadows on the ground.

Cassielle imagined the experience of a normal soul first gazing upon this gate. The imposing wrought iron, entwined with ghostly white flowers, seemed to breathe with an eerie life of its own. She pictured Baron Samedi in his otherworldly attire, standing there, waiting to guide the souls through. His skeletal face, with its wide, toothy grin and dark voids for eyes, would be a terrifying sight for those who deserved the fear of the next life.

A shiver ran down her spine as she thought of Samedi's skull face, his presence a harbinger of the unknown beyond the gate. She hoped that when spirits like her mother arrived, he would wear a kinder visage, something less terrifying. She imagined her mother's gentle spirit approaching the gate, her heart heavy with the recent departure from the physical world. Cassielle fervently wished that Samedi's gaze would soften for such souls, his skeletal grin replaced with a more comforting expression.

The gate was flanked by two colossal statues of Baron Samedi himself, each one a mirror image of the other. Their skeletal faces bore wide, toothy grins beneath top hats, and their eye sockets were dark voids that seemed to peer into the depths of her soul. They stood as silent guardians, their bony hands resting on canes that appeared to be carved from ancient, gnarled wood.

Beyond the gate, the path into Guinee stretched out, bathed in a spectral light that seemed neither day nor night. The air was thick with the scent of incense and the faint sound of distant drums, creating a rhythm that resonated deep within her. Wisps of fog curled around her feet, and the ground beneath her felt both solid and ephemeral, as if it existed in multiple dimensions at once.

She took a deep breath, feeling the weight of the moment.The atmosphere was heavy with the presence of countless spirits, their whispers brushing against her ears like a soft, mournful breeze. As soon as she could feel them, she then saw them passing through. She caught a glimpse of someone telling them where to go.

The air seemed to hum with the energy of the Loa, a reminder that she was now in a realm governed by ancient and powerful forces. As Cassielle's eyes adjusted to the otherworldly glow, a figure emerged from the mist, radiating an aura of both warmth and authority.

Maman Brigitte stood before her, an imposing yet comforting presence. Her skin was strikingly pale, almost luminescent in the dim light of the spirit world. She wore a dress of deep red and black, the fabric flowing around her like a protective cloak. The colors seemed to pulse with a life of their own.

Cassielle's gaze was drawn to the intricate cross that Maman Brigitte wore around her neck, the silver catching the ethereal light and gleaming like a beacon. It was a powerful symbol of protection, a reminder of her role as a guardian of the dead. Her fiery red hair framed her face in wild, untamed waves, a stark contrast to the calm wisdom in her eyes.

In one hand, Maman Brigitte held a bottle of rum infused with hot peppers, the dark liquid swirling ominously. The other hand rested gently on a tombstone beside her, its surface covered in ancient, unreadable inscriptions. The ground around her seemed to respond to her presence, the mist parting respectfully and the shadows retreating as if recognizing her authority.

Her eyes, deep and knowing, met Cassielle's, and a smile touched her lips. "Welcome, child," Maman Brigitte's voice was melodic. "You seek to walk the path of the spirits, to bridge the realms of the living and the dead. Know that this journey is fraught with peril, but also with great purpose."

Cassielle felt a wave of trepidation and resolve wash over her. She nodded.

"I have to rescue Nick," Cassielle said, her voice steady.

Maman Brigitte stepped closer, her eyes never leaving Cassielle's. "I imagine Samedi was not thrilled that you were going to spirit walk?" She shook her head and Maman Brigitte laughed softly, "Well, let's get this done quickly so he doesn't have to fret much longer. You carry the blessing of the Loa, and with it, the strength to face what lies ahead. Just speak with Papa Legba once you cross over. You must be respectful and he will point you down the correct path."

Steeling herself, Cassielle stepped forward, her hand reaching out to touch the cold iron of the gate. As her fingers made contact, a ripple of energy surged through her, and the gate slowly began to creak open. The path lay before her, and once she entered, she would not turn back until she found

Nick, or was lost forever.

Cassielle took a deep breath, then stepped fully into the realm of spirits. The air was thick with energy, pulsing with the whispers of ancient souls. She could feel their eyes upon her, curious and watchful. This was it-the point of no return.

"Be safe," she whispered to herself, steeling her resolve. "I'll find you, Nick. I promise."

CHAPTER THIRTY-FOUR

Cassielle set off down the road. This place was so different from the real world. Looking around, there was mist as far as her eyes could see and then just darkness, leaving her senses disoriented. She slowed as she saw what looked like a fork in the road, just as Maman Brigitte had told her. She paused and peered into the fog. A dark shape slowly emerged. The figure was stooped over and moving slowly. An old man leaning on a crutch. He wore a broad-brimmed straw hat that cast a shadow over his eyes, adding to his air of mystery. A pipe hung from his lips, and the faint smell of tobacco smoke wafted through the air. She could see why he was described as a Grandpa-like Loa. He wore old tattered clothing that reminded her of a farmer's outfit. Some old blue jean overalls and a plaid button-up tee shirt underneath. His brown boots looked old and dirty as well.

"Ah, if it isn't the prodigal child herself," he said cheerfully, leaning heavily on his crutch. "Cassielle. What brings you to this side? You are not dead, I hope?"

"No," Cassielle shifted her feet. "I need to go rescue my friend."

"Ah, the young man lost in limbo?" He drew in slowly from his cigar, removing it from his mouth and blowing out a ring of smoke that curled and twisted in the air.

"I'm guessing yes? I'd hope there aren't a lot of them lost down there?"

The old man chuckled, "Luckily no. We do pretty well keeping those who do not belong there out. But when a posession happens... well, I can't quite explain it, but they sometimes wind up there."

"Okay, well... I need to go get him. So... Papa Legba, right?" The old man nodded. "Right, okay, well Papa Legba, if you wouldn't mind just pointing me in the right direction, I'll be off."

Papa Legba, leaning on his crutch watched her with eyes twinkling with mischief, "So you've come seeking passage to Limbo, have you? Before you tread those murky paths, a choice awaits. You can take the easy road with a price, or face the trials ahead with your own strength. What will it be?"

"Well, if I've learned anything from all of this nonsense, it's that the price is always too steep. I'll take the trials." Cassielle's expression hardened. "I'm not one for shortcuts. I'll face whatever comes."

Papa Legba puffed thoughtfully on his cigar, "The road to Limbo is treacherous, child. Beware the shadows that twist truth and lies. Nicholas's plight is not just a trap but a test. Trust your instincts, for they will guide you where light cannot."

"Will do."

Papa Legba's smile widened. "Ah, very well. Proceed with caution then. I hope to see you return." He gestured down the path to her left and stepped back into the fog, slowly disappearing from view. The mist curled around her as she started down the path he had pointed to.

She walked and had no idea how much time was passing. She didn't feel tired. She didn't feel anything at all. It just felt like she was going down an endless road.

"Hey!"

Cassielle turned quickly to look behind her, but she didn't see anyone so she started to turn back.

"Down here," she turned her gaze downward to behold a surprising sight. A pink pig with shimmering wings, perched near her feet, looked up at her with intelligent eyes. It was a peculiar yet comforting presence in this bewildering realm.

The pig's voice, gentle and melodious, echoed in her ears. "Do not fear. I am here to guide you through this journey. Together, we will navigate the realms of spirit and fulfill your purpose."

As Cassielle's eyes met the gaze of the pink pig, astonishment painted her face. The question escaped her lips before she thought to hold it back. "A pig? Really?"

The pig's eyes sparkled with amusement as he nodded in response. "Indeed, a pig," he replied with a hint of playfulness. "But do not let my appearance deceive you. I am a wise and capable guide in these realms."

She raised an eyebrow at him and he shook his head, "I'm your spirit guide."

Cassielle hesitated for a moment, her mind teetering between skepticism and acceptance. Yet, something in the pig's demeanor reassured her, inviting her to take a leap of faith. She vaguely recalled her mother saying something about spirit guides. If Limbo was real, and everything else from her mother's stories was real, then it was entirely in the realm of possibility that this was, too. She found herself captivated by the depth of his gaze and the earnestness in his voice.

The pig's narrowed eyes conveyed a hint of offense. "If you don't want my help..."

"No, no!" Cassielle quickly interjected, her voice filled with sincerity. "I'm sorry. I was just a bit taken aback."

A mischievous glint danced in the pig's eyes as he straightened himself. "What did you expect?" he retorted. "A human, perhaps?"

Cassielle shook her head, her expression reflecting a mix of awe and uncertainty. "I don't know... I didn't anticipate you being a pig..."

The pig erupted into laughter, a cackling sound that merged with a playful snort. "Ah, my dear, this isn't my only form! I can manifest as anything I desire."

The pig instantly vanished into a swirl of ethereal smoke, transforming into a sleek, dark cat-a magnificent cougar. He gazed at Cassielle, his tail twitching with an air of curiosity. "Is this better?" he inquired, his voice resonating with a feline grace.

Cassielle offered a half-hearted nod, still adjusting to the astonishing nature of her spiritual companion. "I guess."

With an exaggerated roll of his eyes, the cougar, introduced himself as Hannibal. "Enough dawdling. We've wasted ample time. It's time to proceed." He stepped forward, nonchalantly leading the way.

"If you are willing to help me," Cassielle finally said, "Then, I'm happy to have you here."

The cougar's gentle smile widened as he nodded. "Very well. Let us venture through the ethereal realms, unraveling the mysteries that lie ahead. Lean on my counsel, and we will accomplish what must be done."

After walking for a bit they came upon the edge of a sheer cliff, overlooking a vast expanse that stretched into the unknown. The world before them was enveloped in darkness, yet paradoxically more evident than the chamber they had left behind. The velvety sky above shimmered with many stars, their ethereal glow akin to the mystical dance of the northern lights.

As Cassielle's eyes widened in awe, Hannibal, broke the silence. "This is the celestial path to various destinations-the gateway to Limbo, the cycle of reincarnation, or the ultimate union with the universe."

Aware of the pressing matters at hand, Hannibal redirected their attention. "We don't have time for sightseeing. Our focus is finding your task, your destined path, your bon homme."

"I need to find Nick's spirit," Cassielle looked at the different paths. Which way to go?

"Of course. Let us go then."

Cassielle followed Hannibal as they ventured down a

narrow path that descended into the mysterious world below the cliff. The atmosphere grew sparse and desolate, instilling a sense of unease within her. This place had an unsettling absence of sound as if the essence of silence had enveloped this realm. There was only the echoes of their own ethereal footsteps reverberating through the darkness as they ventured deeper into the unknown.

With each step, the surroundings grew progressively darker until Cassielle noticed a faint glow from Hannibal. Curiosity prompted her to glance at her hands, revealing that she was also radiating a soft, ethereal light. Sensing her unspoken question, Hannibal spoke up.

"We glow because we are not of this realm," he explained, his voice carrying a tone of caution. "Your friend, hopefully, will bear the same glow. Yet, the longer one remains here, the more their inherent goodness wanes, trapping them alongside those who truly belong. His glow will fade until it is all gone. It seems the Loa have this place under control. Bondye and Heylel run a tight ship. But they offer no protection for souls like yours, should you venture here. It's a perilous place where the risk is yours to bear. We must ensure your ti bon ange remains intact."

It was then that she realized she felt no temperature in this realm. Though she would have imagined it was cold, she remained unaffected. No warmth, no chill-just an absence of sensation. Breathing seemed unnecessary, and she couldn't detect any scents or tastes.

Hannibal, perceptive to her thoughts, spoke up. "Down here, devoid of a physical form, your senses are absent. You hear me because we communicate soul to soul through a different mode of speech."

Their journey continued, seeming to stretch on indefinitely. Time has lost its meaning in this otherworldly domain. Had they been walking for mere minutes or endless days? Would her physical body still be alive by the time they returned?

Eventually, the terrain leveled out, and figures materialized amidst the darkness-shifting, elusive, and insubstantial shadows. Cassielle realized that she and Hannibal stood out conspicuously, their luminosity contrasting with the surrounding obscurity. Distinguishing spirits from other entities became a daunting task.

"How will we ever find him?" Cassielle's voice wavered with doubt. "It's so dark here... How vast is this place?"

"Stay close to me," Hannibal reassured her, his voice a steady anchor in the eerie abyss.

Yet, a lingering unease gnawed at Cassielle's mind. As she followed Hannibal, she strained to unravel the source of her disquiet. Was it the oppressive atmosphere, the limited visibility that restricted her sight to a mere few feet ahead? Then, a word surfaced in her thoughts.

Baka.

What did that word mean? She collided with Hannibal abruptly, who had halted and now regarded her with an unfriendly expression on his feline countenance. Had he heard her thought?

"Does that word hold significance for you?" she whispered, her voice tinged with trepidation. Hannibal's smile twisted into a mischievous semblance reminiscent of the Cheshire Cat.

"Baka," he muttered, cackling. "Do you recall nothing of what your mother taught you, child?"

Taken aback, Cassielle took a step back. How had she been so sure that he was her spirit guide? Was it solely based on his appearance? Baka... The meaning flooded her mind-malevolent spirits taking the form of various animals.

"You're a baka," she uttered, her voice quivering.

"Look who's talking!" he laughed, his form morphing from a cougar to that of a towering bear. "What will you do now? Where is your spirit guide to keep you safe?"

Hannibal's glow vanished, replaced by a fluid darkness that matched the others that were slowly closing in.

Surrounded by a relentless onslaught of malevolent Baka and other dark spirits, Cassielle felt her spirit being drained, inch by inch. Their menacing hands reaching out to snatch her positive energy, trapping her in their clutches. Panic surged through her veins, threatening to overwhelm her.

Amid the chaos, a flicker of clarity emerged from the depths of her mind. She grasped onto the prayer her mother had taught her, her only weapon against these relentless forces. With each breath, she recited the sacred words with unwavering determination.

"Gracious St. Joseph, protect me and my family from all evil as you did the Holy Family. Kindly keep us united in Christ's love, ever fervent in imitation of the virtue of our Blessed Lady, your sinless spouse, and always faithful in devotion to you. Amen."

The prayer spilled from her lips, a desperate plea for divine intervention. The words reverberated through the spectral realm, and for a moment, the encroaching darkness wavered. The Baka hissed and recoiled, their twisted forms retreating from her radiant light.

But they were persistent, like a relentless tide crashing upon her spirit. Cassielle realized that a single recitation would not repel their insidious presence. With fierce resolve, she repeated the prayer, each utterance strengthening her conviction and creating a fragile barrier of protection.

Over and over, she recited the words, her voice growing louder, emboldened by her unwavering faith. Her glow increased and the Baka recoiled further, their grip loosening, giving her a sliver of opportunity. Sensing a momentary respite, Cassielle seized on her chance.

She darted through the darkness, her prayer echoing through the void as she repeated it over and over. The Baka, weakened and disoriented, struggled to pursue her. With each step, Cassielle could feel her connection to the divine growing more potent, her spirit imbued with a renewed sense of resilience.

She raced through the shadowed realm, her heart pounding and her spirit aflame with a strength she had almost lost. The Baka's relentless pursuit continued, but her repeated recitations of the prayer acted as a shield, repelling their malevolence and providing her with a path to escape.

In a burst of courage and sheer willpower, Cassielle plunged through a rift in the darkness, emerging on the fringes of the ethereal plane. Gasping for breath, she turned back to face the abyss, the Baka snarling and fading into the bleak expanse.

Relief washed over her, mingled with a lingering sense of trepidation. She knew the Baka would not give up easily, so she continued to recite the prayer as a shield whether she could see them or not.

As she stood on the fringes of the ethereal plane, catching her breath and contemplating her next move, she scanned the vast expanse before her. The spirit world stretched out in all directions, mysterious and teeming with unknown dangers. Cassielle forged ahead, her glowing spirit illuminating the darkness around her. The spirit world was a kaleidoscope of surreal landscapes where reality and dreams intermingled.

She traversed shimmering meadows adorned with phosphorescent flowers that seemed to pulse with otherworldly energy. The air was alive with whispered secrets, teasing her with fragments of forgotten knowledge. Strange creatures flitted in and out of sight, their forms ever-shifting and elusive, challenging her with riddles and enigmatic clues.

Cassielle encountered treacherous rivers of shimmering mist, their currents swirling and tugging at her incorporeal essence. She deftly navigated the ethereal waters, resisting the temptation to be swept away by the haunting melodies that echoed from unseen sources.

Moving deeper into the spirit world, she entered a labyrinth of swirling mists and shadowed corridors. Each twist and turn brought her closer to her goal and deeper into the clutches of formidable beings who lived here.

She came around a corner and found herself again face to face with the Baka and other dark spirits.

Hannibal, let out a malicious laugh that echoed through the ethereal realm. "Ah, so you've managed to recall fragments of your mother's teachings," Hannibal sneered. "Silly Mambo, thinking you can defy us. The time of our triumph is at hand. The Loa's reign will crumble, and we shall rise."

Cassielle's eyes narrowed as she took a deep breath. She stood tall, radiating a light that pierced through the darkness around her. The Baka and his zombie-like minions recoiled, their decaying limbs shrinking away from her brilliant aura as if her touch seared their undead flesh. Unfazed, Cassielle pressed forward, her spirit ablaze with her unwavering resolve. "I will not be deterred. I will find Nick and bring him back safely, away from your clutches."

The Baka sneered, his voice arrogant. "You underestimate the perils of this realm, little human. Your mortal frailty cannot withstand the relentless forces that seek to consume you."

A smile played on Cassielle's lips, a glimmer of defiance in her eyes. "No, I am more than just a mere human. I am the daughter of Heylel, the one whom you fear the most. I am neither human nor deity. The power of my lineage courses through my veins, and it shall be my shield against your darkness."

As she spoke, an immense energy surged within her, like a dormant volcano awakening. She harnessed the power she had been suppressing, channeling it into a concentrated force that crackled around her. With each step she took, the ground trembled beneath her, the spirits of the departed stirring in anticipation.

The clash between light and darkness was inevitable, and Cassielle stood at the precipice, ready to strike. Her eyes blazed with an otherworldly fire as she raised her hand, fingers aglow with celestial energy. The power surged forth, a brilliant beam of light that streaked towards the Baka with undeniable force.

The Baka recoiled, his dark form quivering under the onslaught of pure, divine energy. Doubt flickered in his eyes for a fleeting moment, his malevolence wavering in the face of Cassielle's indomitable spirit.

"You will not prevail," Cassielle declared with unwavering conviction. "I am the light that banishes darkness, the beacon of hope in this realm of shadows. Nick's spirit will be free from your grasp, and you shall remain trapped within the realm of the dead to suffer for all of eternity."

Cassielle's spirit whirled and clashed with the spectral foes that dared to challenge her. Each battle was an explosion of vivid hues as her glowing essence clashed against the darkened shades of her adversaries. Shimmering light erupted from her ethereal form, slicing through the shadows with precision and grace.

CHAPTER THIRTY-FIVE

Again, time and direction remained elusive, but she allowed her instincts to guide her onward as she ran. A compelling force urged her in a particular direction, whispering that Nick awaited her. She ran as quickly as she could, miraculously without fatigue. She didn't feel sore, or tired. It just felt as if it was taking a long time. With each step, her energy surged, growing more robust and vibrant. She could sense the certainty within her core that she would find him, and this conviction fueled her onward. Her luminous light expanded, causing the souls lurking in the shadows to scatter, seeking refuge in the safety of their own darkness.

After an indeterminate time, a faint glimmer of light beckoned from the distance, distinct from her radiance. Aware of the dark spirits' ability to mimic her light, Cassielle slowed her pace, approaching the source with caution. As she drew closer, the truth became clear: this light was no deceitful apparition. It lay on the ground, motionless, surrounded by the zombie-like creatures that appeared to be draining its essence. Cassielle hurled her ball of light towards them with an unleashed fury she never knew she possessed.

The creatures scattered in panic, and her radiant projectile collided with the prone figure, enveloping him in its luminous embrace. Cassielle slowed her steps, kneeling beside him. Time had not been kind to Nick in this realm; the toll of his experiences was etched on his face. His hair had grayed, and his complexion appeared pallid. She reached out, her fingertips brushing against his weathered skin.

"Nick," she spoke softly, her voice filled with tenderness. "It's time to go."

Slowly, Nick's eyes fluttered open, confusion clouding his gaze. "Cassielle? Is it really you?"

She smiled, nodding with certainty. "Yes, it's me. Come, let's get you back home."

"Home?" His voice echoed, and he allowed her to assist him into a seated position. He looked around, his brows furrowing. "But this is home. I was just taking a nap under this tree. It's sweltering out today."

Cassielle's brow furrowed in concern as she surveyed the desolate darkness surrounding them. The eerily silent landscape sent a shiver down her spine. She began to argue, but a realization struck her: perhaps Nick's mind was shielding his soul from the harsh reality of their situation. Would he be able to maintain his sanity if he truly comprehended where they were? With a mix of understanding and apprehension, she decided to play along.

"Why, of course," she replied, feigning a light tone. "I'm sorry, Nick. It's been a long and tiring day. Hey, would you mind walking me home? I'm not feeling so great. Maybe I should cut back on the drinks."

A flicker of eagerness to help others sparked in Nick's eyes. "Claro! I'd be glad to help you." They rose together, Cassielle looping her arm around his waist as his knees threatened to give way. "Ay!" he exclaimed, a glimmer of concern crossing his face. "Maybe I should go inside and rest, too. I'm not feeling too well."

"You've had a long day," she agreed, masking her worries. "Come on, let's go."

Silent prayers whispered from Cassielle's heart, seeking guidance from the universe to lead them on the right path. She had nothing to follow but her own instincts and hope she was headed in the right direction. As they walked, Cassielle maintained a cheerful banter while silently beseeching Bondye to show them the way. She pressed forward, her steps growing heavier as the strength she had gained gradually slipped away. The weight of protecting Nick, herself proved more burdensome than she could have ever anticipated. She could no longer muster enough energy. They were truly alone.

Their journey went on for so long, Cassielle wondered how much time would have passed once they returned to the land of the living. However, when the ground started to incline, Nick suddenly dug his heels, resisting the direction they were headed. "No," he protested.

Cassielle halted, her grip on his arm loosening as she regarded him with concern. "What's wrong? We need to go home."

"Home isn't that way," he insisted, his gaze darting around as if searching for the correct path. Cassielle could feel her protective light waning, and a surge of panic threatened to rise within her. She swallowed it down. Taking a moment to compose herself, she devised a new strategy.

"I need to go this way," she appealed, her voice filled with urgency. "Can you make sure I reach where I'm going safely? You've always been so good at keeping me safe." Inside, she crossed her fingers, praying for his cooperation.

"You've never needed me to keep you safe, Cassielle," he replied, his steps veering in the opposite direction.

"Nick, please!" She moved swiftly, planting herself in his path. "Please, we can't go back there."

He frowned, his confusion evident. "I don't understand what's gotten into you."

"Me? Look around, Nick! Really, look around! This isn't New Orleans!"

Nick's lips escaped with a strange laughter tinged with madness. Cassielle drew a deep breath, closing the distance between them until they stood chest to chest. "Nicholas, I'm not playing games. We have to go this way. Now."

"Let me help." Cassielle nearly jumped out of her skin.

Standing behind Nick was someone who took her breath away. But it couldn't be her. She wouldn't be in this horrible place. However, she recognized that voice so well, and the phantom scent that accompanied it caused butterflies in her stomach and unwelcome tears in her eyes. "It's okay, Cassielle, Che mwen. Ti mwen."

"Mom...?" She couldn't figure out if this was real or if the place was toying with her again. The woman approached, bathed in light. Her skin was darker than Cassielle's. She had long and thick, curly black and blonde hair tied back from her face. Her mother had always loved balayage hair, even before it became popular. She wore a flowing white gown that seemed to float around her rather than touch the ground. Adorning her were large gold hoop earrings and a long necklace with a charm dangling at the end. Though Cassielle couldn't see the charm clearly, it would symbolize protection and love if this woman was indeed her mother.

The woman came over and took Nick by his other arm. "Let's go, no time to waste." Cassielle grasped Nick's other arm, but he appeared bewildered by the turn of events.

"I thought your mom was dead?" Nick's bluntness was too much. She needed to get him out of there. She didn't particularly like this version of Nick. Cassielle and the woman guided Nick up the hill. Nick began resisting as they approached the top, screaming and cursing at them. The woman seemed unperturbed by his behavior, while Cassielle's thoughts were struggling to comprehend the possibility that this woman was her mother's spirit. Yet, the spirit was aiding her, and Cassielle felt a surge of strength in her presence.

When they reached the top, she spotted Papa Legba and the gate. He stood, leaning against his crutch and watching as they made their way back to the fork in the road. The gate remained in the exact location as when she had left, emanating a soft light.

As they approached , his face broke into a smile. "I am pleased to see you made it back in one piece."

"You and me both," Cassielle adjusted Nick's arm on her shoulders.

Papa Legba stepped back and gestured for them to pass. "Go with peace and protection, Cassielle, daughter of Heylel. We are all rooting for you."

She smiled and she and the woman escorted Nick, who had calmed down slightly, toward the exit. Nick was looking around himself with wide eyes and mumbling incoherently. She reached out and opened the gate. Once they crossed over, the gate swung shut behind them. Cassielle could sense herself being drawn back to her physical body lying on the ground with Samedi still sitting next to her.

"How do I get him back to his body?" Her strength was waning, unable to resist the pull that would reunite her with her body.

"I'll see him back to his body. Go on, child."

Nick slumped to the ground, his fight extinguished. Samedi patted him on the back but remained quiet.

"But first, Che mwen." The woman removed her necklace and extended it to Cassielle. "Put this on, child. I don't know what you did with the one I gave you when you were young, but this will protect you as you fulfill the rest of your duties here. Don't worry, child. I am always beside you."

Cassielle accepted the necklace and placed it around her neck.

"Mama...?" she queried.

"Go now, child."

Cassielle felt mixed emotions welling inside her as she stood before her mother, the ethereal presence bathing the area in light. Tears streamed down her cheeks as she tried to steady her voice.

"Mama... I can't believe it's really you," Cassielle whispered, her voice trembling with a blend of joy, longing, and grief.

The radiant figure smiled, her eyes filled with love and understanding. She reached out and gently brushed a tear from Cassielle's cheek. "My sweet Cassielle, my darling. I have never left your side. Even in the darkest moments, I've been watching over you."

Cassielle choked back a sob, her heart aching with sadness and relief. "I missed you so much. I've needed you."

Her mother's embrace enveloped her, a gentle warmth emanating from her being. "I know, my precious child. But you have grown into a strong and resilient woman. I am so proud of you."

Cassielle clung to her mother, seeking solace in her presence. "I wish you could be with me. I wish I didn't have to say goodbye."

Her mother's touch was soothing, her voice filled with reassurance. "I am always with you, my love. In every beat of your heart, in every breath you take. Our bond transcends this realm. Remember that."

Cassielle's tears flowed freely now, mingling with a bittersweet smile. "I will carry you in my heart always."

Her mother's gaze held an indescribable tenderness. "And I will be there, guiding you, protecting you. You are never alone."

The ethereal realm around them seemed to shimmer with love and connection as they held each other. The weight of grief and loss lifted slightly, replaced by a deep sense of love and a renewed strength within Cassielle.

With a final kiss on Cassielle's forehead, her mother gently stepped back. "It's time for you to go, my dear. Fulfill your destiny and bring Nick back to the land of the living."

Cassielle nodded, her voice filled with determination. "I will. I'll do whatever it takes."

Her mother's smile radiated pride and unwavering belief. "I know you will, my brave girl. Remember, love conquers all. Trust in yourself and the strength within you."

With a heavy heart, Cassielle stepped back, her hand clutched the necklace her mother had given her, feeling its protective energy.

"I love you," she whispered, her voice filled with sorrow and gratitude.

"I love you too, my precious child," her mother whispered, her voice carrying on a gentle breeze. "May your journey be guided by love and find the happiness you deserve."

As Cassielle turned away, she allowed her soul to be pulled back towards her body. Though their physical separation remained, their eternal connection would forever light her path.

Her fingers instinctively found the necklace adorning her neck, tracing the contours of the protection charm.

"Thank you," she whispered.

Samedi sat beside her, watching her with his eyes wide and anxious. He reached out to touch her but she held up her hand, stopping him. Seeing her mother had reawakened her sorrow at her loss of her. But her mother was right. She needed to move forward. She couldn't keep dwelling on what had happened or be afraid of what might come. She needed to live in the moment. Love those she could, and live life to her fullest.

She looked down at her hands and marveled at how she could see a blue-black light coming off of her skin. It was almost mist-like. Somehow, it looked faded and weak. She looked at Samedi who had no light coming off of him.

"That's your aura," he offered. "I don't have one as I don't have a human soul. You'll be able to tell if someone is possessed by a human soul or malevolent spirit by the presence or lack of an aura." He smiled, "I'm glad to see you've fully awakened your abilities."

She opened her mouth to ask him to elaborate, but she was interrupted by the ringing of her cell phone.

Reaching into her pocket, she retrieved her phone and answered the call. "Yes?"

"Nick's spirit is here. Come back," Nibo's voice came through urgently.

She couldn't help but express her surprise. "You know how to use a phone?"

Nibo let out an exasperated sigh. "We don't have time," Nibo's voice turned stern, abruptly ending the conversation.

Cassielle and Samedi swiftly packed up the blanket. Cassielle closed her eyes, her breath steadying as she visualized the room where Nick was held captive, bound on the floor with Nibo keeping watch. She pictured every detail, focusing on the faint glow she had noticed earlier-two figures standing nearby. Her mother had indeed fulfilled her promise.

A gentle tug on her consciousness guided her as she stepped into the shadows. Emerging into the room, she saw Nibo and Nick's body. Nick's spirit stood behind his body, looking bewildered. Cassielle's gaze shifted, and she noticed a glow emanating from Nick's body-a swirling mist of red and black.

Samedi had told her she would be able to see auras, the essence of individuals. She hadn't expected to see one coming from Nick, but it made sense. DeLuca, a malevolent essence, was inhabiting Nick's body. The sinister aura confirmed his presence, making the gravity of their task even clearer.

"Welcome back, ma cherie," Nibo greeted.

"Okay. Let's do this," Cassielle dramatically cracked her knuckles.

Nibo turned to DeLuca, who glared at them in the chair. Nibo waved at him with a mischievous smile, provoking a growl that rumbled from deep within the man's chest. Chuckling, Nibo refocused his attention on Cassielle, whispering comforting words to Nick's spirit. Nick's spirit was looking around himself with wide and confused eyes. He ran his hand through his ethereal hair and looked at his hand with alarm.

"When I give the signal, you'll shove him back into his body. Samedi and I will extract DeLuca from the vessel and return him where he belongs."

Samedi nodded.

"You will be weakened after having expended so much energy not just shadow walking, but fighting off the baka,"

Samedi said, gently placing a hand upon her lower back. A comforting warmth spread through her body from the point of contact.

"How did you know about the Baka?" She turned to look at him and he simply smirked at her.

"I have my ways," he grinned mischievously at her.

"We don't have time for this," Nibo's voice pulled her out of the moment with Samedi. She mentally kicked herself for getting distracted. What was wrong with her? She recognized that Samedi was right, she felt like she'd just finished running a marathon through a bog. Her limbs felt leadened and her eyes felt grainy like they do when you haven't slept in a long time.

"Okay, let's do this," Cassielle moved towards Nick who growled at her. "Seriously? You're growling at me?"

Samedi offered her a reassuring nod before turning his attention to Nibo who nodded that he was ready as well.

Nibo took a deep breath, his expression steeling as he prepared to initiate the extraction. Cassielle's heart pounded in her chest, her senses heightened with anticipation. She reached out, her fingers trembling slightly as she prepared to assist in guiding Nick's spirit back into his body.

With a determined nod from Nibo, they sprang into action. Cassielle focused her energy, channeling it into a force that gently nudged Nick's spirit toward his physical form. She could feel the resistance emanating from DeLuca' essence, a malevolent force that threatened to resist their efforts.

Inch by inch, Nick's spirit edged closer to his body, guided by Cassielle's steady hand. DeLuca's soul started to come out of Nick's body, kicking and screaming. Samedi stood ready with his cane and hat. Cassielle gave Nick's spirit another little shove while Nibo pulled DeLuca again.

The black and red imbued soul was ripped from Nick's body and caught at the end of Samedi's cane. Samedi threw it with a flourish into his hat where it seemed to vanish. She looked at him with surprise. She had expected a portal to be opened and the soul to go through there.

"Heylel wanted him to go to a special place," he explained and nodded to Nibo who gave Nick's spirit a final push.

Just as they were on the verge of success, a sudden disturbance shattered the fragile balance they had achieved. A dark figure materialized in the room with a burst of energy, Cassielle's heart skipped a beat. She recoiled, her senses overwhelmed by the sinister presence that now filled the space.

It took her a moment to gather her wits and recognize the looming figure before her. The form twisting and contorting into a monstrous visage. His appearance was unmistakable to her-his head resembled that of a lion, its fierce mane flowing around him like a dark halo. Six cloven-hoofed legs extended from his body in all directions, giving him the appearance of a grotesque spinning wheel.

Each hoofed leg seemed to move independently, creating an unsettling sensation as he moved closer. His eyes, glowing with a malevolent light, fixated on Cassielle and her companions with an intensity that sent a shudder through her body. He was grotesque and moved in an unnatural way. Buer.

The air crackled with dark energy as he advanced, his presence filling the room with a suffocating dread. Cassielle and her allies stood their ground, steeling themselves for the inevitable confrontation with this formidable adversary.

It was only after a lingering moment of dread that Cassielle's mind clicked back to life. It was then, too, that she realized even though she could feel his energy, he did not have an aura. Obviously inhuman.

Cassielle's heart skipped a beat as she locked eyes with Buer, his gaze burning with malice. She knew she was outmatched. She was tired. She felt as if her energy was depleted to the extent that if she tried to fight him now, she wouldn't survive it. But she had to. She had to, for Nick.

"We have to go," Samedi's grip closed around her wrist

and pulling her towards safety. But she resisted, her feet planted firmly in a defensive stance, her whole body vibrating with a mixture of fear and adrenaline. Her heart raced in her chest with the strain. She could feel her energy waning, drained by her trip to Limbo, but she refused to back down now.

"No," she shook her head. "We have to stop this. This has to end now!"

"Samedi's right, Cassielle. You're not strong enough right now," Nibo's voice cut through the chaos, his tone urgent but tinged with concern. "We need to retreat. Now!"

But Cassielle's resolve hardened as she faced the looming threat before them. With a primal scream building in her throat, she prepared to unleash whatever remaining strength she possessed. However, before she could make a move, Buer struck with terrifying speed and ferocity.

A gut-wrenching horror gripped Cassielle as she watched helplessly, her scream echoing through the chamber as Buer engulfed Nick's body in a dark, swirling vortex. She felt a surge of desperation, her mind racing to comprehend the unfolding nightmare before her.

Cassielle's heart pounded with terror as her anguished cry pierced the air, her voice trembling with raw emotion as she watched the nightmarish scene unfold. Desperation clawed at her insides as she attempted to lunge forward, to reach Nick before it was too late. But Samedi's firm grip around her waist yanked her back with unyielding strength, lifting her off the ground and hauling her into the shadows.

CHAPTER THIRTY-SIX

"Nick! No!" Her voice cracked with anguish, the sheer agony of the moment threatening to overwhelm her. Each word was a desperate plea, a futile attempt to reach him, to save him from the encroaching darkness that threatened to consume him whole.

Her limbs thrashed against Samedi's hold, her struggles futile against his unyielding grasp. She fought against the crushing weight of despair that threatened to suffocate her, her screams echoing off the walls in a chorus of anguish and despair. She kicked and punched but Samedi was too strong. He held her as they traveled through the shadows and released her once they emerged.

Only when they were out of the shadows did Cassielle's senses begin to return, her surroundings coming back into focus as the haze of panic slowly lifted. She gasped for air, her chest heaving with exertion as she realized where they were. She sat on the ground, exhausted, and consumed with fear and grief. She glared up at Samedi who had stepped away from her.

"What the actual fuck!?" She leapt to her feet, fully intent on beating Samedi or running back to the abandoned plantation.

Cassielle's rage surged through her like a wildfire, hotter and more intense than anything she had felt since the night her mother died, the killer slipping through the cracks of a failed investigation. Now, standing toe-to-toe with Samedi, she screamed at him, her voice raw and piercing, the words spilling out in a torrent of fury and betrayal.

"How could you do this? You've killed Nick! I will never

forgive you!" Her fists clenched at her sides, nails digging into her palms. "We had the stone to protect Nick from Buer! I just needed to put it on him!"

Nibo tried to intervene, his voice a tentative whisper in the storm of her anger. "Cassielle, he saved you from getting killed too, and I-"

"Stay out of this!" she snapped, her glare sharp enough to cut. Nibo closed his mouth shut and stepped back with his hands raised in a surrender position.

Samedi stood in silence like a wall taking the gusting winds, watching her with calm, patient eyes. Nick's spirit stood looking forlorn in the middle of the clearing. Cassielle hadn't registered that he'd been brought with them. She'd had no say in where they went since she'd been dragged away by Samedi.

Her curses eventually faded, exhaustion overcoming her like a tidal wave. Her head throbbed on one side as if someone were repeatedly stabbing her. The sun was just coming up and just the light of that was enough to send pain shooting through her eyes.

"I brought Nick's spirit with us," Nibo said softly after she had quieted for a bit.

She collapsed to the ground, pulling her knees to her chest and wrapping her arms around them, resting her forehead on her folded arms. The clearing was quiet, save for the morning birds calling and the cicadas and toads settling in for another hot Louisiana day.

"Cassielle?" She lifted her head. Nick's spirit stood beside her, his voice distant as if it were fading away, yet he remained, looking bewildered. She could see through him to the trees behind him, giving the scene a surreal, Hollywood-esque ghost movie feel. His clothing and hair seemed to ruffle from a breeze that couldn't be felt by her. "Is this a dream?"

"I wish it was," she said softly, watching him as he looked around himself. "I tried to tell you when we were in the police station, but you didn't believe me."

"He's not going to remember what you're saying," Nibo said, settling next to her. "He's in a different sort of limbo right now. He can't stay there. He's between worlds. It's not good for the dead to stay there..."

"He's not dead." She narrowed her eyes at Nibo, too tired to physically lash out.

"Of course," Nibo agreed, holding up his palms in a defensive gesture. "I merely meant, the state he is in now is as if he were dead. His body, I hope, is still alive."

"He is," Samedi chimed in, leaning against one of the many trees surrounding their clearing. He gazed up at the sky, watching it change from dark blue to pink, purple, and orange as the sunrise moved forward. "Unfortunately it won't be for long. Cassielle, you need to sleep. Rest. Regroup. And then we can go after Buer. Nibo can keep an eye on Nick's spirit."

"And what are you going to do? Isn't there some sort of magic thing I could do to get my energy back so we can go save Nick now? Some sort of Bibbidi-Bobbidi-Boo? We're wasting time just sitting here. I'm so fucking tired of resting and not doing. You don't need to rest. I'm Heylel's child, I shouldn't need rest!"

Samedi turned his gaze back to her, his eyes filled with a pity that made her blood boil. She could hardly stand to look at him. He was attractive, yes, but she felt such deep anger that she wasn't sure she could ever forget this. And yet, a part of her understood why he'd done it. She was exhausted. He was probably right. But she wanted to sit in her fury. She wanted to burn him with her eyes. She wouldn't swoon over him. Not now. When this was all said and done, she was going to be done dealing with the Loa and their callousness towards human life. Nibo seemed to care, but not Samedi. Nibo had at least saved Nick's spirit. Perhaps Nibo managed to retain some of his human spirit when he was made a Loa.

"Magic, as you'd like to call it, though I don't know that I would discern it as such, has a price," Samedi began, his voice steady and measured. "Everything comes with a price.

The power you wield uses energy. It's like trying to run a car with a battery that's dying. Sure, you may be able to turn it on, but how long will that last? If you keep using your power past your exhausted point, you could use up your life force. It's too dangerous." He moved toward her, but she shook her head and he stopped.

"I would risk my life to save Nick's. He would do the same for me, or anyone else," she said softly, her voice trembling with conviction. She'd seen him do it before.

Samedi's expression softened, a profound sadness flickering in his eyes. "I'm not willing to do that," he said quietly. "Your life holds value beyond what you see now. Sacrificing yourself isn't the answer. Sometimes, the hardest part is putting the needs of the many above those we care for and then living with the difficult choices we make."

"This happening to Nick wasn't my choice," she looked down, studying a blade of grass as she tried to hold back the tears building in her eyes.

Nibo stepped forward, his usually playful demeanor replaced with a rare seriousness. "Sometimes, we have to trust others to make the difficult choices when we can't," he said, his voice steady and gentle. "It's not always about the one, but about the many. Your life, Cassielle, affects more than just you. Sacrificing yourself might save Nick, but it could hurt countless others who rely on you, who love you. There are many who will need you in the coming days and years as the veil becomes thinner. There are more malevolent spirits out in the world than just Buer. You can't sacrifice yourself against him to save one person. We need you to help fix it. The strength to make the hard choices, the ones that look beyond immediate pain and loss, is what makes a true hero."

She looked up at Nibo, her eyes reflecting the turmoil within her. "I don't want to be a hero, though. I just wanted to..."

"You just wanted to live your life hiding from who and what you are and cutting out the people around you so that if something happened and you lost them it wouldn't hurt you as much because you'd let them go?" Nibo's words struck deep, hitting home with a precision that left her momentarily speechless. He had cut through her defenses, exposing truths she had been trying to bury beneath layers of denial. She had to admit, begrudgingly, that he was right. It was a bitter pill to swallow, but in the stark light of his observation, she couldn't deny the validity of his words. She'd been so wounded by suddenly losing her mother that she had never truly let anyone get close. And, as her power grew, she became afraid of it and used that as a reason for pushing them all away.

She looked over at the spirit of Nick who had sat, looking lost and forlorn. She swallowed the lump in her throat. It was time to make the difficult decisions.

"Okay. So I will sleep, but then what?"

"Then we go after Buer," Samedi said with a glint in his eye. "As I said before, Nibo will watch Nick, and I need to go report back to Heylel where we are at." He seemed to wince a bit at the thought. Cassielle noticed that the bluster and bravado Samedi carried with him seemed to wane when he was faced with interacting with her father.

"Okay."

Nibo helped her set up her blanket, and she laid down to get some rest. Samedi took one last look at her before stepping into the shadows to face off with what was to be an unhappy Heylel. They'd made their choices. They'd suffer their consequences. But these choices would work. They had to.

As Cassielle closed her eyes, the weight of the world pressing down on her, she wasn't sure how long it took, but she eventually found herself drifting into an uneasy sleep.

And as the first rays of dawn pierced through the darkness, Cassielle drifted off to sleep. Her dreams were haunted by visions of Nick, trapped in some liminal space between life and death. She tossed and turned, the turmoil of her emotions following her even into the realm of sleep.

Yet amidst the darkness of her dreams, a faint light

flickered, a glimmer of hope amidst the chaos. She held onto it, a beacon guiding her through the storm that raged within her soul. For in that light, she found the strength to face the challenges ahead, to confront the demons that lurked in the shadows.

Cassielle's senses gradually stirred to the sounds and scents of the bayou as she opened her eyes, greeted by the dappled sunlight filtering through the canopy of trees above her. The brightness cast a warm, golden glow over the clearing. The earth beneath her felt cool and damp, a stark contrast to the warmth that embraced her skin. She inhaled deeply, savoring the scent of wet soil mingled with the delicate fragrance of wildflowers nearby, a symphony of nature's perfume.

As she stretched her limbs, a sense of unexpected refreshment washed over her, as though the very essence of the wilderness had revitalized her weary body. The rustle of leaves and the chirping of birds provided a soothing backdrop to the tranquil scene, punctuated by the occasional croak of a nearby frog.

Without the aid of a clock, she estimated the time to be early afternoon, maybe? The stillness of the air seemed to indicate the lull before the time when the afternoon's heat would reach its peak. She glanced around the clearing, taking in the sights and sounds of the bayou's embrace, feeling a sense of peace settle over her until she remembered what had happened.

She reached for her phone, only to find it lifeless in her grasp. Maybe those ghost shows were right and spirits draw upon the batteries of electronics. She'd have to ask Nibo sometime.

Nibo's voice echoed from the other side of the clearing where he and Nick sat. Nick, despite his spectral form, remained a poignant reminder of the trials they faced, his expression mirroring a sense of lost innocence that tugged at

Cassielle's heart. She watched as Nibo, engrossed in a book, seemed to be immersed in a world of words, whether reading aloud to Nick or merely allowing him to absorb the pages over his shoulder as he read aloud.

The scene before her unfolded like a tableau of peace amidst chaos, a fleeting moment of respite before the storm that loomed on the horizon. Cassielle stood and stretched her arms above her head, working out her cramped muscles from her slumber. She must have been still while she slept as her muscles seemed to have cramped up, but as she moved they were loosening.

The peace of the clearing shattered when a dark fog developed in the center of the clearing. She recognized it instantly. She had no surprise as Samedi stepped out, the fog clearing up once he was through. Shadow walking was becoming so normal to her that she wondered if she would ever just walk or drive places again. Though she supposed she would have to. Probably best not to advertise that kind of stuff lest she wind up being talked into doing some kind of traveling Victorian era spirituality type of tour.

"Your father is coming," Samedi said gravely. "He's not thrilled with how we moved forward with things, but he wanted to check on you before you go face Buer."

"Well, if he wants my help with all of this, he's going to just have to accept that I have free-will to do things my way," she bent to gather up the blanket that she had been sleeping on.

"There are many things that I and other fathers must accept," the voice coming from the shadows of the trees made her heart leap into her throat. Her father stepped out. He wore that same finely tailored suit, molded to his form perfectly an aura of authority radiating off of him. His cravat around his neck was red while the top hat perched on his head was black and embellished with a miniature skull. His hair was tied back as it had been before, the curls cascading down his back.

His one eye peered at her through his glasses. She took

a steadying breath, readying herself to face off against him.

"I am not thrilled that you disregarded my commands," Heylel strode into the clearing, his long legs making short work of walking to where Cassielle stood. They were roughly the same height, so she was able to look him eye to eye, or eyes to eye as it were. "Papa Legba told me he met you. Of course, he waited until after you'd returned safely to this world." He held up a hand towards Nibo who had opened his mouth to say something. "I am not angry." He continued to look at Cassielle. His gaze was making her uncomfortable, but she wasn't going to break eye contact first. She was determined to stand her ground and maintain eye contact as one would do with a dog. She wasn't going to be intimidated by him.

His face broke into a broad smile. "You've come a long way, my child," he said softly, raising a hand to brush a stray curl out of her face. "You have the power in you, my power in you. You can defeat Buer. I must go and tend to some of the other inhuman spirits. When you finish with Buer, Samedi can help you make a plan on which inhuman malevolent spirit to go after next. We have many to catch and return. I'm sure you've been too busy with this to keep an eye on the human news, but it certainly isn't looking good." He sighed and ran a hand over his face. "Bondye is most displeased. We need to do this before he decides to act... I'd like to avoid a second coming of Jesus." He rolled his eyes. "That man was insufferable with his positivity."

Cassielle refrained from laughing. The idea that the devil would not like Jesus was amusing as from what she knew, Jesus and Bondye were the exact opposite to Heylel. Did that mean that she was also the opposite of Jesus?

She thought on that for but a moment before deciding no. She could choose to be a good person. Heylel likely would have preferred that she go all guns a blazing and tear down the world in an attempt to recapture the demons, but she wouldn't do that. Human life was sacred and valuable. She wouldn't go as far as to say she was following in Jesus's footsteps precisely, for she certainly had plenty of sins she had committed over the years, but she wasn't as dark as Heylel, either.

"Are you ready?" Heylel seemed to have been giving her some time to gather her thoughts, or he was lost in his own. Either way, she could feel that it was time. Her stomach clenched with anxiety, and she could feel her heart begin to race as if she had drunk a cup of espresso. She couldn't speak over the lump in her throat, so she settled for nodding.

"Good," Heylel said, his voice carrying a tone of reassurance. He turned to Samedi and Nibo, his presence commanding attention. "Might I recommend Nibo and Nick remain here while Cassielle and Samedi go after Buer?"

They nodded their agreement, and Cassielle watched as relief washed over Samedi's face. His eyes, usually filled with a mischievous spark, now held a glimmer that matched the resolve she felt building within herself.

"Splendid. Now let's go catch some demons, shall we?" Heylel grinned at her, his expression a curious blend of paternal pride and devilish enthusiasm. Cassielle took a deep breath, steeling herself for the challenges that lay ahead.

She observed the subtle difference in Heylel's departure compared to that of Samedi and the other Loa. As he tipped his hat and stepped into the shadows, it was as if he merged with a swirling vortex of black and red, emanating heat that brushed against her skin. The sight left her momentarily transfixed, but the urgency of their mission snapped her back to reality, prompting her to tuck away her observations for later contemplation.

Turning her attention to Nick's spirit, Cassielle felt a pang of longing to reach out to him, to feel the warmth of his touch. But she knew that without his corporeal body, such a gesture was impossible. She reminded herself of the purpose that drove her forward - to save Nick - and pushed aside the overwhelming fear of Buer's threat to the world and everyone she held dear. One step at a time, she told herself, focusing solely on the task at hand.

"Shall we?" She hadn't noticed Samedi approaching her.

"Stay here, Nick," she whispered, her gaze locking with his. She hoped her words didn't sound as shaky as she felt. Facing off against a demon sounded like the most terrifying confrontation one could have. "I'll find a way to return you to your body soon. With any luck, you won't remember any of this." She hesitated, the weight of her words sinking in. "But if you do, we'll figure it out."

"You will need Nick there as soon as you get Buer out," Nibo looked anxiously between Cassielle and Samedi.

"Samedi will come get you."

"I'm not leaving you alone with Buer," Samedi's face darkened.

"We have no other option. We can't bring Nick with us-"

"We'll just have to figure it out," Nibo interrupted. "We don't have time to argue."

With a final nod, Cassielle turned to Samedi. "Let's go."

CHAPTER THIRTY-SEVEN

As Cassielle cautiously stepped into the abandoned plantation, a sense of unease settled over her like a suffocating blanket. The room exuded a bone-chilling coldness that seemed to seep into her essence, a stark contrast to the oppressive heat of the bayou outside. With each hesitant step, the floorboards groaned beneath her weight, adding to the eerie atmosphere that enveloped the derelict building. She felt chilled with the sweat that had gathered on her skin and in her clothes during her day-time slumber in the bayou.

The walls, adorned with peeling floral wallpaper, bore the scars of neglect, riddled with mysterious holes and patches of decay. The absence of glass in the windows puzzled her, allowing the stagnant air of the room to mingle with the humid breeze outside, creating a disconcerting mix of temperatures. It felt as though the walls held secrets, whispering tales of bygone days long forgotten.

"Well, this place certainly is charming," Cassielle kicked at a discarded beer can.

"As charming as a one eyed snake," Samedi agreed, his voice, solemn and reverent, drawing Cassielle's attention to the broken remnants of a once-grand mantle. Amidst the shattered picture frames and the rusted remnants of a clock frozen in time, she felt a pang of sadness for the forgotten memories trapped within these walls.

If Nick's body had been taken by Buer, there would be

no trace to follow. But if Buer had possessed Nick, perhaps there were clues to be found. Cassielle hurried to the back door. Stepping onto the porch, she scanned the ground, her eyes searching for any sign of disturbance amidst the overgrown weeds and decaying remnants of human habitation.

The path, lined with weather-worn stones, bore witness to the passage of many feet, each step a testament to the building's dark history. Cassielle moved cautiously, her senses on high alert as she followed the winding trail towards the dense thicket of trees that bordered the estate.

As she ventured deeper into the woods, a sense of foreboding settled over her like a heavy shroud. The air grew thick with the scent of damp earth and decaying vegetation, a stark contrast to the crispness of the bayou. Every rustle of leaves and every snap of a twig beneath her feet sent a shiver down her spine, as if the forest itself was alive with unseen watchers.

Just as despair threatened to consume her, a glimmer of hope caught her eye. A flash of blue fabric, caught on a jagged shard of glass, beckoned to her like a beacon in the darkness. Dropping to her knees, Cassielle studied the dirt beneath her, her heart pounding in anticipation as she traced the faint outline of footprints leading deeper into the woods.

"Samedi!" Her voice sliced through the stagnant air, a sharp note of urgency and relief reverberating through the stillness like a ripple on a placid pond.

"Hush, Cherie, I am here," came Samedi's voice, so surprisingly close it seemed to materialize from the very shadows themselves.

"We must tread carefully," he cautioned, his tone a low murmur that seemed to blend with the rustle of leaves in the breeze. "The darkness conceals many dangers."

"I thought I told you to stop doing that?" Cassielle hissed, her frustration tinged with a hint of amusement.

"You didn't," Samedi replied, a playful smile evident in his voice as he chuckled softly.

"I must have thought it," she retorted, gesturing towards the path ahead, "Regardless, we have a trail to follow. And if something were lurking, wouldn't we sense it?"

Samedi shrugged, a fluid movement barely visible in the dim light filtering through the trees. "Not necessarily. Buer's minions could mask their presence with his dark magic. And in a place saturated with residual energy like this, even the most vigilant can be caught off guard."

Cassielle chewed on her lower lip, a knot of nerves forming in the pit of her stomach. "Okay, then we need to be on guard," she whispered.

"Always," Samedi agreed.

Cassielle led the way as they followed the footprints in the mud. She lost them here and there as he must have stepped on rocks or more firm grass, but she was able to find the path again after taking some time to search. She could feel the time ticking away, taking Nick's life with it. She had to hurry up, but the day was growing later, and soon she would lose the light.

"You know, this would be so much easier if everyone's lives weren't at stake," she remarked, her voice tinged with forced lightness.

"Where's the fun in that?" Samedi replied with a grin.

They reached the road and Cassielle took several minutes pacing and studying the tracks in the road. This street wasn't used much, so there weren't many, but she could tell the footprints ended here. He must have gotten a ride from someone.

Cassielle ran her hand through her hair in frustration, feeling the thick, humid air cling to her skin. "There's no way I can track him if he went in a car." She paused, pressing a hand to her forehead as she stared down the dusty back road, her thoughts spinning.

The heat was oppressive, wrapping around her like a suffocating blanket. The sun blazed high in the sky, casting long, shimmering waves of heat off the pot-holed asphalt. Sweat trickled down her back, her shirt clinging uncomfortably to her skin. The occasional buzz of a cicada was the only sound breaking the heavy silence, and even the trees seemed to droop under the weight of the sweltering afternoon.

If they went back to New Orleans, she could charge her phone. But then what? Call Nick? That was ridiculous. Would Buer really waltz up to her to talk? Chances were high that he could have ditched Nick's body anywhere and gone on his merry way, leaving her none the wiser.

Her anxiety churned in her stomach, making her feel sick, and a headache began to throb at her temples. The stakes were too high for her to lose focus now. "Where could he have gone?" she whispered to herself, her voice barely audible over the hum of the insects.

"Could Nick's partner help?" Samedi's voice cut through her thoughts.

"Rebecca?" She looked at Samedi, furrowing her brow.

"No, his work partner. Fontenot. I think Marcus was his first name?"

"Samedi, you're a genius! If I can convince Fontenot that Nick's in danger, he can get the IT guys to track down his cell phone. But, I need to charge my phone for that to work. Let's go to my office. I can also check my emails-"

"We can't go to your office," Samedi interrupted, his tone hesitant.

"Why not?" She demanded, her patience wearing thin.

"Well, it's entirely possible that it is inaccessible at the moment." Samedi avoided her gaze, staring down the road instead.

"What do you know, Samedi?" She could feel her annoyance flaring. "We don't have time for coy games."

"While you were in the bayou training with Nibo, some of the followers of Buer may or may not have burned down your office building."

"What?!" She grabbed Samedi by the shoulders, her voice rising. "And you didn't think that was important to tell me?"

"We had more pressing matters."

Cassielle's head throbbed in time with her heartbeat, and the relentless sun pounded down on her back. She was almost certain she would have a sunburn if she didn't already. She was starting to reconsider her love of Louisiana summers. She'd never been particularly outdoorsy, and they'd been spending a lot of time there. The heat was nearly unbearable, even in the shade of the trees.

Cassielle let out a long sigh, running her hand through her hair again before folding her hands on top of her head. "Okay... well I guess we'll go to my apartment then..."

"Probably not the best idea."

"Don't tell me that's gone too!" Panic rose in her chest. Everything important to her was there, save for her mother's journal in her bag. Reflexively she placed her hand on it as if making sure it was still there before putting a hand to her forehead and the other on her back.

"No, but Buer's followers will know to look for you there. Let's go to Rebecca's."

"For one, I don't know where she lives, and for two, didn't you want her out of all of this?"

"I did, but I know where she lives, and Buer's followers won't be expecting you to go there. They'll expect you to go to your house, office, or LaFitte's. Or even Brittany's house."

"Okay. Then I guess we go to Rebecca's and hope she has a phone charger that will work with my phone... or has the number for Nick's partner." She dropped her hands to her hips. "I guess you'll have to take us there."

Samedi smiled mischievously, and she knew what was coming.

"I'd be more than happy to take you anywhere, cherie," with one swift move, he quickly swooped her up into his arms before stepping into the shadows.

CHAPTER THIRTY-EIGHT

They stepped out of the shadows into a spacious living room with high ceilings and hardwood floors that looked to Cassielle as if they were original to the home. Large windows flooded the room with natural light. Across from the kitchenette, an exposed brick fireplace added a rustic touch. The room was a tasteful blend of modern and vintage, with mismatched furniture clearly chosen to add character and warmth to the space. The walls displayed local artwork, reflecting the vibrant cultural tapestry of the neighborhood.

In one corner of the room, a computer desk was nestled, its surface cluttered with papers and a glowing monitor. Rebecca sat there, hunched over her keyboard, typing furiously. Her intense focus on the screen rendered her oblivious to their sudden appearance. Cassielle's heart raced with embarrassment and alarm at having intruded so abruptly.

"What the hell?" she hissed at Samedi, barely managing to contain her irritation.

"Greetings, Rebecca," Samedi said, his voice loud and clear, leaving no room for doubt that he intended to be heard.

Rebecca spun around in her chair, eyes wide with surprise. Her hand darted to the nearest object for defense- a gun that had been sitting close to her hand that was controlling her mouse. The sharp glint of metal caught the light as she held them up, ready to defend herself.

"Cassielle?! What the fuck?!" Rebecca's face reddened with fury. She didn't put down the gun, keeping it pointed at them. But she also didn't move from her chair.

"I'm so sorry Rebecca, Sam here has a bad habit of breaking and entering-"

"We don't have time for games," Samedi cut Cassielle off unapologetically. He stepped forward, and Rebecca turned her gun towards him. He smiled, eyes glinting with amusement. Cassielle could practically hear him thinking, 'That's not going to do shit to me.' But Samedi didn't talk like that.

"When we met with you before, we told you that all the strange murders were tied to Voodoo and otherworldly events..."

"You mean I told her," Cassielle interrupted. Rebecca moved her gun to Cassielle who raised her hands in a defensive gesture.

"... You didn't believe us then," Samedi continued, ignoring Cassielle's interruption. "You can believe us now on our word, or I can show you something that will likely terrify you. I'd rather not."

"Trust me, you'd rather not see it," Cassielle agreed wryly. "But you did see Nick behaving in a manner that is entirely unlike him-"

"How did you get in here?" She looked between the two of them. "I'm shocked a detective... sorry, former detective, would break into someone's apartment."

We didn't break in," Cassielle said with a smile, her voice calm despite the tension in the air. "We walked in... we stepped through the shadows. Like this." With a fluid motion, Cassielle summoned the shadows before her, the darkness swallowing her form as she stepped into it, only to reappear two feet to Rebecca's left.

To her credit, Rebecca didn't jump, but Cassielle noticed the color draining from her face, leaving her pale and rigid. The gun in Rebecca's hand quivered slightly as she redirected it towards Cassielle. Cassielle shot a quick glance towards Samedi, whose expression had turned serious, the glint of amusement replaced by caution.

Sensing Samedi's intent to intervene, Cassielle subtly shook her head, signaling him to hold back. She didn't believe Rebecca would actually pull the trigger, and she couldn't blame her for being cautious in such a volatile situation. After all, in today's world where even your partner could turn on you, one couldn't afford to trust even those they knew well.

"Okay... I'm listening," she said softly, moving her chair back a bit as if to put space between herself and Cassielle.

"We don't have a lot of time-"

Cassielle cut Samedi off and quickly started rattling off everything that had happened since Samedi first stepped into her office up to just before finding out Nick had been possessed. She wasn't sure how to break it to her. By the time she finished, Rebecca ran a hand through her long blonde hair, clearly trying to process everything she'd just been told. After a few moments, she seemed to give up on that endeavor entirely.

"Let's ignore the massive pile of what the fuck you just dropped at my feet," she started carefully. "And go to the obvious questions - Why are you here? Why couldn't you just call or email like a normal person?"

"My phone's dead and we don't really have time-" Cassielle began.

Samedi jumped in and told her about Nick's possession by DeLuca, and the either possession or abduction and murder by Buer after that. Rebecca's jaw dropped open in horror as she stared wide-eyed at Samedi.

She looked quickly back to Cassielle, "so, you're saying when I saw you and Nick in the bar..."

"He was possessed," Cassielle finished. She let out a breath as Rebecca lowered her gun and set it on the computer desk next to her.

"Well, that would explain his behavior..." Her voice faltered momentarily as she seemed to reconsider her words, then she quickly redirected, "not that I'd be surprised to see him flirting with you. You two have history. But he's so committed to monogamy that even if he still had feelings for you, he wouldn't pursue anything without ending things with me first. We made an agreement."

"You have an agreement to break up with each other before going back to exes?" Samedi arched an eyebrow.

Rebecca fixed him with narrow eyed glare, "Not specifically about exes, but if we ever were to think of cheating, we would have a heart-to-heart about-" she shook her head. "No, it's not important. So we need to find Nick."

"I need to call Fontenot... Marcus," Cassielle clarified in case Rebecca didn't know him by his last name.

"Sure, I have his number here... but how's he going to help? If you two have all this power to use, can't you just... I don't know, do a spell to find him or something?"

Samedi growled in frustration, "Woman, we don't have time-"

Cassielle cut him off, "I'd love to explain everything in extreme detail, but obviously time is pressing. Please, can I use your phone to call Fon... Marcus?"

Rebecca agreed and pulled up Marcus's contact and handed Cassielle the phone. The phone rang twice before he picked up.

"Rebecca?" He sounded confused. She could hear sirens in the background as well as screaming and crying. She'd almost forgotten that the city had descended into Chaos before she'd gone spirit walking.

Cassielle dove in before he could say more, "No, this is Cassielle. I'm borrowing Rebecca's phone. Listen, Nick has gone missing, I need someone in IT to track his phone. I'm not sure if he's alive or dead-"

"Nick's not missing," Fontenot sounded stressed. "And he's most certainly alive." He cleared his throat. "Listen, now's not a great time..."

"Fontenot, spit it out," Cassielle grasped the phone with

both her hands, resisting the urge to scream at him.

"Nick currently is holding the Mayor and some of his staff hostage," Fontenot sounded as if he couldn't believe the words he was saying. "He's had some sort of psychotic break..."

"He's possessed," Cassielle breathed out a sigh of relief. She was a bit surprised she was relieved, but if Nick was holding people hostage, then either Buer or one of his followers was possessing him, so his body was still alive. There was still a chance.

"Well that explains it," Fontenot muttered sarcastically.

"I wish I could explain more-" Cassielle began, but Fontenot interrupted her.

"Get your ass down here," Fontenot pressed urgently. "I don't have time to go into detail, but here's the gist." Cassielle listened intently as he rattled off information before concluding with, "I'm fairly certain you're the only one who could talk him out of this. There isn't a lot of time. We're at city hall. Hurry."

The call ended abruptly, leaving Cassielle to digest the terse message. She'd need to work with what she had and hope for the best. This was becoming an all too familiar tactic. It wasn't her preferred approach.

Taking the phone away from her ear, she stared at it, unsure of her next move or how to convey the urgency of the situation. Samedi's throat-clearing brought her attention back to the room. He gave a subtle nod toward Rebecca, signaling Cassielle to address her next. Turning to Rebecca, she expected horror was etched across her face so she made a concerted effort to arrange her face into something she hoped resembled calm determination.

"Cassielle?" Rebecca said from her chair, gripping the arms as if they were keeping her rooted in her spot.

"He's alive," she said quietly. Samedi stood staring at her. The look on his face told her he wasn't going to be surprised when she dropped the bombshell. Rebecca, however, looked like she was just barely holding on to her sanity.

"But..."

Cassielle's heart was in her stomach. She felt sick and terrified. "He's holding the Mayor hostage and they're about to send in the SWAT team. They're going to shoot him."

CHAPTER THIRTY-NINE

Rebecca's face was a canvas of turmoil, reflecting the storm of emotions Cassielle felt inside. Her lips were pressed into a line, and her eyebrows knitted together in concern. Her knuckles had turned white as she gripped her knees, the tension in her body palpable.

"How are you going to free him?" Rebecca whispered, her voice trembling.

Cassielle took a deep breath, her eyes meeting Rebecca's. "I have a stone that can capture Buer, but we need Nick's body there to put him back once we extract Buer," she said, glancing at Samedi.

Samedi shrugged, his expression troubled. "I still haven't figured out how to get Nick there."

Rebecca's gaze darted between them, confusion and urgency in her eyes. "What's the problem?"

Cassielle quickly explained, her voice hushed but intense. "Nibo is back at the clearing with Nick's spirit. We need to summon Nibo to bring Nick."

"Why don't you just call him?" Rebecca asked, her brow furrowing deeper.

"Dead phone," Cassielle replied, holding up her useless device.

Rebecca didn't hesitate. She bent over and rummaged through her work bag, her movements sharp and decisive. She pulled out a cell phone and grabbed her phone from the desk.

"Give me your phone, I'll charge it. You can use my work phone and personal phone. Give this Nibo guy my personal phone, and you take the work phone and call Nibo when you need him to come."

Cassielle took the phones, her eyes wide with gratitude. "Are you sure?"

"It's for Nick. I would do anything for him," Rebecca said softly, her voice breaking. "I know I've only been with him for a short period of time, but he's a wonderful person. He doesn't deserve this... no one does, but you know..."

Cassielle nodded, feeling the weight of Rebecca's words. "Yes, I know what you mean. Okay, this will work."

She handed her phone to Rebecca, who immediately started charging it. Meanwhile, Samedi stepped into the shadows, his form blending seamlessly into the darkness. Moments later, he reappeared, his presence as sudden and unsettling as ever.

"Let's go," he said with a flourish, bowing dramatically. His usual theatrics were a stark contrast to the gravity of the situation, but it brought a fleeting smile to Cassielle's lips.

Cassielle took a deep breath, setting Rebecca's personal number to speed dial and slipping Rebecca's work phone into her pocket. "Alright, let's do this," she said, steeling herself for the battle ahead. She had been to the Mayor's office once before and recalled a bathroom not far from it. Samedi took her by the hand, his grip firm and reassuring, ready to follow her lead. Together, they stepped into the shadows, the darkness enveloping them as they emerged in the women's bathroom.

The bathroom was stark and sterile, the kind of utilitarian space designed for function over form. The overhead fluorescent lights buzzed faintly, casting a harsh, unflattering light over the white tiled walls and floor. The air was cool and carried the faint scent of antiseptic cleaner mixed with a hint of lavender from an automatic air freshener mounted on the wall.

Cassielle's eyes quickly adjusted to the bright light after

the deep shadows. She noted the row of sinks with spotless mirrors above them, reflecting her determined expression and Samedi's composed demeanor. The stalls lined one side of the room, their doors slightly ajar, revealing their pristine interiors. A faint dripping sound echoed from one of the faucets, creating a rhythmic background noise heightening the tension in addition to the sound of sirens in the distance. She moved and looked out the window. She could see the police barricade seven floors below, blocking people from going in or out of the building. She could see the SWAT van, but didn't see the SWAT team. She wasn't sure how much time they had.

She turned to Samedi, her voice barely above a whisper. "We need to move quickly. The Mayor's office is just down the hall from here."

Samedi nodded, his eyes focused on her. "Lead the way."

Cassielle pushed open the bathroom door, peering out into the hallway. She could hear yelling coming from the office at the end of the hallway. It sounded like Nick, but not like Nick. Her heart raced in her chest. She could feel the weight of the stone in her pocket, a small but potent weapon against the chaos Buer intended to unleash.

With a final glance at Samedi, who gave her an encouraging nod, Cassielle stepped into the hallway. The corridor was quiet, the tile floor did nothing to hide their footsteps. As they moved closer to the office, Nick's words became more understandable.

Cassielle glanced behind her towards the elevator and stairwell half expecting the SWAT team to come charging out and plow them over in their attempt to take Nick out. Yet there was no one. It was silent except for Nick's yelling.

"Your world is coming to an end!"

Cassielle and Samedi crouched to the side of the open office door, their breaths shallow and tense. Inside, Buer's voice boomed, dripping with malevolence.

"Your God, your beloved Bondye, won't save you! He doesn't care about you!" He laughed maniacally, the sound chilling Cassielle to the bone. "And your feared devil? Lucifer? Heylel? He couldn't care less about you either. None of your Gods or Deities give a shit!"

Cassielle cringed at the foul language spewing from Buer's mouth, the corruption of Nick's voice adding to the horror. It was Nick's voice but with a weird deep voice undertone. IIt reminded her of something out of one of those B-Rated possession horror movies she and Jamal used to watch. She took a quick peek around the doorframe and saw a camera and its operator. The Mayor must have been giving a speech, probably trying to calm the public amidst the rampant violence, mistakenly thinking it would work to settle things down.

"Abandon your useless religions, your hollow morals. Rules are for the weak and the submissive. Your world is ripe for revolution! You have shown through your wars and your hatred that you reject the teachings of the pathetic Bondye. If you truly believed in his 'love thy neighbor' nonsense, your actions would reflect it."

Cassielle's heart pounded in her chest, each word from Buer heightening the urgency of their mission. She took another deep breath, steeling herself. It was time to end this nightmare. She exchanged a tense glance with Samedi who nodded. Together, they silently slipped into the office, careful not to draw attention to themselves amidst the chaos. The scene before them was one of sheer pandemonium. Papers flew through the air like confetti, and furniture was overturned as if caught in a tempest. At the center of the maelstrom stood Nick-or what remained of him-his eyes glazed over, his body contorted in unnatural ways under the influence of Buer's possession.

There stood a man behind a camera, unfazed by the chaos unfolding before him. She could see a black and blue aura surrounding him, too dark to be the man's actual aura. She was sure if she was in front of him she'd see his black eyes. Amidst the pandamonium, the Mayor remained the sole un-possessed figure, trembling behind his desk as he stared at the scattered papers, likely intended for his interrupted video conference.

Cassielle's heart ached at the sight of Nick's torment, but she pushed aside her emotions, focusing on the task at hand. With resolute steps, she approached Nick, the stone clutched firmly in her hand, while Samedi stood steadfast beside her, a beacon of reassurance amid the turmoil.

Buer's attention honed in on them, his gaze piercing Cassielle with a chilling intensity. "Ah, the meddling mortal returns," he sneered, his voice dripping with contempt.

"Always ready to stir things up," Cassielle shot back.

"It's truly pitiful to see Heylel's own blood walking the path of righteousness. You harbor such darkness within you, daughter of Heylel," Buer spat with venomous disdain.

"You'd have a different tune if Heylel stood before you, Buer," Samedi warned.

Buer snickered, a twisted grin curling his lips. "It's amusing, Samedi, how you remain loyal to your master," he jeered, his laughter ringing through the room. "Does Heylel even realize you've taken a liking to his own daughter?"

Cassielle felt a shiver run down her spine as Buer's mocking laughter filled the air, his words cutting deep. How did he know?

"Oh, what would he do if he knew?" Buer taunted, his laughter sending chills down Cassielle's arms.

"I doubt he'll give it a second thought once we rid ourselves of you and your ilk," Cassielle retorted lightly, refusing to show how much his words unsettled her.

"Enough talking," Buer snarled. "I assume you're here to rescue your beloved Nicholas?" His laughter echoed through the room, chilling Cassielle to the bone. "The only way I'm relinquishing his body is if you fulfill my demands."

"And what might those be?" Cassielle's voice was steady despite the fear gnawing at her insides. She noticed Buer's attention had shifted solely onto her. Samedi had started to move, his steps calculated as he edged closer to the cameraman who continued to capture every moment of their confrontation, the red light indicating its ongoing broadcast. Cassielle couldn't comprehend why they hadn't turned it off. Maybe people at the station were possessed too? It didn't make sense to her.

Buer's response cut through the tense silence like a blade, his words dripping with malice. "I'll release your precious Nicholas," he taunted, "but not before you pledge your unwavering loyalty to me with a blood oath."

Cassielle wanted to say Buer was out of his mind, but she needed to be smart in how she dealt with him. Samedi was now close enough to the cameraman to pull the soul out of him. She had to keep Buer and the cameraman distracted. Once the cameraman was neutralized, they could target Buer.

Feeling the weight of the stone in her pocket, Cassielle pondered how to approach Buer. Perhaps a change in strategy was in order to close the distance between them. She subtly slid her hands into her pockets, adopting a contemplative demeanor.

"And what, pray tell, would be my reward for such a generous pledge?" Cassielle posed the question, her voice laced with skepticism. "Freeing Nick hardly seems like an equitable exchange. After all, committing myself to you would essentially mean forfeiting my own life for someone who may already be lost."

With careful movements, Cassielle shifted to the side, edging closer to Buer while maintaining an air of nonchalance. Her every step was calculated to conceal her true intentions as she prepared to confront the demon head-on.

"What is it you mortals usually want? Riches? Power? I could give you all of that," Buer said with a sly smile. The way he moved in Nick's body was unsettling, an uncanny valley of distorted familiarity. Nick's rugged charm and easygoing demeanor were twisted into something malevolent. His warm brown eyes, usually reflecting kindness and integrity, now gleamed with malice. The casual yet smart outfit of jeans and a button-down shirt that once complemented his physique now seemed like a cruel mockery of his former self, ripped and dirty. It wasn't Nick.

"What if I don't want any of that?" Cassielle countered, inching closer. She was near enough now if she pulled out the stone and used her power, she could force Buer out of Nick's body. She was ready. It was now or never.

"Are you planning on using that little rune stone in your pocket against me?" Buer's words froze her in place. "You're so predictable. I'd have hoped Heylel's daughter would be a more formidable opponent. But you're just sad."

Cassielle's heart pounded, but she refused to back down. She tightened her grip on the stone, knowing she had to act swiftly. The struggle was about to become physical and magical, and she needed to be prepared for whatever came next. With a quick glance at Samedi, who was ready to act, she steeled herself for the battle that was about to unfold.

"I'm not afraid of you, Buer," Cassielle said calmly, keeping her feelings in check with as much control as she could.

"Your pounding heart says otherwise, girl," Buer sneered.

Cassielle saw Samedi move out of the corner of her eye and knew it was time to act. With a swift, decisive motion, she pulled the stone from her pocket, holding it aloft before her. She unleashed a surge of power, far greater than she had intended, an explosion of energy erupting into the room. The light emanating from the stone was a brilliant, blinding red, pulsating with an intensity that would have incapacitated anyone else. It reached for Nick, attempting to grab Buer and force him out of Nick's body.

Simultaneously, Samedi sprang into action. His cane, a seemingly innocuous accessory, was transformed into a weapon of spiritual extraction. With a deft, fluid movement, he hooked the tip of the cane into the aura of the cameraman.

The possessed man's eyes widened in shock and fear as Samedi yanked, pulling the dark spirit free from its host. The cameraman's body convulsed, then went limp, crumpling to the floor like a puppet with its strings cut.

Cassielle heard a crash from the hallway behind her. She couldn't look to see what it was. The room had become incredibly hot as Nick's body convulsed, Buer was fighting and resisting leaving Nick's body. She couldn't worry about him right now. She needed to get Buer out of his body.

"Get away from him!" a voice from behind her commanded. She didn't recognize it, but the look of relief on the Mayor's face suggested it was someone he thought was meant to help. Yet, her instincts screamed at her to be on her guard. She dared not take her eyes off Buer, focusing all her energy on pulling the demon from Nick's body.

Suddenly, hands gripped her arms, yanking them back with brutal force. Cassielle watched in horror as the stone slipped from her grasp, falling to the ground and dimming instantly. The rune's glow faded, and Buer's swirling mass solidified, taking on his proper demonic form: a monstrous visage of a lion's head with goat legs protruding grotesquely from it.

Turning her head, Cassielle saw a man in a SWAT uniform restraining her on one side. Glancing to the other side, she found another similarly dressed figure holding her just as tightly. The room filled with the chilling presence of Buer, now fully manifested and leering at her with malevolent glee.

"Samedi!" she shouted, trying to signal him to fetch Nibo and Nick's soul. If they couldn't succeed at getting rid of Buer, maybe they could at least save Nick.

He looked at her with a conflicted expression, his eyes betraying his refusal. He couldn't abandon her, but by staying, he was dooming Nick as his body lay lifeless on the ground. They were killing him.

Cassielle struggled against the iron grips of the men

holding her arms, silently pleading with Samedi, who stood on guard, torn between the captors and Buer.

"Oh, poor Samedi," Buer hissed, his voice an eerie blend of gravel and elongation, emerging from his true demonic form. "Can't leave your precious pet, lest Heylel get angry. But by staying, you're condemning poor innocent Nick to death. I wonder if dear Cassielle will ever forgive you for this? Too bad your presence won't do her any good."

Buer's voice dripped with malevolence as he continued, "I had hoped Cassielle would willingly give me her power, but her stubbornness has forced us to do this the hard way. If you won't give me your power, I'll take it from you. Then dear Samedi will have to explain to Heylel why his only child is now dead. But hey, at least you'll get to join your beloved Nick. Think of it as a win."

He laughed maniacally, his eyes gleaming with sadistic delight, and nodded towards the Mayor. "Get rid of him and tie her there."

Cassielle took a breath, turning off her panic. Panicking wouldn't help. She needed to rely on her training-both her police academy training and what she had learned from Samedi and Nibo. As Heylel's daughter, she had to have some of his strength. She stopped squirming and focused her energy and attention on the little flame inside her that she had been using to try and capture Buer. Now, she would need to make herself impossible to hold on to.

Drawing from deep within, Cassielle harnessed her latent power, feeling it surge through her veins like molten lava. The air around her crackled with energy, an almost visible aura forming around her body. She concentrated on the flame, willing it to grow, to envelop her.

"Samedi, now!" she shouted, her voice echoing with newfound strength.

Samedi, catching onto her plan, moved with lightning speed. He drew upon his own power, creating a shadowy barrier that momentarily disoriented the SWAT officers holding Cassielle. They flinched, their grips loosening just enough for her to break free.

Cassielle didn't waste a second. She twisted out of their grasp, reached one hand in her pocket to speed dial Rebecca and lunged for the stone on the ground. Buer, realizing her intent, let out a roar of fury and sent a blast of dark energy towards her. She wasn't quick enough to dodge and was knocked back, her body slamming into the desk, a wave of pain radiating through her side. But she couldn't stop. She wouldn't stop.

Ignoring the agony, Cassielle rolled over the desk, landing on the other side and crashing into the Mayor. The collision knocked the wind out of her, but she pushed through the pain, driven by sheer determination. She pulled the Mayor onto the floor with her and not very gently shoved him into the space under his desk. She quickly speed dialed Rebecca's personal phone and looked up at the Mayor.

"Stay here," she commanded before crawling to the edge of the desk. She could hear the snarls and hissing of Buer on the other side. She had no idea what Samedi was doing or what had happened to the SWAT. She had to come up with a plan to get the stone back. She wasn't going to be able to do anything without it.

Cassielle peeked around the corner of the desk, assessing the chaotic scene. Buer, now fully manifested in his demonic form, was a terrifying sight-lion's head with goat's legs protruding grotesquely, his eyes burning with hatred. He was flanked by the possessed SWAT officers, their movements jerky and unnatural.

She spotted the stone lying on the floor, tantalizingly close yet impossibly far given her current predicament. Her mind raced, trying to formulate a strategy. She couldn't take them all head-on, not in her weakened state.

"Samedi!" she hissed, hoping he could hear her over the din. "I need a distraction!"

Samedi, sensing her desperation, created a swirl of

shadows engulfing the room, momentarily confusing Buer and his minions. Cassielle seized the moment, crawling out from behind the desk and inching closer to the stone. But Buer quickly recovered, his demonic gaze locking onto her.

"You think you can stop me, Cassielle?" he sneered, his voice echoing with unholy power. "You're nothing without that stone."

Cassielle's heart pounded as she reached out, her fingers brushing the stone's cool surface. Just as she was about to grab it, Buer sent another blast of dark energy, more powerful than the last. It struck her squarely in the chest, sending her flying backwards, her body skidding across the floor.

She lay there, gasping for breath, the pain overwhelming. Buer advanced, his monstrous form looming over her. "It's over, Cassielle," he hissed, his voice a chilling whisper. "You've lost."

Cassielle's vision blurred, but she refused to give in to despair. This wasn't the end. She would fight, and she would find a way to save Nick. With the last of her strength, she glared up at Buer, her resolve unbroken.

"You haven't won yet," she spat, her voice hoarse but defiant. "This isn't over."

Buer laughed, an echoing sound filled with pure evil. "We'll see about that," he said, turning his attention to Samedi, who was still battling the possessed SWAT officers. "Enjoy your last moments, Cassielle. The real battle begins now."

As darkness began to close in, Cassielle clung to the hope this wasn't the end. She would either get a hold on that stone, or take him out without it. She wasn't done yet.

CHAPTER FORTY

"Come out, come out, wherever you are," Buer teased, his voice dripping with sinister amusement. Cassielle could hear his footsteps approaching the desk, an eerie blend of scrambling claws and unnaturally heavy thuds. The air thickened with the acrid stench of sulfur, invading her senses and heightening her dread.

Bright daylight poured in through the windows, casting stark relief against the encroaching darkness on the other side of the desk. The contrast was almost blinding, a harsh reminder of the ordinary world just beyond the nightmare she was trapped in. The scratching of claws against the wooden surface of the desk sent a painful screech reverberating through the room, each sound a jolt to her nerves.

The overhead lights flickered erratically, casting unsettling shadows that danced across the room. Cassielle had no doubt Buer was draining every ounce of energy he could to amplify his power. She needed to act swiftly to take him down. The air was charged with a palpable tension, like the oppressive stillness before a thunderstorm, adding to the suffocating atmosphere.

Her side throbbed painfully, each breath sending jolts of agony through her body. She was certain she must have cracked a rib, but she couldn't afford to stop now. She needed a distraction to give her the opportunity to retrieve the stone. The mayor's whimpering behind her only added to the urgency of the situation; clearly, he hadn't anticipated his day turning out this way.

"Give up now, Cassielle, and I'll make your death painless. Or, we can keep playing this cat and mouse game. I find it rather fun!" Buer snarled, his voice dripping with malice.

"Dream on!" Cassielle shouted back.

She knew she needed to create a diversion. Summoning her remaining strength, she reached deep within herself, seeking out the flicker of power that aided her before. If she could generate a strong enough distraction, it might just buy her the time she needed.

With a deep breath, Cassielle channeled her energy, feeling the flicker of a flame ignite within her. She shot a blast of energy in one direction, simultaneously darting in the opposite direction. Her gamble paid off. Buer, drawn by the surge of power, turned and fired his dark energy towards the false target, missing her entirely.

Taking advantage of the momentary diversion, Cassielle moved swiftly, her eyes locked on the stone lying on the ground. She had to reach it before Buer realized his mistake. As she lunged for the stone, she kept her focus, pushing through the pain radiating from her side. Every second counted.

Her fingers wrapped around the warm stone just as she felt the blast of dark energy hit her in the back. She curled into a protective ball around the stone, refusing to let go despite the searing pain lancing through her. The dark energy felt like icy fire against her back, but she gritted her teeth against the pain.

A snarl sounded from behind her, followed by a thud. Slowly pushing herself up to her hands and knees, Cassielle saw Jamal on the ground with Buer in a horrifying mix of inhuman limbs intertwined with human ones. Alba stood just a few feet behind him, chanting and holding out a stone similar to the one Cassielle had.

Through the haze of pain and confusion, Cassielle could see Samedi beyond Alba in the hallway, battling other SWAT team members. Their auras glowed with a sickly hue, betraying the possession gripping them.

Now was her chance. Ignoring the pain threatening to overwhelm her, Cassielle fought through the agony and lifted the stone, pouring her energy into it with every ounce of strength she possessed. The stone glowed brighter with each passing moment, pulsating with power as she struggled to draw Buer into its confines.

"Dig deeper!" Samedi's voice echoed from the hallway, a distant yet urgent command spurring her on.

"What?!" Cassielle's gaze darted towards Alba and Jamal, who were guiding the mayor and pulling Nick's body out of the office as best they could while staying low to the ground.

Buer roared in defiance, unleashing a blast of dark energy towards her. The room grew colder by the second as Buer sapped the energy from the air, channeling it into his relentless assault. Dodging his attacks, Cassielle focused her energy on drawing him into the stone, every fiber of her being dedicated to the task at hand.

The room erupted into a clash of black and brilliant red and white light as they battled, their energies intertwining in a deadly dance. Cassielle could feel her strength waning, her reserves dwindling with each passing moment.

Out of the corner of her eye, she caught sight of Samedi, his lips forming silent words.

"What did you say?!" Cassielle shouted at Samedi, desperation creeping into her voice as she struggled to maintain her grip on the stone.

"Fully unleash your power! You're still resisting who you are!" Samedi's voice pierced through the chaos of battle, carrying a sense of urgency resonating deep within Cassielle.

Her initial impulse was to argue, to deny she was holding back. But a flicker of realization stirred within her, a nagging truth.

It was time to stop fighting. For the sake of everyone who depended on her, she had to rise above her fear and uncertainty. Cassielle pushed herself to her limits, drawing upon every ounce of strength within her. As the battle raged on, she felt a surge of power coursing through her veins, a raw and primal force begging to be unleashed.

With a primal scream, Cassielle unleashed her power in its entirety, unleashing a torrent of energy enveloping the room in blinding light. In that moment of raw power, she tapped into her true heritage as Heylel's daughter. That little flicker of a flame had just been one tongue of the roaring fire she'd kept deep inside of her.

As the light faded and the dust settled, Cassielle collapsed to the ground, spent but victorious. Buer's demonic form writhed and screamed in agony as he was drawn inexorably into the stone, his malevolent essence trapped for eternity.

The room descended into an eerie stillness, broken only by the ragged breaths of those who remained. Cassielle's heart thundered in her chest, the weight of her accomplishment settling heavily upon her shoulders. It took a moment for her to register the absence of noise from the hallway beyond.

Forcing herself onto her knees, she trembled uncontrollably, caught between sensations of searing heat and bone-chilling cold. With faltering movements, she began to crawl across the floor, too weak to rise to her feet.

As she neared the hallway, her eyes searched desperately for Samedi, but he was nowhere to be found. Instead, she was met with the sight of men strewn across the ground, groaning and slowly stirring from their stupor, their expressions lost and bewildered in the aftermath of the chaos.

Doubt gnawed at Cassielle's mind as she crawled, her thoughts racing with concern and frustration. Where was Samedi? Had something happened to him in the chaos? She pushed the worry aside and focused on finding Nick and his spirit. The dust and chaos in the room made it hard to see. Maybe Nibo, Samedi, or Nick were in the hallway.

As Cassielle's hand reached out, fingers grazing the threshold of the hallway, a faint sound pierced the heavy silence. "Cassielle?" The voice, barely more than a whisper.

Her heart skipped a beat, and she turned, her eyes widening in disbelief. There, amidst the destroyed office, lay Nick, his voice feeble but unmistakable. For a moment, time seemed to stand still as their gazes locked, the weight of the moment hanging heavy in the air.

CHAPTER FORTY-ONE

The room lay in ruins, a chaotic aftermath of the fierce battle. Debris littered the floor, the once-stately desk now a mere heap of splintered wood, the curtains torn and tattered, chairs strewn about like discarded toys. It was as if a tempest of fury had swept through, leaving destruction in its wake.

Amidst the wreckage, Nick lay sprawled on his stomach, his gaze locking with hers across the disarray. Nibo and Samedi stood behind him, their expressions a blend of relief and pride, akin to proud parents beholding their child for the first time. Despite the triumph of their victory, Nick appeared as worn and disheveled as Cassielle felt.

"Coño! How the hell did I get here?" His voice was stronger, though beneath the surface, there lingered a palpable sense of bewilderment and confusion.

Cassielle began to crawl towards him, but before she could reach him, Samedi and Nibo were at her side, assisting her to her feet. Together, they approached Nick, who had rolled onto his back, his eyes scanning the room with a mix of confusion and disbelief.

"Nick?" Cassielle's voice was soft, laced with relief and concern as they drew closer to him. His bewildered question hung in the air, a testament to the uncertainty of their circumstances.

Nibo and Samedi assisted her in lowering herself to the floor beside him. Drawing upon her first responder training,

Cassielle instinctively began assessing his condition, checking for any discernible signs of distress despite the lack of medical equipment. However, Nick swatted her away in irritation.

"I'm fine," his tone was edged with annoyance. Yet, when she glanced at his expression, she detected a glimmer of gratitude mingled with his irritation. She realized she was still clutching his hand, which she had grabbed to check his pulse. Flustered, she released it and averted her gaze, searching for Alba and Jamal. Before she could inquire, Samedi provided an update.

"While you were engaged in the confrontation with Buer, I managed to neutralize the Possessed SWAT members," he explained. "Then Nibo, who arrived with Nick's spirit and assistance, escorted Alba and Jamal, along with the Mayor, to safety with unaffected SWAT members."

Her response of "Oh" felt simplistic and unhelpful, so she sat in silence afterwards, unsure of what she should do next. It was only then she realized she had dropped the stone in the middle of the floor after her battle.

Samedi moved quickly to pick it up.

"We'll secure it in a safe place. However, these stones aren't, and never were, intended as permanent prisons for demons. They can regain their strength and attempt to escape. I'll ensure it's kept deep in Limbo, so if he manages to break free again, he'll have quite the journey ahead to find his way out," Nibo grinned.

"Cassielle, what happened?" Nick's voice pulled her focus back to him. She struggled to find the words to convey everything they had experienced.

"He doesn't remember," Nibo interjected softly. Cassielle refrained from a sarcastic retort like 'thanks, Captain Obvious', recognizing Nibo's attempt to offer a gentle reminder.

How could she explain to Nick he had been possessed, journeyed to Limbo, and been rescued by her, only for her to battle a demon to ensure his safe return to his body? She had been terrified countless times of losing him. She had pushed him away to shield him from her darkness, yet here she was, fully embracing her true self after saving him from the real darkness. Would he accept her as she truly was? She wouldn't know unless she tried. It was time for her to be honest.

As the EMTs swarmed into the room, Samedi and Nibo vanished. Cassielle felt a rush of relief mixed with a twinge of apprehension. Samedi and Nibo's sudden disappearance left her feeling exposed, vulnerable in the presence of the bustling medical team. She hoped the Loa were nearby in case any dark souls tried to possess the people here. However, she suspected, with Buer gone, the remaining ones may have scattered.

The ensuing hours passed in a whirlwind of activity. Cassielle found herself grappling with a barrage of questions from police detectives, her mind racing to piece together the fragmented events of the day in a way that wouldn't make her sound crazy. Beside her, Nick seemed equally bewildered, their inability to provide coherent answers only adding to the frustration of the law enforcement questioning them.

Rebecca's arrival brought a bittersweet undercurrent to the chaos. Cassielle watched silently as Nick and Rebecca shared a tender moment, a pang of longing tugging at her heart. It was a stark reminder of the unspoken feelings she harbored for him, feelings she could no longer ignore.

Another thought hit her as she watched them. Despite the attraction she felt to Samedi, they couldn't ever really be a thing, right? He wasn't human. Though she was half her father's child and half human, she didn't fully belong to that world, and she never would. Her mother had told her once Loa liked to dally with mortals. Was that all she was to him? An assignment and a dalliance?

Accepting herself meant accepting her emotions, no matter how painful they might be. It was time to confront the truth, to acknowledge the depth of her affection for Nick and try to come to terms with whatever it was she felt for Samedi. The prospect of rejection from Nick loomed large, yet she knew she owed it to herself to try. After all, she'd had so much time with him, she'd been a fool to throw it away. Yet, at the same time, she wasn't wholly human. Was it right for her to pursue a relationship with him?

She felt lost and confused and there was no one she could talk to about it. Samedi wouldn't understand, nor would her father or any of the other Loa. She needed to tell Nick what she truly was, but would he reject her even if they could have been something? And wouldn't that hurt more? But would they really be something if she didn't tell him the truth?

But as she sat in the back of the ambulance, the EMTs bustling around her, her doubts swirled through her mind. Did she want to disrupt the budding connection between Nick and Rebecca? Was she prepared to risk a possibility of a friendship with Nick for the sake of her own desires? Lost in her thoughts, Cassielle remained silent, allowing the medical examination to proceed without protest.

Would he even believe her about what she was? He'd have to, right? Rebecca could attest to the validity of the strange supernatural truth she'd come to realize and accept. But he hadn't believed her about the possible connection between all of the murders.

Cassielle took a deep breath, trying to steady her racing thoughts. She had faced demons, both literal and metaphorical, and survived. She could face this too. She had to.

Alba and Jamal, through an interpreter, explained to the police about what they'd seen and their involvement. As soon as they were free, they rushed over to her.

"Cassielle! Are you alright?" Alba signed and hugged Cassielle tightly, eliciting a wince from her.

Jamal tapped Alba on the shoulder so she would look at him. "Give her space," Jamal suggested, realizing Cassielle was injured.

"Oh dear, I'm sorry. How do you feel, child?"

The medics informed Alba and Jamal that Cassielle needed to go to the hospital for further evaluation. Alba wanted to ride with her, but Jamal convinced her to go back to Brittany at her apartment. He promised to stay with Cassielle.

Once Alba reluctantly agreed and without thinking Jamal turned to the medic, moving his hands quickly, "Could I accompany her?"

"Sorry, I -I don't... what?" The medic stuttered.

Cassielle interpreted for him and the medic agreed Jamal could go with her.

In the ambulance, Cassielle signed to Jamal, explaining what had happened. She detailed the possession, the journey to Limbo, and the battle with Buer. He'd managed to keep his reactions minimal, mindful the medic was watching their interaction. The medic glanced at them curiously as he went about his tasks. Cassielle could see his brows furrowing as he tried to follow what they were discussing. He didn't know sign, so they had no fear of eavesdropping.

"There's something else troubling you, isn't there?" Jamal's eyes keen and perceptive.

He was good at reading people.

Cassielle nodded, her thoughts a whirlwind of uncertainty. How could she explain the complex feelings she had for Nick and the complicated attraction to Samedi? The confusion of her dual heritage and the fear of rejection from someone she cared about deeply?

Jamal watched her intently, waiting for her to find the words. Cassielle took another deep breath. She had faced so much already. It was time to confront her feelings head-on, no matter how terrifying it might be.

Her movements were quick with her meandering thoughts.

Jamal watched her patiently. He smiled and reached out to touch her arm, stopping her from continuing moving her hands around with a flat hand as she tried to think of what to sign.

"What do you truly want?" Jamal asked simply.

That was a good question. What did she want? She

thought for a few moments.

"I think, right now, I don't have the luxury of romance. There are still evil spirits and demons loose, and I need to stop them." She looked out the back window of the ambulance for a moment before turning back to Jamal. "I'll have to pull a Miss Scarlett and think about that tomorrow."

Jamal smiled. "I'm here for you, whatever you decide and whatever may happen. But I do think you need to tell Nick."

Cassielle nodded, recognizing the truth in Jamal's words. She would have to talk to Nick soon. The lingering evil spirits and demons weren't confined to New Orleans, and she might need to leave for a while. That necessitated an explanation, at the very least.

Jamal stayed by her side during the long wait at the hospital. His presence was a steadying force as they navigated the chaos of the emergency room, its sterile lights and antiseptic smells a sharp contrast to the battles they had faced. After a thorough examination, the doctor confirmed her fears: she had a cracked rib, accompanied by numerous cuts and bruises.

The doctor prescribed a regimen of pain medications to manage her discomfort. Rest was crucial, with strict instructions to avoid any strenuous activity that could aggravate her injury. Once the initial healing phase was over, she would need to start physical therapy to strengthen the muscles around her rib cage, ensuring a full recovery.

As the doctor explained her treatment plan, Cassielle's mind wandered to the daunting tasks ahead. She would need to balance her recovery with her responsibilities, both to the people of New Orleans and to Nick. The weight of her obligations pressed heavily on her, but she knew she couldn't avoid them.

Jamal stayed with her through the entire hospital stay until she was discharged. At her doorstep, Cassielle signed to Jamal, asking him to check on Alba and Brittany. He hesitated, concern etched on his face. She insisted, her movements firm and deliberate. With a reluctant nod, he turned back to the waiting Uber.

She made the trek up the stairs, grateful for the pain medication. Her apartment, a haven of tranquility amidst the chaos of her thoughts, remained unchanged since her departure. The dim lighting cast long shadows, a silent testament to the storm raging within her. Cassielle sat upright in her living room, the weight of the day bearing down on her shoulders.

"I wonder how long it's going to take before a Loa shows up..." she mumbled, looking out the window.

It couldn't have been more than a few minutes before a swirl of shadows appeared before her and Samedi stepped out. Dressed in his customary attire, he exuded an air of enigmatic charm, but even his charismatic smile faltered at the sight of her troubled expression.

"What's wrong, cherie?" He started towards her but she raised a hand to stop him.

"I've done a lot of thinking," Cassielle began.

"Sounds dangerous," Samedi quipped. She shot him a look and he smiled sheepishly.

"Given the presence of other demons beyond Buer, it's clear our work is far from over. But before I commit, I have a few conditions." He waited for her to continue this time. "I've come to a decision. I think, at least for now, it's best we maintain a professional relationship." She studied him for his reaction. "I wouldn't want to drag you into any complications with my father."

His face faltered a little, but he nodded. "What are your conditions, then?"

"Firstly, I need assurances Brittany won't be held accountable for Michael's death," Cassielle stated firmly, her voice unwavering despite the weight of her words. "And secondly, I need to speak to Nick. I need to know where he stands, what he believes happened. I owe him that much."

"May I speak now?" Samedi's voice was calm.

"Go on," she lifted her head to watch him.

"I did speak with your father after today's endeavors. He's pleased with how you did and thrilled you tapped into your total power. That said, it's time we up your training so the things that went wrong don't happen again. Yes, I think it's a good idea to speak with your Nick and see what we can do about ensuring Brittany is safe from criminal prosecution. Though I would caution you about reminding Nick of everything his soul has been through. That's not an easy thing to accept," He moved to sit next to her on the couch. "He may have some difficulty coping with it."

"I think he'll be okay. He has Rebecca now," she did her best to push the pain out of her voice when she said it, but she could tell by Samedi's face he knew.

"Okay, let's go see them, then."

"Okay," she agreed before pulling her phone out and sending a text to Rebecca and Nick. She received a response from Rebecca letting her know Nick was at her place and she was welcome to come over to talk.

Cassielle steeled herself before standing up. She and Samedi stepped into the shadows and out in front of Rebecca's door.

She hesitated a moment before knocking. Rebecca answered after a minute. Judging by her face, Cassielle could tell Rebecca wasn't surprised they'd arrived so quickly. Nick, however, was looking at her as if he thought she was stalking him.

"Thank you for letting us come over," she started cautiously.

"Of course! Come on in," Rebecca stepped back to allow them to enter.

"Would it be possible for me to talk to Nick?" She began, her voice steady despite the emotions churning within her. She looked at him standing by the kitchen counter. He looked as if he'd taken a shower. He had on a clean grey tee-shirt and some basketball shorts. His hair still looked wet. "There are things you need to know about what happened today, about what I've discovered about myself."

Nick's brow furrowed in confusion, but before he could respond, Cassielle took a deep breath and began to recount the events of the day, sparing no detail as she revealed the truth about her heritage and the role she played in the battle against Buer.

As she spoke, she watched Nick's expression shift from disbelief to shock, his eyes widening with each revelation. She could see the turmoil within him, the struggle to reconcile the truth with the reality he knew.

When Cassielle finished speaking, there was a heavy silence hanging in the air, broken only by the sound of their breathing. She waited, her heart pounding in her chest, unsure of how Nick would respond.

Finally, after what felt like an eternity, Nick spoke, his voice quiet yet filled with emotion. "¿Qué?" Nick's face betrayed no emotion, leaving Cassielle uncertain of his reaction.

"Do you really want me to repeat all of that?" Cassielle's sinking feeling deepened, realizing the situation was spiraling and unlikely to improve.

"Have you lost your mind?" Her stomach churned, threatening to abandon her body altogether.

"I'm assuming that's a rhetorical question?" Cassielle responded, her voice heavy with resignation.

"I... I don't know what to say," he began, his gaze locking with Cassielle's. "Fontenot spun a similar tale... so did Rebecca." He took a steadying breath, "It's not that I don't trust you all... and I recognize I lost a lot of time... but I'm not sure I can believe this whole demon possession thing." He held up a hand to stop Rebecca who had opened her mouth to argue. "That said, I can assure you no one plans to press charges on Brittany. There isn't enough evidence to support it was her, and we spoke to the neighbors, and one had a video camera that caught a hooded figure going into the courtyard after Brittany had. The people in the other apartment said they hadn't been there, and a footprint lifted from the porch didn't match anyone there. Fontenot pressed the DA who said there's no way they could, not with the fact she would have had trouble lifting him, and someone else may have been there. It doesn't add up." He sighed, "we're going to keep pursuing the stranger. I have a feeling if we can find that person, we may have our answer."

Cassielle felt a wave of relief wash over her, gratitude flooding her heart as she realized that despite the challenges ahead, she didn't need to worry about Brittany. But this was quickly followed by fear. Was Jamal the hooded figure? That would be another issue to deal with in the future.

"Has anyone told her yet?"

"Fontenot went to talk to her at Alba's place. They're still shaken by whatever has been happening," he rolled his eyes, "he said there was incense and all sorts of nonsense everywhere like they were trying to keep the devil himself out."

"Okay, well, that's good then..." Cassielle looked to Samedi who appeared to be pretending to be fully interested in something outside the window. "On that note, I need to go away for a while." She looked back to Nick.

"There's more out there to deal with, huh?" Rebecca said, looking between Cassielle and Samedi. "I've been reading the news..."

"Yeah."

"And what are you really going to do, Cassielle? Don't tell me you think you're some sort of Demon hunter now." Nick looked almost angry. She couldn't quite figure it out. They stood there, locked in a silent exchange for several moments.

Cassielle felt a surge of frustration rising within her at Nick's incredulity, but she forced herself to remain composed, meeting his gaze with a steely resolve.

"Nick, I understand this is difficult to accept," she began, her voice calm yet tinged with urgency. "But I assure you, what I've told you is the truth. And whether you choose to believe it or not, I need you to understand there are forces at play beyond our comprehension, and we can't afford to ignore them."

Nick's expression remained impassive, but Cassielle could see the flicker of doubt in his eyes, the hint of uncertainty betrayed his stoic facade.

"I know this is a lot to take in," she continued, her voice softening with empathy. "But I need you to trust me, Nick. We're in this together, whether you believe it or not."

Before Nick could respond, Samedi stepped forward, his presence commanding attention as he fixed Nick with a penetrating gaze.

"Nicholas," Samedi's voice was low yet commanding, his tone tinged with an otherworldly authority. "You would do well to heed Cassielle's words. The danger lurking in the shadows is very real, and you would be wise not to dismiss it lightly."

Nick's eyes widened in shock as Samedi's features shifted before him, his once-human visage contorting into a grotesque skull-like face that left Nick speechless and stuttering in disbelief. "¿Qué coño?"

Cassielle watched in silence as Nick struggled to process what he had just witnessed, the reality of the situation finally sinking in as he stared into the abyss of Samedi's true form. After a few moments, Samedi shifted back to his human guise, leaving Nick stunned and speechless in his wake.

Turning to Nick, she offered him a reassuring smile, her eyes reflecting the unwavering resolve burning within her.

"We'll figure this out," she said, her voice soft yet filled with determination. "Together."

With a nod of agreement, Nick finally met her gaze, his expression softened with a newfound sense of understanding.

"Yeah," he replied, his voice tinged with uncertainty. "Together."

As the weight of their conversation hung heavy in the

air, Cassielle felt a sense of closure settle over her, knowing despite the challenges ahead, they were one step closer to facing them together. With the support of her friends and the strength of her convictions, she was ready to face whatever challenges lay ahead, armed with the knowledge she would not have to face them alone.

ABOUT THE AUTHOR

S. J. Winter

S.J. Winter is not only a devoted wife and loving mother but also a passionate writer who finds inspiration in the beauty of storytelling. With a deep love for reading, writing, music, and aiding others, Winter cherishes moments with her family while exploring the boundless realms of imagination. Her debut novel, "Legacy of Shadows: The Keeper's Rebellion," is a captivating exploration of identity, resilience, and the power of embracing one's true self. Now, with the release of her second novel, "Devil's Hope," Winter delves deeper into the realms of mystery and intrigue, where dark forces threaten to unravel reality itself.

BOOKS BY THIS AUTHOR

Legacy Of Shadows: The Keeper's Rebellion

"Legacy of Shadows: The Keeper's Rebellion" is a captivating fantasy novel that delves into a world where magic and humanity collide. Follow Blythe, a young woman burdened by her unique heritage, as she faces accusations of a grave crime by the ruling council of witches. Forced to confront her identity and navigate treacherous alliances, Blythe joins forces with Quentin, an enigmatic Fey, to uncover the truth and challenge an oppressive hierarchy. As tensions rise and their feelings intertwine, Blythe must embrace her dual heritage to become a beacon of hope in a world on the brink of chaos. Prepare for a thrilling journey of resilience, self-discovery, and the extraordinary power within.